"Thoroughly enjoyable. It's like those rare 'great' B movies—a fast, fun time."
—*OtherRealms* on *Necroscope*

Door number 666 slid swiftly, silently out of sight—and hell itself became visible behind it, red and orange flames rumbling and roaring. A great shaft of fire belched out like a thick, dripping tongue and licked Clayborne for long seconds, head to heels. He disappeared, screaming, in liquid light and heat.

Then the tongue of fire was retracted and the door hissed shut to contain it, and the thing that had been Clayborne screamed again as it fell in a smoking, steaming heap upon the scorched earth.

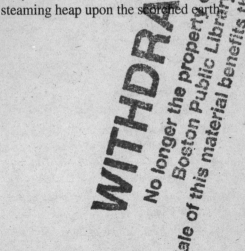

TOR BOOKS BY BRIAN LUMLEY

BRIAN LUMLEY

THE HOUSE OF DOORS

TOR®

A TOM DOHERTY ASSOCIATES BOOK
NEW YORK

THE HOUSE OF DOORS

Copyright © 1990 by Brian Lumley

Cover art by J. Thiesen

A Tor Book
Published by Tom Doherty Associates, LLC
175 Fifth Avenue
New York, NY 10010

www.tor.com

Tor® is a registered trademark of Tom Doherty Associates, LLC.

ISBN: 0-812-50832-7

First edition: March 1990

Printed in the United States of America

0 9 8 7 6

For:
John and Sigi,
Terry and Sheila,
Dixon and Mady—with
many fond memories
of fourteen
sun-drenched days,
and quite a few
ouzo-drenched
nights!

CHAPTER ONE

Hamish Grieve, as his surname might suggest, had been a gillie for the Laird of Earn for forty-four years. Before that he'd been apprenticed as a joiner, receiving his signed indentures and freedom on the attainment of his twenty-first birthday; at which point he'd given up working *with* woods to work *in* them. And from then until he was sixty-five and pensionable, like many a good Scot before him, he'd cannily managed his affairs and silted away a percentage of his middling but not entirely insubstantial wages.

Biding his time, he'd kept his contempt for the Laird well hidden, until the evening of his sixty-fifty birthday (the 2nd May, 1984), when, leaving the stables and crossing the paddock for the last time, he'd walked up to the great granite house at the heart of its many acres of woods and entered his master's rooms. There Hamish

1

had checked the contents of his wages envelope, laid down in a neat bundle his shotgun, notebook, dog whistle and certain lesser appointments of his profession, and resigned. It was his right, for he was sixty-five and there'd never been a written contract.

"But . . . what'll I do?" The old laird had been flabbergasted. "And more's to the point, what'll *you* do, Hamish?" Hamish was head gillie; the others in the Laird's employ, for all their years of service, weren't nearly so experienced and much less trustworthy.

"Ah shid imagine," Hamish had grunted, "that ye'll do as ye've done for the last forty-four years—*verra* little! As for maself: there's a wee property come available in Lawers overlooking the water. Ah shall buy it and spen' ma time fishing and reading—what time's left to me." And he did just that.

For the next ten years he would get up each day, breakfast, open his windows over Loch Tay and do his deep-breathing exercises. At nine o'clock he'd get his bicycle from the lean-to and, weather permitting, peddle a fairly leisurely seven miles down to Killin at the eastern end of the loch, there to visit an old sickbed friend who'd been dying for fifteen years and never got any closer to the actual box. Hamish's mongrel dog, Barney, would trot alongside; which in the main was how the two of them got their exercise.

But on this Sunday morning in mid-June of 1994, a few weeks after Hamish had clocked up seventy-five years, things were to work out just a little different.

The morning was bright if somewhat chilly

for the time of year, and Hamish found the bike ride invigorating and even exhilarating—to a point. That point being reached when, in a moment, his emotions switched from exhilaration to astonishment. He saw it as he cycled round a gentle right-hand bend in the road: that which could not possibly be there to see. And his gnarled hands at once gripped the handlebars that much tighter, causing his front wheel to wobble. Barney, trotting alongside, yelped and narrowly avoided a trapped paw, by which time Hamish had brought his machine to a halt.

He sat there astride his bike, one foot on the ground, jaws agape and eyes staring their utter disbelief. The object of his amazement, what he could see of it, was a house, or even a mansion by its size; indeed, more a castle, with its turrets and battlements. It stood midway between twin spurs coming down from the lordly Ben Lawers, its base hidden by the ridge of a scree saddle and its back to a steep incline where granite outcrops came thrusting through the thin turf. A castle, yes, and not unlike many another of much the same size, period and general construction; in itself, hardly a matter for astonishment. Castles abound in Scotland, and to a native dour as Hamish Grieve one castle seemed much like any other; unless you were talking about the really grand jobs, like the one on the Mount of Edinburgh, for instance.

No, the building itself (in any other circumstance) would hardly take Hamish by surprise. But the fact that he'd found it here, now, would and did—for as recently as yesterday morning it had *not* been here! Neither then nor any other

3

morning for the last ten years, and for all the long years of time gone before that!

Hamish shook his head, rubbed at his eyes, frankly couldn't accept the evidence that his senses were offering him. But the longer he stared, the more undeniably solid the castle looked to him. Could it be, he wondered, that the thing really had been there all of this time, and he simply hadn't looked that way before, hadn't noticed it? But that was to ignore the facts, indeed to ignore his own especially lucid memory. Last summer, on these very slopes, he'd seen French and English botanists examining Ben Lawers' rare alpine plants. Six months ago there'd been skiers up there, coming over the crest of that very scree-filled depression. Hamish had always hated these periodic incursions of tourists and foreign riff-raff, but now he thanked the Lord for these memories of them. Without such memories his sanity itself must be suspect.

Or perhaps it wasn't so much his sanity but his sight. He'd heard of people damaging their eyes like that, but never thought it could happen to him. "Barney," he said, still gazing at the castle rising there over the scree less than three-quarters of a mile away, "have ah been hitting it too hard? Is a couple or three wee drams of a nicht too much, d'ye think? Could it be that an accumulation o' malt's addled ma brains, eh?" But Barney only wagged his stump of a tail and whined, as he always did when he was worried.

"Well, ma laddie," said Hamish, more to himself now than to the dog, "it seems we'll just have tae look into this, you an' me."

There was a track climbing from the road to

a spot maybe halfway between Hamish and the object of his curiosity, climbing in fact along the sharp, narrow ridge of the eastern spur. Hamish left the road, cycled a little way up the track until the going got too heavy, then leaned his bicycle against a boulder and continued on foot. Barney stayed right to heel, uncomplaining, perhaps wondering at this rare break in the tradition of so many years.

Finally, climbing above the scree ridge, Hamish paused for a breather and studied more closely the mysterious castle. And despite the fact that there was a great deal wrong with that enigmatic structure, at least Hamish was no longer in doubt of his eyesight.

The place most definitely *was* there; its squat foundations going down into scree, its frontage like half a hexagon, forming a flat face with flanking walls angling sharply back; and the frowning granite walls themselves, going up maybe fifty feet to the turrets and crenellated battlements. And all grandly set against Ben Lawers, rising majestically to its cloud-piercing four-thousand-foot crest; all very impressive, solid and powerful seeming. And very, very wrong.

For there was no road to the place, not even a track, and no windows in it that Hamish could see. And perhaps most peculiar of all, no doors . . .

Up here, with a breeze tugging at his light coat and the sun warming his neck, space seemed to open up for Hamish Grieve and time to stand still. Long moments passed while his breathing settled down and his heartbeat slowed. Barney sat at his feet, stump of a tail wagging a very little, small whines sounding now and then from deep in his chest.

Finally Hamish shivered. His neck might be warm but the rest of him felt unaccountably cold. Or perhaps not unaccountably. It wasn't every day that something like this happened.

Before he could begin shivering again he started forward, skirted the castle, began to climb the ridge of the spur towards its rear. Down there, sheep clambered in the rocks at the castle's base and chewed on the coarse grasses. Hamish paused and stared at them. If sheep weren't afraid of the place, whatever it was and however it came to be here, he didn't see why he should be.

Scrambling down from the spur onto the level, overgrown scree, he moved right up to the base of the inexplicable edifice. Hexagonal, yes; he followed the planes of its walls to the rear. And it was here, close up, that he first noticed the shimmer.

The walls shimmered—very faintly, almost unnoticeably—as though viewed through thin blue wood smoke, or the heat reflected from a tarmac road. It wasn't hot enough for that, to be sure, and there were no fires that Hamish could see, but still the castle shimmered. Like . . . a mirage?

The base of each section of wall was perhaps thirty-five feet long; pacing to the rear, Hamish gazed along the entire length of the back wall where the stony hillside rose up and away from it. There were sheep back there, who lifted their heads to look at him curiously, before returning to their munching. But one of them stood half-in, half-out of the shimmer.

Hamish's jaw fell open. The sheep, a fat ewe, was browsing on the coarse grass at the foot of the wall, but its rear quarters disappeared *into* the granite! Which could only mean—

"It really *is* a mirage!" Hamish gasped. "Unsolid, unreal!"

He approached the castle's wall more closely yet, with Barney right behind him, whining ever more loudly and persistently. The shimmer was faint but quite definitely there; the wall, for all that it was opaque and seemed thoroughly dense, must be entirely matterless, a trick of the light and freakish Nature; that sheep there, not ten paces away, was surely all the evidence one required.

Hamish put out a slightly trembling hand until his four fingertips touched the shimmer. He felt something like the very mildest of mild electric shocks—but in the next moment the shimmer disappeared and the wall was suddenly real. Hamish knew it as surely as he knew that he stood here. What had been or might have been a mirage had suddenly stiffened into reality, becoming solid. In a single split second—occurring simultaneously with a shrill, terrified, and agonized bleat—the tingling in his fingertips had been replaced . . . by pain!

He snatched back his hand, clutched it, gazed bug-eyed at his fingertips. They looked like he'd rested them for a moment on the surface of a rapidly revolving drum of sandpaper. Blood welled up from four flat discs of flesh at the tips of his fingers.

"What?" said Hamish to himself, scarcely able to accept what he couldn't hope to understand. "What?"

Along the now entirely solid wall something had happened. Something lay crumpled there, still twitching. Clutching his hand, Hamish stumbled to see what it was, went to confirm an awful suspicion. Barney went with him, sniffed at the freshly dead ewe and backed away from it stiff-legged. For the animal was only half a sheep now, the front half, lying there where its body had been sliced through like a worm by a straight-edged razor. Collapsing, its severed trunk had left a swath of blood like fresh red paint on the hard granite wall.

Hamish Grieve held his breath, took all of this in, felt his heart beginning to hammer in his chest. The "mirage" wasn't a mirage, and the castle wasn't a castle, and nothing here was even nearly right.

He backed away from the blank, looming wall and began to climb the side of the stony spur to its narrow ridge. But because he went backwards his progress was slow, and not for a single moment did he shift his gaze from the castle that wasn't a castle.

Barney was right there with him, yipping and snapping a little to hasten him on. Then Hamish's heel came down on a loose stone and it threw him; flat on his back he tobogganed to the bottom again, numbing himself where hard projections banged his spine. Barney, very nearly frantic, came scrambling after, tugging at his master's sleeve to get him mobile.

Hamish sat up. In front of him—but *directly* in front of him—the wall's surface was shimmering again. And its base now came right up against the foot of the spur!

Breathing raggedly and feeling he was going

to faint—for the very first time in a long and, until now, entirely mundane life *knowing* he was going to faint, but not daring to—Hamish began to climb again. He climbed like a youth, soaring up the side of the spur, and without pausing glanced fearfully back over his shoulder. The castle was expanding, its wall flowing forward to engulf boulders where they held back the sliding scree not six feet behind and below him.

At the top, burned out, Hamish heaved himself up over the rim and lay facedown, sucking at the air and gulping harshly in a throat dry as a granary. Sheep, likewise fleeing, stampeded past him and away, up and down the spur. A breeze blew on him and gradually cooled the heat of his exertions.

Down below, the castle was as he'd first seen it; solid seeming and ordinary enough at first glance, but now, to Hamish, totally alien.

Barney was nowhere to be seen. . . .

CHAPTER TWO

New Year's Eve, 1995, 11:45 P.M.

Jon Bannerman, who had been known to describe himself as a tourist, stood at the top of the Royal Mile where its cobbles met the tarmac of Edinburgh Castle's esplanade, and gazed with dark and mildly foreign eyes down the long, steep, narrow way at the laughing, thronging, frenetically weaving crowds where they sang and danced, celebrating the death of the old and the imminent birth of a brand-new year. He leaned against a wall which bore a plaque commemorating the burning of the last of the Scottish witches on this very spot. It hadn't been so very long ago, not in Bannerman's eyes.

Bannerman had recorded the plaque's legend; now, with the recorder still working in his pocket, he concentrated his attention on the crowds. Their celebration was a rite, very nearly barbaric, not too far removed from a

10

state of orgy. Men and women, for the most part total strangers, embraced and kissed quite openly; in darker doorways lovers who didn't even know each other's name panted and groped fumblingly; the bitter cold air reeked of the alcoholic exhalations pluming from laughing mouths no less than from the small-paned windows of a nearby pub, where inner lights told of a private party still in progress.

Young men and women with bright eyes and gleaming teeth roamed to and fro, shouting and joking, seeking partners, while bottle-hugging drunks teetered this way and that, jostled from one gyrating group to the next.

To Bannerman the whole seemed a very decadent scene, and he dutifully recorded it. Then a girl came bursting from nowhere and bumped into him, jerking him erect from where he leaned against the wall. "*Whoa!*" she said, her brandy breath whooshing in Bannerman's face. She clutched at him for support, tried to focus on the dark face frowning at her. "Head's spinnin'," she said. "Canna seem tae stan' on ma aen feet!"

Bannerman steadied her, held her upright, hugged her close. It was the easiest way to keep her from falling while she found her balance.

"You've had a few," he told her, without accusation.

"Eh? A few? Ah've had a *lot*, laddie!" Her eyes swam and she was dizzy again. Then she screwed up her pretty face. "God—the noise! Ah'll be sick." She buried her face in Bannerman's overcoat.

"Not on me, I hope!" he said.

This time when she lifted her face she was

steadier; her eyes focused more readily; she cocked her head on one side and managed a smile. "You're no frae here—frae Edinburgh, I mean?"

"I'm . . . a tourist." He shrugged.

"In Edinburgh, in the winter?" She seemed astonished. Then, still hugging close to him, she burst into easy laughter. "The Bahamas," she said as her giggles subsided. "You should have gone there. Lord, what ah wouldnae gi' for a spot o' sunshine!"

He pulled gently away from her, steadied her elbow with only one hand. "Are you okay now?"

She swayed a little, got a grip of herself, looked towards the crowds of milling people. Most of them were heading in a crush now down the Royal Mile. "Ten to midnight!" someone shouted, and the crush moved that much faster.

"They're all off to the Auld Cross!" The girl was breathless, excited. She smiled at Bannerman. "Shall we no join them?"

"The Auld Cross?" he repeated. "Is it something special?"

"What, the Mercat Cross? You're no much of a tourist, eh?"

Again he shrugged. "Are you on your own?" he asked. Strange if she was, for by local standards she'd be very attractive.

The smile left her face in a moment. "Ah say I am," she muttered, "but the two who filled me wi' drink would probably dispute it. Aye, and ah know what *they* were after, too."

She glanced again at the receding crowd, peered into the crush of faces and figures—and gasped. She drew Bannerman into the shadows.

12

"They're there," she whispered. "Lookin' for me!"

He peered out from cover. The "two" she was afraid of stood out clearly in the crowd. Where all else was drunken or half-drunken or at the very least tipsy merriment, these two were sober, furtive, sneaky, intent. All eyes were bright but theirs were even brighter. Their smiles were frozen on their faces until they were little more than grimaces painted there. They'd lost something, someone, and were intent upon finding her again.

In the local parlance they'd be "hard men," Bannerman reckoned, and eager. They'd sniffed the spoor, come close to snaring the game, and now the chase was on for real. And he, Bannerman, might easily get caught up in it. Of course, he could simply walk away. But on the other hand . . .

Across the narrow road, stone steps went steeply down into the darkness of a maze of streets. With everyone heading for the Mercat Cross, the levels down there would be deserted. Bannerman looked back into the shadows, took the girl's hand. "Come on," he said. "Let's get out of here."

She shrank back, whispered, "I don't want they two tae see me!"

"They've gone," he lied. For in fact the two men were standing in the doorway eyeing the stragglers, their eyes flitting this way and that.

"Gone?" she repeated. "No, they'll be waitin' doon the Mile. At the Cross. It's only five minutes now."

"Then we'll cross the road and go down those steps there."

13

"We? Are ye comin' wi' me, then?"

Again Bannerman's shrug. "If you wish."

"No verra eager for it, are ye?" Again she'd cocked her head on one side. She had dark hair, gleaming green eyes, a lush mouth. "No like they two. But ah know *them*. They like a' sorts of weird games, them. Well, are ye keen or no?"

Not very, Bannerman thought—but out loud he said, "Come on."

They left the shadows, crossed the road. Even the stragglers were thinning out now. The girl's pursuers were moving off, their faces angry, following the crowd. Then one of them glanced back, saw Bannerman and the girl starting down the steps and out of sight.

Bannerman thought, *Maybe now that she's with someone, they won't bother her*.

Down the steps they went, the girl much recovered now, almost dragging Bannerman after her. "This way, this way!" she hissed back to him, leading him through the dark alleys between high stone walls. She knew the maze of streets intimately, and the urge was on her to know Bannerman that way, too.

In his pocket the recorder worked on, noting every smallest detail of what was occurring here. Then—

"Here," said the girl. "Here!" The alley was narrow, dark, cold and dry. In the shadows on one side stood an arched-over alcove. There'd been a door here once, now obliterated with mortar and smooth stone. She drew Bannerman in, shivered, swiftly unfastened the buttons of his coat, and crept in with him. Her clothes were flimsy and he could feel her body pressed to him. "There," she said, opening her blouse for him. "See?"

Bannerman saw, even in the dark. Her breasts were perfectly shaped, brown-tipped—utterly repulsive. He forced himself to weigh the left one in his hand. *Incredibly massive; heavy; full of blood; but the temperature so low it seemed impossible that life—*

"Hot!" she gasped, breaking his chain of thought. For the first time she'd felt his body heat. "Why, you're like a furnace! Have ye got the hots for me, then?"

Her long-fingered hand shifted from his chest, slipped down the front of Bannerman to the zip of his trousers, lowered it in a smooth, practised movement. A moment later she said, "No underpants! Were ye perhaps expectin' something?" She chuckled coarsely—and froze. He felt the fingers of her cold, searching hand stiffen. For down there in the crotch of his legs she'd found nothing! Just hot, smooth, featureless flesh, like the inner contours of a sharply bent elbow.

"Jesus!" she cried, leaping from the recess in the wall, her breasts swinging free. "Oh, sweet Je—"

Her pursuers were in the alley, creeping there. One of them grabbed her from behind, one hand over her mouth and the other fumbling roughly at her breasts. "Heard us coming for ye, did ye?" he whispered, his voice a threat in itself.

While she kicked and snorted through her nose, the second man lit a cigarette and held his lighter close to the alcove. Its flaring light caught Bannerman there, coat unbuttoned and fly open. "Laddie," said this one. "We're not much round here for strangers feelin' free with our women. Now you'd best hold your breath, son, for ye're about to lose your ba's!"

He snapped his lighter shut and lashed out with his left foot, driving it straight to Bannerman's groin. In the next moment, clenching his heavy lighter tightly in a balled fist to stiffen it and give it weight, the thug swung for Bannerman's face. The blows were delivered as swiftly as that—one, two—exactly where they were aimed.

Thrown back by the force and suddenness of the attack, Bannerman snatched what looked like a fountain pen from his top pocket.

The girl had meanwhile broken free. The man who had held her tried to strike her in the face but missed his aim. Her fingernails had opened up the side of his face in straight red lines. At first she gasped for breath, but then she started to shout. But not for help. She shouted *at* the men:

"Leave him! For God's sake leave him be—*or he'll have ye!*" Animals they might be—but they were human animals. Then she turned and fled into the night.

"Oh, a big-yin, is it?" said the one with the threatening whisper and the bleeding face. "Well then, let's be seeing the bastard!" He reached into the alcove, caught hold of Bannerman's lapels and bunched the material in a huge scarred fist.

His friend, however, had drawn back a little. When he'd kicked the stranger and struck him, Bannerman hadn't gasped or cried out. He hadn't even grunted. He should be on his knees, crippled, but he wasn't.

"Out ye come," said the one holding Bannerman's coat. "Out here where we can stomp on ye a bit and—" He jerked his arm out of the alcove, but Bannerman didn't come with it. Neither did the thug's hand. Severed at the wrist, his stump sprayed his companion's face with hot blood.

Then Bannerman came out. He breathed and his breath whooshed like a great bellows. His eyes glowed internally, swinging like searchlight beams to scan the men and the alley. Something gleamed in his hand and made a soft whirring sound. He swung that something in an arc and opened up the one who had struck him in a curving line across the chest.

Bannerman's weapon sliced through clothing and the man wearing it down to a depth of five inches. It slid through skin, flesh, cartilage, ribs, heart, lungs, with as little effort as an egg slicer. His victim didn't draw another breath; he was dead before he sagged to the cobbles; his companion was still gaping in disbelief at his own crimson-spurting stump.

Bannerman waved his weapon again, almost dismissively, and decapitated him where he stood. The cut was so clean and effortless that the man's head remained upright on his neck until a moment after he began to topple sideways. . . .

CHAPTER THREE

The pubs in Killin—the old pubs and the three new ones alike—were doing a roaring trade, as they had been since the arrival of the "Killin Castle" some twenty months ago. In the main bar of one of the new ones, called simply The Castle, Jack Turnbull and Spencer Gill got better acquainted. Turnbull was a minder looking after his boss from the MOD (Ministry of Defence), and in that capacity he'd earlier attended a briefing given by Gill to the two dozen or more VIPs currently here to make this or that decision in respect of that weighty phenomenon guarding and now guarded on the lower slopes of Ben Lawers.

"Lackluster?" Gill repeated Turnbull's terse but not deliberately unfriendly critique of his talk. Turnbull was outspoken, that was all. Gill shrugged. "I suppose it was. Hell, it always is!

If you tell the same story twice weekly with occasional matinees for the best part of a year, it's bound to get boring, isn't it? I mean, it isn't *The Mousetrap*. And it's not like a joke where you can spice up or tone down the story to suit your audience. I can't embellish the facts: they are what they are. And the Castle is what it is: a machine. That's what I was telling them, and I did it as best I could."

"It wasn't a criticism," Turnbull told him. "Or at least I didn't mean it that way. But I just sat there listening to you, and I thought: This bloke's knackered, and it's showing. He's saying something exciting and it comes out dull as ditchwater."

Gill smiled wryly. "Actually," he said. "I don't have much to be excited about. Not a hell of a lot, anyway. Maybe that's why it comes out so dry. You see, you don't know all the facts."

"Actually," Turnbull mimicked him, but unsmilingly, "I do know the facts. Most of them. I know more about you than you'd believe. Want to hear?"

Gill raised an eyebrow, nodded. "Why not?" he said. "I'm flattered that my confidential reports are that interesting! Go right ahead."

Turnbull looked at him almost speculatively. A curious look. It wasn't appraisal; perhaps it was an attempt at understanding what must be going on in there; or maybe he was simply remembering what he'd researched or been told. Gill thought: *There can't be all that much of the intellectual in him, not in his line of work.* But Turnbull looked at Gill anyway, and took a mental photograph of him, his way of remembering. Now, if he saw Gill again ten years from now, he'd know him on the instant. Except, of course, Gill didn't have ten years. He'd be lucky if he had two.

Gill was maybe five-eleven, a little underweight at around eleven stone, thirty-three years old but already looking more like forty. And he was dying. Fifteen years ago as a teenager he'd caused something of a stir; they'd recognized him as a new phenomenon, a quantum leap of Nature to keep pace with Science. Gill had "understood" machines. His great-grandfather had been an engineer, which seemed to be Gill's only qualification for the trick his genes or whatever had played on him. But nothing his great-grandfather had done could possibly have anything in common with Spencer Gill's ability.

"In the Age of Computers," some sensationalist journalist had written, "there will have to be minds which are *like* computers! This young man has that sort of mind. . . ." Of course, he'd had it wrong: Gill's mind wasn't like a computer at all. It was simply that he understood them, them and all other machines: by touch, taste, smell, sight; by listening to them and feeling for them. He was a mechanical empath; or rather, he had empathy with mechanical things. And people had first taken note of him when, at the age of eighteen, he'd described Heath Robinson's mobiles and mechanisms as "soulless Frankenstein monsters." He hadn't understood them, because *they* hadn't understood themselves. "If they were men," he'd said, "they'd be idiots."

"Well?" Gill prompted now, when Turnbull's

stare began to irritate him. "Are you going to tell me the story of my life, or aren't you?"

Turnbull's eyes seemed suddenly to focus and he said, "You're the Machine Man."

Gill grinned sourly and nodded his head. "You've a good memory," he said. "No one has called me that in ten years!" He brushed back unruly grey-flecked sandy hair from his forehead, picked up his drink and sipped at it. It was brandy: his doctors had told him not to but he'd reached the stage where he believed that if you enjoyed it you should have it. *Not* drinking brandy wasn't going to save him, so what the hell?

"And is that it?" he asked Turnbull. "Is that the lot? Hardly a dossier."

Turnbull continued to study him. Gill was a little thin in the face, had a high forehead, unfathomable eyes which were green one moment and grey the next. His teeth were even behind thin, slightly crooked lips; his skin overall, while generally unblemished, wore that certain pallor which spoke of severe physical disorders. Problems which were surfacing and wouldn't stop until Gill himself was submerged.

"You have a rare blood cancer," Turnbull finally said, and looked for Gill's flinch but failed to detect it. "That's the other reason you're up here: the air is good for you."

"Scotland," said Gill. "Somebody called it the last bastion of air-breathing man. I'm here for that, yes, but you're not one hundred percent right. It's not leukemia I have but something else. My system's all to cock. When I breathe in poisons, my lungs pass them right on into my blood. They're not blocked or filtered, and I have trouble voiding them. Also, I've no great tolerance for them. Just breathing is killing me. In the cities it's a fast train to the next world, but up here it's a bike ride—the object being not to pedal too fast, of course."

"And yet you take a drink now and then," said Turnbull. "You come into places like this where people are smoking, where even the fumes off the alcohol have to be bad for you."

Gill shook off the gloom he could feel settling on him like a heavy cloak. He'd had all of these arguments (with himself) many times over. He didn't need reminding. "The cities are one thing," he said with a shrug. "I can do without them—never liked them anyway. But I won't give up the things I do like. Is it worth it for an extra week or two? I don't think so. I just thank my lucky stars I never got hooked on smoking! Anyway, can we change the subject?"

"Sure," said Turnbull. "We can talk about everyone's favourite subject, if you like."

"The Castle?" Gill was at once uneasy again. "What's to talk about? It is. It's there. It's a machine. That's it."

"No." Turnbull shook his head. "That's not it. Not all of it. There's something you know that you're not saying."

Now it was Gill's turn to study Turnbull. He did so thoughtfully, narrow-eyed, and for the first time with something other than friendly curiosity. Today had been his first meeting with the man, when he'd been introduced to him by Turnbull's MOD minister. Security was so thick on the ground up here that the Minister had given his minder the weekend off. Knowing that

Gill had rooms in Killin, and that lodgings were otherwise almost impossible to come by, it had been suggested that Turnbull put up at his place. Gill hadn't minded; company was something he'd been going short on. Lecturing VIPs wasn't his idea of company. And anyway the big man interested him. Perhaps even more so, now. An intellectual he wasn't, but shrewd he most certainly was.

Turnbull was just over six feet tall, shaped like a slender wedge, with a bullet head supported by very little neck to speak of. His hair was black, fairly long, and swept back into something of a mane; he kept it stuck down with something that gave it a shine without making it greasy. But that wasn't out of vanity, it was just to keep it out of his eyes. Those eyes were heavy-lidded, blue when they flashed a smile or when he opened them in surprise. But his smiles were rare and the creases in his forehead many and deep. He seemed to be always on his guard: his training, Gill supposed. And his hands were huge, blunt, extremely strong and yet very fast and flexible. All of him looked fast and flexible. And efficient.

Gill looked at Turnbull's face. One eyebrow sat fractionally higher than the other, giving him a quizzical look even when he wasn't quizzing. His angular chin was scarred a little, with small white pocks showing through the brown. Brown, healthy skin, yes—from many a trip to the sun with his boss, no doubt. That's where Gill would be if he weren't required here: somewhere in the sun. The Greek islands, maybe.

He controlled his train of thought. He *was* here, and Turnbull had seen through him. Or seen through something of him, anyway. Finally he met the other's blue unblinking eyes behind their heavy lids, said, "What am I to make of a remark like that? Have you been tasked to me or something? Am I under suspicion, even surveillance?" He was only half joking; the security services of the entire world were interested in the Castle, from the CIA to the KGB, stopping at all stations along the way. But when Turnbull's eyes flashed blue in genuine surprise, Gill relaxed a little.

"Hell, no!" said Turnbull. "It's just that I can see you're worried about something—over and above your big worry, I mean. Part of my training was in interrogation. If I got hold of someone who looked like you, the first thing I'd think was that he was holding something back. I thought it during your talk. What you said boiled down to the Castle being a machine. You said a lot, but basically you could have said it in three words: it's a machine. That's what you *said*, but you were thinking something else."

Gill thought: *I've underestimated you!* And out loud, "So what was I thinking?"

Turnbull picked up his drink, shrugged. "Maybe I'm wrong. Christ knows you must have plenty of other things to think about. Plenty of things on your mind."

"Like dying? So we're back to that again. You know, I've just realized why I dislike company. I'd forgotten for a little while, but you've reminded me. People always want to know what it feels like."

Turnbull ordered more drinks. The bar was filling up. There were people here from all over the world, so that Turnbull must raise his voice to make himself heard over the hubbub. But when he turned back to Gill, he was quieter. "Well, I don't. Okay, that subject is . . . finished. Let's try something else. Like, how did you get started?"

Gill raised his eyebrows.

"This machine thing. This trick of yours."

"It's no trick."

"I didn't mean it that way."

"I know you didn't." Gill tossed back his fresh drink in one, gulped, and made a face. "Can we get out of here? This atmosphere really *is* killing me!" He elbowed his way a little unsteadily from the bar; Turnbull drank half of his malt whisky and followed him.

They walked through the bitter late February night, through streets an inch deep in ice-crusted snow, back to Gill's rooms on the outskirts of the village. As they went Gill said, "Look at this place, will you! Killin? You'd think it was Gstaad midseason! Two years ago this was a sleepy little village. But check out these car registrations. They're here from all over Europe—and some from a lot farther than that."

"Like Mars?" Turnbull said.

Now it was Gill's turn to say, "That isn't what I meant."

"But you do think the Castle's alien, right?" Turnbull pressed.

"I didn't say so." Gill was evasive.

"Not in your lecture, no," said Turnbull. "But then you were talking to a whole lot of heavies: Russians, French, Germans, Americans, even a couple of Chinese! You've been told not to be as open with outsiders as you've been with the home team. But my Old Man talks to me now and then when he's not busy, you know? He practices his speeches on me, or just says things to get my reaction. And just occasionally he lets things slip. It may not have been on BBC One—may not be for common consumption—but the word is that you've opted for an alien origin."

Gill snorted, almost laughed out loud. "The whole world has opted for an alien origin, for God's sake! What else would they opt for? It's either that or the biggest damned hoax in the history of the planet."

They had reached Gill's rooms. As he unlocked the door and let them in, Turnbull said, "But it isn't a hoax, right?"

Gill put on the lights. Shrugging out of his overcoat, he looked Turnbull straight in the eye. "No," he said, "it's no hoax."

Turnbull clutched his arm and Gill could feel the big man's excitement. "So where's it from? And why is it here? I mean, you're the Machine Man—the man who talks to machines—so if anyone knows it has to be you."

Gill shook his head (sadly, Turnbull thought) and turned up the heating. Collapsing into a chair he said, "I don't talk to the damn things. I have . . . a *feel* for them, that's all. I understand them like Einstein understood numbers, or like a paleontologist understands old bones. Just like Einstein could find a missing equation, or a fossil hunter put together a dinosaur, I can rebuild a machine. No, even that's not strictly true, for I haven't the skill. But I can tell someone who has the skill how to do it. I sense things about machines. Show me a car engine and I'll tell you what year it was made. I can listen to a Jumbo and tell you if one of the turbo blades is cracked. But as for talking to them . . ."

Turnbull looked disappointed. "So you don't know where it's from."

"I know where it's *not* from: it's not from Mars. Nor from any other planet we have a name for."

"It's not from our Solar System?"

Gill was patient. "Ours is the only Solar System. The sun is Sol—hence Solar System. No, it isn't from one of our nine planets or their moons. And that's not me saying so but every cosmologist in the business. We are the only intelligent life-forms in this neck of the woods. The Castle is from . . . somewhere else."

Turnbull was excited again. "You know, I've been daft on science fiction ever since I was a kid. But this isn't SF, it's real! You said you can tell the age of an engine on sight, so—"

"Not always on sight," Gill cut him short. "But let me touch it, let me sit with it for a while, and . . . I'm not usually far wrong."

"Well fine. So you've been up here sitting on this machine of yours for a year! So here comes the obvious question—"

"How old is it?"

"Obviously."

Gill's pàle face was suddenly even more gaunt. His eyes were grey now and empty as space. "I don't know," he said. "I've nothing to measure it against. I mean, I wasn't here when it was made—when what's inside it was made. *We* weren't here. How old? How old is the earth?"

Turnbull sighed. And after a long time, he said, "So what's it doing here? All right, I know you don't know. So guess."

"I *do* know," said Gill, "I think. It's watching, and it's listening, and it's waiting. But I don't know what for. . . ."

CHAPTER FOUR

"You asked me how it started," said Gill. "I honestly don't know. It's as much a mystery to me as to anyone else. It's something that grew in me, that's all. But I'm not unique. It's as if, in some people, nature makes up for a deficiency by introducing a supplementary talent. People who are blind from birth or soon after can often 'see' as well as you and I. Musicians as deaf as posts compose masterpieces—without ever being able to hear them! Do you know what I mean?"

Turnbull frowned. "I think so. And you think nature knew she'd played a dirty trick on you, so gave you this thing of yours to balance the scales. But what good is it to you? It strikes me the scales remain pretty much out of kilter. I mean what the hell *good* is this talent of yours—

this rapport with mechanical things—if it doesn't solve *your* problems?"

"It's been a lot of use to other people." Gill defended his "talent." "I check out faulty jet engines. I have a knack of programming computers to crack security codes—Eastern Bloc codes, that is. I can look at a piece of Russian equipment and say how it was made and, if it's any good, the easiest way to duplicate it. I've just helped Elecorps reduce their microchip to micromicro, and working with Solinc we developed a solar energy panel thirty-five percent more efficient than the next best. No, it hasn't helped me much, not personally—not if you discount the money. I'm not short of money, believe me! But even without the financial side, I'm still a sight better off than that kid in Cyprus."

"Cyprus? Your father was in the army, wasn't he? He served there?"

Gill nodded. "I was just a kid," he said. "I schooled in Dhekelia, a British sovereign base. I was lousy at sums. One day out shopping in Larnaca, my father showed me a local kid standing on a street corner. 'Son,' my father said, 'stop worrying about your sums. Some people have it and some don't. You see that Greek Cypriot kid? He has it. But he's also a cripple, with one leg four inches shorter than the other, and he stammers like a machine gun.'

"I asked what it was that the kid had and my father showed me. He wrote down a three-figure number and multiplied it by itself twice. Like two times two times two equals eight, but using three figures instead of just one. We went to the Greek kid and my father told him the first number and asked him to cube it—but in his head. Mental arithmetic! The kid said the number twice to himself, scratched his head, then took my father's pencil and wrote down the answer. The one-hundred-percent-correct answer. Now tell me: what good was his talent to him, eh? On a street corner in a fishing village?"

Turnbull had to agree. "Not much."

"Then there were the so-called 'Rubik Twins' just nine or ten years ago. A Manchester father bought his twin sons a cube. No matter how complicated he'd mix up the squares, his sons would solve it in seconds flat. Let him totally sod up the combinations, still they'd unscramble the thing. Each son was as good as the other. So the father complained to the makers that he'd been ripped off; their cube was too easy. They came to see these prodigies for themselves, concluded that the twins were naturals at it—as simple as that. Word got out and other kids turned up who were almost as good. But the beauty of the twins was this: they invariably solved the thing in the *least possible* number of moves!

"The media explanation: 'their minds work in three dimensions!' My personal response to that: crap! That's as bad as saying I talk to machines. *All* of our minds work in three dimensions! We *live* in three dimensions! But the fact is that multidimensional or otherwise, their minds did work differently. And so does mine."

"What about computers?" Turnbull was insatiable. "That's where you really shine, isn't it? You can hear them thinking."

The look he got then told him he was wrong. "No." Gill sighed again and shook his head. "I can't because they don't. They solve problems but they don't think. They can only give out what's first put in. Oh, they can extrapolate, if they're asked to—and they do it all a lot faster than any human mind—but they can't think. Not yet anyway. Look: if you want to make a three-minute egg timer, put some fine sand in your funny bottle and let it run out. And time it. When you have exactly three minutes worth of sand in there, seal the bottle. After that, every time you want a three minute egg, the timer will give you exactly that. Does that make it intelligent? A better example: if you want to know the time you check your watch, right? Day or night it gives you the right answer at a glance. But has your watch got a mind? It's programming, that's all."

"My watch is programmed?"

"Certainly, to tick away one second every second."

"See," said Turnbull, grinning, "that's why I was so good at interrogation."

"Eh?"

"Methinks you protest too much. Have you *tried* listening to the Castle think?"

Gill found himself smiling a real smile for the first time in too long. "You know, Jack," he said. "I liked you the first time I saw you. Something about you—a bloke I could get on with. But I didn't tag you as brilliant. You are, though, in your way. Or if not brilliant, very clever."

"You *have* heard it thinking?" Turnbull sat up straighter.

"I've heard it doing . . . something." The smile slid from Gill's face.

"Listening, watching, waiting?"

Gill nodded. "Yes."

"But you didn't tell that to the VIPs." It wasn't an accusation, just a statement of fact.

"Most of them already know," said Gill. "Those who are worth their salt."

"Come again?" Turnbull's heavy eyelids came awake and propped themselves wide open. "I don't recall hearing anything about that."

"Scare mongering," said Gill. "That's what I'd be accused of if it was public knowledge. That's what the government would be accused of. What? This pile of alien masonry up here on a Scottish mountainside, sitting watching us, waiting for something? Perhaps making its mind up about something? They'd yell, 'What's the government thinking of? Why aren't they protecting us?' And then they'd have to be told that the government is protecting them—or that they're prepared to, anyway. And when they knew just *how* prepared . . ."

"So-called 'tactical' nuclear weapons," said Turnbull, low-voiced. "CND would have a field day!"

"Hey! You're not supposed to know about that!" Gill was alarmed.

"Damn right I am," said Turnbull, matter-of-factly. "How am I supposed to play the game if I don't know the stakes? We both have talents, Spencer, and mine's minding. I look after the Man Responsible, remember?"

"Anyway, enough's enough," said Gill. "I'm tired and I'm turning in. I may read for a little while. Will the light bother you?"

"Not me." Turnbull shook his head. "I won't sleep for a while anyway. Too much to think about."

Gill had the bed and Turnbull a long, wide settee. He'd slept in worse places. When Gill switched the light off, Turnbull said, "Just one more thing."

"Shoot." Gill's voice was weary in the darkness of the room.

"You said the Castle was perhaps making its mind up about something. Now what did you mean by that? Machines don't have minds, you said, and they don't think. A bit contradictory, isn't it?"

"Yes," said Gill, after a little while. And: "It was a figure of speech, that's all."

Unconvinced, Turnbull nodded thoughtfully to himself. "Computers can't think, you said—not yet. But you were talking about our computers, made here, on Earth. This thing, this alien thing, has to be way ahead of anything we've got. It would have to be just to have come from—wherever." He waited for a response, and when none was forthcoming: "Gill?"

"Yes," said Gill, very quietly. "It would have to be. . . ."

Turnbull left it at that. And now he had even more to think about before sleeping.

The time scheduled for selection was close now. The time of the choosing, when the House of Doors would take and commence its analysis of a handful of specimens. Nothing must be allowed to interfere with that; there was no margin for error; and so the Thone Controller must now seek out and deal with the watcher: the one who was aware. To some Thone Controllers that awareness in itself would have signalled an end to any further intrusion, but Sith of the Thone was not one of them. This world was a good one, eminently suitable, and Sith very much desired to please the Grand Thone. He must, for he himself was one of the contenders for that all-powerful office.

Which was why, tonight, in the cold and the dark, he was out in the shining, frosted streets of Killin. The hour was late and few people were about, but it wouldn't much concern Sith if they were. In his human construct guise, and armed, he was close to invincible. Human flesh and blood just couldn't stand up to him. Outside of his manufactured shell, of course, the bitter cold of this planet would kill him off in a matter of seconds. And even a human child would find little difficulty in pulling him to pieces.

What he contemplated—the murder of an innocent—was entirely against every Thone law, but this was no-man's-land and as far as he was concerned the law didn't apply. The man called Spencer Gill was or might prove to be a serious threat, and every threat must be taken into consideration. Since Gill was the *only* threat, the simple solution was to eradicate him. He couldn't be allowed to stand in the way at the time of the taking.

Sith had graphed Gill on the last occasion his interference had registered inside the Castle, and now he let his locator guide him unerringly to Gill's lodgings. Sith had calculated that since Gill was a mind alone—possibly one of a sort— it was likely that he'd also be a man alone. But even if there were a woman or a friend, it would make no difference. Surprise was on his side; that and his near indestructibility—the fact that face-to-face with an unarmed man he would be quite simply invincible—gave him supreme confidence, so that he failed to even consider the possibility of resistance or retaliation.

Gill was asleep when his doorbell sounded, ringing insistently and with short, regular breaks. Someone was either very impatient or extremely methodical. He woke up thinking just that, and putting on the light saw Turnbull shrugging into a dressing gown. "It's okay," said the big man. "It's bound to be for me. I'll give you odds something's come up and we're wanted in London on the double. Me and the boss, I mean."

"What?" said Gill, only half-awake.

Turnbull went through a bead curtain and headed down a short, dark corridor to the door. The curtain jangled behind him, falling back into place. "Eh?" Gill mumbled, swinging his legs out of bed. The doorbell was still ringing. Gill heard it stop abruptly as Turnbull unlocked the door. Then—

Out in the night street a tall, blocky figure stood with something in his hand that shone and whirred. Turnbull didn't even have time to focus his eyes. An arm and hand shot out, caught him under the left armpit and yanked him out into the street. His bare feet skidded on ice, shot out from under him. As he went down, so the hand holding the whirring thing sliced the air where his face had been. Turnbull scrambled frantically away, his hands and feet shooting off in all directions as they tried to find purchase.

Sith scarcely gave him another glance. His locator said that Gill was still inside. This man wasn't Sith's target. He stepped inside, into the corridor. At the other end, Gill's shambling figure was coming through the bead curtains. "Who is it?" he said, blinking owlishly.

Sith stepped towards him.

"Hold it!" Turnbull yelled.

Sith paused and looked back, and Turnbull saw the fires behind his eyes. Turnbull's dressing gown hung open and he was wearing a shoulder holster over a crumpled shirt. He was holding a gun in both hands, levelling it on Sith. But Gill was already halfway down the corridor.

"Spencer, go back!" Turnbull yelled. Sith put up his free hand before his face, lumbered back out into the street with his shining weapon swinging this way and that.

Turnbull backed off, triggered off a round. In the crisp night air of the dreaming village, the sound was a deafening roar. Turnbull saw the hand holding the whirring thing fly apart into so many red sausages, and the shining weapon went spinning into a pile of snow at the side of the road. It was lost in chunks of glittering ice crystal.

Sith charged Turnbull, who got off another round before the blocky figure was on him. Then he went down like a truck had hit him, hammered to the icy cobbles, and the intruder fled on across his prone form and away into darkness.

Turnbull lay where he had fallen, senses spinning, and tried to work out what was happening. Then Gill was there beside him, helping him to sit up. "Are you all right?"

Turnbull gingerly fingered his ribs. "Something in here's a bit— *uh!* —banged about. But . . . yes, I think I'm all right. Bruised ribs, that's all. I was lucky. Jesus, he was strong as a horse!"

"Who . . . who was he?" Gill's face was white, shocked, a pale blur of astonishment.

Turnbull got up. Lights were coming on behind curtained windows up and down the street. "Inside," said Turnbull. "Quick! We don't want to become a focus of attention." But before joining Gill in the corridor, he limped over to the snow pile and fished about for a moment. Then he followed on; Gill closed the door and locked it; they went to the flat's tiny kitchen. Almost automatically, Gill made coffee.

Pouring hot water onto brown, swirling granules, he said again, "Well, who was—"

Turnbull cut him short. "I was rather hoping you could tell me," he said. He glanced at Gill curiously, then began examining huge bruises across his chest and down his left side. Already they were starting to darken.

"Eh?" said Gill. "How would I know? I met you for the first time this morning, and now this. You're the Dangerman around here. It's pretty plain to me that he was after you." He was plausible but didn't sound too certain. Indeed, Turnbull thought his voice sounded just a fraction more shaky than it should be, even in these circumstances.

"He could have killed me when I opened the door to him," Turnbull said. "He almost did! But then he left me and started after you. It was you he was after and I just happened to get in his way."

They took their coffees into the bed-sitting-room, where Turnbull put something down on a small occasional table. "What do you make of that?"

Gill picked it up. It was six inches long, blunt-tipped at one end, like a silver pocket torch or thickish fountain pen, otherwise featureless apart from a very small scar and dent halfway along its cylindrical length. Gill fingered the dent.

"A freak shot," Turnbull told him. "I hit it in his hand. There'll be a fistful of fingers out there in the snow. These bullets I'm using are stoppers!"

"My God!" said Gill.

"It's a hard world, son," Turnbull grated. But then he saw that Gill's remark hadn't been directed at him. Gill was staring at the thing in his hand. As he stared so it began to whir, but gratingly, like something was broken. Its blunt tip shimmered with an almost invisible vibration. Gill quickly held it away from himself, towards the table. For a moment its vibrating tip touched the dark oak of the tabletop—then sliced through like it was cheese!

Gill gave a small cry and let go of the thing. Inert, it fell to the carpet. . . .

CHAPTER FIVE

Gill and Turnbull came to a mutual understanding, put away the alien weapon and called the police. This action coincided with the wailing of a siren from fairly close at hand. Before the car could actually get to them, Gill went back out (covered by Turnbull from the shadows of the corridor) and gingerly retrieved a bloody finger. He had time to hide that, too, before the police began ringing the doorbell.

The two men gave identical statements:

Turnbull had been attacked by an intruder who had then threatened Gill with a gun. Recovering from the initial attack, Turnbull had drawn the intruder back out into the street, shooting at him before he himself could be shot at. He believed he'd hit him in the hand. That was all there was to it.

A quick telephone call to Turnbull's Minister

(he was at the home of an MP in Edinburgh, returning to Killin tomorrow) had authenticated Turnbull's identity and explained his possession of a weapon. Fingers had then been gathered up from the snow outside, substantiating the story; by then, too, it was snowing again, huge soft flakes an inch across. There was no blood to mention, and no tracks anyone could hope to follow.

By 2:45 A.M. the police were satisfied they'd covered everything and went off to make their report. They'd considered putting a guard on the house but higher authority had dissuaded them: pointless to put a minder on a minder. Gill should be safe as long as Turnbull was here. Instead they would insist on covert police protection for Turnbull's Minister, at least until Turnbull had been recalled to the job. It could well be that the Minister had been the real target. Turnbull had pretended agreement: maybe he had been at that. But neither he nor Gill believed it.

When Turnbull and Gill were alone again and as the latter made more coffee, Turnbull growled: "Okay, Spencer, let's talk."

"Talk?" Gill repeated him.

"Do you know this American word, 'meaningful'? Well, it's time you and I had a meaningful conversation. Before, when we talked, we were finding our way, fooling around, feeling each other out. You were, anyway. I was just being me. But I was right about you: that is, I know you're not telling everything you know about the Castle. And tonight's little visit proves it."

Gill was jumpy, surly. He didn't like being squeezed into a corner. "What does it prove?"

"For one, it proves that there's a lot more going on here than meets the eye. Was that guy tonight an alien or what? I know his weapon is!"

"I didn't see him well enough," said Gill. "Didn't get close enough—thank God! And anyway I don't know what an alien looks like. You're right about the weapon, though. That certainly *is* alien. It was made where the Castle was made—where it was designed, anyway."

"You know that for a fact?"

"No, but it's too much of a coincidence."

"I agree. As for our intruder"—Turnbull shrugged—"it was all too quick. He came, got spiteful, didn't like what he'd bitten into, went. And I'm not much clued up on aliens either. But I'll tell you one thing: he was strong!"

"We have the weapon, anyway," said Gill, with some satisfaction. "That goes to the people upstairs."

"Like hell!" said Turnbull. "Who the hell are the people upstairs, anyway? My boss gets it. If we're going up against aliens, we can use the know-how."

Gill scowled at him, yet not in antagonism. "One minute I think you're smart," he said, "and the next you're a dimwit!"

"Eh?"

"What do you think your Minister will do with it if you give it to him?"

Turnbull frowned, gradually eased off. "Eventually it'll come right back to you, right?"

"Not eventually, immediately. See, my people *are* your people! I had assumed you knew that. It's how your boss and I come to know each other. Ministry of Defence. We're not only on

42

the same side but also the same team. Or maybe you thought I was up here solely for my health?"

Turnbull slowly nodded. "Maybe I should have guessed," he said, "but you're not on any list. Which makes you Cosmic. In this capacity, anyway. Top secret. *Top* top secret, in fact. See, I had you tied up with one or another of the intelligence services."

"In the right place, at the right time, you'd be right," said Gill. "We're all hand in hand anyway. But here there's not a lot of intelligence to gather. The Castle's here and that's about the only clear fact. So I'm MOD. Also, our intelligence agencies are geared for spying against other human beings—not against aliens."

Turnbull brought out the weapon from its hiding place down the back of the settee. He sniffed suspiciously at the thing, kept it at arm's length. "What do you make of it?"

"Busted," said Gill, taking it from him and holding it as before. "It's power source—its converter, anyway—is damaged. Your bullet."

"Converter? Power source? Like a battery, you mean?"

Gill shook his head. "Have you ever used a battery-powered shaver? I shouldn't think you have, not with your chin. Bristles like that would be too much for it. Or can you imagine a battery-powered circular saw? Running on a couple of pencil-slim flashlight batteries? Of course not! No, this thing takes its energy from somewhere else, converts it, releases it destructively here at the tip. It's like a portable power drill—except it doesn't need a cable. Its energy is beamed to it. It's constantly available—like a

TV picture or a radio signal. They're there, just waiting for you to switch on the set. I think so, anyway."

"Beamed to it," said Turnbull, scratching his chin. "From the Castle?"

"We can only suppose so, yes."

"For twenty months they've sat up there on that hillside, doing nothing, just checking us out," said Turnbull thoughtfully. "As far as we know, anyway. So why should they suddenly decide to come on strong now? The media have got used to the idea that they're friendly observers—if they're there at all. Was that it, do you think? Lull us into a state of false security? Familiarity breeds contempt?"

"Like a mousetrap?"

"Eh?"

"A mousetrap sits there in the night doing nothing. The mouse has his run, which he knows intimately. All of a sudden there's this object right in his way, something new, which he never saw before. And it appears to be harmless. It doesn't do anything. So he approaches it from all angles, cautiously at first—and still it does nothing. Then he spots the food, the trigger. Except he doesn't know it's a trigger. He takes the bait, trips the spring, and . . ."

"Have we tripped some kind of spring?" Turnbull lifted his angular eyebrow a shade higher.

"We've brought tactical atomic weapons up here," said Gill. "I think we can assume they know that. *If* the Castle contains aliens, that is. I mean, we don't know that for sure. For an alien, tonight's visitor looked pretty human to me. And his finger is . . . a finger!" The digit he spoke of was now in a jar in his fridge.

"That's the other thing I'd meant to ask you," said Turnbull. "Why?"

"The finger? Why did I want a piece of him? To give to forensic, naturally. Our forensic. Oh, the police will take prints from their bits, no doubt—but myself, I'd like a rather more in-depth study."

"You mean, just because he looked human, it doesn't mean he was human."

"Something like that." Gill managed a fragile grin. "Hell, *you* look human!" And before Turnbull could answer: "My guess is that if that finger is from another world . . . well, there will have to be differences. Small, maybe, but obvious—to someone who knows what he's looking for."

Turnbull nodded, said, "And then of course, there's you."

"Me?"

"A spring-tripper," said Turnbull, his eyes glooming on the other.

Gill suddenly felt cold. "Go on."

"You've been here a year. Before that you were up here half a dozen times checking the Castle out and making your reports, until they decided to station you here permanently. Right?"

Gill nodded.

"Whether there are intelligences inside the Castle, or whether it in itself is an artificial intelligence, maybe doesn't matter. You say it probably knows we've brought atomics up here. So maybe it knows that you're here, too. Maybe it's been reading you like you've been trying to read it. . . ."

Gill's telephone rang. It was Turnbull's boss, asking for him. Turnbull took the phone and listened for a while, and when the Minister had finished filled in some of the details of what had happened at Gill's place. When their conversation was over, Turnbull replaced the handset and said, "Curiouser and curiouser."

"Oh?"

"He's just tasked me to you! Spencer, my boy, you now have a minder all your own!"

Gill was surprised and not a little grateful. The big man knew his job, and in the shortest period of time Gill had been made to feel very vulnerable. His relief showed on his face when he said, "Because of tonight?"

But Turnbull only frowned and half shook his head. "Yes and no," he said. "The boss will pick us up tomorrow morning and fill us in then. All he's saying for now is that things are 'coming to a head.' The way I see it . . . you're an ace card, Spencer. Maybe someone's just realized that we can't afford to lose you."

Gill didn't attempt to fathom it any further than that. In any case, it only served to verify what he'd suspected for some little time: that indeed things were rapidly coming to a head. . . .

CHAPTER SIX

Angela Denholm checked herself out in the mirror. The bruising had almost disappeared now from her right eye, but she would continue to wear her dark glasses. With their help, and snug in her new white parka and black ski pants, she would at least feel disguised. She supposed she might only be fooling herself, but there was always the chance that Rod would also be fooled. The new clothing had been the best idea she'd had since running out on him.

She checked the bruising again, the faint, fading, telltale blotch where his fist had struck home, and gave a small, involuntary shudder. She had always loathed physical violence, never would have believed that she'd become just another victim. And yet that's exactly what had happened to her—or would have. But being a battered wife hadn't been Angela's scene. She had more going for her than that. And when finally love had fled, so she'd fled, too.

That had been a little more than three weeks ago, since when she'd been on the run. Pride had stopped her from seeking help, kept her from going to the police, screaming for a divorce; the divorce would come later. Pride and what little loyalty she'd had left. Rod had been warned off more than once already about his drinking; another incident was all it would take for him to lose his job; Angela considered that he'd paid enough in losing her. He was a technician with a local TV station in Edinburgh, and a new job wouldn't be easy to find. But . ... it was painful to her that he would be hurting. She hadn't taken her marriage vows lightly. On the other hand, he'd only be hurting inside. And there'd been times when Angela had hurt all over.

She looked at herself in her bedroom's full-length mirror and nodded, strangely relieved that she still recognized the woman in there. For a time she'd felt irrevocably changed, but now the old Angela was coming back again. At least married life—life married to Rodney Denholm—had kept her in good trim. Little chance there of becoming fat and contented!

Small, leggy, slim, and pretty, with elfin ears half-hidden in tight black ringlets, a not-quite-perfect mouth, pert nose, and slightly tilted, deep, dark eyes, she looked almost Eurasian and was often taken for it. But in fact she was as English as they come. Or British, anyway, since her father was a Scot. But she'd inherited her mother's face and slender figure, and mercifully something of her independence, too.

Dressing, putting on her very feminine under-things, Angela felt something of the sadness again, but also a lot of the freedom. Rod would get tired of the chase eventually, and then he'd have a choice. Straighten up and kick the habit permanently, and maybe find someone new who he'd have to treat right—or keep hitting the bottle until it hit him back, and go down and out without a friend in the world. Sober, he could be a most sensitive, even a tender man, but only give him a drink—just one—and everything he kept suppressed would surface on the instant and he'd be all hell let loose. The thing he'd kept most suppressed had been his jealousy. . . .

The thought of that, Rod's maniacal jealousy when he'd been drinking—his totally unwarranted, almost homicidal jealousy—drove out the last dregs of sadness. For in the end that was why she'd run: because at times it had been so bad that she'd feared for her life.

Waiting one morning until he'd gone off to work, she'd packed a few things, left their flat in Edinburgh's Dalkeith Road for the last time and caught a train down to London. She had friends there from her years at university. She had left Rod on a Friday, but by the following weekend he'd tracked her.

First there had been telephone calls: Rod, desperately looking for her, pleading with her friends that if they knew where she was they must tell him. He had been to see her parents, too. Of course, she'd kept them in the picture by telephone right from square one; they'd been supportive and offered her every assistance; when Rod went to see them, they'd played the worried parents (which of course they'd been) for his benefit, or more properly for Angela's, and kept her whereabouts secret.

Then there had been the long, rambling letters: letters to her friends, explaining to them how sorry he was (wasn't he always?) but that her leaving had shocked him back onto the rails, the straight and narrow, and all he wanted now was that she'd forgive him and come back. He would make it all up to her, he promised.

But Angela knew better. She was in hiding and intended to stay that way, for now anyway. The people she was with had their instructions to play dumb and never admit that she was there; Rod's letters to her, to be forwarded through them, were returned to him unopened with sympathetic little notes saying that they couldn't be forwarded because it simply wasn't known where Angela was. All of this because she had needed the time to get herself—her thoughts, emotions, her plans for some kind of future—sorted out.

But then Rod had found her.

She was staying with Siobhan and George Lynch. On the Monday morning ten days after Angela left Edinburgh to travel down to their house in North London, when George drove down early to Finsbury Park to take the first tube train into the city where he worked, Rod had been waiting for him. The station had been almost empty: a bum with his bottle, moaning in a plastic bag stuffed with newspapers; a black workman in coveralls and a headset, jiving with himself at the far end of the platform; and Rodney Denholm, unshaven, with whiskey on his breath, following George from the ticket machines down onto the platform and grabbing him there. George wasn't much physically, had never been a fighter to speak of ... but at least when Rod was through with him he'd managed to telephone Angela and warn her. Apparently her husband had been keeping a watch on the house since Saturday evening.

Now, shrugging into her parka, Angela thought back on that telephone conversation with the husband of her best friend. Siobhan hadn't been out of bed yet (thank God! For she was the hysterical type) and so Angela had left her breakfast to answer the phone herself. If it had been Rod, she could simply jiggle the handset about a bit and put it down, to give the impression that the telephone wasn't working properly or that the connection was a bad one. Except it hadn't been Rod but George.

"Angela?" his tinny voice had croaked. "You'd better get—*uh!*—out of there, love, and run for it! Rod's—*uh!*—here, and he's just had a go at me!" George had been out of breath, sounded like he was in pain. Angela's heart had almost frozen inside her.

"George? Has he hurt you? Could you smell drink on him? Oh, God, he's been drinking! Where *are* you?"

"Finsbury Park," his choking voice had come again. "God! He has fingers like a steel vise, that bloke! He accused us of having an affair, you and me, and said he could kill me! But he wouldn't because it's you he wants. If he killed me, they'd put him away, and you'd be free to go on running around and, well, fucking whoever you want!"

"George!"

"That's what the bastard *said*!" George had

rasped. "He accused you of being—*uh!*—a bloody vampire, said you'd suck any man you could dry as a stick. So he was going on a crusade for all men. He was going to get you and settle with you for good! He pitied me, he said, because I was just the latest in your long line of victims, and he wanted to know why my 'poor cow of a wife' wasn't complaining about it. Or maybe I was having both of you away in the—*uh!*—same bed."

"George, but you know none of that's true!"

" 'Course I do, love, but he thinks it is! Angela, this bloke is as barmy as they come. So you get out of there. There'll be motors on the roads by now, but even so he'll still be able to bus it up there in about twenty-five minutes. And if he has a car, it'll be even quicker. Just tell Siobhan not to answer the door to anyone, and then make yourself scarce. Do you need money?"

"No, that's one thing I'm not short of."

"Off you go, then. Me, I'm calling the police."

"What? Did he hurt you?"

"I'm not a hospital case, if that's what you mean. But he scared the shit out of me, yes. And I'll likely have bruises on my windpipe for a week! You should know what he's like if anyone does."

Angela had fingered her own slender throat. "But the police, George!" she'd protested. "It's all over for him if you call them."

"Better if it's all over for him than for you or some other poor sod! Now you do what you want to, Angela, and I'll do my own thing. But right now, love, get the hell out of there. You're wasting time!" And with that he'd put the phone down.

Then, no longer concerned whether Siobhan had hysterics or not, she'd rushed about the house bundling her few things into a travel bag, and as her friend had stumblingly followed her about trying to get orientated, told her what was happening.

"Rod, coming here?" Siobhan had finally got the message.

"Lock the door after I've gone," Angela had breathlessly told her. And she'd left her with a kiss on the cheek. She hadn't even had time to say thanks.

At midday, from Waverly Station in Edinburgh, she'd phoned Siobhan and got the story. Rod had arrived a little after the police, and George had been a few minutes behind him. Except there'd no longer seemed to be any anger left in Rod, just tears, exhaustion, shame. Siobhan even sounded a little sorry for him. George hadn't brought charges; the police' had shrugged and called it "a domestic," and they'd asked Rod if he wanted to report Angela as a missing person; George had finally gone off late to work and Rod . . . had fallen asleep in the spare room! In fact he was still sleeping there now.

Well, he *had* been, but he'd heard Siobhan on the telephone. And suddenly, instead of talking to Siobhan, Angela had found herself talking to Rod. He must have had a good dose of whatever he'd been on, because she could still hear it in his voice. She recognized and knew that tone only too well, and also that any remorse he'd shown had been make-believe, conjured to pacify the police and perhaps to give himself a break from the pursuit.

"Hello—Angela? Sweetheart, you can't go on

running forever," he'd said. Not: "I love you, forgive me." Not: "Angela, I'm going mad and I need you so badly. I can't live without you." Not: "I'm sorry. It doesn't have to be like this. Let's try it this way: do your own thing for three months and then see me. And if you see no change in me, then we'll go our own ways. And if we do, then no hard feelings, only soft ones." If he'd said any of those things . . . she couldn't think how she might have reacted. For she had loved him desperately—once. But he didn't, just:

"Angela, sweetheart, you can't go on running forever." And there'd been that in his use of the word "sweetheart" which had told her a lot, and a threat in his words that said, albeit obliquely, "And when you finally stop running, I'll be right there behind you."

"Rod . . ." she'd at last answered. "Rod, I—"

"Where are you, sweetheart?" he'd cut in. And God, she'd almost told him! But saving her: "Who is he?" Rod had continued, his voice cold, lacking the emotion she might expect in any normal man. "Who has taken my place, Angela? Does he love you any better than I did? Does he *make* love to you any better?"

And that was when she'd slammed the phone down, for she'd heard that loathsome leer creeping into his voice, and she'd recognized that, too.

"Love?" Rod didn't know the meaning of the word. "Sex," he knew, and "lust." But looking back, Angela could only remember a handful of times when Rod had actually made "love" to her. In the early, tender times, when he'd courted her, and in those few short weeks after

they were married. But then there had been difficulties with his new boss, and Rod couldn't
hack any sort of competition or threat. He'd had
trouble with the bottle before (Angela hadn't
known about that) and now leaped right back
on the hook. Toss tenderness out of the window! With a drink inside him, Rod was an animal. Since when, with only the occasional,
merciful break, Angela's life had become a long
unending nightmare.

Make love to her? He had once upon a time,
yes, but not anymore. Now, when the bottle
hadn't killed it in him entirely, it was no longer
love but rape in the ugliest, fullest meaning of
the word! Instead of lashing out at his boss, he
lashed out at her. Instead of tearing up his files
and his contract, she'd thought he was trying to
tear her. And it had become a matter of survival—and of pride, for her parents had tried to
warn her off him—to recognize his every mood,
sense the slightest imbalance in his emotions
before it could go right out of kilter.

But his drinking, his rages, and worst of all
his insane accusations hadn't improved; finally
Angela had woken up and asked herself, "Do I
need this?" She hadn't, and so she'd run.

Yes, and now she was running again. But she
promised herself, this was the last time.

Her parents had their place in Perth, where
they'd retired early. From Edinburgh she'd
gone there—or rather, she'd come here—and
her folks had done the sensible thing and "gone
off to visit friends down south."

"We've had it planned a long time, my dear,"
her father had told her—lying in his teeth, the
darling. "And now that you're here to caretake

for us . . ." They'd known what was best for her: to be on her own with plenty of time to think things out. Then she could be herself, without worrying what they were thinking, or about them worrying about her. But before they'd left Rod had called them on the phone, and Angela's mother had taken the call. So that Angela had discovered how both of them could lie if it was important enough.

With the voice of an angel her mother had told Rod that Angela was in the southwest of England, Torbay, with friends of hers. That was all she could say; Angela hadn't told her any more than that; why didn't Rod just give it a rest now and let things work themselves out in their own good time?

It had been a clever move, for it had given Angela another ten days of peace and quiet. Oh, the phone would ring every now and then but she'd trained herself not to answer it. She could make calls if she wanted to, keeping them short, but she must never answer one. She'd come to an agreement with her parents that they wouldn't call her; any legitimate calls she might ignore probably wouldn't be important anyway.

After ten days, and no telephone calls at all for the last three, Angela had really started to relax, even to blossom a little. It had been the quietest and the best holiday of her life—until this morning, half an hour ago, when she'd been dragged out of bed by the telephone's insistent ringing, ringing, ringing. She'd had a letter yesterday from her folks; they would be back Monday; she was left with a last weekend to herself. This would be them on the phone, she'd thought, making sure all was well. But it hadn't been them, and all was far from well.

Rod's *hiss* of discovery, of—anticipation?—when she answered the phone had almost made her drop the thing. And when he'd spoken, she'd recoiled from his voice like it was a snake.

"Angela, you've cost me a lot," he said, slurring his words. "My job, my friends, my pride—everything. My job through my absenteeism while I've been chasing around after you, my pride because you've driven me lower than any man should go, and my friends because they were screwing you. But now—"

"Rod," she'd cut him off, her voice a gasp, "there's no way I'm coming back to you. It's over."

"—now we're going to have it out," he'd continued as if she hadn't even spoken. "The Great Lay of Edinburgh and London, eh? Well, *sweetheart*, before we're through you're going to know what screwing is all about!" And that was all, for then *he* had put the phone down. Angela had known that Rod's cracks had opened into chasms. There was no more pretending now, for his threat had sounded very real. Possibly he was only trying to frighten her; well, if so he'd succeeded.

But she had one more place to run to: her uncle's house in Killin. If Rod followed or threatened her there . . . then it would be time to call in the police, and to hell with him!

So now she scribbled a note to her parents saying she'd gone down south (they'd guess she hadn't, and would understand), went out and locked the door, hugged her parka to herself, and climbed into the driving seat of the Volvo. Her parents had left the car for her use.

Crusty snow crunched under her tyres as she turned right out of the drive into the road and headed west for Comrie and Killin. She didn't notice the battered VW Beetle that stayed back a hundred and fifty yards to her rear, sticking there like glue as she picked her way through the light, early-morning traffic and out of town. . . .

CHAPTER SEVEN

Turnbull's Minister, David Anderson, had arrived to pick up Turnbull and Gill at 7 A.M. sharp. He'd had coffee with them before they'd trooped out to his car. Over their coffees, Turnbull had shown him the finger. The big minder had tried often enough in the past to shock his boss (it was a thing they had between them) but he'd never quite succeeded. While Anderson had nothing of Turnbull's military background, still he didn't shock very easily. All a matter of being in control, Turnbull supposed. Anderson had picked up and studied the digit in its jar, shook it pale and stiff this way and that, and gone on drinking his coffee.

Anderson was jowly and overweight, wore fancy, almost feminine spectacles with ornate wings, and a white silk handkerchief flopping from his pinstripe pocket.

"Probably the index finger," he'd finally commented, taking out his handkerchief and dabbing at his thick lips, his voice dry, well-bred, but not especially superior. "See how the tip is tilted to the right, inclining inwards towards the nail? Compare it with your own. Yes, right-hand index, I'd say. His trigger finger. So he'll not be shooting at anyone for a while—unless he can grow a new one!"

"He didn't shoot," Turnbull had reminded him. Anderson had been told the details, but the finger looked so human it was easier to connect it to an orthodox weapon.

"This is what he used," said Gill, producing the dented silver cylinder.

"Alien?"

"Yes," said Gill. "I . . . caused it to work. For a few seconds, anyway." He indicated the cleanly sliced tabletop.

The Minister had looked—looked under the table, too—and frowned. "Have you tidied up since last night?"

"No."

"No sawdust," Anderson had pointed out. "No . . . debris? And yet there's a slice an eighth of an inch thick missing from the table. This— well, whatever it is—disintegrates, totally. Can you dismantle it?"

"I haven't tried." Gill had shrugged. "If it will X-ray, that might give us a clue. I didn't want to do it any more damage."

"Good!" Anderson had nodded. And he'd pocketed the thing. "I'll get it right back to you."

"You should have some top people look at the

finger, too," said Gill. He placed the jar and contents in a plastic bag, handed it over.

Anderson placed the bag between his feet, nodded his agreement. Then, hurrying now, he'd said to Gill, "Listen, Spencer, things are happening. Our monitors have been picking up an all-round increase in activity. And you?"

"For seven or eight days now," Gill had answered. "I told you about it."

"Hmm. Well, give yourself a pat on the back. You twigged it before the instruments. Right now it's hitting a new peak of activity. Any ideas?"

Gill shook his head. "I can't say," he said. "Not for certain. But—"

"But?"

"I've had this feeling it was gearing itself up."

For a little while there had been silence; then Anderson had grunted, nodded, and that had seemed to be that.

Through all of this Turnbull had been all ears but hadn't made a lot of what was said. But as Anderson had stood up, ready to leave, he'd blurted, "Can you break that down into tiny little words for me?"

Anderson had looked at Gill. "He's your man. It's up to you."

Getting their coats on and as they went out in the frosty morning to Anderson's car, Gill had explained, "We have monitors, up there on Ben Lawers behind the perimeter fence. Dug in. Unobtrusive. If you look hard, you can make out their aerials."

"Monitors?"

"Ultrasonic, infrared, radio, other radiations—anything we know how to measure. The harder a machine works, the more energy it consumes—and the more it radiates. Heat or whatever. As you rev a car, so its engine runs faster, gets hotter."

Turnbull had nodded. "Or as a mass of fissionable material moves towards critical, so the radiation levels go up."

"Right," said Gill. "*Exactly* right."

"And we're going up there—now?"

"The Castle isn't a bomb," said Gill.

The Minister got into the driving seat, said, "I want to have another look at it. It fascinates me. But it's not just idle curiosity. I want *you* to have a look at it, Gill. See if there's anything at all—anything new—you can tell us. Then I'm off back down to London. They're very concerned about things down there. Evacuation models I have to check over, you know?"

"He said it wasn't a bomb," Turnbull pointed out.

In his ear, Gill quietly said, "In case we need to use ours."

"By the way," said Anderson too loudly as Gill and Turnbull got into the back of his Mercedes, "this gentlemen is Jean-Pierre Varre." His voice returned to its normal tone, became dry as tinder as he added, "Er, from France. He's here to see you, Spencer. But I don't have to remind you—or you, Jack—that the Castle is a sensitive subject."

Waiting for them in the front passenger seat, Varre nodded curtly. He was small, slim, looked a little peeved. "Talk all you wish," he said. "About whatever subject. I am not interested in your Castle—not especially. But as the Minister said, I am here to speak with you, Mr. Gill."

Since talking about the Castle was now out, Gill said, "Fire away. How can I help you, Mr. Varre? Except, well, don't take that as a promise."

"Mr. Gill is a very busy man," Anderson added. "And his time is limited."

Gill stared at the back of Anderson's neck but said nothing. He knew—hoped—Anderson hadn't meant it that way. On the other hand, he knew he wasn't much for mincing his words, either.

They drove northeast out of the village to the first barrier on the loch road. As they went, Varre started to explain what he wanted. "Mr. Gill, I'm told you have a rare talent."

"Unique, we think," the Minister corrected him.

"Very well, unique." Varre nodded. "Some few years ago your government opted out of the European Space Programme. It had to do with finance—a certain tightness of the purse strings? They couldn't see their way clear to put up the necessary funds. Also, since the USA and USSR were already in the driving seat, as it were . . . well, there's no use shutting the gate after the horse has bolted. This was their reasoning. Some decisions of this sort might be seen as reasonable, others as sheerest folly—like abandoning HOTOL."

"Go on," said Gill.

"During the course of the last twelve months, however," Varre continued, "your government has been trying desperately to get back in. The so-called Castle may have much to do with that; it is generally accepted as an alien artifact, some sort of spaceship; it begins to seem likely that in the not too distant future intercourse with alien worlds is to become a reality—and of course Great Britain would not wish to be emasculated in that area."

"Not in *any* area!" Turnbull muttered, but to himself.

Gill had already decided he didn't much care for Monsieur Varre. There was something overly unctuous about the little Frenchman; he spoke openly enough, and his accent was only faintly French, but still it was as if his words sidled, instead of coming head-on. Politicians can be like that and get away with it, but Varre wasn't a politician. His eyes, like Turnbull's, were heavy-lidded—but that was where any similarity ended. For the eyes themselves were too bright, shifty, possibly devious. A snake's eyes, or those of a clever cardsharp. In any event, a sharp operator.

"Get to the point," said Gill.

"So far," said Varre, "the efforts of your government to get back into space have proved futile: ESP's contributors have put in a lot of trust, goodwill, money, and success can't be too far away. In less than three years our shuttle will be a reality—and far and away superior to the current American vehicle. But . . . of course there are problems. Not insurmountable. Time, alas, is the great enemy. Technical problems, yes: small faults in ballistics, in computer linkage, perhaps even in basic engine design. In many instances our only recourse is to a system of trial and error. And time slips by, and costs rise. If we could enlist your aid, however, and if your, er, *rapport* with machines is all they say it is . . ." He let it tail off.

Gill stared again at the back of Anderson's neck, and this time the Minister must have felt it. "Not my line, I'm afraid," he said, without looking back. "Hardly SDI, is it? Not yet for a while, anyway." And to Varre: "You realize of course that Mr. Gill's fees would be quite astronomical?"

Varre smiled, and Gill felt sure that if he'd had moustaches he would have rolled their ends in his fingers. "His fees and the difference between what ESP members have put in and what Great Britain has not put in might easily balance themselves out—er, if his work in this respect is fruitful, of course."

Gill thought: *The Frog is assuming that it's all over bar the shouting, that he's made me an offer I can't refuse. If I'm lucky, I have maybe two years left, and even now I don't have enough time to do my own things. If it wasn't that the Castle fascinates me, I'd be out of here. Why should I waste what time's left skipping to and fro between here and Paris?* What was more, he knew he couldn't help. And so out loud he said:

"I assume you've stolen or cannibalized what you could of HOTOL, and imitated what you've had access to of the American designs, right?" And before Varre could wax indignant or whatever: "Two wrongs don't make a right, Mr. Varre. HOTOL is a solution looking for someone to solve its many problems. The spin-offs will be worth more than the project, if that's any consolation. The American shuttle is working again now, okay, but it's still dodgy. I had a look at their launch system for them, and the new one they're building will be better."

"Is that classified, Spencer?" The Minister's

voice had a hard edge to it. He'd brought his car to a halt at the barrier. A uniformed policeman was coming forward, clipboard in hand.

"Possibly," Gill answered. "Will you sue me?" Sometimes the pressure ruffled his fur.

"What?" Varre looked from one to the other of them, his mind trying to catch up with what Gill had said. "Are you trying to say that—"

"Not trying," Gill cut him short. "I'm saying that if you haven't radically improved on everything you've borrowed so far, then you won't even get that heap of junk off the ground—with or without my help! And in any case the Minister is right: my time is strictly limited. I don't believe I have any left over for you."

Varre's jaw had fallen halfway open. He slowly closed it, shrugged, and said, "Then I go away empty-handed."

"Not at all," said Gill. "You go and tell them to cut their losses, save them billions."

The policeman had checked Anderson's pass. He signalled to the barrier's operator and the red-and-white striped pole began to crank aloft. From here to the second barrier half a mile short of the Castle itself the road was patrolled and strictly out of bounds to unauthorized traffic. There were patrol boats on the loch, too. Across the water some enterprising landowner had opened a restaurant; the sharp winter sunshine glanced from the lenses of a hundred pairs of binoculars all sighted across the water at the Castle's enigmatic masonry.

The Minister eased his car into first, started to drive forward before the barrier was fully up. As he did so, he became aware of a sudden flurry of exterior activity. On the unrestricted side of the barrier a circular car park with a perimeter track was filling up with the cars of disappointed tourists and sightseers; from here on in, their only route to the Castle lay in climbing Ben Lawers itself. From a vantage point halfway up they could look to the northeast, and if there wasn't any cloud cover they might even spy it down there. But barbed-wire fences would stop them from getting any closer than that, and from that height and distance even powerful binoculars would only succeed in making the Castle look like a fairly ordinary . . . castle.

The disturbance had its origin in the car park. A metallic green Volvo had come bursting out of the herringbone patterns of parked cars, slewed wildly onto the loch road and raced up alongside the Minister's Mercedes as it crept under the barrier. Gill saw a girl, wild-eyed and white-faced, hunched over the steering wheel. The policeman had to jump for it or might well have been struck. Then the Volvo cut sharply across the road and directly into Anderson's path, so that he was forced to slam on his brakes.

"What the hell . . . ?" the Minister had time to gasp, before three things occurred almost simultaneously.

One: the girl lost control of her car, which careened up a steep verge a little way before stalling and tilting over onto its side. Two: there came the sharp *crack!* of an automatic pistol and the rear window of the spilled Volvo became a glass jigsaw puzzle which collapsed in upon itself. And three: a second car, a beaten-up black VW Beetle, came slewing out of the car park to slam side-on into the barrier as it was lowered.

While Anderson, Gill, and Varre sat like lumps of stone, Turnbull was out of his door, kneeling on the tarmac, bringing out his gun. The Volkswagen's haggard-looking driver staggered from his car, hung himself half over the barrier, began to take aim for a second shot. Turnbull squeezed one off first and hit the man in the upper right arm, which served to pluck him upright off the barrier and toss him face-down in the road.

Meanwhile, Gill had also got out of the Mercedes. He saw the front passenger door of the Volvo crack open and a slender hand emerge, trying to throw the door all the way open. Since the door was uppermost, its weight was hampering the girl's efforts. Whatever else was going on here, and whatever part she played in it, the girl was in difficulty and might well be injured. Certainly she'd be shocked and very frightened.

Gill hurried to help her. He wished he could run faster but didn't have the strength. . . .

CHAPTER EIGHT

"Just keep him away from me!" Angela sobbed as Gill helped her out of the Volvo. "He followed me to Killin. I saw him, tried to hide my car among the cars here. But then he came, prowling the parking lanes in that Beetle. I saw the barrier going up and made a run for it. Oh God! Oh, my *God*!" She was half in shock, incoherent (to Gill), and obviously hurt. She kept touching her right shoulder and working it in a circular motion, but gingerly.

Gill looked at her and thought: *She's very lovely.* She looked a little like Marie-Anne, Gill's "girl next door." That had been two years ago and they'd made serious plans. But then he'd discovered that his time was running out and he'd let Marie-Anne off the hook. There'd been no one since.

"That lunatic was shooting at you?" Gill

looked from her towards the man on his face in the road, where Turnbull sat astride him on the other side of the barrier. At first Gill had thought that this must somehow be connected with last night, but now that idea was slipping away.

"My husband." She nodded, sobbing as he led her stumbling to Anderson's car. "Was, anyway. No, still is—but it's finished now. He's the jealous sort—insanely! He's been tracking me down for three weeks. I suppose he thinks if he can't have me no one else will. That's how his mind works. But I didn't think he'd try anything like this." She winced and held her shoulder again. "Ow! I think something's out of joint in here."

"Get in the car," Gill told her. "In the back."

Anderson leaned out of his window and patiently asked, "Spencer, what are you doing?"

"There's a first-aid post up at the Castle," Gill answered. "They're fully equipped. Someone should have a look at her shoulder."

Turnbull had disarmed Denholm and handed him over to the barrier policemen. Denholm was conscious and on his feet but bleary-eyed, slope-shouldered, and staggering. Now Turnbull came running, stuck his head inside the car. "He's okay, I only creased him," he said breathlessly. "The police witnessed the whole thing. They want statements from me and from the girl."

"Tell them later, when we come out," Gill told him. "We're taking Mrs. er . . . ?"

"Denholm, Angela Denholm." She sat propped in the corner of the backseat.

"Taking her for treatment at the Castle. The bloke who was shooting is her husband."

One of the policemen, approaching the car, had heard all of this. Anderson forestalled any protests by introducing himself and stating their intentions. "We should be out again in about two hours," he finished off. "Maybe less."

"Very well, sir." The officer was amenable. "But don't forget to stop and let us have a word with Mr. Turnbull and Mrs. Denholm, now will you?" He waved them on.

Gill and Turnbull got into the car. As Anderson started the car moving again, he turned and glanced at the girl. "I take it that what just happened here has nothing to do with the Castle? That it was an entirely, er, private and personal affair?" His instinct, too, had been to connect this latest incident with last night's business at Gill's place.

"Yes," she said. "I mean no—it has nothing to do with anything." Taking her weight off her right shoulder, she leaned a little against Gill where he sat in the middle. He was very much aware of her there. Her parka's fur collar held her perfume. "I've broken up with my husband," she continued, "and now it seems that he . . . well, that he wants to break *me* up!"

"Hmm," said Anderson. "Well, I should hardly think he'll be in any position to do that for a while."

Through all that had happened, Jean-Pierre Varre had sat in the front passenger seat very stiff and silent and a little pale. Now he coughed, cleared his throat and quietly ventured: "What on earth are things coming to?"

In a voice so dry it might easily have been

Anderson's own, Turnbull said to him, "What? Don't people try to kill each other in France, then? It would have been a crime of passion, surely? I always thought Frenchmen were supposed to understand that sort of thing."

Varre said nothing but merely turned and stared at him for a second or two. Looking into his eyes, Turnbull made a mental note that perhaps, in this Frenchmen, anyway, there wasn't a deal of passion to spare. . . .

At the second barrier Anderson asked the men on duty to phone ahead to the first-aid post and have someone waiting. And a minute later, driving round a bend in the loch road between the water and the mountain—

"Is that it?" Angela asked in a small, hurting voice.

Up on the slopes of Ben Lawers, the Castle had come into view. At its foot, about fifty feet to the fore, a high fence had been erected like the perimeter of some fort out of a Hollywood western. It had wooden towers, a catwalk and observation points, searchlights, and a wicket gate guarded by uniformed policemen. Behind the Castle the steep mountainside had been enclosed in barbed wire, and even up there were wooden towers with roofed-over observation platforms. The entire place was staffed by policemen, members of the security services, and men in plain workaday clothes who looked like nothing so much as soldiers—which in fact was what they were. Little of these people could be seen from the outside, however, for in the main they were within the enclosure, in various fortified workplaces both above and below the ground. Slender metal masts stuck up here and there from the fortress walls: the aerials Gill had spoken of to Turnbull. Between the lake-side road and the massive fence, a cable lift had been constructed with two open cars each capable of carrying four people.

"That's it," Gill finally answered the girl, hearing his own voice as faintly as if it came from some distance away. And even though he'd spent so much time here, still he found himself staring as in some fatal fascination up the slope as the mountain's contours unwound and the Mercedes swept them closer to the great enigma which was their destination. For impressive as the perimeter structure and its entirely man-made facilities were, the alien Castle itself drowned them in solemn stone, in a sort of cold, implacable patience. That was how Gill thought of it, anyway: as something old as the mountains and impersonal as ... as what? As the hangman's rope? As the terminals on an electric chair?

Now where did that thought spring from? he wondered as Anderson pulled off the road and brought his car to a halt in the car park midway between the spurs.

"I should very much like to go with you," said Varre as they all got out of the car. "This is my first time here."

"By all means," the Minister told him. "But as you'll discover, there's not a lot to see."

Gill said, "We'll go up in the first car, if that's okay? The sooner she gets this shoulder seen to the better."

"Fine," Anderson told him, holding back a

sigh of annoyance. He gave Turnbull a nod. "Jack, you go with them."

The three narrowed their eyes against a cold wind, followed the threads of cable receding dizzily away up the steep slope and looping between the lift's pylons. The whole setup was distinctly utilitarian; the Castle wasn't yet a tourist attraction, and not likely to be for a long, long time. They got into the stationary car and fastened their belts, and up above chains started rattling as the car gave a lurch and a sway and commenced its ascent.

Midway, the number-two car passed them on its way down. It contained four Americans, conversing in less than boisterous tones, all round-eyed and obviously still in awe of what they'd been looking at. They wore lapel badges which proclaimed them members of SCOPE.

"SCOPE?" Turnbull looked at Gill quizzically. "Sounds somehow military?"

Gill shook his head. "Society for the Correlation of Paranormal Experiences," he said. "But I agree, it gives the wrong impression. So does ESP, for that matter."

"Paranormal experiences?" Turnbull didn't attempt to conceal his bewilderment. "Ghost-busters, up here?"

Gill shrugged. "Apparently the American vice-president's cousin is a member—or something. Someone pulled some strings, and that's a fact. Anyway, they're listed amongst this week's VIPs. A dozen of them."

Getting out at the landing stage, Gill escorted the girl through the wicket gate in the high perimeter fence. Turnbull entered with them but remained at the gate while Gill took the girl to the first-aid post—a marquee which reminded Turnbull of nothing so much as a field hospital.

Inside the marquee a muscular, short-cropped paramedic type was waiting for them. He introduced himself and got right on with it. "I'm a physiotherapist"—he smiled at Angela—"when I get the chance, anyway. But I've been up here for three months now and you're my first case. I've been hoping one of the cable cars would crash!"

While he spoke he sat her down in a chair, took her right arm and extended it horizontally. "Can I see the shoulder?" he said. "Please don't say no or I'll get the sack! Sir, will you open her parka?" He must take Gill for her husband or something. Gill thought: *What's a joker like you doing in a nice place like this?* But he did it anyway. "And the blouse—just the top button." Again Gill obeyed. Angela said nothing, just sat there white and hurting.

The medic's hard fingers slid gently under the collar of her blouse onto her shoulder and worked there, exploring the bones. He shook his head, frowned, said, "Nothing broken, anyway. One or two things are a bit out of line, that's all. Ma'am, can you lean forward just a little?"

Her arm was still extended, held there where he grasped her wrist. As she tentatively leaned her weight forward he turned her wrist sharply and her shoulder made an audible *click*! She cried out, slumped down in the chair, and the medic stopped smiling and clowning, gently folded her arm and laid her hand in her lap. "Done," he said. "I hope!"

"Ah—*oh*!" she said. But there was more surprise than pain in her tone. She slowly rotated her shoulder, then glanced at Gill and smiled. He saw small tears in the corners of her eyes and felt an unreasoning urge to hit the medic on the nose. If he had, he knew the man would probably break him in half—but he wanted to anyway. It was a peculiar feeling, an emotion he'd never experienced before. . . .

Turnbull, Anderson, and Varre were waiting for them at the foot of rough concrete steps leading up to the base of the Castle. As Gill and Angela made towards them, he said to her, "Will you wait down here for me, at the gate?"

"Can't I come up?" Only a little over five foot tall, she was obliged to look up at him. "It's only a dozen steps away. . . ." As their eyes met something passed between them. They both felt it; and Gill thought: *She's like a beautiful doll! How could anyone want to hurt her?*

He smiled to hide his bewilderment, shook his head half in annoyance—at himself—and said, "You shouldn't even be here!"

"I'm not here because I wanted to be," she reminded him. "But . . . I'm glad anyway."

He nodded and took her left arm. "You can come up if you want to."

Climbing the wide steps, the group of five made way for a party of Americans coming down. All were wearing SCOPE badges. One member of their group remained at the top, at the foot of the Castle's blank, frowning wall. He stood there unmoving except for his head and eyes; the latter scanned slowly up and down the wall, absorbing the featureless lower face no less than the high, apparently pointless upper battlements.

"No windows, no doors," he was drawling to himself as they came up behind him. "Weird as all get out!"

Weird is right! Gill thought. He came to an abrupt standstill and Anderson, immediately to his rear, bumped into him. "What?" Gill mouthed, out loud. The Castle—this great machine—had suddenly woken up. Gill knew it if no one else did.

But in fact there were others—other human beings—who did know. Down in a sandbagged dugout under the perimeter fence, someone was yelling incoherently, and from the foot of the steps a man with a walkie-talkie was shouting up at them, "Sir? Mr. Anderson, sir—Mr. Gill? The activity has gone right off the register. Off *all* the registers!"

There was no time to do anything. Someone Gill didn't know, a tall, sturdy man, was climbing the steps directly behind them, walking right into it. Gill—the only one of them who knew that something was about to happen— might have made a run for it, but this stranger was in his way. Also, all the strength had gone out of him. He was afraid—because he knew that the Castle was suddenly *intent* upon something.

"Oh, God!" he said, his voice very small.

The others just looked at him: a sea of round, uncomprehending eyes. No, for one of them at least seemed aware of something. The American from SCOPE, shouting: "Shit, shit, oh *shit!*" and trying to run.

But Turnbull grabbing him and holding on, asking, "What the bloody . . . ?"

Gill wanted to shout, "Let go of him! Let him go!" But all that came out was, "Oh, God! Oh my good God!"

And the Castle's wall shimmered and began to expand, eating up the ground as it rushed to engulf them. . . .

CHAPTER NINE

The shock threw them off their feet. They weren't hurled down physically, just reduced to such a state of imbalance that they fell of their own accord. All of their senses clashed with what had happened to them, fought against the unbelievability of it, and lost to its reality. They had *moved* or had been moved between an "A" and a "B" with neither physical nor mental perception of distance covered or time expended. And human minds aren't built to take that sort of treatment. The sensation it produced was a sort of drunkenness without the alcoholic confusion. Confusion was there, certainly, but it was that of minds confronted—indeed surrounded—by the Unacceptable.

What Gill had seen as he staggered and collapsed to all fours was this:

Square grey clouds moving with an almost

mathematical precision across a domed sky of blue hexagons, like a cross-section through a honeycomb but vast as the vault of heaven itself. In the distance, mountains formed of a myriad pyramidal and similarly upward-pointing and angular geometric shapes stood heaped against a horizon of hexagon-formed sky, whose colour darkened to a pure indigo in which square stars radiated white flashes of light from their corners. And a pale ten-sided moon was hanging over the rim of a flat plain of green graph squares, which marched all the way from the left of Gill's visual periphery and dwindled away to the horizon of his right.

That was what he had seen. Before that: he remembered that the Castle had rushed down upon him and enclosed him and the others, following which it had apparently *moved* them somewhere. Somewhere else. Between being engulfed and emerging here, there had been an impression of intense white light—like the flash as a nuclear weapon explodes, which precedes the appearance of the stalk and boiling white mushroom head—and that was all. Gill's instinct had been to close his eyes and he had done so as he fell to all fours, but not before the weird landscape had impressed itself upon his retinas, remaining there as his senses ceased their spinning. And when he opened his eyes again, everything was quite different.

The stranger who had been last to climb the steps to the Castle was already on his feet, helping Turnbull up, and the world around seemed more nearly normal—or at least normal by comparison with that first entirely alien landscape of rigidly geometrical designs. But still,

Gill saw, totally abnormal by any mundane orientation. It was, quite simply, an alien scene.

Angela saw it where she lay sprawled, gave a small cry, and squeezed her eyes shut, then threw herself in Gill's direction. He caught her, cradled her in his arms and said: "It's all right. You're all right now." And thought: *God, where are we?*

"Where are we?" someone whispered, and Gill wondered if perhaps he hadn't after all uttered the words out loud. But it had been Anderson, pale as a wraith, round-eyed, cringing down into himself where he lay curled on the . . . grass?

Gill got up, helped Angela to her feet. No sooner up, she flew into his arms again. In other circumstances he would have been pleased— even here her nearness gave him something of pleasure—but he'd sooner be lover than protector. Was that how she saw him, he wondered? A man of strength? He hoped not. Any one of the others could probably do a better job of protecting her than he could.

"Mon Dieu!" Varre lay where he had fallen, pointing. All eyes followed his trembling hand and finger.

Behind them, maybe fifty yards away, stood the Castle. But it was a Castle with a difference. It now had doors. Indeed the great hexagon of its base contained entire rows of doors along all three of its visible walls.

Turnbull said, "Anyone hurt?" He was being practical, but his voice wasn't as deep as it might be. He stepped between Anderson and the man from SCOPE and helped them to their feet. Varre remained where he was, moaning a little as he hugged the ground, his eyes wide in terror.

Anderson brushed himself down—an entirely involuntary, habitual, and meaningless action, for there was no dust—and again asked, "Where are we?"

Gill had the answer to that one. He could feel it all around him, like a vast invisible factory. He was something bacteriologically small stuck to a continent-sized microchip in the guts of an incredibly complex machine. Almost without thinking, he answered Anderson's question. "We're inside the Castle!" he said.

"Jesus, have I gone nuts?" the American with the SCOPE badge whispered. He looked at each of their strange, strained faces in turn, then more fearfully at his alien surroundings. "Is this . . . it?"

"It what?" Turnbull wanted to know. He was more alert now, in control of himself, as close to normal as could be in the circumstances.

The American shook his head, shrugged hopelessly, said, "What I've been looking for—no, avoiding—all of my life. Well, it seems that I've finally found it. Or it has found me!"

"You're talking nonsense," said Turnbull. He turned from him and almost dragged Varre to his feet. "As for you," he growled, "well, you'd better face it, Varre. We're in trouble—but we're all in the same boat."

"But I . . . I'm claustrophobic!"

Turnbull gave a harsh laugh. "You're what? Look, this may not be exactly what we're used to, but we're certainly not closed in!"

"Leave him alone," said Gill. "He's right, we

are closed in. His phobia is doing a good job for him."

"Closed in?" Anderson clutched Gill's arm. "Spencer, what do you mean? You said we were inside the Castle—but isn't that the Castle over there?" He inclined his head towards the enigmatic structure.

Gill said, "It is and it isn't. Let's say it's part of it."

Anderson stared hard at him for a second, then scowled. "Damn you!" he suddenly snapped, jerking his hand away from Gill's arm. His face had turned an angry red. "All along you've known more about this than you were saying," he accused.

Gill was taken aback. "Don't be a fool, Minister," he said, his own voice tight. "Wherever we are—whatever has happened to us—do you think if I'd known about it I'd be here voluntarily?"

"But just *look* at this place!" Angela's words left her in a gasp where she clung to Gill's arm. So far they'd all avoided really looking, but now they did. It was a world, certainly, but it wasn't their world.

Far away, the mountains had lost a little of their angularity. There were rounded foothills, hazy with distance, beyond which the peaks themselves were quite majestic, whitecapped above and pale purple at their bases. But still there was that about them which suggested that they'd been painted on some fantastic backdrop. The stars above the mountains were no longer square, but in the deepening twilight they glittered more brightly than Earth's stars—almost like the stars in a Disney cartoon. As for the great flat plain: its "grass" was underfoot, a carpet of evenly cropped green stretching away as far as the eye could see, presumably to the very mountains. That left only the moon, which was a perfect disc now, yellow as Earth's moon but entirely featureless.

"The sky was honeycombed," said Angela. "I . . . I thought it was, anyway."

"Me, too," said Turnbull. "I got one good look at the place before it knocked me down. My eyes must have been shaken all to hell or something. Christ, it looked like computer graphics!"

He's got it in one, Gill knew it at once. They'd arrived here while the place was still in the process of filling itself in, before it had built a compatible picture. Now they were seeing what it (it what, the Castle?) wanted them to see, something which was bearable by their standards, which had been prepared for them. But did that mean it wasn't real? Not necessarily. Is a picture on a screen any less real because it's a picture? And surely it's more real if you're actually *in* the picture!

That thought conjured another, and Gill was suddenly awed. This was one hell of a big screen!

"Spencer, is something wrong?" That was Turnbull, too.

"Something wrong?" Gill looked at him, glanced all about, and snorted. "Are you kidding?"

"Your face had a weird look."

"You should see your own!" But Gill had decided to say nothing that might add to the confusion or aggravate the group's worries. There'd be time later to think it all through. Maybe . . .

"Introductions," said Anderson, very nearly in control of himself again. But his face twitched a little as he awkwardly held out his hand to the American. "David Anderson, from the MOD—er, Ministry of Defence, to you. I shall probably take charge here. Someone will have to, certainly, and I believe I'm best qualified."

"Miles Clayborne," said the other. "President of SCOPE. Er, that's—"

"The Society for the Correlation of Paranormal Experiences," said Turnbull.

"Ah, you've heard of us!"

Gill said, "Is that what you meant? About something you'd been looking for or avoiding all your life? This place, the ultimate paranormal experience? If so, forget it. We're having a close encounter, Miles, but with nothing supernatural."

"But—"

Turnbull cut in. "I'm Jack Turnbull, and this is Spencer Gill. He's kind of bright. I've been sort of looking after him—but not very well, it seems. The young lady is—"

"Angela Denholm." She spoke for herself. "I'm, well, nothing special."

Gill wouldn't have agreed with that.

Varre introduced himself, too, and then it was the turn of the other stranger. They all looked at him. "My name is Bannerman," he told them, shaking hands all round. *Rituals*, thought Gill, *at a time like this!* "Jon Bannerman." Angela thought he had unusually warm hands.

"And what is it you do, Mr. Bannerman?" Anderson enquired, politely.

Bannerman shrugged. "Nothing very much. Right now I'm a tourist. . . ."

CHAPTER TEN

Gill and Turnbull might have studied Bannerman more closely; for without at present knowing it, they felt a mutual interest in him. A not necessarily flattering interest. But this was neither the time nor the place and each member of the kidnapped (extracted? *Abstracted*, Gill thought) group had now recovered somewhat from the initial buffeting and was eager to voice his or her opinion. They had all started to babble at once: excited, shrill, mainly incoherent mouthings. Each with the exception of Varre, who now commenced to run, or stumble, in the direction of the second Castle.

"It's . . . a house!" he was gibbering. "A House of Doors. It took us in, and now we've to find our own way out!"

"Stop him!" Gill yelled, feeling an electric fear tightening his skin. "That thing's active!"

He knew it with an instinct that wouldn't be denied.

Turnbull raced after the Frenchman. "Why stop him?" he called back. Before Gill could answer he'd caught up, brought the little man down in a rugby tackle within a few paces of the looming walls.

Gill and the others came after. Breathlessly Gill said, "If there's a way in—or out—he may have triggered it."

"A way out?" Anderson looked at him. "A way back . . . home, do you mean?"

"I don't know what I mean yet," said Gill. "Look, the original Castle shut us off from our world. If Varre had gone through one of these doors, maybe he'd have been shut off from us."

"His lookout, surely?" said Turnbull, holding the struggling, panting Frenchman.

"And maybe ours, too," Gill answered. "What if he found his way home—on his own—and we were left here?"

"We'd follow him," said the American, Clayborne, shrugging.

"If we were able to," said Gill. "If the door he used could be used more than once."

"But of course it could!" Anderson was angry again, afraid and angry.

"We don't know that." Gill rounded on him. "We don't know *anything*! Not about this place or this . . . Castle. No, this House of Doors. I like Varre's term better. And just suppose he used a door and we all pile in after him. Who says we'd be going home? Why not somewhere . . . else?"

"But why *not* home?" said Turnbull, his voice

cracking like a whip. And Gill knew how tight the big man was.

"Maybe home," he told him. "Just maybe, Jack. But if that's all this was about—a simple return ticket—then why does this damned thing need *so many doors*?"

Varre had been listening to Gill's reasoning. Now he stopped struggling in Turnbull's arms and said, "You people don't understand. *Sacre bleu!* you don't understand!"

"What don't we understand, Mr. Varre?" Angela spoke gently, reasonably to him.

"We're *inside* the Castle—the first one," he answered, seeming equally reasonable. "All of this"—he waved his arms about, indicating the darkening sky, distant mountains, vast green plains, and enigmatic Castle—"is *inside* the first one. Don't ask me how, but it is. I can feel it weighing on me, crushing me"—his voice speeded up—"and I have to get out!" And in another moment he was fighting again, struggling to be free of Turnbull's overpowering, imprisoning arms.

"You heard what I said," Gill told him. "One of these doors may, just may, take us home again. And maybe not. But there are an awful lot of them. Suppose one of them is the right one, how do we discover which one? Do we guess? What if we guess wrong? Where do all the *wrong* doors lead to?"

"Anywhere would have to better than this," Varre gasped, still struggling.

"Would it?" Gill growled. He'd lost patience with the little Frenchman. Beside which, there was always the chance he was right. Gill nodded at Turnbull, a tight, curt nod. "Okay, Jack—turn him loose."

"Wait!" Anderson snapped. "Before any one of us does anything rash, can't we at least rationalize? What are we, rats in a trap?"

Gill thought: *The "are we mice or men" bit!* He knew the truth of it was that they were all scared stiff. But after all, Anderson was—or had been—a leader of men. And any form of leadership had to be better than none. Didn't it?

"What do you suggest?" Bannerman wanted to know. The unaccustomed sound of his voice caused all of them to look at him. He spoke quietly, without their general panic. Indeed, so far he'd been the quietest of them all; perhaps the entire episode had simply stunned him, and being a stranger to everyone present, he'd felt even more out of things. "I mean," he continued, "what is there to rationalize? Is any of this rational?"

Overhead, more stars were coming out; the moon was brighter now, and the angular mountains darker on night's horizon; the House of Doors was throwing a soft velvet shadow over the group.

"Something of it might be," said Miles Clayborne, shivering as he felt the gloom imperceptibly deepening. "I mean, I'm all for getting out of here, but I'd sure as hell like to know where to!"

"I agree," said Angela Denholm, in the smallest voice of all. "We should try to make sense of everything we've experienced and everything we see here, before trying to move on somewhere else."

Varre had stopped struggling. Exhausted

physically and emotionally, he hung almost limp in Turnbull's arms. "Very well," he said, "let it be your way. I . . . I panicked. But believe me, you don't know what it's like. I feel . . . buried alive!"

Turnbull relaxed a little, let the Frenchman go. But he opened his coat and showed him his gun. "Varre," he said, "I'd like to think we were all going to make it back home. But Gill says if you go for broke you could spoil everyone's chances. So don't, or I just might spoil yours."

"You . . . threaten me!" Varre gasped, astonished.

"Damned right I do!" Turnbull was vehement. "You're only one man, and you're outvoted." And the thought occurred to him: *Come to think of it, this gun of mine carries the biggest vote of all.*

"Jean-Pierre," said Anderson gravely, "Gill and Turnbull are absolutely correct. And to be coldly clinical about it—as Gill would seem to be"—he glanced at Gill thoughtfully for a moment—"might be a very sensible solution. If your phobia is going to prove troublesome, become a danger to us all, then perhaps you should go on alone."

Gill nodded. "That way when you put a foot wrong, we'll just very carefully step round whatever's left of you," he said.

Angela at once let go of his arm and stepped away from him. It was the first time she'd parted company with him since they'd arrived here. "Are you really that cold-blooded?" Her eyes held disappointment.

He looked away, said nothing. He wasn't cold-blooded and meant the Frenchman no harm, but Varre must be made to see sense.

"We're agreed upon a rationalistic approach, then," said Anderson. "Very well, so where do we begin?"

Clayborne said, "Bannerman asked if any of this is rational. If it's paranormal—that is to say supernatural—then none of it is rational. My society has explored dozens of cases, and there's never been anything remotely—"

"Sorry," Gill cut him off, "but you're wasting time. Believe in ghosts all you want, er, Miles?— and who's to say you're not right to?—but this isn't that sort of thing. The Castle grabbed us up and brought us here. Or rather, it enveloped us. Varre is right to believe he's inside it. We all are—lost in the guts of a machine. So let's have no more about ghosts, right?"

Clayborne's jaw jutted a little. "And what the hell are you? Some sort of expert?"

"Yes, he is," said Turnbull. And to Gill: "Okay, so we're inside a vast machine. The Castle has snatched us into itself. But why? How? To what end?"

"I only wish I knew," said Gill, shaking his head. "But I don't. The whys and wherefores will have to wait. We *are* here."

"Inside a machine . . ." Anderson shook his head, suddenly snorted his derision. "Somehow I don't think I can buy it."

"That's a fair comment," said Bannerman. "What? A machine that's bigger on the inside than the outside?"

"It might only seem to be." Gill was cautious. "Alien technology. And as you've all seen for yourselves, it's far and away superior to ours."

Turnbull stopped and plucked a blade of grass. He sniffed at it, chewed on the tip, spat it out. "Grass." He shrugged. "I think. It tastes and feels like it. But flat as a billiard table? Now, if this is an alien world, why grass? Why a moon, stars, mountains?"

"To make us feel at home?" Angela ventured.

"Sister," said Clayborne, "I for one do *not* feel at home!"

"But it is bearable," Angela persisted. "It's not as alien as it could be—is it?"

"She's right," said Gill. "Human beings are strong in some ways, frail in others. Maybe this place is like this so as not to scare us to death. It's different enough for us to notice, but not so bad as to knock us sideways."

Again Anderson's snort. "Are you suggesting it has been built for us?"

Gill might have answered in similarly sarcastic terms and tones, but Angela was already speaking. "A moon, stars, mountains," she mused. "Presumably there was a sun, too. It seems there must have been, but that it's gone down now. This is twilight rapidly turning to night."

"Why weren't we snatched at daybreak?" said Clayborne, nervously. "Answer me that, Mr. clever bloody Spencer Gill! Oh, you're right: the Castle was a visitation from another world— but not another planet. It's a spectral world, impinging upon our own. The Castle was its focal point—and we've been sucked into it!"

Gill gave up on him.

Anderson took Gill's arm. Gill could feel the nervous tension causing the other's hand to tremble. "Gill, the girl's right. There was a sun and it's gone down. But can't you see why I'm so skeptical? All of this *inside* a machine? It stretches the imagination too far."

"Not mine," said Gill. "I know what I feel."

"But . . . the light is going," Turnbull pointed out. "A sun must have set. She's certainly right about that."

"Not necessarily," said Gill. "Maybe someone is turning the lights down—and turning the moon and stars up. . . ."

"The same s-someone," said Clayborne, his voice trembling as he backed stiff-legged away from the House of Doors, "who just this minute put numbers on all the doors, right?"

They looked.

The base of each of the two facets of the hexagon which were visible to them had four doors maybe six feet wide and nine high, with two feet of rough, mortared stone between each door. The doors were set back about fifteen inches in arched recesses. They seemed constructed of some sort of hardwood, possibly oak by its grain, with heavy jambs, mullions and panels. No one had noticed the numbers before, but now they shone with a ghostly yellow light: numbered one to eight in an anticlockwise direction.

"Widdershins," Clayborne gasped, still backing away. "A sign of evil, of Satan himself!"

"I wish you'd cut out all that crap," Turnbull rumbled, feeling a driving urge to lash out at something, anything. His instincts were all physical, but there was nothing physical here to focus on. Or there was—the House of Doors itself—but that was Unknown and therefore Untouchable. Turnbull wasn't truly afraid, but he was frustrated. In his case, perhaps the two were the same.

"There are no doorknobs," said Varre. "I couldn't have used one of these doors anyway."

"But there are knockers," said Bannerman.

There were: great hinged iron rings set seven and a half feet high, with the numbers central in each ring.

"The light is going," said Anderson, "and the more it goes, the brighter these numbers shine out. Some sort of luminous paint, maybe?" He looked at Clayborne. "Have you never looked at your wristwatch in the dark? Ghosts!" The last word was a sneer.

"There must be a reason for the numbers," said Angela. She was back beside Gill again. "Maybe they're there to tell us something—or at least to suggest something. Maybe we should try number one first."

No one argued. They walked along the base of the wall to the first door. "But no handles," Varre repeated, when they stood there under the glowing number one.

"Why don't we just ... knock?" suggested Bannerman.

It was almost dark.

Turnbull looked around at the others, took out his gun and released the safety. They stood clear as he reached up, took the iron ring, and swung it against the central panel. The effect was like someone had banged on the great door of a mighty, sounding cathedral. But that was only the first effect. The second was that in the next moment the door swung silently inwards!

Mist swirled in there, great banks of it that came gusting out in a dank, bitterly cold blast.

A wind howled out from the open door. It was like opening the slab over a centuries-forsaken tomb: the door exhaled its pent gasses into their faces, blew out its damp, clinging mist upon them . . . and then was still.

"Mist?" said Angela, when she had her breath back. "Highland mist?"

Anderson pressed eagerly forward. "Scottish mist?"

From somewhere within the swirling fog beyond the open door—from somewhere a hundred yards or a thousand miles away, it was impossible to tell—came the mournful, unmistakable howl of a lost dog. They all froze, gazed at each other with wide, astonished, even hopeful eyes. For a moment. Then—

A figure tore abruptly through the mist in the oblong of space before them, came sobbing and reeling out to crash into Anderson where he stood in the forefront. Anderson screamed like a woman; Turnbull snarled and pointed his gun; Gill shouldered the big man aside even as he pulled the trigger. The bullet sped harmlessly away into unknown space while the echoes of the shot came thundering back to them, gradually diminishing.

One breathless moment later and the door slammed itself shut again—slammed as if in a fury—leaving a tattered, bloody, staggering figure to sink to its ragged knees, sobbing on the alien grass. A male, entirely human figure, with flame-yellow eyes that burned on them all where they gasped and gaped.

"Thank God!" the man cried, raising his arms to them. "Oh, thank . . . *God!*" And then he fainted. . . .

CHAPTER ELEVEN

Angela got down on her knees and cradled the crumpled figure of the man from door Number One in her arms. "I think he's all right," she finally said, without looking up. "Just exhausted."

"And bloody," said Turnbull.

"And scared half to death!" Clayborne added.

Turnbull looked at Gill. "I almost shot him."

"That's because you're all geared up to be a minder," Gill said. "And in a place like this you're bound to be edgy. I was just seeing a bit clearer than you, that's all."

Anderson was still white, his face gleaming with cold sweat in the light of the high-sailing moon. "What was that place, Gill?" he said. "The mist, the howling dog, and then this fellow . . ."

"Well, it wasn't Scotland," said Gill. "Scotland's not everyone's cup of tea, I know, but nobody hates it *that* much!"

"Is that your British sense of humour?" Varre was perplexed. His claustrophobia seemed to have abated a little; paradoxically, to him the night had always made everything seem somehow larger, less enclosed. "How can you find anything funny in these circumstances?"

Turnbull answered him. "See, Spencer here has just had a big lift. Oh, this whole thing is a downer, no denying that, but for him it isn't so bad. Before this, we had an advantage over him. Just about everybody was better off than Spencer. We were all going to live out our lives in full, but Spencer knew he didn't have too much time left. What's happened here is like the Big Equalizer. Now it looks like we've all got exactly the same amount of time left. Namely, not a lot."

"Whatever do you mean, Jack?" Anderson snapped.

"Work it out for yourself," Turnbull answered.

"He's talking about little things like food and water," said Gill. "And about staying alive. He's talking about our continued existence in an alien environment. Or environments."

"Environments?" Clayborne repeated him. "Plural?"

Gill shrugged. "It speaks for itself, doesn't it? What's the sense of all these doors if they all lead to the same place? But as far as I'm concerned that's not a bad thing. I mean wherever this bloke came from, it's no kind of place for me!"

"He has a lot of bruises," said Angela. "He's

thin, too. Starved, I'd say. But his cuts are fairly superficial. The blood is mainly dry on him. He looks worse than he is. I'd say he's been on the run, long and hard." What she didn't say was that she knew how the unknown man must feel. Something of it, anyway. She'd been on the run, too.

And that was when the battered stranger woke up.

He opened his eyes and by moon and starlight looked up at them, and they down on him. Then he gave a choking cry and hugged to Angela for dear life. He clutched at her as if she were the sole source of sanity, light, a rope dangling from a sheer cliff. His cliff. "Back!" he finally croaked, his voice high-pitched and yet cracked. "God, I've come back! I'm really . . . back?" But a note of doubt had entered his voice, and the life had seemed suddenly to go out of his eyes as they fastened on the alien moon.

"No," he said then, the word strangled in his throat, bitter with disappointment. "No, I'm not back. . . ." He struggled free of Angela's embrace, pushed to his feet and tottered there. And now the group could see him more clearly. Colours were difficult in the yellow moonlight, but a general description was possible:

He was small, no more than five-seven. Youngish, he'd be maybe twenty-six or -seven, and there wasn't a lot of flesh on him. His copper hair, once crewcut, had gone a little wild; he had small, piggy eyes, gangling arms, puffy, petulant lips and a weak chin. His clothes were hard to make out. The wide lapels and padded shoulders of his tattered jacket might be considered smart in certain circles; likewise his stylishly baggy trousers; but his appearance generally, allowing for the damage, seemed somehow false. In pristine condition he and his gear might look just a shade too flash. In any case and whatever he'd been before, now he looked like he'd just come through a forest of thorn trees. The collar of his silk shirt was dark with blood, sweat, and fog.

He staggered this way and that, held up his arms as if to ward off the House of Doors. And: "No," he sobbed again. "I'm not back at all. I'm still . . . here!"

"Who are you?" Anderson stepped close to him.

The stranger went at once into a half crouch, backed away from the group, made ready for instant flight. He wouldn't be able to run far, but still he'd run if he had to. "Don't you worry about me, mate," he answered, his voice high and panting, his accent all London. "I know who I am all right. But who the fuck are you?"

Turnbull took two quick paces forward and caught him by the arm even as he made to race away. "We're the ones who let you out of there, son," he said quietly, inclining his head towards the looming House of Doors, specifically door Number One. "We're the good guys, okay?"

"What were you running from?" Angela asked him.

The stranger's eyes went wide in a moment, flashing his terror. "The crab!" he gasped. "The bloody lobster! The scorpion—whatever it is!"

Varre whispered to Gill, "Is he sane?"

"Did I come out of there?" The stranger pointed a trembling hand at the door. They all nodded affirmatives. "Then I'm not far enough away from it!"

He at once jerked himself free of Turnbull's grasp, ran to door Number Two and leaped for the iron ring. The clang of heavy metal on hardwood resounded as before and the door swung inwards and stood gaping open.

Sunlight blasted out! Impossible! With the moon and stars overhead? Totally impossible—but real for all that. A shaft of golden sunlight oblong as the door itself, almost solid in comparison with the darkness it thrust back and invalidated, fell warm on the group where they leaped in pursuit of the fugitive, bringing them crashing together and to a halt. But not the stranger. He had paused for the merest moment on the threshold, and with one arm thrown up before his eyes had sobbed, "Warm! Oh, Jesus, no—*warm*!" And then he'd hurled himself through.

"Go on in," Turnbull yelled at the others. Frantically he waved them forward. "After him, quickly—*come on*!"

They might have faltered, argued, but the big man had already left them, stepping out of a shadow world into a world of blinding bright haze. Bannerman was right behind him, and like lemmings the rest quickly followed. The door at once slammed shut behind them—and vanished! When they turned their heads to look back, there was no door there at all. Neither door nor House of Doors. Just . . . jungle! Green things growing everywhere, and sunlight turning the air to a dappled golden haze.

Again the instantaneous and simultaneous assault upon every human sense was terrific.

Angela, Anderson, Varre and Clayborne felt their senses spinning and fell to their knees, collapsing together in loam and leaf mould and creeper. But Gill, Turnbull and Bannerman remained on their feet. Though they staggered a little, they quickly regained their balance. And without pride Gill thought: *Obviously we three learn faster—we're more adaptable—than most people.*

"Why, Jack?" Anderson gasped, clutching Turnbull's leg to steady himself where he kneeled on the forest's floor. "Why did you follow him? There may be danger here." Suddenly he was furious. "Who the *hell* authorised you to follow him?"

Turnbull stared down at him, frowned and shook him off. "I need someone's authority to stay alive? Why did I follow him? Because he's been a prisoner here longer than us, that's why. And he's survived. He must have learned a few things while he's been here. I say stick with him, at least until we know as much as he does."

Anderson took several deep breaths, finally looked away. "You're probably right," he said, however grudgingly. "But in future let's try not to be too . . . precipitous."

"He is right." Gill was on Turnbull's side. "That bloke was scared witless, but not like Varre and Clayborne—no offence meant. He was scared of something real."

"You'd better believe I was," said the stranger, emerging from a clump of undergrowth. "And I still am. I was listening to you lot, making sure you weren't just part of all this. You can't trust anything in this place." He licked his lips, looked nervously all about. "We should be okay now, for a little while anyway. But let's get away from here, see if we can find a clearing or something."

Turnbull had snatched out his gun; he put it away again and said, "For someone who's obviously knackered, you're in one hell of a hurry. Don't you ever stand still?"

The little man scowled at him. "We just came through a door and landed here, didn't we? If something follows us through, it'll land here too. *Right* here! You do as you like but I'm moving on."

"But you must be dead on your feet." Anderson carefully stood up.

"No," said the other. "I'm *alive* on my feet! And I intend to stay that way."

He moved off in a fashion suggesting a certain familiarity with this new environment, and the group quickly followed suit to stay close behind. The green growth was more forest than jungle, close but not densely grown. Ducking his way beneath low branches or hanging festoons of vines or creepers and weaving between or around clumps of thorn trees and brambles, the stranger led on. He seemed to be aiming at the sun.

Despite the fact that Gill was growing very tired now, he stuck as close to the little red-haired man as possible. That way he could talk to him as they traversed the forest's ways. In any case the going wasn't too bad: the stranger's own exhaustion made keeping up with him no great hardship.

"I'm Spencer Gill," Gill at last introduced himself. "I work for the government—or I did.

It was my job to study the Castle, the House of Doors, on Ben Lawers' flank. Now it seems the House of Doors may be studying me, and these others with me. The girl is Angela Denholm. Her being here is pure bad luck. The others— Anderson, Turnbull, Bannerman, the Frenchman Varre, and the American Clayborne— were just too close to the place at the wrong time."

"Castle?" said the other. "I can understand 'House of Doors' easily enough, but 'Castle'?" He frowned for a moment, then snapped his fingers and said, "Hey, I remember reading about that! A spaceship or spook house or something, which grew up overnight on a Scottish mountainside, right?"

Anderson and Angela were right behind and listening to the conversation. Anderson said, "Do you mean you don't know?"

"Know what?" The stranger didn't look back.

"You don't know that this *is* the Castle, and that somehow we're inside it?"

At that moment they emerged from under the canopy of trees at the forest's edge onto the banks of a sparkling river. It wound out of the trees on a bed of bright, rounded stones between green banks cut through declining meadowland. Fifty yards ahead the water turned white over a series of shallow falls, and where bare rock thrust up through the thin soil, there the rushing river became a waterfall. From two hundred yards away the deluge roared its futile challenge to gravity, sending aloft a fine, drifting spray that fell soft and welcome on itching, sweaty faces. At the edge of gapped, jutting cliffs a rainbow bridged the void between earth and sky; and in the sky, halfway towards its zenith, there hung a ball of fire too bright and searing hot to allow more than a glance.

Wearily approaching the chasm, the little redhead laughed a raucous, almost hysterical laugh and finally answered Anderson's question. "Inside it? We're inside something, are we? Just how big is this bleeding castle of yours, mate? I mean, do you really believe there's one big enough to pack all of this into?" He stood at the edge of the cliffs and opened his arms.

Beyond the rim were plains, forests, mountains, and rivers, reaching away into a distance where the world's curvature was plainly visible. Gill looked at it all, and for the first time in a long time felt like a great fool. No wonder the little redhead was laughing at what Anderson had said, at what Gill had caused Anderson to believe. Here was an entire world lying open before them. How could you build a wall round that? Where *was* that wall?

Gill's shoulders slumped a little and he sat down on a flat stone, chin in his hands. Anderson scowled at him and moved off to find a place to rest his heavy frame. Turnbull and the others likewise. Angela sat close to the stranger where he spread himself sighing on soft grass between a pair of leaning boulders at the very rim. But Varre sat close to Gill and touched his arm. Gill looked at him.

Over the thunderous roar of the waterfall, the Frenchman said, "You are right. You and I, we both know it. All of my senses are in order, working for me, telling me that what I'm seeing, hearing, feeling is real. It is real—but so is my phobia! I can feel the Castle pressing down on me, all of its many tons."

Gill nodded but said nothing. He sat and listened to the Great Machine. He sat *in* the machine and tried to understand what it was doing.

What it was doing to them . . .

CHAPTER TWELVE

The little man slept for an hour, a sleep of utter exhaustion, while around him at the edge of the cliffs the group for the most part aired their views.

Turnbull had recently suggested: "How do we know this isn't our world? For all we know, this could be somewhere in South America, or Africa, maybe." He looked at Bannerman (whom he'd already looked at several times, but cautiously, out of the corner of his eye) and tried to draw him into the conversation. "What do you say, Jon?"

The other shrugged. "You could be right," he said, in an even tone. "I wouldn't know, for I've never been there. But it strikes me that wherever we are, we're lost."

Excited, Anderson jumped to his feet. "I go along with the idea, Jack," he said. "Why do we keep on assuming that this is some weird, alien world? Maybe the Castle has simply spat us out again not in a different world but a different place! I mean, so far as I can tell this grass is more nearly grass; the sun is *the* sun; this water is absolutely real." He stooped, dipped his hand into a clear pool, slaked his thirst.

But Varre shook his head. "Botany was a hobby of mine," he said. "That's one of the reasons I jumped at the chance of seeing Ben Lawers: rare plants grow on its slopes. But none so rare as these. Oh, the grass is grass—but I'll wager it's not our grass. And the trees back there in the forest. They weren't too different, but different enough that I've never seen anything like them before. Also, I've been watching the birds. They're not quite right. Neither were the small creatures in the forest. No, this isn't our Earth. Now that isn't guesswork; it's science. But even without it, I'd know we were still in the Castle—or the House of Doors, as Gill prefers. Why don't you ask him? I'm sure he'll verify what I'm saying."

Angela said, "How about it Spencer?" It was the first time she'd called him that.

"Varre's right," he answered simply. "Leave it at that. I can't explain the inexplicable."

Turnbull nodded, grew gloomy in a moment. "You're both right," he grunted. "Sleeping beauty there knows it well enough. I should have realized. When we came through that door he showed no sign of relief, pleasure, joy. He'd seen it all before, or something very much like it. He *knew* he wasn't home and dry."

Anderson sighed, shrugged, and sat down again. He glanced at his watch. "Stopped," he announced. "It hasn't worked since the start of all this."

"Nor mine," said Clayborne. "A classic sign of paranormal interference."

Gill said nothing but turned away in disgust. He took off his own watch and hurled it over the rim.

"Why did you do that?" Clayborne asked.

"Something for the spooks," said Gill. "When you're invited to a party, it's impolite to go empty-handed!"

"It will soon be noon," said Angela. "A few more hours and we'll all be hungry."

"I'm hungry now," Varre answered. "There were fruits on some of those trees. Nuts too." He glanced at the redhead where he slept on between the boulders. "Maybe this fellow knows which ones are edible."

Gill nodded. "That's something we'll have to ask him. Me, I have a couple of other questions."

Turnbull cocked his head enquiringly. "Go on?"

"What he remembers prior to finding himself here," Gill answered. "He was genuinely surprised when he learned where we believe ourselves to be, so I want to know how he got here."

"What else?" said Anderson.

"Why he shouted 'warm' as the door opened. He seemed worried about it. He sobbed, 'Oh, Jesus, no—warm!' And then he jumped right in. Also, I'd like to know more about this crab something or other he's scared of. He seemed afraid it would follow us here. Does that mean it's intelligent? An intelligent crab? Oh, there are a few things he can tell us."

"His name might be nice for starters," said Turnbull.

Right on cue, the little man started awake and jerked into a seated position. "What?" he gasped. "Where . . . ?" Then he saw them all looking at him, relaxed, and fell back again. And after a little while: "How long was I out?"

"About an hour," Angela told him. "Are you okay?"

He looked at her, brushed sleep from the corners of his eyes, and managed something of a smile. Gill considered it more a leer. "I'm okay," said the redhead. "Going a bit short of . . . all sorts of things. But okay. And you? You going a bit short, are you?"

He smiled again and she saw the bad, crooked teeth behind his puffy lips. She wasn't close enough to tell, but she guessed his breath would be foul. She looked away.

Anderson said, "We let you get your rest, what you could. Now that you're awake, however, there are some things we'd like to know."

"Oh, yes?" said the other. "Well in my old game as was, I'd get paid for valuable information. So what have you got that I might want, eh, Mr. Anderson? See, we're all pretty much in the same boat here—in the shit, that is. Except some of us are likely to be more in it than others. And some of us have learned a bit about how to keep out of it. Knowledge like that has to be worth something."

Anderson frowned. "You have us as a group," he answered. "You're one of us now. Safety in numbers, you know? Also, there are some keen minds here, Mr.—er, whatever your name is. What you know, plus what we might deduce from it, could make all the difference."

Gill spoke up. "What is your name, anyway?"

"Haggie," said the other. "Alec Haggie. 'Smart' Alec Haggie, they called me. Born and bred in Mile End, East London. But not so bloody smart after all, as it turns out!"

"How long have you been here, Alec?" This was Angela again, determined to be pleasant and make the best of an entirely unpleasant situation.

"The time would have flown if you'd been here with me, darling," he drawled, leering again. But then, when he saw her expression, he turned sour. "About a week, near as I can judge it." He scowled. "Seven, eight days, maybe. Days as was. But here it's hard to keep tabs. I'll tell you about it, if you like. Maybe your gaffer there is right." He glanced at Anderson. "Maybe those 'keen minds' he mentioned can make some sense of it. Damned if I can!"

"Before you start," Varre cut in, "is there anything here that's safe to eat? You must have lived on something."

Haggie looked the Frenchman straight in the eye and grinned again. He tapped the side of his pug nose with his right index finger, said, "Now that has to come under the heading of very valuable information, right? We'll get to that later—maybe. Anyway, from where I'm sitting, I don't see too many hunger pangs. Not yet. If you want to know what hunger is, then you'll just have to hang on a bit."

Varre pursed his lips. "Have it your own

way," he said. "It will make no difference in the long run. What you eat, I shall eat."

"One other thing, before you start," said Clayborne. "You say you've been here for a week or more. In your judgement, what is this place, this ... experience? Is it an alien world or the spirit world? Is this a visitation from some other planet, or from some underworld, some parapsychological hell?"

Haggie looked at him for a long moment. "I don't know." He finally shook his head. "I've thought about it, but I just don't know. There is something like a ghost here, I can tell you that much. A jelly thing. Something strange and clever. But I never really believed in spooks and I don't care to start now. Alien? You mean spaceships and like that? I don't know about that either. It's just like everything is out of joint here. And the worst of it is not knowing where bloody 'here' is! At first I thought I'd gone off my head. I thought if I just sat still I'd wake up one morning in a padded cell. And another time I thought I'd died and this was hell. But then along came the crab—and I ran! I've been running ever since. And now along comes you lot, in the same boat, so I suppose I'm not crazy after all. . . ."

As he had spoken, so Haggie's eyes had gradually taken on a sort of glaze. Now he snapped out of it, said, "Anyway, do you want to hear about how I got here or not?"

"Just one more thing first," said Gill. "After that, no more interruptions. What did you mean when you shouted 'warm'? I mean, when you opened the door and came through into this place. You shouted, 'Oh, Jesus, no—warm!'"

"Warm?" Haggie repeated him. "Did I do that? See, I'd started talking to myself, I know that." He shrugged. "Maybe I did it out loud sometimes, too. But I think I know what I meant. It's this: the jelly thing—the spook, if you like—doesn't much like the cold places. I know that for a fact 'cos I've never seen him in a cold place. So me, I *prefer* the cold places— except there's usually not much to eat there." He looked at Varre. "So it's a choice of two evils: a warm place and food, but probably the spook will be there; or a cold place and nothing to eat, but no spook to bother me. See what I mean? Nothing's easy here."

Gill slowly nodded. "I'm getting something of the picture," he said. "So you were on the run from the crab, and took the first door that was available, even knowing it was warm and that the spook might be in there. Has he—it—ever threatened you?"

Haggie shook his head. "It usually just sidles away from me, runs off somewhere. But I know it's, well, *thinking* things. I know it's clever— and weird!"

Gill nodded again and looked at the others. They were all very quiet.

Finally Anderson cleared his throat and said, "Maybe you'd better tell us your story. . . ."

CHAPTER THIRTEEN

"Seems I've always been on the run from one thing or another," Haggie commenced, "even as a kid. My Old Man, my stepfather, was a real bastard. I was often on the run from him! Never did know my real father, and I don't reckon my mother did, neither.

"I got in with the gangs early, knew all the really bad ones, too. Most of 'em are gone now—paid the price in full, or locked away—or under new management, you know? But I survived. I was never big stuff, eyes and ears mainly. Smart enough not to get in too deep, not hard enough to demand my fair share when it was due. And not so stupid I'd ever stick my neck out. Nobody was frightened of me, and so I didn't need to be frightened of anyone. But I knew it all, everything there was to know about gangland, and bought and sold information for a living. Bought it cheap, or stole it, and sold it to the highest bidder. That's why they called me Smart Alec. It's not easy to keep your fingers clean *and* make a living.

"But . . . a year ago the Specials got hold of me on a little thing. Well, maybe not too little. See, I'd made a fatal mistake and done lookout on a security vault job. And the Specials picked me up and said they'd fingered me for it. But I was only small fry, they said, and it wasn't me they wanted really. So they'd give me a choice. Spill the beans—names, addresses, the lot, you name it— and go free. Or keep mum and eat slop in the cage for ten long ones. Not much of a choice, eh? And I've never much fancied porridge.

"So I gave them what they wanted. And they laughed in my face, said they hadn't had anything on me anyway, tossed me out in the street! I tried to play it cool, but when the lads started to get picked up one by one . . . it was a nervy time. Thing is, my nerves were never too good for that sort of thing. All of the lads went away except one, and that was the Big One. He started asking around, putting two and two together, and finally came looking for me. I was the only one who'd been in on it who was still on the loose, see? Him and me. And he knew he hadn't let anything slip, nor any of the lads inside. After all, if one of them had wanted to do him up, he'd be right in there with 'em.

"Looking back, that was my one mistake. I should have fingered that big bastard, too! But I hadn't, because of his nasty ways with a hacksaw. You've heard of Harry Guffin? Hacksaw Harry? No? Well, of course you wouldn't, would you? Upper-class types like you lot . . .

"Anyway, I ran for it, came north to Newcas-

tle and laid low. That was a year ago. First time
I'd been out of London in my life, it was. And
lo and behold, I found Newcastle just like London as was ten or twelve years ago! The same
gangs, con men, crooks. Maybe a bit harder, but
playing all the same old games as used to be.
And so I worked in with them, and things
started to look up a bit.

"But Hacksaw Harry, he hadn't given up on
me. A month ago a carload of lads—big, sour-
looking types—came up from the Smoke on a
tip-off. Someone had mentioned to Harry that I
was up North, and he'd sent this bunch to have
a word with me. But when they started asking
around after me, I got word of it. I looked 'em
up—from a distance, you understand—and
knew 'em straight off. I wasn't likely to get any
change out of that lot!

"I scarpered to Edinburgh for a fortnight, but
the readies were dwindling pretty smartish.
When I was skint there was nothing for it but
to go back down again. There were lads in Newcastle who still owed me a few quid. Ah, but
Harry's boys had had a word with them, too.

"A couple of days I was down there—ducking
and weaving, you know—before they caught up
with me at my place. My place—*hah*! I'd settled
for a smelly little hole on the river where you
couldn't swing a cat and life was a nightly battle with the silverfish! God only knows how
they'd found it, but there they were, waiting for
me that night.

"At first I thought it would be a concrete wel-
lies job—the river was right next door—but that
wasn't the way of it. Harry had a house in Edinburgh and would be up there in a few days'

time on business. He pushed a bit of snuff now and then, you know? So they drove me up to his place to wait on his pleasure. Except I really would have preferred the river, 'cos from what they told me Harry would be bringing a couple of his hacksaws up with him. A couple of the rusty ones . . .

"I'll cut it short. I got loose on the first night, nicked their car, headed north for this blip on the map called Crieff. They'd expect me to go south again, I thought—London's a big place—and so I took the opposite direction. The chances were their car was dodgy anyway and they wouldn't want to draw attention to themselves by reporting my little larceny to the police. But they were clever ones, those lads. Clean as whistles, they must have been, with no form to mention. And their car, too. They put the Law on me! Can you believe it?

"The next night the Filth came looking and I almost bumped into them in the foyer of the place I was staying. But I saw 'em in time and skipped it. But Harry's lads were there, too, outside, waiting. It turned into a chase. I nicked another car and ended up in Killin. The lads were right on my tail. I had no choice but to hotfoot it cross-country. I knew that if they caught me again I was a goner—I mean there and then! And in fact I was nearly a goner anyway. What? The dead of night, and the middle of winter—up there, in those mountains?

"When I was just about done in, I saw a big house down there in the valley. I was up on the slopes of a mountain, and down there was this big dark place and a lake. There were some lights round the house, a high fence at the front, some figures moving about which I took to be Filth. Maybe it was a government place, a defence establishment or something. I didn't know and couldn't care less. By then I'd decided that the Law had to be better than Harry's lot. I was ready to give myself up.

"Somehow I got down off the mountain without breaking my neck or tearing myself on the barbed wire—barbed wire, right! Like Fort Knox, the bloody place was!—and staggered up to the wall of the big house. And . . . bingo!" He paused.

"Bingo?" Anderson repeated him after a while.

Haggie looked at him and nodded. "That was it," he said. "All there was to it. I figured I must have tripped and banged my head, 'cos when I came to, there was no big house and lake, no mountains, nothing like I'd ever seen before. I was in . . . oh, a place I can't describe." He shook his head, waved his arms helplessly.

"This big house," said Gill. "It sounds like the Castle to me—as you'd see it from Ben Lawers after dark. As for the place you woke up in— try to describe it."

Suddenly animated, Haggie screwed up his face and snarled at him, "But I just told you I *can't* describe it—'cos it wasn't like anything I ever heard of before! How do you describe a bad dream you can't wake up from? How can I explain what it was like to feel legless drunk when I knew I was stone-cold sober?"

Gill smiled wryly, said, "Seems like you're doing okay to me! Look, I'm not asking you for scientific terms or descriptions, Alec. Just tell it your way."

The other scratched his head and thought about it. Finally he said, "Okay, I'll try it. Do you remember when you were a kid and you looked in one of those tube things that made coloured patterns? Like a cardboard telescope, with a little hole for your eye? You just had to turn the end and the patterns would change, forming different shapes every time?"

"A kaleidoscope." Gill nodded.

"That's the thing. Well, it was something like that. But room size, and I was in it. Inside a damn big weird room. The floor was white, soft, spongy—I sank up to my ankles in it. It was like walking in snow. I mean it didn't cling, but it was as tiring as walking in snow. Except it wasn't anything like snow 'cos it was hot. In fact the whole damn place was like a sauna—almost too hot to bear! I thought I was going to dry up and blow away! The ceiling was one big light. I mean it was a sort of bright haze. You couldn't see any actual ceiling for all the light up there. Not blinding light, like the sun, but just making everything up there indistinct. Do you understand?"

"I think so," Gill answered. "What about the kaleidoscope effect? Where does that come in?"

"The walls," Haggie answered. "That's where *that* came in! The walls . . . *crawled*! It was like the kaleidoscope, yes, but underwater. Moving patterns, flowing, ever-changing. Like the walls were just big screens showing a lot of liquid movement. But they weren't screens. It was like . . . I mean . . . can you imagine a television picture without the TV set, without the screen? That's what it was like, on all sides. And I could walk through it all I liked and never seem to go

119

anywhere. I thought I walked for a mile or more and nothing changed. Except the patterns, which changed all the time . . ." Haggie paused again and looked at the ring of faces all around him. "Is this crazy?"

"No," Gill answered him, shaking his head. "I don't think it's crazy. So how did you get out of there?"

Haggie took a deep breath. "That happened the first time I saw the jelly thing," he said. "See, every now and then, in this room, I'd come across things like pillars. I thought of them as pillars because they went straight up from the floor presumably to the ceiling. They were, I don't know, maybe six feet right through. But as for their shape—square or round or whatever—don't ask me. I can't say what they were in cross-section because they were the same as the walls. Their surfaces were full of this coloured motion, which made them look like they were revolving or . . . or melting. Hey! That's right! *That's* what they looked like, the walls and the pillars; like a gang of crazy painters were melting colours onto them and blowing it in all directions, until the walls themselves were molten!"

"That's a good picture," said Gill encouragingly. "And the jelly-thing?"

Pleased with his description, Haggie had been grinning, however nervously. Now the grin slipped a little. "The spook?" His puffy lips trembled. "He was behind one of the pillars. I came round it . . . and I saw him. He was like—like—"

"Go on." Clayborne was fascinated, bottom jaw hanging slack. "What was he like?"

Haggie swallowed and said, "There's this stuff spooks are made of."

"Ectoplasm," said Clayborne, nodding.

"Yeah? Is that it? Like funny putty, or goo, or the slime of a jellyfish? Well, if you piled stuff like that up say four feet tall—but thin, very thin—and split its bottom half three ways—"

"Tripedal?" said Gill.

"Three legs, yes. And if you gave it four or five thin, ropy, dangling arms, all snaking down from its top . . . then you'd more or less have it. As for motion: it flowed like an octopus. I've seen them move the same way. Not jet-propelled, mind, but flowing sort of. But eyes, nose, mouth, any sort of face like we have—forget it. It was the same all over: blue-grey, a jelly, fluid as the walls. But . . . I knew it lived, and I knew it was thinking things. I mean, if you saw it you'd know it too. You'd know it was . . ."

"Sentient," Gill prompted him. "It had intelligence."

"Christ, yes! Sly too. Anyway, I saw it; it saw me; I took off. We probably both took off, I don't know. But I've seen it a couple of times since then and I *think* it avoids me. Which is okay by me.

"Anyway, I ran. There were places where there were holes in the walls. I mean, you couldn't *see* these holes, for there was nothing there. But that was just it: there was *nothing* there, surrounded by motion. Panicked, I ran into one of these spaces. Not deliberately, mind. I just sort of collided with it. And . . ."

"And?" Angela prompted.

"And the hole was a door." Haggie shrugged helplessly. "A kind of door."

Turnbull frowned. "What kind of door?"

Haggie jumped to his feet. "There you go

121

again!" he accused. "I don't bloody know what kind of door. Shit, when is a door not a door? When it's a jar? Christ, I never understood *that* one, either!"

"Not a jar," said Gill. "Ajar—when it's half-open. It's a play on words."

"Oh, play on my dick!" Haggie scowled. "Anyway this bastard door was *fully* open. And I ended up . . . somewhere else." He stepped carefully to the rounded rim of the cliffs and looked down. "Actually, I came out in this place." His eyes focused on forests far below, and on a green plain that sprawled beyond them, maybe six or seven miles away.

"Right here?" Anderson got up and followed him. The others followed suit.

Standing there with the sun warm on his back, outlined against the sky and the curve of the world, Haggie's shoulders were shuddering; he had started to cry; silent tears of frustration, of impotent rage, welled from his eyes and ran down his grimy, haggard face. He pointed out and down and his arm was visibly trembling. "No," he sobbed, "not here. Not this very spot. It was down there, see?"

They looked, and they saw. Before, there had been nothing to see. But now there was. Down there on the green, distant plain, a great house like some airy country mansion.

A House of Doors . . .

CHAPTER FOURTEEN

"It's a never-ending circle," said Haggie, regaining control of himself. "A great big bloody circle, and I just keep running round and around it." He sat down again on naked stone, with his calves and feet dangling over the rim. "If I had the guts," he continued, "I'd put an end to it right now and just throw myself down."

"That would be one way to the bottom, I suppose," said Gill briskly, "but I don't much fancy it for myself." And to the others, more seriously: "The descent shouldn't be too difficult. The cliffs don't appear to be sheer. There are plenty of outcrops, rock chimneys, overgrown fissures. In some places the foliage looks pretty dense. We can split ourselves into teams, go down in stages. Then, if one team's route becomes impossible, they can retrace their steps and work round it until they join up again with another team—and so on. We must of course stay within hailing distance of each other." He craned his neck to glance at the sun standing almost directly overhead. "I suggest we start right now."

Clayborne had gone deathly white. "Go down?" he said. "Climb? Why the hell would we want to do that?"

"But isn't it obvious?" Anderson looked at him curiously. "That house down there is one of two things: a mansion built by people not unlike ourselves, or another kind of Castle."

"It's only one thing," said Gill and Varre almost in unison. And the Frenchman continued, "Since it wasn't there an hour ago, it can only possibly be one thing."

Angela looked from one of them to the other and back. "A doorway?"

"Several," said Gill. "Even from this distance you can see its doors. We're being invited to try our luck somewhere else."

"But what's wrong with this place?" Clayborne wanted to know. "If we can find food here we'll be okay. Good climate, water, possibly meat. Some of those fruits back in the forest should be good. What's the big hurry to move on?"

Turnbull looked at him suspiciously. "What, are you planning on settling here or something? What is it, Clayborne? What the hell's wrong with you? Not so long ago you were trying to convince us that this was the spirit world! Something about a metaphysical hell? Have you decided your ghosts aren't such a bad lot after all, then?"

Clayborne licked his lips and glanced fearfully over the rim. He at once went weak at the knees and backed off. "Vertigo!" he gasped. "I can't stand heights!"

"I'm not much for heights myself," Angela told him, "but if that place down there means a chance to get back home, then I'll just have to risk it."

Haggie looked up from where he sat. "That's what I keep telling myself," he said. "Maybe it's a chance to get the hell out of here. Except it never is. . . ."

"Teams, then," said Anderson. He glanced at Clayborne and frowned. "Miles, you won't mind me saying it, but since you're bound to be something of a liability, I'm going to suggest putting you with two of our strongest. Strong-nerved, that is, as well as physically. Jack?" He looked at Turnbull. "And, er, Jon?" He turned his gaze upon the ever silent Bannerman.

Bannerman shrugged and said, "I'm easy."

But Turnbull wasn't. "Listen," he told Clayborne, "and let this sink in. I don't mind giving you a hand, but take some well-intentioned advice and don't go throwing any fits of the screaming ab-dabs. Not when we're climbing. I can sympathise and all that, but putting my own life in jeopardy is something else. I don't intend to die for someone I've only just met who's incapable of helping himself. So if your nerves get a bit wobbly, just you keep them to yourself. Don't go setting me off, right? Hysteria can spread like wildfire in a bad situation." He turned to Bannerman. "Jon, can you climb?"

"I'll get by," Bannerman answered. He seemed steady enough.

125

"Okay." Turnbull turned back to Anderson. "We're a team."

"Next," Anderson continued, "I propose to team myself up with Jean-Pierre. He's lightweight and should be able to scout the way ahead; I'm beefy and can use myself as an anchor where the going gets a bit steep."

Varre nodded his agreement. "I have done a little rock climbing," he said. "I foresee no great difficulties."

Gill said, "That leaves Angela, Alec, and myself." He shrugged. "I think we're all three agile enough. I tend to tire easily, but in any case I can't see us doing it all in one go. In fact I think we'll be lucky if we're down by nightfall. We might find it's as easy to camp on the cliff for the night—that's if we can find a safe staging area. We'll have to wait and see how it goes."

"Very well, then," said Anderson. "So if everyone's ready, let's split up into our teams and start looking for the easiest way down. . . ."

An hour later the sun had gone down a little, throwing various slopes and projecting facets of the great escarpment into shadow. This caused no real problems as there was still full daylight; in fact with the sun out of their eyes the descent became that much less dangerous, and in the near-tropical climate they might otherwise have found the going too warm.

To the north (taking directions from the path of the sun) Turnbull's team followed a diagonally slanting fissure which split the cliff's face to an as-yet-undisclosed depth and gradually closed the distance between them and the other teams; with a little luck the fault might go all the way to the bottom. The great crack was stepped in places, with horizontal fractures, rock chimneys galore and wide, scree-littered ledges where shallow-rooted flowering creepers grew greenly lush in weathered crevices. Even Clayborne had to admit that the going was fairly easy; the way was by no means sheer, and all he had to do was follow in the steps of his companions and keep from looking out over the unknown deeps below.

Anderson's two-man team was located central between the other two. He and Varre had descended fairly quickly and were a hundred feet or more deeper than the others. They picked their way down a steep slope of piled boulders where in ages past part of the cliff face had collapsed onto a great jutting ledge. For them it was mainly a matter of testing each protruding rock before trusting their weight to it, and of keeping their balance when scree threatened to shift underfoot. It was more a test of nerves and patience than of skill; to become impatient and make too much haste here could well prove fatal. Varre, aware of Anderson's greater bulk, made every effort to keep to one side of him or bring up the rear. . . .

Gill and his party were to the south, clambering along the side of a jagged spur of granite-like rock with no sliding scree to worry about but precious little of vegetation for handholds. As a boy Gill would have romped down this section, but now he found the going very difficult. His weakened system was suffering under the constant strain on wasting, unaccustomed muscles; his lungs worked like a battered bellows, sandpapering away in his chest.

Angela, carrying her parka tightly bundled on her back, was also in some difficulty. She wasn't lacking in strength, but being small, she found it hard to stretch for the various hand- and foot-holds. Both she and Gill were aware that Haggie could simply put on a little speed and leave them behind if he so desired. They didn't consider this likely, however, and certainly wouldn't worry about it anyway—it was just frustrating that he should be so much more capable. During his time in this place he'd grown accustomed to its hazards; his wiriness helped and his quick thinking, and yes, his criminal instinct for survival had readily adapted to these more basic levels of existence. For in fact he *was* a survivor, and the despair he'd displayed at the top of the cliffs had been entirely transitory. If no one else made it to the bottom, Smart Alec Haggie most certainly would. If he didn't, then it would be through the intervention of something completely beyond his control.

Already the three teams were more than a third of the way down, so that it began to appear that Gill's assessment had been pessimistic. Each group was within hailing distance of the next; on the spur, Gill and his team were visible to Anderson and Varre; Turnbull and party could follow the progress of the other two teams visually while themselves remaining for the greater part out of sight in the recessed caves and convolutions of their fissure. But in fact Turnbull's team was on a ledge out in the open when their first real confrontation with this alien world proved almost fatal.

The fissure had finally closed up—this section of it, anyway—becoming little more than a descending crack in the face of a cliff. Obliged to leave its protection, the three now worked their way along a ledge formed of the projecting lower lip of the fault. Some three to four feet wide, the ledge was neither an overhang nor itself overhung, so that Clayborne found his vertigo more or less containable. In places creepers hung down from above and closed the team in, making it appear that they descended the ramp of a steeply sloping tunnel. But abruptly and when they least expected it, as they rounded a jutting promontory of fractured rock, there the ledge, creepers and all, had been swept away, leaving only a sheer, glistening face that plunged into a misted abyss—misted by virtue of the waterfall whose wide white spout fell in a seemingly solid sheet down this section of the escarpment.

Turnbull was in the lead, followed by Bannerman, with Clayborne bringing up the rear. But seeing what lay directly ahead, Turnbull stopped, looked back and shook his head. "End of the road," he called back over the roar of the thundering waters. "We'll give ourselves a few minutes' break, then go back and up a little. We'll have to find a route across the water higher up—or maybe a route under it?"

"Under it?" Clayborne's voice was faint, hushed, barely audible.

"That's right," Turnbull answered. "Like where it leaps an overhang, maybe." He leaned back as the others crushed forward to gaze out at the obstruction.

When Clayborne saw the waterfall rushing into eternity, his mind froze; the great spout set his senses whirling; his vertigo struck at the worst possible time. Drawn as if by a magnet toward certain death, arms windmilling, he took a staggering pace forward. Turnbull caught his upper arm, used his own body as a pivot to swing Clayborne back against the face of the cliff. In so doing he tripped and sat down heavily on the ledge, and with his free hand automatically grasped at a nodule of projecting rock. But it wasn't a rock.

Outwardly it was like a large, oval, deeply domed limpet as big as a man's clenched fist— but underneath it was something else. Caught unawares and dislodged by Turnbull's side-swiping hand, the thing fell from the cliff face onto the ledge close beside him, lying there for a moment on its back. Turnbull caught a glimpse of bright purple, strangely jointed, twitching chitinous legs, pincer claws, venomously yellow mandibles and glittering diamond eyes—before the thing righted itself and sprang astride his outstretched hand!

Galvanized by shock and horror, Turnbull tried to snatch his hand back. But the thing had extended its many legs and driven them deep into the compacted scree and rootlet-forced cracks of the ledge. The creature's carapace had closed on his hand like a vise, clamping it down. Doubtless this was how it trapped its victims before eating them. No sooner had this thought dawned on Turnbull than he felt the thing's bite. It was the acid-etched pain caused by the spines of a stonefish, the white-hot sting of a scorpion. And it was . . . *agony!*

Turnbull screamed and his eyes bugged as he frantically drove the fingers of his free right hand down into the soil under the rim of the domed shell. Still shrieking, he jackknifed to his feet and tore the creature free of the ledge. It came loose and left three of its legs still jerking where they'd fixed themselves to the rock. Continuing his movement, Turnbull hurled the crustacean thing out into space; but his swing was so desperate and agonized, and he was so dizzy—by virtue of the poison already working in his system—that he overbalanced and took a stumbling backward step out over the abyss. He would have fallen, indeed he *did* begin to fall, but Bannerman reached out, caught his left wrist and closed his fingers round it in an iron grip. In the next moment Bannerman lay spread-eagled on the ledge, peering over its rim, and Turnbull hung at arm's length, slowly turning, looking up into the face of the one man who could save him.

He saw Bannerman's face and shoulders in silhouette against blue sky and black rock, and even as the venom in his body began to exert a freezing paralysis, so his brain worked that much more coherently. Bannerman's silhouette matched up *exactly* with another until now hidden in memory. A silhouette seen framed in a doorway on a certain dark night in Killin. Last night, in fact, and Gill's doorway!

Turnbull looked at the hand grasping his left wrist and his brilliantly clear brain ran a replay; he saw the hand fly apart into so many crimson-spraying sausages. And then he looked into Bannerman's face, directly into his eyes. Bannerman was smiling.

Turnbull fought his fear, fought the numbness in his limbs to raise his right arm and hand. He would reach inside his jacket, take out his gun, and point it into Bannerman's face. And he would say, "All right, you bastard. Go on, let me fall. But the split second after you drop me I'm going to pull the trigger and blow your fucking head off!"

Except . . . Bannerman wasn't smiling but straining, and Turnbull could feel himself being lifted up, up, up to safety. He got a leg over the ledge, flopped over onto his back. He was alive—safe! *Thank God for Bannerman!* he thought.

But even as he passed out, still he wasn't sure. . . .

CHAPTER FIFTEEN

"Stay here," Bannerman told Clayborne. "Wait for me."

They had moved back maybe fifty yards to a spot where the ledge was roofed over in tangled vines and the rushing of the cataract was just a dull, distant booming. Bannerman had carried Turnbull over his shoulder, only putting him down in a place which was absolutely safe.

"Here?" Something of his previous terror had gone out of Clayborne's eyes; now, in a moment, it was rekindled. "Stay here?" he repeated. "But . . . are you leaving me?"

"I'm leaving both of you," Bannerman answered, without emotion. "I can move faster and more safely on my own. I'll find an easy route down and come back for you. Meanwhile, you stay here and look after him."

"But . . . what can I do for him?" Clayborne

got down on his knees on the ledge beside Turnbull and looked into his pale, drawn face. Turnbull's breathing was shallow, ragged. There was
a patina of cold sweat forming droplets on his
upper lip and in the hollows of his cheeks.

Bannerman shrugged. "I don't suppose
there's a lot you can do for him," he said, "but
it's a certainty you can only hinder me. So stay
and watch over him."

"But—" Clayborne began, yet again.

Bannerman dismissed his protest before he
could give it voice, saying, "I'll be back." And
without another word he began retracing their
steps up through the dusty, vine-enclosed zig-
zag of the fissure.

In a little while he came out into open air,
abandoned the fault, and doubled back along a
narrow, horizontal striation which had weathered into the merest strip of a ledge. The way
took him in the same direction but on a higher
elevation than their previous route. It wasn't a
path which Clayborne might even have contemplated, but that didn't stop Sith-Bannerman. Finally he reached a jutting, striated spur and
climbed it to a vantage point from which he
could scan almost one hundred percent of the
scene below and around.

No more than a hundred yards to the south,
Anderson and Varre were returning *up* the bottom part of the boulder slope in search of another route. The reason for this manoeuvre was
plain to see: below them the slope had given
way to a sheer, moisture-slick face descending
blindly into the waterfall's spray. From their
position directly overhead, the two hadn't been
able to see what Sith-Bannerman could see.

Even if they had seen it, he doubted if they'd have reached or responded to the obvious conclusion.

What he saw under the cataract was this:

About sixty feet below the vertical spout of shining water, a misted pool lay in a deep stone basin hollowed from a wide ledge or false plateau. It was hidden from the pair overhead by the spray and the almost sheer angle of the cliff, just as it had been hidden from Turnbull's party at the spot where their route had petered out. And at the edge of the pool—which overflowed gently at several points around its perimeter, to continue its fall in a series of frothing white rills and curtains of spray and foam—the girl Angela Denholm sat bathing herself in the shallows, plainly relishing the laving effect of the cool waters after the heat of her climb. Gill and Haggie were down there, too, seated on a flat boulder at the pool's rim. Obviously their chosen route down the side of the spur had turned out to be the best one.

Like members of most of the galaxy's sentient races (with the notable exception of the dark-minded Ggyddn) Sith-Bannerman had a sense of humour, though in his case sardonic. He chuckled inwardly at the thought of how the three of them down there at the pool would react to his, Turnbull, and Clayborne's abrupt arrival in their location—and from such an unexpected direction! It was something he looked forward to.

Meanwhile, Anderson and Varre had crossed the boulder slope diagonally to the base of the next spur, where now they made the connection with Gill's recently used trail. They had also spotted Sith-Bannerman, and paused to wave at him across the depression between spurs. He waved back, pointed out and confirmed the route they should follow, and continued to observe them as they commenced that section of their descent. Finally, satisfied that they would arrive safely at the pool, he went back for Turnbull and Clayborne.

Once move retracing his steps, Sith-Bannerman automatically checked that his recorder was working and pondered the strangeness, the ambiguities and contradictions of these self-proclaimed "human" beings. And what a mass of contradictions they were, what a hodgepodge of strengths and weaknesses, mores and immoralities, faiths and faithlessness.

Short-lived and yet inflated and bombastic as immortals (but elastic, too, and resourceful, and at times even remorseful) he pitied their apparently futile existence—while at the same time almost envying them. For all their phobias and neuroses, and their physical as well as mental disorders, still they had come a long way along the evolutionary track—by their standards if not by those of the Thone. Having studied them, however, Sith-Bannerman found it astonishing that they'd reached even their current level of attainment. But they had, and it quite appeared that given time they might yet achieve greatness . . . except that he had made it his business to deny them any such span.

They were, he knew, a fifty-fifty case. That being so, and according to Thone law, he would normally make his recordings and let the synthesizer, which the test group now called the

House of Doors, complete its various analyses, and leave the rest of it to the judgement of the Grand Thone himself. But this was not a normal occasion.

Nor was it normal or even deemed acceptable that Sith should use his Bannerman construct guise to insert himself into the synthesizer's analytical programme. But he had his reasons. And of course he would take time later to go over the records carefully and to edit himself out. A grand falsification of the facts, obviously, but he was the only one who would ever know, and he was quite sure he could live with his conscience.

If there had been more time and another way ... but there wasn't. This was the single guaranteed stairway to the pedestal room of the Grand Thone. And that was Sith's driving ambition: to occupy that crystal pedestal. Ah, but there were others just as ambitious, and their feet, too, were set upon that spiral stairway. What? And should he let a race of self-tormented Neanderthals stand in his way? Of course not! Not when the nearest Higher Authority was half a million light-years away, anyway ...

By now Sith-Bannerman was back on the ledge under the vines, descending the dusty slope to where Clayborne waited with the unconscious Turnbull. Clayborne looked up, startled, at his approach. "That was quick. Any luck?"

Sith-Bannerman nodded. "We were right on it," he said, "but we couldn't see for looking." He stooped and picked up Turnbull, hoisting his dead weight to his shoulders. As he did so he felt a warning tremor of unequal motion in the liquid elastic motor in his construct's back. That would need attention.

"Something we missed?" said Clayborne, frowning. "You mean on our way down?"

"I said we were right on it," Bannerman answered. "On top of it. Up ahead."

Urging Clayborne on before him, he followed the same route as before and once again they came out at the spot where the ledge had been washed away and spray rose up from the thunder of falling water. Clayborne went deathly white; despite the fact that the ledge where he stood was at least three feet wide, he clung to the cliff face almost as tightly as the creature Turnbull had dislodged.

Deep inside his Thone self, Bannerman smiled the alien equivalent of a cruel smile. These people were here to be tested, weren't they? According to the rules of the game, Clayborne should now be given a choice, and his decision would count for or against him in the tally when the tests were completed—but they were playing this game by Bannerman's rules.

That was why he'd become a player: to manipulate the game and make sure that Clayborne and the rest lost. But in his own good time, after he'd first reduced them to fighting, tearing, mindless animals and turned them against each other. Of the six of them, Clayborne would be the first to crack, that was obvious. And in his case Bannerman had no objection to speeding up the process.

Closing with the gasping, trembling man where he stood spread-eagled to the cliff, Bannerman said, "This is it."

"This is what?" Clayborne gulped, his Adam's apple bobbing.

"Gill, Haggie and the girl are directly down below. I mean, *directly* down below."

"What?" In his extremity of terror, Clayborne wasn't taking it in. Bannerman had supposed it would be so.

"Explaining my meaning wouldn't make it easier for you," said Bannerman. "And it wouldn't change anything, either." He yanked Clayborne from the cliff and shoved him into space. Clayborne didn't have time to draw breath for a scream; he simply disappeared into boiling spray and tossing water. And without pause Bannerman lobbed Turnbull from his shoulder into the waterfall slightly to the right of where Clayborne had fallen, and he himself jumped a little to the left. . . .

Five minutes earlier, Haggie had said to Gill, "Known her long, have you? The bint?"

"Bint?" Gill answered, absentmindedly. He was toying with the silver cylinder, frowning as he concentrated his attention on it and turned it in his hands. He knew (in that way of his) that he should be able to dismantle it, but there were no seams, no screws, no external mechanisms of any sort that he could see. Finally Haggie's question got through to him and he looked up.

The redhead's piggy eyes were on Angela where now she stood up and began wading back towards them through the shallow water at the edge of the pool. *"Brr!"* she said. "I'm afraid it's cooled me down a bit faster than I intended."

"Yeah?" said Haggie under his breath. "Well, it's done just the opposite for me!" Gill had heard what he said, and he saw where the small man's eyes were looking.

Angela's black ski pants were tight-fitting and had shown her legs off to their best advantage right from square one; but now she was showing even more, for her white, frilly blouse was of a material which turned almost transparent in water. She couldn't know it, however, or she would realise that her half-cup bra was now plainly visible, holding firm to her tip-tilted breasts.

"God, but I've been missing a bit of that!" said Haggie, again under his breath, while still she was far enough away not to hear him. But she did see his eyes fixed on her body and the way he licked his puffy lips, and she was aware of Gill's agitation.

She looked down at herself and gasped, and covered herself by crossing her arms over her breasts. "Spencer," she said, coming to a halt, "will you bring me my parka, please?"

The garment lay between the two men in a hollow in the rock. But Haggie was quicker off the mark. He snatched up the parka, grinned at Gill and jumped down from the boulder into inches of water. Three paces took him to the girl, and he tentatively held out her coat to her. She made to take it but he at once backed off.

"Try it with both hands," he advised, grinning.

She stood there undecided, biting her lip, her colour rising.

"What, are you ashamed of them?" he taunted. "Believe me you don't need to be! Not with tits like those!"

Gill climbed down from the boulder. "Haggie," he said, "you have a dirty mind, and it's so full of crap that it's dribbling out of your mouth! Give her the parka."

"What, have you laid claim to this piece?" Haggie half-turned towards him. Angela saw her chance and snatched the parka, then climbed up out of the water. Gill went to her, helped her into her coat.

"You know," said Haggie, "I've been watching you pretty carefully, Mr. Gill. Er, Spencer? Now me, I've never been much physically, you know what I mean? But I reckon I've got your measure any day. In fact, you're a bit of a wreck, aren't you? So from now on, if you have any more real cool, real hard comments to make, you keep 'em to your frigging self, right?"

Normally Gill would know how to keep a tight rein on himself. He'd learned to control his temper some years ago, when his disability had first begun to affect him. But not this time. Even knowing he'd probably take a beating, still he couldn't let things stand like this. If he did, the situation could only get worse. He bunched his fists and took a pace into the water in Haggie's direction—and in the next moment the entire scheme of things changed!

CHAPTER SIXTEEN

Anderson and Varre were just in time to witness the whole thing. They had come down the side of the spur at the narrow, southern extreme of the shelf, and had been obliged to pick their way around the scattered debris of huge boulders where they had fallen or been washed down from above. Now, as they approached the main pool over a terrain of smooth, humped rocks, where smaller pools glinted in weathered hollows, they saw Angela where she stood with her back to them, and beyond her Gill and Haggie squaring up to each other, ankle-deep in the shallows.

Fifty feet beyond the two men where they stood poised for battle, a shining spout of water crashed down and made the surface of the pool boil where it was deepest. Lesser spouts and rills cascaded down the slick cliffs behind the main deluge, sending up spray which drifted as it climbed from the tossing pool; the face of the escarpment overhead was for the greater part obscured behind its shifting milky curtain. But even as Gill and Haggie were on the point of hurling themselves at each other, so there came a diversion.

Down from the unseen heights, borne by the main spout like matchsticks down a gutter, a trio of whirling human shapes came crashing, plunging one after the other in rapid succession into the pool's deepest part. First to surface was Clayborne, who came choking and floundering, kicking feebly for the shallows. Bannerman's head next appeared from the spray, only to submerge again as he went in search of Turnbull. A moment more and Gill was wading out into the deeper water, offering his outstretched hand as Bannerman resurfaced with Turnbull's limp form in tow.

Anderson and Varre reached the pool in time to relieve Bannerman and Gill of the unconscious Turnbull, drag him out and commence pumping the water out of his lungs. Angela assisted them as best she could, and in so doing was the first to notice his poisoned left hand.

Turnbull's hand had puffed up to about twice its normal size, making it look as though he'd perhaps broken his wrist and all the fingers. But when she carefully turned the hand palm down, then the true story revealed itself.

Gill saw the look on the girl's face and examined Turnbull's hand. He saw the yellow, soft puffy flesh, and right in the centre of the hand's main pentagon, twin incisions white as good-quality paper. They were half an inch apart, each a quarter inch long, dark slits as keen as razor slashes between the pulsing purple veins—which they'd barely missed.

Gill looked at Bannerman where he sat on his own, testing his right shoulder with probing fingers. "What bit him?"

Bannerman looked up. "A crustacean sort of thing, something he accidentally disturbed. It was, oh, so big." He described its size and shape with his hands. "It clamped itself to his hand and did that."

Clayborne could be more descriptive than that. He'd got his breath back, something of his colour, too, and lay where he'd dragged himself onto a patch of shingle between rounded boulders, clinging to the earth as if it were a pillow. Now, shakily sitting up, he said, "The thing was . . . nightmarish! I mean, I've never much been bothered by bugs and the like—Christ, back in the States I've seen cockroaches as big as your thumbs in five-star hotels!—but this thing was a real monster. Facedown it was like a rock, but faceup it was something else. Its legs were like a crab's but extendable, and it had too damned many of them! It had sharp, bright little eyes . . . it was all yellow and purple . . . it moved about as fast as lightning. Yes, and it looked venomous as hell!"

"It was venomous, all right," said Gill. "How long ago did it happen?"

"No more than half an hour," said Clayborne. He got up and moved quietly to where Bannerman continued to massage his shoulder and exercise his back. "Just before this bastard threw me off the goddamn cliff!" Without warning he lashed out with his foot, catching Bannerman under the chin and knocking him flat. He went to kick him again but Anderson got in the way, trying to placate him.

"He threw you off the cliff?" The Minister repeated Clayborne's words. "What on earth do you mean? That he tried to kill you?"

Clayborne stood there clenching and unclenching his fists. "No," he finally said. But in the next breath: "Yes—yes he did. He damn near frightened me to death!"

Bannerman sat up, and now his right shoulder was hanging a little limp. He touched his jaw and looked at the blood on his fingers. "I shoved him into the waterfall," he said. "If I hadn't, he'd be up there on that ledge right now. And he'd stay there. He was in a state of shock. His phobia. I couldn't waste time, look for a new way down, carry Turnbull *and* look after Clayborne. It was the easiest way—and by far the quickest."

"Easiest for you!" Clayborne snarled.

"Should I have left you there?" Bannerman's logic was unshakable. "Should I have left Turnbull there, or risked my life trying to carry him down—and him probably dying? Were you fit to help me carry him down? You weren't fit to carry yourself."

"That's okay for you to say," Clayborne snapped. "You've no idea what vertigo is like."

"I know one thing," said Bannerman, without emotion. "If you ever move to strike me again, you'll wish you hadn't."

"All right, all *right*!" Anderson shouted. "That's enough. What the hell is everyone fighting about? We're two-thirds of the way down and only one casualty. Let's thank our lucky stars it wasn't worse. It could so easily have been much worse."

Varre had meanwhile been to the edge of the pool where the water overflowed down the escarpment. "From here on down it's not so hard," he informed. "Even carrying Turnbull, it should take us no more than an hour, an hour and a half. Or we can wait here and see what happens."

"See what happens?" Angela was cold now in the shadow of the cliffs; she hugged herself and stamped her feet to keep the circulation going.

"To him," said Varre almost negligently, indicating Turnbull with a nod of his head.

"He needs to be kept warm," said Gill. He had considered Turnbull the one man he could really trust and get on with, and now the big fellow was in a bad way. "In fact we all need to keep warm. I've noticed how it's been getting colder. It's this spray, clinging to everything. Look, do you see how long the shadows have grown? This isn't our world. The sun seems to be racing and the days will be correspondingly short. Another hour or two and it will be dark. I suggest we move along the shelf away from the water, get some fires going, dry ourselves out. Maybe we can find a place to make camp for the night. But in any case, we shouldn't try to move Turnbull too far while he's like this."

Oddly enough, Haggie sided with him at once. "He's right. We don't want to be too eager to get down into the forest for nightfall. You can't be sure what you'll meet up with down there."

Anderson looked at him curiously. "You said you'd been here before," he said. "Does that mean you *know* what's down there in the forest?"

Haggie scowled. "No," he answered, "I don't know them. And I really don't want to. It's bad enough just listening to them howling and killing each other in the dark...."

Gill woke up and knew something was wrong. And also, paradoxically, he knew something was amazingly right. Or at least that it felt right.

He felt right! For the first time in five long years he wasn't cramped; he wasn't bursting for a pee; his lungs weren't on fire, and his bones didn't feel like they'd break if someone spoke to him. He was a little stiff, yes, but he didn't feel like he was coming apart at the seams. It really would be a miracle if he didn't at least feel stiff! There was a word, "well-being", whose meaning he'd almost forgotten, because it hadn't applied to him. But he was sure it was meant to describe something like this.

He would have liked to dwell on this amazing new sensation and analyse it, but he knew that it wasn't what had brought him awake. So what had?

The place they had found for themselves wasn't really a cave, or at best it was a shallow one under something of an overhang. It was simply a place in the cliff where a massive boulder had rolled free and toppled forward, leaving a concavity to its rear which it protected with its bulk. Centrally on a sandy floor, the embers of their fire were still glowing. Clayborne had had a book of matches which by now should have dried out, but Anderson had had a cigarette lighter. Thank God for Anderson's lighter!

Close beside Gill, Turnbull groaned in his sleep. Was that what had brought him awake? Had he heard the big man moaning—or had it been something else? Movement? Was that what he'd sensed?

Gill abandoned his amazement at his own sense of, yes, well-being, laid aside his overcoat and sat up. He reached out and touched Turnbull's forehead. It was cool, dry. His fever had broken. Gill quietly stood up (still no aches and pains, and his lungs gratefully drinking in the chill night air) and looked around. Anderson's lumpy figure lay coiled close to the fire's dying embers; Clayborne lay flat out on his back, his large hands twitching in some dream or other; Haggie was ... where was Haggie?

The unpleasant little redhead had gone to sleep there on the opposite side of the fire. Now there was just the depression he'd cleared for himself in the sand. Bannerman had also slept over there, and there was no sign of him, either! What the hell was going on? Was it morning already?

Gill moved a little apart from the main sleeping area and looked into the shadowy corner where Angela had curled up in her parka. The parka was still there ... but no Angela. Of course, it could be that Bannerman or maybe Haggie was relieving Varre, and that the other two were getting a breath of fresh air. Perhaps they'd found it difficult to sleep. Calls of nature?

Varre should know. The Frenchman had volunteered himself for the job as watchkeeper—

outside the cave, of course. He had declared that he could never sleep anyway, not cooped up in there. He would keep watch, and perhaps later one of them would relieve him. If not he'd wake them at dawn, then snatch a little sleep himself while the rest of them made plans and preparations for the day ahead.

Gill decided to speak to him. He should know about the others. Especially about Angela. Even her temporary absence from this place made Gill's mouth go dry. He didn't know what their chances were, but having just found her he wasn't about to lose her if he could help it.

He fed some broken lengths of dry, brittle creeper into the fire, then made his way swiftly and silently out of the hollow behind the great boulder. He came out into starlight (no moon that he could see) and for a moment was stunned by the night sky. He'd never seen stars so large, so colorful, so many. They filled the sky like jewels, making the night live and breathe. The skies were literally glorious! And of all those amazing constellations blazing up there, not a one that he recognised. Which shouldn't have surprised him, but did anyway.

Varre had propped himself up in a leaning, hollowed rock, covering himself with his coat. Gill went to him and found him fast asleep. *Some watchdog!*

"Spencer!" Angela's voice split the night from somewhere close to the shelf's rim. Gill held his breath, felt his heart begin to hammer. Again she called out, this time urgently, breathlessly, "Spencer!" And: "Oh, take your . . . filthy hands . . . *off* me!"

And another voice—Haggie's—low, dangerous, and warning: "Listen, Angie doll, we're not getting out of this. Not you, not me, and not your bleeding Spencer. None of us. So we have to get what's going now, while it's still warm!"

Gill rushed in the direction of the voices, uncaring whether he broke his neck or not. Caring only to break Haggie's neck. He saw them outlined against the sky: Haggie clutching her from behind, with one hand over her mouth and the other tearing at her blouse as she tried to break away.

And then he saw something else coming up from beyond the rim. Something black and glinting and monstrous beyond belief!

CHAPTER SEVENTEEN

"Angela!" Gill shouted then as the sight of the thing clambering up over the rim of the escarpment stopped him dead in his tracks. "For God's sake—*look out!*" But she'd already seen it, and so had Haggie.

The little redhead let out a single, bubbling, inarticulate shriek which rose into the night and came echoing back from the face of the escarpment, and started running. Angela fled with him, not caring where she was going but only that she put distance between herself and the glittering, metallically tinted monstrosity which had now dragged itself fully onto the rock shelf. And still Gill stood frozen with his jaw hanging slack, staring at the thing in the starlight.

It was . . . an elongated crab, a rearing scorpion or mantis, a nightmare given form and substance and grown to monstrous proportions. Nine feet long, five wide, four high, with stalked eyes, incredibly articulate claws, antennae, a stinger arced over its back, and other appendages whose functions could only be guessed at. It was blue-gleaming chitin, ivory mandibles, feathery, flickering feelers. All of these things and something else, for Gill knew beyond any shadow of a doubt that it was also Haggie's pursuer.

For as he'd stared at the creature in stunned amazement, so in its turn the thing had gazed at him. Its feelers and antennae had strained in his direction, and its glittering faceted eyes had seemed to focus upon him—but only for a second. Then it had rejected him, turned like a living tank on its own axis and gone scurrying after Haggie and Angela. Except Gill guessed it wasn't especially interested in Angela. She wasn't its target. But she was in its way.

"Angela!" he yelled again, his voice hoarse with fear for her. "Come back. Get away from Haggie. It isn't coming for you. It's after him!"

If she heard him it made no difference; and then it dawned on Gill that of course she hadn't heard him. She'd been panicked, at first by Haggie and now by this thing. Also, they were running towards the falls; Gill's voice would have been mainly drowned out by the thunder of the waters. Cursing under his breath, he ran after them.

He glanced back once and saw that Varre had at last come awake. Anderson and Clayborne were there, too, stumbling about like lost souls in the starlight. Clayborne carried a flaring brand taken from the fire. Only Bannerman was still missing—but right now Gill didn't have the time or inclination to worry about Bannerman or anything else. His head (and his heart, too?) was full of Angela. Gnawing fear for Angela.

The lobster-scorpion thing was now directly in front of him; always choosing the easiest route, it scurried around and between a pebble-dash smatter of domed boulders where they littered the wide shelf. The thing didn't seem capable of a lot of speed; it was terrifying mainly by virtue of its looks, and awesome in its determination, its single-minded concentration upon the job in hand. No wonder Haggie feared it so. For already Gill knew—as Haggie himself knew—that the monster wasn't going to give up the chase until it had achieved its aim, which was to take the redhead. But why?

He drew parallel with the scuttling creature but a little apart from it, skirted it and clambered across crumbling ledges of rock and domed boulders to get in front. His intention was to reach Angela first and separate her from Haggie. But then . . . disaster!

Scrambling across spray-damp boulders, he slipped; his feet shot out from under him; he crashed down on soft, wet shingle directly in the creature's path. Winded, almost exhausted by a combination of panic and unaccustomed exertion, Gill lay on his back and looked up at the thing as it bore down on him.

It jerked to an uncertain halt; great pincers swung high and poised there; the thing's stalked eyes swivelled to peer down on Gill, angling this way and that to encompass his whole body. Its mandibles clashed inches from his face as its blue-glinting legs straddled him, firmly anchoring the monster where it stood astride him.

And Gill thought: *It's breathing right into my face and I can't smell a thing! Not anything animal, anyway . . .*

And then, as surely as he was gifted with a sixth sense, he knew what he was up against. He knew what it was, and why it pursued Haggie with such grim intent: because it had been programmed to do just that. Programmed, yes—for it was a machine!

A pair of pincers came swinging down and Gill's flesh went cold. He batted uselessly at the hinged crab claws with both fists; they ignored him, took him by the waist, lifted him to one side and dumped him. Unharmed in any way, he fell mere inches to the shingle at the rim of the cataract's pool. Without more ado, the monster lumbered by and splashed many-legged into the water. And from across the pool: "Oh, Jesus! *Jesus!*" Haggie's shrill shriek of terror rang out over the thundering of the water. "It's after me—it's coming!"

Gill got to his knees. He saw Angela and Haggie at the very edge of the pool, where the water flowed over its smooth rim and down the face of the escarpment. Wreathed in spray, they crouched there—and the nightmare machine wading or swimming towards them—and in the next moment Haggie grabbing Angela and throwing her bodily down. No, throwing her *over* the edge! Gill cried out, *"No!"*—felt an emotional agony tearing at his insides—as Haggie himself slipped over the edge and followed Angela down out of sight.

No! Gill said again, but this time to himself.

And in the next moment he was in the chilly water, swimming for all he was worth in the wake of the grotesque machine; and only vaguely was he given to wonder how his weak, dying body could possibly sustain him through all of this. Or perhaps that was why he was able to do it: because he was dying anyway and it would make no difference. But the thought of Angela dying was something else.

The machine trailed its rearmost limbs in the water; Gill made a supreme effort and grabbed one of them, then hung on panting and gasping until the hunting thing reached the rim of the pool and rose up from the water. Its eye stalks swayed out over the gulf, directing its gaze downward. Faceted eyes focused, swivelled this way and that, and appendages at the front and rear of the body elongated, extending themselves silently but with pneumatic precision. Claws clamped to rock and the creature (even knowing it for a machine, still Gill thought of it as something alive) tilted sharply forward. It was preparing to go down—headfirst!

Gill stood up in the pool so close to the thing that he could reach out and touch it. The plated rear of its carapace was towards him, but even if he'd been visible to it, he suspected it would not interfere with him. It tilted more yet and inched forward, flattening itself to the ledge.

Gill knew a raging frustration; he stood there undecided with his jaw jutting, fists knotted. This damned thing was going to follow Haggie to the bitter end. If the redhead lived, it would find him. And if Angela lived, it would probably find her with Haggie. The one thing Gill wanted now was to find Angela, which meant that he must make an impossible decision. But impossible or not, he made it. As hoarse, shouting voices reached him from the far side of the pool, he climbed up onto the hunter's back and clung there, deliberately snagging his clothing on its many sharp projections. And not a moment too soon.

With a sickening lurch the machine upended itself, turning through ninety degrees and into the vertical as it began its descent. Gill felt his clothes start to tear as he slid forward, was brought up short with a bump when his shoulder rammed up against the hunter's stinger. Arcing forward over its back, that otherwise menacing scythe of chitin and arachnid-insect-crustacean flesh was something Gill could cling to. He did—for his life!

After that . . . all was a nightmare of lurching limbs, of gravity defied—but barely, Gill felt—and of claws and pincers grasping projecting rocks with such fierce energy that they occasionally burst asunder. That would be bad enough in itself—the fear that at any moment the machine could err and carry itself and its limpet passenger into oblivion—but there was a further complication. While it was an entirely mental thing, still it was a distraction which Gill couldn't afford; and yet it insisted upon distracting him. It was this:

He was astride a machine, in closest possible contact with it, and his talent was confused to the point of breakdown. For he "knew" in his way that there was never a machine like it—not on Earth, anyway. What, an *un*mechanical machine? Unheard of! Or if there was something like it, then what it was was the mighty and enigmatic structure which men had called the Castle—now the House of Doors. He had sensed, felt, experienced these alien machines working, and for the first time in his life had failed to understand *how* they worked—because they were alien. Given time he might understand them, though that wasn't something which would come easily.

But now there was something else, something which hitherto Gill had sensed only as a vague awareness. The House of Doors and the hunting thing both solicited the same response from his machine-oriented mind: he had accorded them the same instinctive recognition. Them and one other piece of . . . machinery? Previously he had put it down to the environment, to the fact that he was inside the House of Doors, which must be affecting or deflecting his talent as a magnet deflects a compass. But now he wasn't so sure.

The thing that had been disturbing him was Bannerman—and the fact that he could no longer be sure that Bannerman was a man.

But a "tourist"? Possibly . . .

CHAPTER EIGHTEEN

Sith of the Thone was mainly liquid, as most living things are. But since the Thone were essentially low-gravity creatures, in them the proportion of liquid to solid was far higher than the norm; in a low-grav situation, it is easier to flow than to walk. He did have microscopic solids in his chemical soup of a makeup, of course, but the only really "solid" thing about him now was a cylindrical exoskeletal sleeve of superflexible plastic protecting that midsection of his person which contained his three vital organs: brain, primary motor system, and the spongy cartilaginous siphon-cum-nerve chain that linked them, corresponding in Earth-type creatures to the spinal column.

He was in aspect very much as Smart Alec Haggie had described him: an upright jellyfish going on three tentacles. Of eyes, ears and nos-

trils he had none; bands of sensors formed an intricate pattern of luminous blue dots all about his person, and with these he perceived more than adequately of three-dimensioned space and was aware of time—but not so conscious of it as are men. Men are mainly conscious of it because they have so little. Sith, on the other hand, had already spent more than a dozen human lifetimes in hypersleep alone.

Apart from the protection of his organs, his exoskeletal tube served one other very important purpose: it contained microconverters and gravitic deflection shields which drew energy from the synthesizer and converted it to combat the effect of Earth gravity, thus enclosing Sith's person in a low-grav envelope. Without this envelope he would be little more than a stain on the floor.

Above the "waist", Sith's body contained a secondary motor system which functioned without direct physical connection to his brain. In fact it reacted to inward-beamed messages from his light- and other wave-sensitive sensor spots, thus negating any necessarily tedious brain activity. Therefore, his reactions were literally lightning fast; for the function of the upper motor system was the extrusion and control of manipulators, "hands", with which to operate the synthesizer's controls. Those of them, at least, which required sentient adjustment or instruction.

A second brain, now vestigial, formed a pale grey oval the size of a walnut central in Sith's upper mass. Some Thone individuals extruded their atrophied brains as useless matter; others formed them into sigil-shapes by which they might be recognised without first revealing their names. Since the pinnacle of all Thone ambition was to achieve almost total seclusion and insularity, however, Sith had always considered this a symptom of disordered identity or hereditary inferiority; he had kept his own nonfunctioning brain pristine, retaining it for curiosity value only. Perhaps he would do something with it when (if) he mounted the crystal pedestal to become Grand Thone. By which time he would be above reproach, of course.

The other important difference between Sith's race and mankind was this: their body temperature was more than twice that of men. This came of having evolved on a mainly arid, hothouse world; which in turn meant that their basic body fluid was closer to mercury than to water. It was not mercury, however, and having a curious molecular structure was indeed very much lighter than water. In short, Sith was very insubstantial by human standards. Physically, if not mentally.

The Bannerman construct, on the other hand, was just the opposite.

The original Jon Bannerman had in fact been a Portuguese tourist. Having an older, retired friend in Scotland, he had visited him during a tour of the British Isles. His friend had been something of a local dignitary with connections sufficient that Bannerman was granted a visit to the Castle in the secure area at the foot of Ben Lawers. That had been four months ago, when first Sith had decided to go out among the native inhabitants of this world. Bannerman's visit to the Castle had coincided with Sith's preparations.

Since a model was required (on which Sith would base his construct) Bannerman had been taken. It could just as easily have been someone else, but it was him. Standing alone at the base of a side wall, he had known a moment's dizziness—and that was all. His reception within the synthesizer had been well organized; in the space of mere moments he had been copied; anyone watching him might well have been puzzled by a trick of the light which made him seem to disappear for a few seconds, only to reappear moments later.

The Castle hadn't greatly impressed Jon Bannerman—indeed it had given him a headache which persisted for a day and a night. But he was grateful for having seen it anyway. And at the end of a week he'd gone back home to Portugal.

Outwardly the construct *was* Jon Bannerman. Tall and by local standards slightly foreign-looking, especially its dark eyes—strong, with a blocky figure and broad chest, and a sturdy neck bearing a moderately handsome head; with dark, short-cropped, prematurely greying hair, and having a straight nose and a narrow, serious mouth—it (he) would not go entirely unnoticed in the streets. But neither would he attract too much attention. There seemed nothing especially unusual about him.

But his external appearance was entirely superficial, a cosmetic shell for Sith's life-support system, and inwardly there was little or no similarity to a human being. Cut Bannerman or hit him on the nose and he might bleed. Tear off a finger (or indeed all of them) from one of his hands and you would get blood, bone, apparently human flesh—all of it synthetic, but close enough to pass merely cursory inspection. Cut him a good deal deeper in the trunk or a major limb, and there you'd find the grey fluids of an incredibly versatile microhydraulic system—which would not be recognised as such, but as "ichor". There would be no time for analysis, because the fluid would rapidly devolve. Remove an eye and you'd find sensor membranes which a biologist *might* identify but never fathom; likewise within his ears and nostrils.

His chest cavity contained not only sufficient space for Sith's upper body but also for energy receptors and a powerful converter. He was . . . neither a robot nor an android, for these were human terms describing types of mechanisms, and Bannerman wasn't any kind of mechanism which human science could yet understand or even credit. He *was* a vastly efficient engine, composed in its entirety of fluids, whose only limitations lay in the strictures of its size and shape.

This, at least, is how a human scientist might have viewed him. But to Sith of the Thone . . .

By analogy, Bannerman was in fact something between a deep-sea diving suit and an aqualung, synthesised by Sith for his own use, and as cumbersome to him as the analagous mechanisms are to men. And being a brand-new model and as yet only partially tested, it was only to be expected that there would be minor problems.

For unlike the human body it imitated, the Bannerman construct wasn't self-repairing. It could have been, but not within such rigid space limitations. In all honesty, Sith couldn't blame the current malfunction on design alone; nor would he, for it was his design. But in fact Bannerman had taken several hard knocks, and it was doubtless these which had brought on the trouble.

First there had been the brief but vicious attack of those thugs in the alley in Edinburgh, and more recently the climbing, carrying, leaping into waterfalls and such, and finally Clayborne's display of savagery. Add to all of this the aggravated wear and tear of high gravity, and . . . it shouldn't have been difficult to foresee the development of small problems.

As for that other incident—the loss of a hand—that must not be forgotten either. Oh, the hand had been repaired easily enough, but not Sith's pride. The man Turnbull had taken him by surprise that time, but that wouldn't happen again. While carrying his unconscious body, Sith-Bannerman had removed and disposed of his gun.

Sith still felt anger that he had let a primitive get the better of him. But of course, that *had* been the fault of the construct: the fact that it so restricted him. Alas, but movement in the world of men were entirely impossible without it.

The world of men, yes . . . but for how much longer? While he programmed several small design modifications and instructed the synthesizer to carry out the required restructuring, Sith reflected on his mission: the discovery of new worlds for the ever-expanding Thone.

Sleeping in the womb of the synthesizer—and

bearing with him a transmat receptor, for use if this world should prove habitable and available—he had crossed countless light-years of space. His findings would determine whether or not the planet was fit for Thone colonization. And in fact he'd discovered that given a minimum of geothermal engineering and perhaps a delicate realignment of orbit around the parent star, it could have been. Such measures would, of course, render the planet quite *un*inhabitable to all of its native species—wherein had lain the source of a bitter disappointment.

For it was a principle of the Thone never to threaten or in any way disturb higher lifeforms, but to distance themselves from them and let them go their own ways in peace. The Thone were neither mercenary nor greedy within the boundaries of their cause; they respected developing species to a point, that point depending upon their *stage* of development, and the likely route further development would take. A race inspired towards barbarism would probably receive short shrift, but not until it had been "tried" and found wanting beyond reasonable doubt.

These things being so, and the rules governing his investigations being strict and nononsense, Sith had soon concluded that indeed the peoples of Earth were sufficiently advanced as to preclude Thone interference: they had made this world their own, and had almost arrived at that stage of development beyond which Thone law and ethics forbade interference. And *specifically* forbade their destruction! A million years earlier it would have been different. Even three or four thousand years ago.

But no longer. Oh, it could still be argued that they were borderline barbarians, but Sith had little or no doubt how the verdict would go—namely, in their favour.

That being so, he had set up and activated the transmat. The matter transmitter would not work in hyperspace, which meant that messages could not be transmitted while the synthesizer was in flight across the void. Now, however, having charted this world and categorised its inhabitants, he could send all relevant details to his nearest Higher Authority. Doubtless Earth would be struck from the list of possible habitats; Sith would receive instructions to move on; his search would recommence at once.

But before he could use the transmat, an incoming message had reached him. And it was this:

The Grand Thone was retiring! The palace of the crystal pedestal was being made ready for a new occupant! The way was now open for Thones of merit to make their once-in-a-lifetime bids for the ultimate seat of power and authority! Sith had long declared himself an aspirant; his work for Thone expansion may have gone unrewarded, but it had not gone unrecognised; he had been short-listed!

He had been granted permission to use the transmat and journey to the palace of the pedestal, there to make the case for his own ascension to Grand Thonedom. The current Grand Thone would of course preside, and there were to be five other contenders. These were named, and Sith saw that he was up against five serious rivals. The choice would be made in (the equivalent of) three years' time, when the presence of all six aspirants on the palace planet would be imperative. . . .

Sith had given the matter a little thought, and had then transmatted a simple answer: in all humility he would be there at the appointed hour. Following which, in something less than humility, he'd considered his position. To have been named as a candidate for Grand Thonedom! But . . . he knew he couldn't win. Two of his opponents were elders, which would weigh heavily in their favour; two more were scientists of astonishing range, one of which descended from Lakkas himself, inventor of the synthesizer! Even the least of the five was arguably Sith's equal—another locator and invigilator, like Sith himself.

Except . . . he might indeed stand a chance—could even possibly win—if only he could take home with him something of extraordinary value. And with that thought in mind, Sith had once more turned his sensors upon this new world, this Earth, to view it in a somewhat different light. . . .

For human minds were not the only devious ones in the universe, and now Sith was discovering that his could be one of the most devious of all.

Some weeks had then passed, during which Sith did very little. Eventually, emerging one period from a brief state of voluntary stasis or sleep—and almost before he was fully awake and knew what he was about—he'd erased all of his records concerning Earth and its peoples and prepared to start afresh. Except that this time his findings would go against humankind, and indeed he would take home a singular prize for the Grand Thone. One which would doubtless make Sith the new, rightful, all-powerful occupant of the crystal pedestal.

He would take home a claim on the planet Earth itself!

CHAPTER NINETEEN

How long Gill's nightmare descent of the escarpment lasted, lodged like a sheep tick on the back of the hunting thing and clinging there for his life, he would never be able to say. Long enough that he thought his arms were going to tear free of their sockets, but that even if they didn't, it would make no difference for he'd never again be able to unclench his bloodless, nerveless fingers. Long enough that he lost all sense of direction and orientation; so that when he did finally succumb, lose his grip on the stinger, and slide unresisting down the curve of the thing's segmented flank, it took some little time for the fact to dawn that instead of falling through space he had flopped down on his back in thick moss, and that the alien stars overhead were paling now in the fast-spreading light of a new dawn.

For the fact that he still lived, Gill hoarsely breathed his thanks to whichever gods applied here, before gritting his teeth and forcing his throbbing muscles to answer his call. From high overhead as he tremblingly, groaningly sat up, he could hear the ringing, echoing cries of his fellow castaways, calling down, "Halloo! Halloo!" But he hadn't the wind or the spit in his dust-dry throat to try for an answer. Later, maybe . . . if there was to be a later.

For as he looked all about in the still-faint but rapidly improving light, he became aware of a massed cracking of twigs and dry branches, and he sensed the presence of some large bulk moving in the dawn. The short hairs stood up on the back of his neck as the sounds grew louder, apparently heading in his direction, and instinct told him that nothing remotely human made them. It could only be that something had sensed him here and was even now closing on him.

Gill got to all fours, tensed himself, held his breath. To the east a rolling bank of ground mist was gradually clearing, and this was the source of the sounds. In another moment something solid formed in the mist, taking on mass as it moved towards him. Then . . . Gill's talent reasserted itself; he knew what the thing was; his gathered breath *whooshed* out of him and he slumped a little, gasping his relief. It was only the hunting machine, scuttling this way and that, proboscis to the valley's floor, for all the world like some awesome hound tracking a scent. And the idea took hold: that was precisely what it was doing. Haggie's scent, of course—and Angela's.

Finally the thing turned towards the near-distant forest; its antennae moved atop its head, locking on something Gill could neither see nor hear; its faceted eyes glinted in the new, misty light and blinked away a film of moisture. And then it moved with renewed purpose, scurrying out from the shadow of the escarpment and towards the faintly stirring, dew-laden canopy of alien foliage. Heading, in fact, in the direction of the mansion, which Gill had little doubt was yet another manifestation of the House of Doors.

He climbed achingly to his feet. *Where you go, my friend*, he silently, grimly vowed, *there go I!*

Keeping a low profile and running through grass and soft mosses on legs which astonished him with their strength (where by rights there should be none), he gained on the alien machine until he was right behind it. Finally he was able to reach out, grab hold and cling to an armoured plate, draw himself up onto its back, and—

—the thing stopped dead in its tracks!

Eye stalks swivelled with all the agility of a chameleon, turning the faceted eyes through one hundred and eighty degrees and directing them to gaze upon Gill. Whether the thing recognised him or not it was difficult to say: it must have memory banks, he supposed. But if not as a person—and one it had seen before—certainly it recognised him as an unnecessary burden. It reared first to one side, then the other, tilting its carapace like some alien, crustacean bronco, trying to unseat him. Had he been some large clod of earth or a fallen tree, then the thing might have succeeded; but he was a thinking being and the hunter's motions were too mechanical and contrived to fool him; he simply shifted his centre of gravity and stayed put. Now he would see how this creature (no, he reminded himself, this machine) coped with an intelligent clod of earth.

He did see, and at once. The great scythe stinger swivelled in its socket, bending its tip down towards him where he clung to the hunter's plated back. Gill twisted his neck to look up and back at the stinger as it elongated itself towards his spine, and he thought: *God, is it going to kill me?* If so, he would guess that it wasn't because the thing found him especially distasteful; and since he hadn't threatened it, he could hardly be considered an enemy. Therefore, it could only be that he was an encumbrance, an impediment.

Jesus! he thought. *I'm going to die because I got in its way once too often! Why the hell didn't you do it back there, when we were coming down the damned cliff?* But of course, the thing made no answer.

He released the base of the stinger and tried to throw himself from the thing's back. But his jacket had snagged on one of its spiked plates. Tugging his sleeve until the material tore, Gill wrenched himself over onto his back. The tip of the stinger was now poised just six inches over his heart. Thick as Gill's thumb, the chitin-plated point was indented at its tip like a navel. As his bulging eyes watched, the "skin" of the navel peeled outwards like the petals of a flower unfurling—and a hypodermic needle emerged, squirting liquid even as it stabbed home!

The needle passed through jacket, shirt, and vest, and into Gill's chest. But the agent it used was so quick that he didn't even feel its sting. . . .

It didn't ditch me on the cliff—Gill's resurfacing mind was still working on the problem—*because it knew that to do so would be to kill me—which wasn't its purpose. Its job concerns Haggie. Only Haggie.*

And carrying his logic a step further: *So if it didn't desire to kill me then, why should it do so now? Answer: it shouldn't. It hasn't. Ergo, I'm not dead!*

"Is he dead?" Varre's voice with its faint French accent got through to him. Which was all the corroboration Gill needed. Someone was fumbling with his jacket; a hand groped around in the region of his heart, touching the sore spot where the needle had gone in.

Gill opened his eyes on blinding light, gurgled, "No, I'm not!" But his mouth felt like something had died in there.

They helped him to sit up. Varre, Anderson—who had been examining him—and Clayborne . . . but where was Turnbull? And where was Bannerman? Anderson saw the question written in Gill's eyes, said: "Turnbull's okay. He's coming out of it. We found an easy way down, took turns carrying—or dragging—him. He's a big man."

Gill felt a sudden nausea welling inside. He gulped and a little bile entered his mouth, causing taste buds to react and fill it with sweet water. He spat the whole lot out. Then he looked around and saw Turnbull propped against the bole of a squat tree. He was still out but his colour had returned almost to normal.

"Where's Bannerman?" Gill asked.

Anderson shrugged. "Gone missing. Haven't seen him since last night when we got our heads down. What about Haggie and the girl—and that bloody nightmare?"

Clayborne helped Gill to his feet and he told them what he knew. Especially about the hunting machine. "So it's just as Haggie said," he finished. "It's after him. Don't ask me why, but it is. It's not a bit interested in us. I would have been easy meat but it just put me to sleep."

Turnbull woke up with a start and said, "Eh? Sleep?" He squinted and looked dazedly around. His eyes were bloodshot in their dark sockets. "I was, *uh*, dreaming!"

Gill went to him. "You're not quite awake even now." He grinned. And then he sobered. "Something bit you, remember?"

Turnbull glanced at his hand, which was now more nearly its original shape and size. "God, yes!" he breathed. "What a monster!"

"I could tell you a few things about monsters." Gill nodded.

Meanwhile Varre had been examining some green and red fruits on a thorny shrub. They looked very much like apples. He bit into one and held the portion in his mouth, carefully tasting it. Then he chewed, but hesitantly, and finally smiled. "Hey," he called out. "These are good!"

Anderson and Clayborne went to him, leaving Gill and Turnbull on their own. Turnbull jerked his head, indicating that Gill should come closer. Gill went down on one knee. "What is it?"

"About Bannerman." Turnbull kept his voice low. "There's something not quite right about that bloke. I've suspected it from square one, and even though I've got no proof, still I'd bet my life he's weird."

Gill looked at him. "He saved your life," he answered. "Got you down off the cliff after you'd been bitten."

Turnbull frowned. "Then that's twice he's saved my life," he said. "But God only knows why! The way I have it figured, he's the one who tried to nail you that night at your flat."

Gill stiffened. That was the other thing that had been worrying him about Bannerman: where he'd seen him before. "But he has both of his hands," he answered, after a moment.

Turnbull nodded, shrugged. "It's got me beat," he said.

"You're probably right anyway." Gill let him off the hook. "I smelled something funny about him, too. And not funny ha-ha. But . . . this is between you and me?"

"Sure."

"I'm not even a hundred percent certain he's a man!"

"*What?*" Turnbull sat up straighter, groaned, and would have slipped to one side if Gill hadn't grabbed him. "God, I'm dizzy as a doped cat!" he said. And in a voice even more hushed: "Did you say Bannerman isn't a man? You mean he's an alien?"

"Yes," Gill answered instinctively. "I mean, no—not unless they're machines."

"He's a machine?" Turnbull couldn't accept it. "But that's . . . crazy!"

"Sounds that way, doesn't it?" Gill was suddenly unsure. "But anyway, that's my best shot. Oh, he wouldn't be any kind of machine we ever met up with before, but . . ." He shrugged. And before Turnbull could begin to argue the point: "Anyway, he's disappeared. Went in the night."

"The night? What night?"

Gill saw the others returning with some of the fruit. Lifting his voice a little, he said, "Yes, he vanished last night. You were unconscious, of course."

Turnbull flexed his arms, legs, said, "Help me up."

Gill got him on his feet, told him, "I'd take it easy if I were you."

Turnbull looked around, squinted into the blue sky where a blazing orb moved towards its zenith. "I don't see Haggie and the girl," he said.

In the presence of the others, Gill repeated what had happened. As he was finishing, Varre bent double and threw up. It was quite the most sudden, most violent upheaval Gill had ever seen, and in the middle of it the Frenchman fell to the grass and rolled there, obviously in agony. Anderson and Clayborne looked at each other with horror written on their faces, and in another few seconds they'd joined Varre.

"P-poisoned!" Varre gurgled through his vomit.

And Clayborne added, "God, what a hellhole! You and your fucking fruit!"

Gill and Turnbull could do nothing. For another half hour they simply sat and watched the three purging themselves. . . .

CHAPTER TWENTY

When the Bannerman construct firmed back into being, Sith observed it with something approaching distaste. He had enjoyed the all-too-brief period of physical freedom here in the synthesizer's vast control room. It was sheer luxury after the confines of the construct. But in fact, even the control room itself was mainly synthesised: a projection of space within space. It was one of many projections, even of entire worlds. But they were transient things, hyperspatial as the faster-than-light continuum whose configurations formed the mainly hypothetical boundaries of the universe. The synthesizer stored them in its memory banks, for reproduction at Sith's will.

He had discovered *many* worlds in his voyage of search and discovery, and all were stored unedited within the memory of the synthesizer. He would store reproducible memories of Earth there, too—but not until after planetary restructuring. He would not want some future Thone scientist wandering about in the synthesizer's memory banks and perhaps discovering that in fact the peoples of Earth had been worthy.

But were they worthy? Really? The question gave Sith pause for thought. He attempted to justify the coming destruction of mankind, and of all the thousands of lesser species inhabiting this world.

Worthy? In what way?

They possessed what to them must seem a haven, a beautiful world. And to the Thone (after modification) it would be even more desirable. And yet these "men" seemed in large part to be trying to destroy it. Internally as well as externally! They tore out its guts, mining it to extinction. Then they burned the produce of their mining, poisoning the planet's atmosphere with their smoke and gaseous by-products. They polluted the oceans with their own wastes and the machine wastes of their cities, and razed oxygen-producing forests to make room for their own heedless, headlong expansion.

Perhaps all of this were pardonable if, like the Thone, they had other worlds to replace this one when they'd reduced it to a corpse. But they didn't. With their solid- and liquid-fuel engines they had only succeeded in journeying to their own satellite—and that for no good purpose that Sith could see. To use as a staging post, a launchpad? To where? The rest of this system's planets, which were plainly uninhabitable by men? To the stars? Out of the question!

Even at the (quite incredible) rate their technology had advanced in the last hundred years, still it would be at least a thousand before they could possibly develop anything like the synthesizer, or some other mode of FTL travel. No, they ran before they could walk, these creatures.

But to use liquid—to *burn* and thus destroy liquid—as a fuel! That were sacrilege. Given another millennium, perhaps they might have come to recognise that liquid, in itself, could be an engine.

And barbaric? There could be no doubting it. They warred, not against warlike alien races (they'd not yet encountered such) *but against each other!* They killed each other—mass murder, attempted genocide—in their wars. And in so doing, they destroyed even more of their planet. What sort of creatures are they who, when gifted with a beautiful house, immediately turn upon each other and in their fighting knock out the very walls from within?

Half of the planet stood at odds with the other half, each of them possessing the means to burn off the atmosphere and reduce the entire surface to rubble many times over; and yet constantly increasing their arsenals, if not of one type of weapon, then of another. As for the lesser nations: no corner of the planet was at peace. Small wars were waged everywhere!

And in their use—their misuse—of nuclear fission . . . here they did not merely run before they could walk, they raced before they could even crawl! They had no notion of safety, no conception of how to dispose of or neutralize their nuclear wastes. Atomics were a primitive, wasteful power source at best, but even *knowing* they erred, still these monsters proceeded to experiment and improvise, and gradually destroy themselves and their world in the painfully slow process of what they called progress.

They *were* indeed destroying themselves—so why shouldn't Sith help them along their chosen route?

But (his inner being, his conscience, spoke to him) *you examined this race, and found it worthy. According to the rules, Thone rules, it was worthy—before your own ambitions got in the way. Before you felt the wonder and the power of personal glory within your grasp. Now who is unworthy?*

Not I! Sith told himself. *My worth is proven: I am accepted as an aspirant to the crystal pedestal!* Against which his conscience had no argument. Or if it did, he stifled it unuttered. But to be doubly sure of his ground, Sith produced yet more evidence against the human race, this time by examination of their own mores, beliefs and taboos.

Given that they were bisexual (a loathsome condition at best) and that for the greater part their religions dictated one woman for one man and vice versa, then their appetites—their lust, along with an enormous capacity for ignoring the law—seemed unquenchable. The promiscuity of their young, even by their own standards, was appalling! As a race they were a mass of sexual contradictions and perversions; and this description applied not alone to their sexuality but to all other aspects of their lives.

Sith had recorded a recent American TV programme, aimed (ostensibly) at the prevention of certain diseases and addictions, in which the principal message had been: CARELESS SEX KILLS! DOPE KILLS! SMOKING KILLS! DRINK KILLS! And yet one of the programme's young presenters had admitted that he himself had "tried out" all of these things, and on occasion still did. Indeed, the overall picture seemed to be that in certain sections of society these known killers were generally considered to be the "in thing" to do— and if done to excess, then so much the better! Approximately two-thirds of the planet's population was killing itself through self-willed wars, excesses of addiction, self-inflicted disease (very often sexually transmitted) as a result of grossly inadequate personal hygiene, and senseless industrial contamination—to name a few.

One of their religions, Christianity, extolled the observance of ten laws called commandments, which by definition had to be the most defiled laws in the world. A majority of so-called Christians actually lived by the nonobservance of these laws!

Nor were Sith's observations a mere overview, for in his studies he'd gone from macro to micro, from the masses down to the individuals of human society. And it was his belief that if he searched from now until forever, he would not find one—not *one*—entirely moral or ethical man or woman. Each one of them thought in terms of "I" and not "we". Each wanted to be at least "as good as" the next step up in their pecking order—or to bring down the one who occupied that step to his own level. Which meant that any real advancement of the race as an entity must be either (a) an accident, or (b) ... the sheerest flight of fancy! Man did not seek to advance his race but him*self*—and any benefits his brother might derive were entirely coincidental.

And so it went; the list was long; the objections of Sith's conscience were gradually eroded and dispersed. To put a final seal of approval on his plan for the race's extermination, he looked one last time at the most puzzling of all human attitudes: their conceit. How might one explain it—except as perversity? What did they have to be conceited about? Physically grotesque and diseased (some even from birth) their minds, too, were wont to break under the pressures of their chaotic existence, or at best warp until their view of reality was twisted and fearful. And as a direct result, their mental illnesses were legion.

Take for example the group of specimens Sith had trapped for testing.

Anderson, for the greater part of his life, had been a winner, a leader of men, a figure of authority. He'd thrived on it. Here in the entirely alien environments Sith planned for the group, the Minister would doubtless endeavor to go right on leading. But only erode his authority, let it be seen that outside of an armchair in a modern office, or the leather upholstered seat of an expensive car with a telephone hidden in the armrest, he was incapable of leadership ... and how long would his facade stand up, his veneer of sophisticated authority remain intact? Not very long, was Sith's guess. And because men in authority were wont to be ruthless—to possess what human beings called "the killer instinct"—how long before that more basic instinct surfaced? At his own level of society, the circles in which he had moved, Anderson need only snap his fingers and his bidding was done. But here, where he must do for himself? In what direction would his "killer instinct" lead him when the result of any amount of finger snapping proved negative?

Then there was Varre, who believed that if it couldn't be bought, begged or stolen, (a) that it wasn't worth having, like honour; (b) that it should be sabotaged, destroyed, so that no one else could have it; (c) that it could only be entirely beyond his understanding and should be given a wide berth. Currently he could neither buy, beg nor steal anything. The old values were gone, reality steadily crumbling, the Unknown closing in—like walls closing on his being. Did the Frenchman realise, Sith wondered, that his claustrophobia wasn't so much a fear of being denied space as a fear of being denied? He was a procurer, but here in the synthesizer he'd find nothing to procure. Take away his ability to wheel and deal, and what then? How long before the invisible walls of his phobia closed in and squeezed him into raving lunacy? Already he showed a measure of contempt for his fellows—whom he deemed worthless because, like he himself, they were helpless—and a growing frustration with a universe in which no bargains could be struck.

As for the woman: she was threatened by her own sexuality. One woman marooned in an alien universe with six men—seven, if Sith included Bannerman? Already Haggie had menaced her, making it plain that if he got the chance he'd not hesitate to press home his advantages of physical superiority and mental degeneracy. Whatever else the girl might or might not fear, she must certainly be aware that physically she was the least of them all, and that any one of these men—or all of them—would have the power to abuse her if (when?) they so desired. Except perhaps for Gill; and here Sith's thoughts narrowed like human eyes, speculatively.

For Gill was the one with the talent—the awareness, the machine-mindedness—which made him not only unique but perhaps even a little dangerous. Apart from anything else (indeed, set against almost everything else) that talent alone might have been the saving of his race, if the circumstances were different. No Thone examiner-invigilator could ever relegate to extinction a race which had produced the likes of Gill. Or at least, none before Sith. But then none had ever been in his position.

The man Gill, yes . . .

There seemed very little wrong with his mind. Quite apart from its uniqueness, it appeared to house no illnesses. Unlike his body, it was mainly healthy. Oh, Gill was short-tempered and he had his frustrations, but nothing which might be termed a phobia or even a specific fear. Unless it was the fear of death itself. If so, then he'd suppressed it—put it out of mind, so to speak. Perhaps he'd grown accustomed to the idea of death; if not contemptuous of it, certainly the familiarity of its gradual encroachment had bred phlegmatism. To a point.

At least he didn't seem to fear it for himself—but for the woman? Ah, but here in the synthesizer, things other than death could be arranged for her. Yes, it would all hinge upon the woman; but Haggie's criminality—his lack of principle and superfluity of undisciplined lust—might not be the only trigger to set in motion the chain reaction of Gill's disintegration.

Haggie was here as the result of a mechanical imbalance in the synthesizer. When the machine had corrected itself, he had been trapped here. And having spent some little time here his instincts, criminal even before he'd been taken, were now grown so coarse as to reduce him to the level of a hunted animal. He believed, not unreasonably, that he *was* hunted; and in a way he was, though not in the way he believed. But having degenerated (or adapted?) so rapidly did not make him any less intelligent. Quite the opposite: his wits had been sharpened. Moreover, he now had the freedom to use them more fully, and to more basic ends. He no longer feared reprisal: where there is no law except the law of survival, there can be no justice. It was down to the survival of the fittest. Dog eat dog.

Being what he was, Haggie had very quickly come to recognise these new parameters. In many ways they suited his mentality. Especially now that he had others of his own kind to prey on. But . . . how long before the others caught on? And where the woman was concerned, how long before their civilised trappings fell free, and they began to look at her not so much as someone to be protected but as legitimate prey? Oh, yes, there were interesting times ahead, Sith was sure.

Turnbull was still something of a mystery. He seemed fearless, but Sith suspected this was a front. If it covered a mental disorder, then be sure it would be an unpleasant one. To have been buried that deeply, it must be. But there was no denying that Turnbull had size and strength, and a certain quickness of thought and response. That had been proved only too graphically on the night Sith had set out to eradicate Gill, when but for Turnbull the man had surely died. Sith had been overanxious that time: Gill had not been that much of a threat. It was simply that Sith had feared his interference—that perhaps he would sense the synthesizer's preparations and cause men to be kept back from it, beyond its perimeter of expansion—at the very time he'd set for the trap to be sprung. That and the fact that Gill was aware, which had made him the principal objection to Sith's plans. He had been the one mote in the eye of Sith's conscience. Remove him and . . . there'd be no further reason why Sith should not proceed. No more obstacles along the route to the crystal pedestal.

But Turnbull had intervened; Gill had been spared and Sith frustrated; and the Thone invigilator had discovered a new facet to his mind. He experienced an almost human reaction. Which was this: that he desired . . . a rematch? Possibly. Turnbull and Gill had frustrated what were otherwise a smooth operation. Without even knowing what they went against, they'd succeeded in thwarting him, and without too much difficulty! For a super-entity face-to-face with Neanderthals, that is a difficult concept to come to terms with. And in fact Sith had not come to terms with it. Instead . . . he had wanted to even the score.

And obligingly, they had given him the opportunity. Now he would test them in the time-honoured tradition of the invigilator. Ah, but not quite in the prescribed manner! They would be faced with all the terrors the synthesizer could conjure; but Sith would record only their defeats and none of their victories, assuming there were to be any of the latter. And it would be seen (after the careful editing of all of his recordings) how just and right it was that this race be terminated to make way for the Thone.

Finally Sith considered Clayborne, and in the American he recognised his trump card. Whatever the mind of man could conjure, the synthesizer could duplicate. As well as the real, it could manufacture elements of the unreal and give them life. And Clayborne's mind was a veritable storehouse of terrors undreamed, or perhaps *only* dreamed. So far.

Clayborne believed in a netherworld—or many netherworlds, called hells—all inhabited by supernatural beings and governed by chaos. He saw the synthesizer, the House of Doors, as a gateway into these dark dimensions. Very well, let it be so.

Men considered themselves the masters of this world, eventually of the universe. And to fulfill their destiny they must only survive against themselves. So let it be: the six would be tested against themselves.

Men (and one woman) against their own worst nightmares. Especially Clayborne's!

CHAPTER TWENTY-ONE

"**I** have to get after Haggie and Angela!" Gill could contain himself no longer. Now that it seemed certain Anderson, Varre and Clayborne would live, more important things had returned to mind. And there were several great swaths of forest and plain to cross before nightfall. A week ago, even a few days ago, the idea would have been unthinkable. And yet now, when by rights Gill should be totally exhausted if not actually bedridden, he fully intended to go on alone and brave whatever terrors this alien place—the heart of this great machine—should hold for him. Moreover, he felt he actually had the strength for it, and maybe even some to spare.

"I'm coming with you," said Turnbull at once.

"What?" Anderson sat and cradled his stomach where he looked from one to the other. His ashen face showed something of his astonishment, and something more of his fear. "Neither one of you is going anywhere!" he stated flatly. "You've seen how deadly this place is—poisonous plants and insects. For all we know *everything* here is poisonous! The very air itself could be killing us! And you, Jack—you amaze me! An hour ago you were flat out, unconscious. We had to carry you down the final stretch. What makes you think you can make it?"

Turnbull shrugged. "I have a good constitution, I suppose." Then he frowned. "So it was you who carried me, eh? No wonder I'm bruised to hell! Anyway, listen: you're not the only one who's amazed. I thought I was done for, too. But my hand's almost back to normal and I feel good for another thousand miles. So don't tell me the air is killing me. It strikes me it's doing all of us a lot of good!"

He could be right, Gill thought, fingering his chin. *It could be that something really is ... improving our condition? But ... the air?* He didn't think so.

Anderson tried to stand, groaned and sat down again. "Anyway," he said, "you're not going." He looked sulky as a spoilt child. "We all agreed that I was to be leader here, and I am. I say we all stay together. Safety in numbers, and all that."

"I seem to remember you saying much the same thing to Haggie," Gill reminded him. "Safety in numbers, and all that. And where's Haggie now?"

"But that's exactly what I'm talking about," Anderson wheedled. "If we keep splitting up, in no time at all each one of us will be on his own. It's best if we stick together."

Varre spoke up. "Oh, for goodness' sake let them go! All this bickering is going to make me sick again." His face was still tinged green.

Clayborne agreed with him. "Yes, go on," he said. "Get the hell on with it. You're heading straight into hell anyway. And when we stumble across your bodies, at least it'll be a warning for us."

"Shit!" said Turnbull, chewing his lip.

Gill looked at him enquiringly.

"My gun," Turnbull explained. "Gone! I can't understand it. The holster's there but no gun. It has a safety strap with a spring release. You couldn't lose it if you tried—and yet I have." He glowered at Anderson and company. "You three got me down. Have you seen it? Maybe one of you thought I wouldn't be needing it, eh?"

"Jack, that's ridiculous," said Anderson. "You must have lost it in the pool under the cataract. You certainly didn't have it when we were pumping water out of you."

"The pool?" Turnbull didn't know about that. "What water are you talking about?"

"I'll tell you about it when we're on our way," said Gill, "if you're still coming." And to Anderson: "Minister, you'd better get used to being just plain mister. You were the one who said he was leader, but I don't recall anyone agreeing with you. I don't recall voting on it. And let's face it, you're out of your depth here. It's not for our safety you want us to stay but for yours. So listen and I'll tell you something. I don't remember much about that hunting thing carrying me down the cliff, but there's one thing I can't forget. In the half hour before dawn, when I was hanging on for dear life, I heard things howling and shrieking in that forest. Haggie mentioned them, remember? Now my advice would be forget your bellyache and follow on after us just as soon as you can. And if you do get caught short when night falls, for God's sake do it in the open where you can see what's happening, or at least find a place that will give you some protection. That's all from me." He turned toward the east and Turnbull made to follow him.

"You just called me a coward!" Anderson cried, enraged. "Well, it seems to me you've just admitted who the real coward is. You want to get to the mansion before nightfall. You've no stomach to stick with us and see it through!"

Gill turned on him. "Aren't you forgetting something?"

Anderson had finally managed to get to his feet. He saw the look on Gill's face and fell back a little. "Eh? What do you mean?"

"I mean that Haggie is alone with that girl, that's what I mean. The man's an animal, you know that. He's like a trapped rat. He's given up hope and all he can do now is keep on running. But with the girl along . . . there's no saying what he'll do next."

"But—" Anderson started.

"But nothing!" Gill spat the words out. "And one more thing—you speak to me like that again and there's no saying what *I'll* do, right?"

He turned away, set off into the forest, and Turnbull right alongside him. . . .

"Thanks," Gill said, when they were under the canopy of the trees and out of earshot.

"No need," Turnbull grunted. "Anderson's a slob, Varre's an arrogant bastard, and the ghostbuster gets on my tits!" He grinned. "That leaves you. And anyway, I'm your minder, remember?"

The forest's floor was divided by animal tracks running at random from and in all directions. The tracks were wide, well trodden, fouled here and there with droppings, some of which were fresh. The pellets were egg-size, black, oily, and sweet-smelling. Taking a rabbit pellet as standard, that would make the howlers—*if* this was the spoor of the things that howled and killed each other—pretty big. Man size at least. But now, with searchlight beams of sunlight falling through the trees and dappling everything golden and green, and the foliage canopy keeping the floor cool, there wasn't even a hint of menace. Unless it lay in the silence. Unlike at night, during the day this was a very quiet forest.

Keeping the sun at their backs, Gill and Turnbull walked and loped in turn (loped because vines and creepers hung down from above almost everywhere, so that the men were continually ducking) and were reasonably pleased at their progress. After a while they came out from the first belt of forest onto a flat stretch of grassy plain. Tall reeds told them where the ground was marshy and they stuck to the drier, shorter grass and patches of springy heather. Behind them, already two miles away, the escarpment went up like a wall in the west; in front was the plain and beyond it more forest.

They saw nervous, hopping things like leathery, flightless birds, which squawked wildly and scattered at their approach; blue snake things with powerful hind legs that fired them down burrows like bolts of living lightning; birds as near as damn like Earth birds but not quite, whose wings were more membrane than feathers. There were insects, too—mainly Earth size but including a species of green, twelve-inch centipede—and clouds of yellow-legged flies which followed after the men in swarms but without landing on them. Turnbull kept a wary eye out for squat limpet rocks but didn't see any.

With few exceptions the flora was as close to Earth type as possible, or seemed to be; since neither Gill nor Turnbull was a botanist, it made no difference anyway. One plant which wasn't earthly looked like a six-foot-tall stand of rhubarb which furled up all of its huge veined leaves at the stomping of their feet. The yellow-leg flies seemed to find this one irresistible, clinging to its stalks in their thousands.

Gill had earlier brought Turnbull up to date on the things he'd missed. Now, halfway across the plain, he said, "We're doing fine. I calculate we're already a quarter of the way there."

Turnbull had been silent, thoughtful for some little time. As they slowed from a jog to walking again where the heather was thick and spongy underfoot, he said, "Sure, we're doing fine." The words somehow didn't ring true. And he continued, "But ... Spencer, you know this is all wrong, don't you?"

Gill nodded, kept walking. "Yes," he answered simply, "I know." And: "Okay, you tell me what you think is wrong, and I'll tell you what I think is wrong. Between us the result might be interesting."

"You're pretty cool about all of this." Now Turnbull's voice held mild reproof.

"So are you, actually," Gill answered. "But isn't that the best way? I mean, it's happened—*is* happening—fait accompli. Would it improve matters if we raved? No, best to be cool. The only thing I'm hot about is Angela. For . . . various reasons." And hurriedly: "Now let's get back to what you think is wrong. Wrong in what way?"

"I mean 'wrong' apart from having been kidnapped and etcetera," Turnbull answered. "Like . . . basically wrong."

"Kidnapped?" said Gill. "As in for ransom, do you mean? I don't think so. Taken prisoner, yes. Why we don't know, not yet."

"Whichever." Turnbull shrugged. "But tell me this: how long have we been here?"

"A little more than twenty-four hours, at a guess."

"And are you hungry?"

"Not especially—but I've seen what the local fare can do to you! Varre seemed to think he was hungry, I remember."

Turnbull nodded. "Now get this," he said. "We've had twenty-four hours of misery—lots of hard work, unaccustomed exercise—been bitten by poisonous crustacea and stung by giant, robot scorpions—you name it. And we're not dead on our feet? We're not especially hungry? Not even tired?"

"I wouldn't say that," said Gill. "Frankly I could happily fall into a bed right now. But you're right, I'm not desperate. So?"

"Eh, so?"

"Your conclusion?"

Turnbull shrugged again and said, "This is going to sound silly."

"Try me."

"Well . . . is this real? I mean, couldn't we be dreaming or something? Now tell me the truth, have you pinched yourself yet? I don't mind admitting I have—hard!"

"And what happened?"

"A bruise."

"We're not dreaming," said Gill. He grinned, however wryly. "If I dreamed something like this, I'd see a psychiatrist."

Turnbull snorted. "Can you be serious?"

"I am serious. But go on, tell me what else is wrong."

"Well, this thing about Bannerman being a machine. Don't get me wrong, I believe you— but then what's he doing? Watching over us or something? Some kind of guardian angel? If so, how come he tried to kill us at your flat? It was him, I'm sure."

"All part of the mystery," said Gill. "For now. What else?"

"Nothing else," Turnbull grunted. "And everything! The whole situation is crazy—and that's about the only real alternative to being asleep and dreaming all of this: I could simply be crazy."

"Am I included in that? Listen, I'm sane—and so are you. If I didn't know the Castle was real, an alien mousetrap back there on Earth, and that it had snatched us, then I might be tempted to think the same way. But knowing what's happened to us, I prefer to think I'm sane but stuck in a crazy situation, undergoing a close encounter, an alien experience, an ... examination?" He paused and frowned. "You know, that might just be it?"

"Something's checking us out? But why?"

"I don't know." Gill shook his head. "But I'm aware that I'm inside a vast machine, and that Bannerman's also a machine, and likewise Haggie's pursuer. And that all of this is happening to us *inside* the Castle, the House of Doors, on the slopes of Ben Lawers. And yet that the mansion we're heading for is also the House of Doors! But that nothing is crazy, no, just different—alien. So for now"—he shrugged—"I'm satisfied."

"You're what?" Turnbull glanced sideways at Gill, perhaps doubting his sanity after all. "Satisfied?"

"That we know more than we did at square one," Gill answered. "Not a great deal, but we're learning. When we've learned a lot more, then maybe we'll be able to do something about it. But right now all we can do is keep going and keep learning. And meanwhile I have some questions for you."

"Oh?"

"You were poisoned, desperately ill. Remember? That was maybe, oh, an hour and a half ago? And maybe five hours ago I was given an alien injection to keep me out of trouble. And yet here we are eating up the miles like we were teenagers again! I don't know about you, but I should be stretched out in an oxygen tent!"

"That's what I've been telling you!" said Turnbull, exasperated.

"But you forgot something," said Gill. "Something just as weird." He started to jog again, making for a track through the next stretch of forest.

Turnbull came up alongside him. "Go on."

"Hair," said Gill. "Facial."

"Eh?"

"How often do you shave?"

"Twice a—what?" Turnbull put up a hand to rub his face and chin. "*Shit!*" he said.

"Like a baby's backside," said Gill. "The only one with excess hair around here is Haggie. How do you explain that?"

They were into the trees. "I don't," said Turnbull. "It's just another—*whoa!*"

They pulled up short. In front of them a cobweb stretched right across the path. It was eight feet high with strands like wire netting—if not in strength, though that was debatable, certainly in thickness. Up above, a series of dark blots obscured the light, making the place gloomy. Straining their eyes, they saw several clusters like great balls of cotton wool up there—and they heard something that rattled with a slow, unmechanical, warning beat. Strands from the web went up to the balls of fluff. And now the web had started to vibrate. . . .

They backed off, found another track, carried on running. But now they were quiet and there was no more talk about things being wrong, and their eyes were everywhere. Otherwise they might have missed it. Gill saw it first and went white as death. It was hanging low down on a thorn bush, trailing on the forest's floor.

Angela's white, frilly, now torn and bloodstained blouse!

CHAPTER TWENTY-TWO

"**I** don't understand," Anderson gasped, jogging alongside Varre and Clayborne. "An hour ago we were crippled, bent double, from eating those damned apple things. But it passed almost as quickly as it came. How could we get so ill, and yet recover so rapidly? It makes no sense. Also, I've lost my spectacles somewhere, but my sight hasn't suffered. Now how can that possibly be?"

"Save your breath," the Frenchman told him. "Gill's advice was good: make it to the mansion before nightfall. The sun is past its zenith, slipping down towards the escarpment. How long have we got? Three, four hours?"

"Both of you save it," said Clayborne. "Why try to understand anyway? Even our striving may be futile. This is the world of the supernatural, evil given embodiment in a landscape, the place of fear. The whole situation is satanic, can't you see that? And we're the playthings of hell's dark forces."

"I can't believe in your spooks!" Anderson snapped. "While this place may be subtropical, it certainly *isn't* a furnace—fiery or otherwise! This is no place of fire and brimstone! But if you're so convinced, then why don't you quit right now?"

"Evil takes all forms," said Clayborne. "Are you tempting me to quit? Temptation is evil. This place has already tainted you. Without even considering what you're saying, you advise me to lie down and let evil overtake me! Now who put those words in your mouth, eh? No matter—I know well enough—but I'll tell you why I won't take your devil's bait. We've all had nightmares, haven't we? Yes, and we woke up from them. If I see a man or a woman knifed to death in the street, I don't lie down and die with them, do I? No, I face up to it and say 'evil exists, but I have to live with it.' While there's that in me which is good—even a small part—I can't surrender all of myself to evil. Life is good and it's precious, mine included, and that's why I don't quit. So keep your advice to yourself and let me live till I die!"

"Well, if we fail to catch up with Gill and Turnbull," Anderson replied, "you might well end up doing your dying sooner than you think. Together they could be our salvation. Gill has a unique mind. If there's an answer to all of this, he's the one most likely to find it. As for Turnbull: he's a survivor. Before he was a minder he was . . . something else. When his nerve started to go, he was taken out of it. But he's stepped naked out of places and situations where you wouldn't go in armour plate!"

Varre glanced at Clayborne, and both of them looked hard at Anderson where he ran on their right flank. He was out of condition, but still doing surprisingly well. But as the three came out of the first belt of forest onto the plain—as if at a signal, though none was given—Varre and Clayborne put on a little speed and began to draw ahead. Anderson tried to match them, quickly gave up and stumbled to a halt.

"What are you doing?" he called after them. "I can't keep up that sort of pace!"

"Try," Clayborne shouted back. "Don't let the devil pull you under."

Puffing and panting, forcing his lungs to draw air and his legs to get moving again, Anderson came on. "You're leaving me behind!" he gasped, panic lifting his voice. "Why are you doing this?"

"We're doing nothing," Varre answered him. "It's you who is not doing enough. But you have managed to convince us, Minister. About Gill and Turnbull. So the sooner we team up with them again the better. Now tell me, should we let you slow us down?"

"Bastards!" Anderson whined through his clenched teeth. He begged his heart, his lungs, his legs for more power—and amazingly they responded. He was still being left behind, but not so badly. Really, he hadn't known he'd got this in him. It was all a matter of willpower, that was all. But they were treacherous dogs, these, to try and deprive him of his leadership. All of them, treacherous. He'd make sure they paid for it if it was the last thing he did.

"Bastards!" he said again, and glanced back once, fearfully, over his shoulder. Already the sun seemed so much closer to the rim of the frowning escarpment. . . .

Gill and Turnbull found the crab-lobster-scorpion—the machine that imitated life and hunted Haggie—stuck in a crack in the bed of a once river. Oddly enough, it gave Gill hope. The thing was fallible. So maybe its makers—or the ones who controlled it—maybe they were fallible, too.

But in that period just prior to finding it:

. . . As Gill reckoned it, they were on the last narrow strip of heath before the final forest barrier. Beyond that, maybe two more miles through the trees, they'd find the big green plain and the mansion. The way had been harder than they'd anticipated, and they'd underestimated the distance by at least three miles. The heather wasn't easy to run on and their shoes, not designed for this sort of work, were hurting their feet. Also, since the episode with the web of the rattling thing (whatever *that* had been) they'd proceeded with a lot more caution. The seven or eight miles they'd covered since leaving the foot of the escarpment had taken maybe a little less than two hours. But the sun was still an hour or two from the escarpment's rim, and even after that there would be a twilight, a brief dusk.

Both of them worried, albeit over different things. Turnbull worried about their next move: when they reached the mansion, what then? Another door? Where to this time? But Gill was worrying more about Angela than anything else.

Angela, with Haggie. About her blouse back there, torn and a little bloodied. Maybe she'd just ripped it on the thornbush, and her flesh a little, too. But if Haggie had had anything to do with it . . .

And Gill had thought: *Alec, my lad, if you've hurt that girl, you'll have more than the hunting thing to worry about. Believe me, Hacksaw Harry would be like an angel of mercy compared with—*

"Look!" Turnbull had grabbed his arm, drawn him back to the present.

Chests heaving from their exertions, they had arrived at a dry, crumbling riverbank. For some little while there'd been a dearth of grass where the soil was streaked with a white crystalline deposit, possibly salt. The river had not been wide; its bed lay roughly north and south, wobbling away into hazy distance in both directions. The dry bed was glittery white and dazzling in the sunlight, riven by deep, wide cracks in its centre. And stuck in one of these cracks, there they'd seen the hunter.

Even at a glance it was plain that the machine had a problem. And as the two men scrambled down the crumbling bank and began to cross the powdery bed, it became obvious just what that problem was. The silted mineral deposits underfoot were about as substantial as talc! Their feet sank in up to fifteen inches deep before finding more solid ground underneath where the stuff had hardened or compacted itself into a chalky consistency. White powder puffed up and drifted like fine ash as they plodded carefully towards the distressed thing. And testing the way before them as they went, it took them some little time to get there.

Finally they stood at the edge of the crevice and looked down on the trapped thing. It was wedged quite firmly, but still trying to free itself from the jaws of the crack. Many of its legs along the left underside of the carapace hung down uselessly into the hole, with nothing to give them purchase. On the thing's right side, farthest away from Gill and Turnbull, two legs had been trapped awkwardly between the carapace and the side of the crevice. They stuck up in the air and waved jerkily, brokenly, doing nothing much of any use. The eye stalks turned this way and that, with their gleaming faceted eyes ogling here and there, apparently seeking a solution.

The great stinger kept leaning first to one side, then the other, elongating itself, pressing down on the rim of the crevice like a lever and straining to raise the carapace up. To no avail. The talc stuff simply crumbled under that sort of pressure. At the thing's front its claws clashed and fought with thin air; its head was tilted downwards into the crack, and the pincers couldn't lift themselves high enough to find the rim.

"Knackered!" said Turnbull with finality.

"So would we be," said Gill, "if we fell down there. No purchase. It would be like digging your way upwards through an hourglass—you'd end up burying yourself! But . . . he makes a pretty handy bridge." He stepped tentatively onto the hunter's back.

"Are you trying to get yourself stung again?" Turnbull was alarmed.

"Just the opposite," said Gill. The eye stalks swayed and swivelled to point the faceted eyes in his direction; the stinger commenced to swing inwards and its dust-coated navel tip opened up; as the needle appeared, Gill stepped quickly to one side and grasped it at its root, wrenching it loose. A fist-sized gob of gooey grey liquid squelched from the "wound" onto his sleeve—then ran up his wrist and hand where he leaned a little against the carapace and transferred back to the hunter! In another moment the thing's solid chitin shell had absorbed the stuff.

"Did you see that?" said Gill. He crossed to the other side and Turnbull followed him. The stinger tried to bat the big man aside but he was too quick for it, and his weight served to push it even further down into the crack.

"I saw it," he answered. "That stuff ran like mercury—but uphill? What the hell—does this thing have living blood?"

Gill looked at the "hypodermic" in his hand. It was simply a large, bony thorn, six inches long, with a three-inch retractable tip made of stuff like flexible glass. Inside the base of the thorn was a rubbery bulb. Gill put a finger inside and squeezed gently. A tiny squirt of glistening fluid sprang from the tip and turned to mist in the air.

Gill looked at Turnbull. "Got any use for that shoulder holster of yours?"

The other shrugged. "I've been hanging on to it out of habit, I suppose." He took off his jacket and the holster, and gave the latter to Gill.

Taking off his own jacket, Gill said, "We now have a weapon—of sorts. Not as powerful or as permanent as your gun, but better than nothing." He pushed the thorn down into the holster until its tip bedded itself in the soft leather cup at the pointed end. Then he put the holster on, and shrugged back into his now badly torn and dishevelled jacket. "Roles reversed, see? Now I'm the minder."

"For myself," Turnbull grunted, "I'd hope we don't get that close to anything!"

Gill glanced down at the holster and thorn hanging under his right armpit. Unnoticed until now, he saw a ring of silver metal protruding from a thin scabbard stitched into the holster's leather. "Eh?" he said, drawing it out. It was a cleaning rod: five inches of steel rod three-sixteenths of an inch through, with the ring at one end and a slot or "eye" at the other, like the eye of a large needle.

"For cleaning the gun," Turnbull explained. "You thread a piece of lightly oiled cloth through the eye, stuff it up the barrel. It collects any dirt, burnt powder, carbon."

"Might make a stabber," said Gill, "if it can be sharpened. Mind if I keep it?"

"Be my guest."

They began to make for the other side of the dry riverbed, but after only two paces Gill stopped. He looked back at the trapped hunter, which waved its eye stalks at him. And he stood there uncertainly, frowning.

"Something?" Turnbull enquired.

"That bloke is hunting Haggie," said Gill, nodding at the trapped monster. "Or he was until the side of that crack caved in when he was making his crossing. And I've a feeling that

wherever Haggie goes, this fellow will know where to find him."

"So?"

"And Haggie knows things about this place that we haven't discovered yet. There are entire worlds in here, where Haggie can lose himself from us, but not from this bloke."

Turnbull sighed. "You want to set it free?"

"I think we better had," said Gill, "if it's at all possible."

"Won't that be murder?"

"He's escaped justice so far—in more ways and more worlds than one!" Gill answered. "And maybe he'll keep right on doing it. But meanwhile this thing can be our tracker dog."

"But it must weigh a ton!"

"Several, I should think." Gill looked around. Close to hand, a cluster of sharp boulder fragments lay half-buried in the talc. "Do you want to help?"

Turnbull sighed again. "As long as you know what you're doing, of course I'll help. But I ask myself, what happens when this thing gets through with Haggie? Will it be our turn? And anyway, are we okay for time?" The sun was falling ever closer to the rim of the distant escarpment, whose face was now black and frowning.

Gill nodded. "I think it's in our best interests to make a little time. It may save us a lot later. Now listen, if we can lob these boulders down right under his nose, sort of pile them up, he might be able to push down on them with his claws. They're pretty powerful, those claws. . . ."

CHAPTER TWENTY-THREE

In fact it didn't take that long. First they took a rock each, straining and grunting them to the edge of the crack and letting them fall where Gill had prescribed. The next boulder fragment in line was too big for one man on his own, however, so between them they wrestled it to the rim, where they paused for breath before standing it up on its heavier end and toppling it down. And watching it fall, they shouted their appreciation when sheer good fortune caused it to jam halfway down, where the walls bottlenecked a little.

As the hunter put down its pincer claws and tested them on the wedged boulder, so Gill and Turnbull backed off. They saw the carapace straining upwards as clouds of talc erupted from points all around its perimeter. Strangely jointed legs scraped and clattered, and the stinger pushed itself down into the talc on the far side of the crack like the snout of a mechanized jack.

As more talc billowed and became a churning cloud, the men backed off farther yet. But in a little while the dust began to settle, and the hunter dragged itself out from the flurries. Its movements were very slow now, and to starboard it trailed a pair of crippled legs.

A little distance from the riven bed of the river, the thing came to a standstill and shook itself. White dust drifted from its flanks like powdered snow, leaving its surface all blue- and black-gleaming chitin, white bone and yellow ivory. In a strange way (and if it wasn't so monstrous) the thing might even seem beautiful.

"A ... a machine?" Turnbull obviously couldn't quite believe it. "It shook itself like ... like a dog!"

"I don't blame you for doubting it," Gill told him, "but take my word for it anyway."

The hunter lowered its carapace to earth on its good left side, lifted up its right on half a dozen stiffened legs. The two useless ones dangled twitching from damaged sockets. Turnbull looked from the monster to Gill, who seemed to be waiting for something. "Well? Time's wasting."

Gill held up a hand. "I'd like to watch this," he said. "It could be important."

It was. Gobs of the grey liquid came spurting and sputtering from the sockets and displaced joints of the damaged limbs, and at the same time Gill jerked stiffly upright as he sensed something happening. Turnbull looked at him and asked, "What is it?"

Again Gill held up a hand. Then he reached slowly into his jacket pocket and brought out the cylinder weapon. He looked at it, weighed it, rubbed it in his hands like it was a lucky stone. He turned his gaze on the hunter, then back to the cylinder in his hand. And a strange light came into his eyes.

"Spencer?" Turnbull was anxious.

Gill nodded towards the hunter. "That thing's drawing power from somewhere. It's fuelling itself. And some of the energy is leaking off—being leeched, maybe—by this!" He held the cylinder up, held it out towards the hunter.

Turnbull licked his lips, shook his head. "I don't understand. But, you know, I think I can feel something, too!"

"They're charging themselves," Gill said, "like rechargeable batteries."

Through all of this the hunting thing had stood there in its lop-sided pose, frozen like stone, with its crippled legs dangling. For a few seconds more Gill held out the cylinder towards it, then slowly drew back his arm. "That's it," he said. "All charged up."

Turnbull made no answer, continued to observe the hunter.

For long moments the thing remained static in its jacked-up mode. Then, suddenly, more gobs of the thick grey liquid were ejaculated from its torn sockets. They flowed outwards over the crippled legs, sheathing them in goo. But in a little while, like nets drawn in, the sheaths of living liquid retracted, drawing the damaged hard parts back up under the carapace and into the body and sealing them in position again in their sockets. Then the goo itself was withdrawn and some of it, where it covered the raw joints, hardened rapidly into a flexible leathery plastic. The entire process had taken perhaps twenty seconds.

Turnbull gulped. "Now if only my car could do that!" he said.

But Gill only said, "Time to go."

They turned and hurried as best they could for the far bank. Looking back as they climbed to the withered, mineral-streaked plain, they saw the hunter lower its carapace into a mobility stance and commence trundling after them. Or if not "after them", at least in their general direction. All of its legs appeared to be working, those on the right perhaps a little stiffly, lacking something in coordination. Even so, it was still something to see.

"Just how fast can that thing move?" Turnbull asked nervously. "I've got this awful feeling I've just helped reactivate Frankenstein's monster!"

"Pretty fast," said Gill, "but not as fast as us. Not over short distances, anyway. We sprint pretty well, but it has stamina. Anyway, you don't need to worry about it—it isn't interested in us."

He turned his face to the powdery plain where its grasses grew more lush towards the final belt of forest. If nothing else delayed them, another hour should see them approaching the mansion, the House of Doors. It was an "if" Gill couldn't be certain about. Only time would tell, and right now there was little enough of that to waste. An image of Angela's bloodied blouse kept filling the mirror of his mind. "Let's go," he said. . . .

* * *

The House of Doors was like some strange, square, squat mastaba, a modern step-pyramid constructed of precise, white stone blocks. Three-tiered, its base was perhaps sixty by sixty feet, twelve high, balustraded at the top with stark square pillars supporting a square rail. It had doors, too, plenty of them: huge numbered slabs of flush-fitting marble, with no hinges or other mechanisms apparent except for the square stone door knockers. And there were no windows.

The second tier was stepped back maybe seven or eight feet on all sides, making it forty-five by forty-five; likewise the third and topmost tier, a featureless plateau of white stone some thirty-seven feet square. In its entirety the structure might well have been designed by some geometrical purist. It was like a giant wedding cake, even to the detail of a bride—but there the similarity ended. For she didn't stand atop the cake but protected its bottom tier against the advances of Smart Alec Haggie, the would-be bridegroom.

There she stood in the slowly fading light—scratched and dishevelled, wild-eyed and primitive in ski pants reduced almost to tight-fitting Bermuda shorts, a flimsy bra, and (mercifully) sensible shoes—silently challenging him to try, just *try*, to climb up to her. And while Haggie taunted in his fashion from below, so Angela thought back on some of the details of their nightmare flight from the thing on the ledge under the waterfall. . . .

She remembered very little of their scramble down from that place; only that before finding a wide, overgrown, descending fault in the cliff, there had been too many times when she'd believed she must surely fall. Indeed, it was a miracle she hadn't fallen—but not, as she'd later discovered, a blessing.

Then they'd been at the bottom, and Haggie half-crazy with terror where he rushed here and there in the gloom; one minute peering at the unknown forest ahead, and the next looking back and up at the escarpment, fearing at any moment to see their pursuer descending towards him. But eventually dawn had started to come, staining the eastern horizon a pale silver with its flush, and the howling of the things in the forest had tailed off, so that at last Haggie was satisfied they could proceed.

She'd held back then, asking about Gill and the others. Shouldn't they hide and wait for them? But he'd told her they would be lucky if they still lived; by now the crab-lobster-scorpion might well have taken them; that no one could hide from it because it would always sniff them out. If Gill and the others had somehow survived, they'd surely meet up with them again at the House of Doors. Indeed, he'd promised they would wait for them there.

And fearing to be left on her own, with the hunting thing coming down from the escarpment to sniff her out, Angela had let him lead her on into the forest.

They had gone painfully slowly at first, hardly daring to breathe, every nerve jumping and senses straining to their limits. She had held his hand and he hers—an entirely mutual, almost involuntary thing—and she'd felt his trembling. That, too, had been mutual, but she'd fancied he was the more afraid. Perhaps knowing something of this place, having been here before, he knew enough to *make* him more afraid. She'd thought of asking him, but in the event held her tongue. Maybe it was better that she didn't know.

Full dawn had come as they left the first belt of misted forest and crossed a strip of heath; and as the light waxed, so Haggie's fears had seemed to wane. He had lived through yet another night with his miserable body and soul still intact, and could now appreciate the advantages of his new situation. So that soon he began to talk to her, to make plans for them. But for *them*—the two of them—with never a word or thought for the others. At that Angela had known that Haggie didn't intend to reunite with Gill and the rest, but she'd made no comment for fear of angering him. That had been a mistake, for he'd seen her silence as encouragement. When his talk had turned more intimate, however, and his piggy eyes commenced to devour her in the full dawn light, finally she'd spurned him.

It was something he'd said—something about "women, like men, all seeming much the same from the waist down"—that stung her into rebuke; that and his statement that she would soon get used to him, once she saw what he had for her. He'd been "saving it all up, because in a dump like this there was nowhere to spend it." It was the sort of thing her husband had used to say to her when he was drunk, and caused her to remember the things he'd used to do to her.

Then, breathlessly, she'd asked Haggie if he

thought she was a bitch in heat, that he could talk to her like that—which of course had been the wrong thing to say to someone like him in a place like this. "In heat?" he'd answered. "Well, you look pretty hot stuff to me. . . ." And straight out with it: "But if that's how you like it—doggie-fashion—that's okay by me."

What she might have said to him then— whether or not she'd have gone for him tooth and nail in her extremity of fear and loathing— would never be known, for that was when they'd reentered the forest and she'd stumbled into the web.

At any other time she couldn't have failed to see that patterned mesh of glistening fibers strung between the trees, but her blood was up and she'd been blinded by anger. In a moment she'd found herself held fast, spread-eagled on the web; and then she'd heard that vibrant, rhythmic, *sentient* rattling—and seen the devil's own worst nightmare falling on her out of the treetops! It had been about as big as Angela herself; not exactly a spider or a wood louse, but something in between and much worse than both.

Her horror had given her strength; somehow she'd torn herself free; and give Haggie his due, he had tried to fend the spider thing off with a branch torn from a thorn tree. But the monster had stabbed at her even as she got loose from its web, and one of its chitin-covered forelimbs had pierced her blouse and torn her shoulder. The blouse, hooked up on the limb's hairy barbs, had been ripped from her cringing body and yanked aloft even as she staggered to safety.

When they reached a brighter patch of forest, Haggie wanted to look at her wound but she said no. Tearing her ski pants from the knees down, she'd somehow fashioned a bandage and even a scrap of a halter to cover her breasts; but Haggie had only laughed, insisting that modesty in this place was for fools. Why should she want to hide what was going to be his anyway? But ... it was up to her. She could do it the hard way or the easy way, take her pick. The easy way would be to do as she was told— *everything* she was told—and he'd take it easy on her. And the other way? Sooner or later, if she chose that route, she'd come crawling to him. And then there'd be no terms but his.

The gash in her shoulder had been an agony, but still she had her pride. Defiantly she had told him that she'd wait right here, for Gill and the others. She believed they still lived—they *had* to! She was bluffing, of course, for she didn't dare wait there in the forest. She had to make it to the mansion—and Haggie knew it. It had prompted him to play a cruel game with her.

"Suit yourself," he'd said, and sneered at her then. "Wait for them if you want to. See if they're alive and if they can help you. Gill was a dying man anyway, couldn't you see that? But if they don't come, or if you miss them, then you're finished. It's up to you: stay here and I'm done with you, I go on alone. Or come on with me to the mansion. If you do come with me, then you're mine. It's the three *F*'s, Angie doll. If I feed you and fend for you, then it seems only right that I take care of the third *F*, too—

when and how and as often as I like!" And with one last contemptuous grin he'd left her.

With tears of frustration streaming from her eyes, crying out her bitter detestation of him, she had stood her ground—for a little while. But life was dear, and now that she was alone the forest seemed even more sullen, silent, alien. And indeed she knew that it was all of those things. She'd caught up with him at last as he entered the final belt of forest, which must have been something over two hours ago. . . .

They'd reached the mansion just as the sun was preparing to touch the purple rim of the distant escarpment, which was also when Haggie chose to commence her subjugation. "It can't wait," he'd hoarsely grunted, coming up behind her where she sat on a stone at the foot of the mansion's wall. And as she heard the naked lust in his voice, her eyes had widened and she'd turned her head to look up at him.

"What?" she had said, unable to credit that he'd try something in a place and at a time like this. She had loosened the knot of her makeshift halter, was examining the burning gash in her shoulder. Strangely, it seemed to be healing very quickly; while still purple and a little puffy, it was no longer so stiff as to incapacitate her.

"You flash your tits about like that and ask me what? This is what!" As he tore the halter from her back and she jumped to her feet, he showed her what he'd been saving for her, throbbing where he worked it with one hand. "Now's the time, Angie doll," he told her. "My way!"

But after that business with the spider thing, Angela had armed herself with the whiplike branch of a thorn tree. She'd kept it close to hand and now snatched it up. Maybe Haggie had thought she was spineless, that she wouldn't dare. But she did. She whipped him back away from her, out of range, where he danced and hooted his delight at this unexpected sport. "Hoo! Hoo! But it's going to feel really nice when I slip it in, Angie doll! This is my little slippy-stick, see? Biggest muscle in my whole bloody body!"

And then she'd run from him around the square base of the mansion. Behind her, he'd laughed all the harder and let her go; but in a little while, curious, he'd come looking for her. "You'll be back," she had heard him calling, "when it gets dark and they start howling and fighting. But don't leave it too long or I might not be here."

At the back of the mansion Angela had found a slender tree with many branches, standing alone in a position close to the wall. The upper half of its trunk leaned inwards, dangling lesser branches and leaves over the high balcony. As a girl she'd been something of a tomboy and could handle trees well enough. She'd launched her thorn-tree weapon like a spear onto the first tier, then scrambled up the tree to comparative safety—from Haggie, at least.

Haggie had found the tree eventually and even tried to climb up after her. But she'd lashed him around the head and shoulders and had the satisfaction of seeing his blood; and then, snarling, he'd retreated back down to ground level. From which time until now he'd wasted no slightest opportunity to taunt and terrorize her. . . .

CHAPTER TWENTY-FOUR

Coming in from the heath in the gathering dusk, Gill and Turnbull heard most of it. If Angela had chosen to look in their direction, where they deliberately kept a low profile, still she just might have seen them; her first-storey vantage point was a good one, giving her a more or less clear view over the scrub all around. But she was more interested in Haggie; or rather, in holding him at bay.

"Well, Angie darling, what's it to be?" he called up to her from the foot of the mansion. "Are you going to wait up there for the bats? Or would you prefer me?"

"Bats?" Her answer was a gasp. It was the first time she'd spoken to him at all since climbing up here, and even now the word sprang from her before she could stop it. Haggie guessed he'd hit on a sore point.

He shrugged. "They fly like bats, anyway. Something like 'em. All leathery wings and big ears. But after that they're more like snakes. Long, whiplash bodies. Oh, yes," he added, as if on afterthought, "and they're big. Big as large house cats. Couldn't say what they eat. I was only here once and I didn't wait to find out. Nor will I this time. You'd better come on down."

She looked nervously all about in the darkening sky. The sun's exit had left a shrinking glow in the west over the dark, elongated mass of the far escarpment. But to the south . . . sure enough she could make out a cloud of gnatlike aerial shapes darting this way and that. They were a long way off but seemed to be coming closer. "Oh!" It was the second time a word had made its involuntary escape.

"Oh?" he repeated her mockingly from below, his voice echoing out into the expanding silence of dusk. "So you see them, do you? That doesn't give you much time then, sweetie. Now come on down before they get here. I mean, I'm telling you the truth. I don't know what the hell they are, but you can bet your backside they're not nice. That is, unless you can think of a better use for that sweet little backside of yours. I certainly can!"

She looked down at him uncertainly, and again at the darting dots in the sky. From somewhere in the forest a far, faint howling reached her—was taken up and answered from another direction—and again from a third.

"The howlers," said Haggie unnecessarily. "But that's not all they do! That's why I'm waiting. When they eat, I eat." He chuckled obscenely. "And you, too, if you want to. You have to eat sometime, if you want to stay on your toes. And good red meat is scarce around here, until the howlers scare some up." Again his obscene chuckle. "You'll see what I mean soon enough—that is, if you're still around."

Angela thought fast. She could try one last time to reason with him. Whether it worked or not, he'd win in the end anyway, because she knew he was right and she couldn't stay up here indefinitely, a sitting duck in the growing darkness. "If I thought you could behave more like a man," she started, "instead of a dog, then maybe I . . . I . . ."

Now his voice turned sour. "Listen, Angie: I've shot my load twice in my pants just thinking about having you. So you're okay from that point of view—for a little while. But I'm telling you, you can't stay up there. Shortly the howlers will be hunting, and what they hunt will run this way. The howlers don't much care for this place, but they won't hold back forever. Now I know which of these doors is which. Some of 'em anyway. I'll just grab up a little food—on the hoof, you know?—and get the hell right out of here. If you're down here with me, all well and good. We eat, you carry right on living, and tomorrow can take care of itself. But if you're still up there, you face the howlers, the bats, whatever."

She shook her head desperately, looked this way and that. He knew he very nearly had her.

"Also," he quickly continued, "I know the place where I'm going. It's not good there but it's not the worst. Except I'll make sure you don't see which door I use. So if you do make it down after I've gone, you won't know *where*

I've gone. You won't be able to follow. Of course, you can always choose just any old door. But you're not stupid—you could have done that already. And you'd better believe me when I tell you that most of these doors lead straight to hell!"

Gill couldn't take any more of this. "It's okay now, Angela," he said, stepping out of the shadow of the wall. "You can come down." Then he turned towards Haggie.

At the sound of his voice the little redhead had drawn breath in a gasp, stooped and picked up a rock. He swung it at Gill's head. Ready for him, Gill ducked, straightened up and slammed a fist into his mouth. Swatted from his feet, Haggie went down—and bounced back to his feet just as quickly. He edged around Gill, ran past him along the front of the mansion.

Turnbull was waiting for him. The big man grew up like a huge dark blot out of the wall, grabbed Haggie by the neck with one massive hand. "Little man," he growled, "I'd say you're in trouble!" He bent Haggie's arm up behind his back until he howled, frog-marched him back to Gill.

Taking careful aim, Gill hit Haggie again, hard and deliberate, flattening his nose. But this time when Haggie hit the ground he didn't come up. He simply lay there and moaned. Gill sat down on him and asked Turnbull, "Can you get her down?"

Meanwhile Angela had burst into tears of relief. "Oh, Spencer, Jack! I—"

"It's okay," Turnbull growled. "Don't say anything. We can imagine. Listen, can you climb over the balcony and lower yourself down? If you can, I'll be able to reach up and grab your legs."

"Round the back," she gasped, trying hard to regain control of herself. "There's a tree."

"Angela," said Turnbull quietly, "forget the tree. Just do as I say, right?" He had seen dark shapes descending out of the amethyst sky, a cloud of them that squirted like a school of winged squid, crisscrossing the first stars. She knew from his tone of voice something was wrong, glanced up and saw them. Haggie's "bats." In another moment she was over the parapet, on her knees, lowering herself to her fingertips. Turnbull got her, said, "Let go." She fell into his arms, hugged close to him a moment, then turned to Gill.

Haggie raised his head and spat out dirt. Gill dispassionately hit him again, behind the ear, and stood up. Turnbull stepped close to the sprawled Haggie and put a foot in the middle of his back. "Just stay put, not-so-Smart Alec," he said, "or I'll smash your spine." And knowing he would, Haggie lay very still.

Meanwhile, Angela had flown into Gill's arms. "Oh, Spencer, Spencer!"

"Did he . . . ?" He let the question hang unspoken.

"No," she sobbed, shaking her head in the hollow of Gill's shoulder. "He wanted to, would have, but—"

"He tried?"

"He . . . I found a way up there. I was safe there."

"It's okay, then." Gill felt his heart slowing down, the adrenaline settling in his system. "I won't have to kill him. But if he had, then I would have." If Haggie heard all of this, he was saying nothing.

Gill could have held on to the girl forever, but he knew they didn't have even the smallest fraction of that. "Jack," he said, "get that little bastard up onto his feet."

Turnbull hauled Haggie upright but held on to him. "No running away," he warned him. "If you make me chase you, I'll fix it so you *can't* run, right?" Haggie hung his head, remained sullenly silent. Turnbull shook him until his head nearly came loose. "Right?" he said again, louder, after he'd stopped shaking.

Haggie nodded. "But listen—" he babbled.

"You listen," Gill cut him short. "First off, there are things we need to know. And no more bullshit about information being valuable. It *is*, if you value your own skin. See, we've had it with you. You try to make a profit—all sorts of profit—out of threats and blackmail. You'd bargain with people for their lives and their bodies, even their souls, if you could. Okay, so we've learned from you and learned fast. So try this on for a threat: if we're going to die in this place, be sure you're going first. Got it?"

Turnbull tightened his grip on Haggie.

Haggie gulped. "Got it," he said. Blood dripped from his nose and the corner of his mouth.

"And don't bleed on me," said Turnbull. "I'm particular."

There were scraping sounds from above, claws scrabbling at smooth stone, where things were landing on the square of the topmost tier. Bat wings furled down, and a line of leathery, big-eared gargoyles looked down on the group of human beings. They were perched on the edge of the top tier, cat eyes glowing gold in black silhouette faces. Angela hissed her terror, shrank back into Gill's arms.

Gill held her tightly and said to Haggie, "These bat things—you didn't say if they were dangerous. Are they?"

"I don't know," Haggie answered. "I was on my own last time. They didn't bother me, just sat watching me."

Turnbull gave him a quick shake. "You mean you were only using them to frighten the girl into coming down?"

"Yes," Haggie said. "I mean, no! Christ, I don't know! They could be dangerous, couldn't they? Almost everything else is. Anyway, I wasn't going to hurt the girl. I only . . . wanted company?"

"You ugly little . . ." Gill released Angela and moved to hit him yet again, but Turnbull intervened.

"Don't you think he should be conscious?" he said, with no reproof but simple common sense in his voice. He didn't have Gill's involvement. "Let me talk to him." And to Haggie: "Alec, son, what about the howlers? Are they dangerous?"

Haggie looked up at him. "Son?"

Turnbull grinned. "I never married," he said. "Any sons of mine are bastards!" The grin slipped from his face. "The howlers?"

"Dangerous?" Haggie gabbled. "Damned right they are! They hunt and kill, and as night comes down they get braver. You can bet they know we're here, but they'll wait until it's really dark before they move in."

"Really dark?" said Gill. "With stars like

these?" He glanced at the sky, which was beginning to blaze. "It doesn't *get* really dark! We've seen that."

"It gets dark enough." Haggie shivered. "The howlers are ... black things. A dull, rubbery black. They don't reflect the starlight. You'll see what I mean."

"When will we see?" Gill pressed him.

"Soon. They hunt in packs, and what they hunt might head this way. Last time I was here, I caught one of them. Then, like now, I was starving. And in this whole damned place—in this entire fucking maze of horrible places—there's only a handful of things you can eat that will stay eaten! But you can eat what the howlers hunt, and it's good. Right now my belly button's making love to my spine. I *need* to eat, and soon! If I didn't ... believe me, I'd already be out of here."

Gill stared hard at him. "You'd face down howlers, bats—even take your chances with that thing that's hunting you—all for a bite to eat?"

"Face them down?" Haggie shook his head. "Take chances with that damned thing that's tracking me?" He looked nervously all about, and his bloodied face was frowning. "What the hell's wrong with you people, anyway? Don't *you* ever eat? I told you, the only reason I'm still here is the chance of a free meal. But if anything nasty comes too close, I'll just duck right out of it!"

"Through which door?" Gill was quick off the mark, giving no warning of what was on his mind. And he watched Haggie's eyes.

The little man didn't even blink. "You're standing right in front of it," he said.

Gill glanced over his shoulder at the nearest of the marble-slab doors. "This one, number seven?"

Haggie shrugged. "Why else would I be this close to it?"

"Just be sure you don't try to get any closer," Turnbull warned. "Not just yet, anyway."

Throughout this conversation the howling in the forest and on the plain had been drawing closer, louder and more insistent. Suddenly, from somewhere out in the scrub, there sounded a thundering of small hooves and a shrill, terrified shrieking, all accompanied by renewed peals of howling and a savage grunting. For a little while, just out beyond the sphere of vision, the night seemed alive with activity; but after a few moments the sounds of the stampede—the hunt?—faded into distance.

Haggie seemed disappointed and struggled in Turnbull's grasp. "Let *go* of me!" he demanded. "That's our supper out there—meat on the hoof—and if any more of it heads this way, I want to get my hands on some!"

CHAPTER TWENTY-FIVE

"What about Anderson and the others?" Despite the circumstances, Angela was almost herself again. Something of hope had returned, and with it anxiety for the safety of the majority. "Didn't they come with you?"

"They were . . . incapacitated," Gill answered. "That's putting it mildly. They tried eating some of the fruit back there, which apparently didn't want to be eaten! They were okay when we left, but not up to moving just then. If they're coming, it should be anytime now. I would think the fall of night—seeing it coming—would spur them on."

Haggie was logical for once. "If they set out an hour after you," he said, "then they should take an hour longer. Maybe more. That Anderson's a bit on the heavy side. . . ."

"We were delayed a bit on the way," said

Turnbull. Then he saw the warning on Gill's face and said no more. Pointless and even foolhardy to scare Haggie right now by mentioning the hunter. They didn't want him bolting again.

"But will they be able to see this place in the dark?" Angela was concerned for them.

Gill glanced at the mansion. "I should think so. It's like a great blob of snow with the starlight on it." Then his voice changed. "*Oh-oh!*"

The others looked up. The bat things had come down a tier, were perched shoulder to shoulder, a row of them, all along the rim of the second storey. Their feral eyes were unblinking, fixed firmly on Gill and the rest.

"We could do with lighting a fire," said Turnbull. He immediately felt Haggie stiffen a little in his grasp. "Oh, and you have the makings, do you?"

Haggie wriggled again and Turnbull caught up his hands. Gill searched the little man's soiled suit pockets. In the inside jacket he found a book of matches—and recognised it. "Clayborne's," he said.

"I . . . I picked them up from where he left them." Haggie searched for a way to excuse himself. "They were beside the fire in the cave. They'd dried out. I . . . I didn't want the fire to set them off and waste them. Precious things, matches."

"You thieving shit!" Turnbull growled. He released Haggie, shoved him away from him. "God, you're probably contagious! But I'm telling you: run for it if you like, but if you do—and if and when I see you again—you're a goner."

"I'm not going anywhere," Haggie answered. "Not yet."

Gill and Angela got a few dry branches and bits of heather together. He tore a strip of lining from his jacket, set fire to it. In a little while the heather caught, then the twigs and branches. Flames leaped. Turnbull found some heavier branches. In little more than five minutes they had a blaze going. Now the only problem would be to keep it fuelled. Meanwhile, however, the bats had retreated to the topmost tier again.

Through all of this Haggie could only protest, "Jesus, you'll frighten them off!"

"We *want* to frighten them off," Gill told him.

"Not the bats and howlers," Haggie snorted. "The things the howlers hunt!"

Turnbull rounded on him. "We lit this fire as a beacon. Now what's more important to you? Your stinking guts or the lives of Anderson and the others?"

Gill looked at Haggie and thought: *That's easy: his guts! Haggie has to be one of the lowest forms of—*

Abruptly, his thoughts were interrupted. From far out in the night, a frenzied renewal or addition to the howling—in screams which could only be human!

"Jack!" Gill grabbed the big man's arm. "Help me up onto the roof there." Turnbull made a cup of his hands; Gill stepped into it, was thrust aloft, grabbed the rim of the parapet and drew himself up and over the low wall. Inside his head, he told himself: *I don't believe I'm doing this! Maybe Turnbull's dream theory isn't so wild after all. Where am I getting all of this strength? Or is this the final flare-up before the candle expires?* "Toss up a brand."

Turnbull yanked a fat, burning branch from the fire, carefully lobbed it up to Gill. He reached out, snatched it from the air. "This way!" he shouted then into the night. "We're over here!" And he waved the blazing branch over his head, this way and that as a signal. As his voice rang out and came echoing back, silence fell like a cloak on the starlit plain and the silvered forest beyond. Gill heard a shuffling and scraping, a flapping of wings from behind and above. He whirled, thrust out his sputtering torch . . .

. . . But no problem. The bat things were cowering back from the rim of the top tier, using their wings to shield their eyes from the burning yellow light. He thrust the torch at them, shouted, *"Hah!"* And they drew back more yet.

But . . . the howlers were still now, utterly silent. And in the threatening night, where the crackling of the fire was the only sound, Turnbull quietly said, "Well, if they didn't know we were here before, they certainly know it now!"

"Listen to that," said Haggie softly. "Silence, yes—but you can almost hear the bastards thinking. . . ."

Gill propped up the branch against the wall to light the way for the three men—if they still lived—and shouted again into the silence, "This way! Follow the fire!" Then he stepped over the wall, lowered himself to arm's length and jumped down. And straightening up, he heard again out in the wild the first faint howlings starting up, and the answering calls from other howlers as they recovered from their astonishment.

Now, too, from out of the night, they heard a human voice, Varre's voice, shouting, "Gill, Turnbull—we see you! We're coming!" They could hear Clayborne, too, but he was incoherent, yelling and gibbering like a madman. But if Varre and Clayborne were coming, so too was something else; for no sooner had Varre stopped calling to them than the drumming of the earth started up again, the mad thundering of hooves.

"This time!" said Haggie excitedly. "Maybe this time!"

Gill had been developing an unconscious nervous habit: at times of stress he would reach into his jacket pocket and clasp the cylinder there. He did so now as the sound of the stampede grew louder and frightened shapes were seen bounding in darkness. He clasped the cylinder and squeezed it, and turned it in his dry, nervous fingers. And . . . *what?*

There was no dent; the "bruise" of Turnbull's bullet had disappeared, smoothed itself out of existence! Gill's jaw fell open. He remembered the self-sufficient hunting thing. Machines that refuelled and repaired themselves. And wonderingly, he drew the cylinder out of his pocket. He looked at it in the firelight, a liquid silver cylinder—and knew!

Liquid, yes—but liquid which could imitate a solid! It would work now, could be used as a tool or a weapon. And Gill knew how to use it. . . .

He was snatched back to the present in a blast of wild, panicked screaming as Haggie's "food" came on the scene. A small herd of four-footed deer creatures burst into the firelight, split up, and went bounding like springboks to left and right. But one of them wasn't so fortunate or so surefooted; screaming, it leaped high over the fire, smacked headlong into the mansion's wall between two of the doors. And it crumpled to earth there.

Angela, Turnbull and Gill had crouched down low, with their arms held up over their heads for protection; Haggie, on the other hand, had known more or less what to expect. He was on the stunned creature in a flash. Maybe it wasn't just stunned but already dead, Gill couldn't say, but Haggie was taking no chances. He held the animal between his legs, twisted its head and neck until something snapped and there was no more resistance.

He was jubilant. "God!" he gasped. "God—I can eat!"

But these things were only the hunted. And now came the hunters!

Perhaps because Haggie knew a little of what to expect, he was the first to see them. All of the jubilation went out of him in a moment. "Oh, Jesus *Christ*!" he moaned. And clutching his prize like a pet dog to his chest, he backed up against the mansion, the House of Doors.

As the sounds of the stampede died away, the others peered fearfully into the gloom where Haggie had fixed his gaze. Gill saw ... *something*—several of them—and thought: *God!* Except where Haggie had blasphemed, with Gill it was a prayer. But where the little redhead was concerned, Gill had learned to be sharp. Now was exactly the time when the little man might try to make a break for it. "Jack," Gill said, low-voiced, never for a moment taking his eyes off the black things that squatted and shuffled and crept closer out there beyond the fire's glow, "watch Haggie!" And to Angela: "Get behind me, quick!"

She crept behind him, trembling like a leaf; and Gill faced front, held the cylinder weapon out before him. It was a close-combat weapon, yes, but deadlier by far than teeth and claws. The howlers shuffled closer still, and out in the night their brothers and cousins kept a deadly silence, with no more howling to cause a distraction. Word had gone out that there would be strange, rich fare tonight.

The fire sputtered and threw up sparks, then sank low. And the howlers advanced again, beginning to grunt quietly among themselves, slowly closing their circle towards the little knot of humans. There were . . . a good many of them.

Gill stared hard at the one closest to the fire, who also seemed to be the biggest of the bunch. Haggie was right: the thing's hide looked black, rubbery. It walked upright on two legs, but crouching low, shambling. Three and a half feet tall, anthropoid but scarcely manlike, the howler was as broad as he was tall and shaggy as a sheep. An alien Neanderthal covered in masses of ropy, matted hair or fur.

It was hard to discern faces, just slanting, red-glowing eyes in black rubber masks—until the one Gill was watching opened its jaws. And then he saw that the great shaggy head of the thing was *mainly* jaws!

Somewhere to Gill's right Haggie sobbed, and

Turnbull's voice was tight, urgent when he whispered, "Spencer, I—"

Gill stooped, picked up a brand, tossed it towards the tightening circle.

And in that same moment, from *beyond* the circle: "Gill! Turnbull!" It was Varre. He came at a stumbling run, heading straight for the fire and seeing little else but the flickering flames and the knot of familiar human forms and faces. Behind him, raving, staggered Clayborne.

"Hell!" the American babbled and shrieked in the night. "The infernal regions. The very *confines* of hell! For I have seen Satan shambling in the dark and hovering on bat wings, and I have seen his eyes yellow and red and lusting for my soul. Yea, though I walk in the shadow of the valley of death, I shall fear no evil, for . . . for . . . *for God's sake!*" He seemed entirely unhinged.

To the howlers it must seem they were under attack from the rear. Gill's firebrand had landed amongst them, scattering both sparks and the creatures themselves, and now these shouting, lurching figures were coming straight at them out of the darkness! Hooting their alarm, the howlers broke and ran—or rather bounded—in all directions; how far couldn't be determined.

Varre and Clayborne came on, collapsing to their knees in the firelight. Gill and Angela searched in the immediate vicinity for more branches to fuel the fire, and Turnbull continued to guard Haggie.

"*Mon Dieu!*" Varre gasped, wild-eyed in the fire's glow. "I thought we were finished. The things we have seen! Great spiders in the forests, and that monstrosity which pursues Haggie, stuck in a bog and sinking. We skirted it and came on. On the heath things thundered by us, and great bats flew overhead. There were eyes everywhere. And the howling, that dreadful howling . . . I think Clayborne is mad."

Clayborne jumped to his feet. "Mad? I'm as sane as any man. Saner than most. Speak for yourself, Frenchie. What? It was my prayers carried us through! Now you people have *seen* these devils with your own eyes. Surely it's obvious to you by now that this is no place of science but the supernatural!"

"You're raving." Turnbull was blunt, as always.

Clayborne growled low in his throat, charged at the big man. Turnbull had not witnessed Clayborne's attack on Bannerman at the pool under the waterfall, but he knew trouble when he saw it. Clayborne was blocky, powerful. And half-crazy, he'd be strong as hell. Releasing Haggie, Turnbull ducked under Clayborne's wildly swinging fists, folded him with a blow to the stomach, then straightened him with another to the chin. Clayborne was sent sprawling with all the wind knocked out of him.

But Haggie, freed, had immediately begun sidling towards door number seven. Gill saw him; if it wasn't for the carcass Haggie carried, he'd have been through the door before anyone could stop him. What advantage this would give him was hard to say: the rest of them would surely follow him through at once. This was the thought that puzzled Gill as he put himself between Haggie and the door, blocking his escape.

And at that point Anderson arrived. . . .

CHAPTER TWENTY-SIX

Anderson came stumbling, trembling, utterly exhausted, out of the dark and into the firelight. Gone for now any semblance of his old guise of authority; the power in which he'd cloaked himself for most of his life had been stripped away; he was only a man fending for himself, and by no means best equipped or in the best possible condition. But seeing Varre crouched there beside the fire, and Clayborne where he sat dazed from Turnbull's blows, he rallied himself and tried to throw out his chest a little.

"That was sheer treachery!" he accused, pointing a shaking hand first at Varre, then Clayborne. "If I hadn't made it, then it would have been nothing less than murder!"

Gill didn't know what any of this was about, but before tempers could flare any further, he said, "Save your outrage for later, Anderson.

You're not out of trouble yet. None of us are."
He turned to Haggie. "It seems we're all here—
those of us who are going to be, anyway. Now
what about these doors?"

"I've told you about them," Haggie answered.
His mouth had swollen up and he mumbled his
words. "I only ever used one of them, this one."
And he looked at door number seven.

"What's in there?" Gill asked him.

"Another place." Haggie shrugged. "Same as
always. But there's water to drink, a few vege-
tables you can eat, and the climate won't kill
you. Don't ask me about the rest of the doors,
for I don't know. But I'd chance any one of them
against this place at night!"

Gill looked at the others. "That's it then. So
what's it to be?"

The howlers had meanwhile started up again.
Red-and-yellow gleaming eyes crowded the
darkness beyond the fire's sphere of light. From
out on the heath there came many small thun-
derings, shrieks of terror, howls of elation, tri-
umph.

"I'm with you," said Turnbull. "It's why we're
here. And if we don't go through, what then?
No way we can live here. Not for very long, anyway."

"He is right," said Varre. "Who cares where
we go as long as it is away from here?"

Clayborne agreed. "A door out of hell? Let's
chance it. The Lord *shall* provide!"

Angela said nothing but simply stayed close
to Gill, and Anderson was already at the door,
staring up at the knocker. "Are we agreed,
then?" he said, as if he were solely responsible
for the arrangements. "Is everyone ready?"

Clayborne shoved him roughly aside. "Let me be first," he said. "I have the strength of my knowledge, the armour of my faith. If there are demons, I shall know them." He opened his arms wide, threw back his head and cried, "In the name of the Lord I make pure, I *exorcise* this gateway out of hell!" And he reached up and knocked.

It was like pulling the plug in a bath full of water, or as if the door were an airlock, with empty space behind it. It fell—was *sucked* flat—inwards, and like ants under the nozzle of a vacuum cleaner, Clayborne, Gill, Angela, and the others were sucked up. All except for Haggie, who had somehow contrived to place himself at the rear and well out of range.

Whirled head over heels and tossed down in something warm and soft, Gill slid to a halt facing the other side of door number seven. The door was a dark oblong set in a white surround, beyond which Haggie was silhouetted against the fire. Gill saw the look on his face where he strained backwards from the door's suction—elation, criminal glee that he'd made such great fools of the six—and thought: *You bastard!*

Haggie was still clutching the carcass of the deerlike quadruped; but then the door sucked harder still and the look on his face turned to one of desperation as he backed off farther yet. But the creature he'd intended to eat was snatched from his arms, drawn through. It went tumbling overhead, and Haggie was left with nothing for his troubles.

He gestured obscenely and his lips formed a pair of parting words. Gill couldn't make them out over the howling of the wind, but he knew what they were anyway: "Fuck you!" And he guessed that this new place wouldn't be as Haggie had described it. He got to his knees, gritted his teeth, pointed at Haggie and shouted some choice invectives of his own . . . then stopped and in the next moment laughed. He looked beyond Haggie and laughed.

The little man's jaw fell open. He whirled about-face. . . .

And the last thing Gill saw before the door slammed gongingly shut and disappeared was the hunting machine, coated in slime, closing its pincer claws on Haggie's upper and lower body.

The last thing he *heard* was the redhead's terrified screaming, echoing off into silence. . . .

"Desert!" Turnbull called down from the top of the dune. "White, glaring desert in all directions. And thataway"—he pointed at something the others couldn't yet see—"is a mountain range. Don't ask me how far, could be five miles or fifteen—or just a mirage. Everything shimmers. But . . . is there something glinting up there? A mirror? A piece of glass or crystal? Windows?" He shrugged. "If we're going anywhere, I'd guess that's our destination. Anywhere else is nowhere."

"Is that it?" Gill called back. "No trees anywhere? Buildings? Ruins?" He sat at the foot of the dune, roughly where the door had been, and gazed at the drifts of sand all about. His jacket felt rough against his shoulders and back, for now Angela was wearing his shirt. It gave her back something of modesty and protected her from the sun. For it was broad daylight here, and hot; something less than twenty minutes had gone by since their arrival; sufficient time that they'd all made their adjustments and recovered their senses.

"That's it," Turnbull answered. "A few kites in the sky far off—birds of some sort, anyway. Nothing else. Oh, and in case anyone was wondering, this isn't Earth. As well as that sun up there"—directly overhead was a small, blinding white orb—"there's another one low on the horizon. *And* a big moon; its craters are clearly visible."

Gill looked at the others. Anderson was already toiling up the side of the dune, with the muttering Clayborne a little to his rear. Give the ex-Minister his due, at least he was making the best of it. He paused for a moment for a breather and wiped his brow. His foppish handkerchief was little more than a silken rag now. "Come on, let's go!" he called down to Gill, Angela and Varre. Apparently he'd got his second wind! People seemed to make very quick recoveries . . . here.

Varre was examining the carcass of the quadruped. He licked his lips. "Haggie said we could eat this?"

Angela went to the thing and looked at it, said, "Oh!" and drew back. She looked shocked or disgusted—or both—Gill couldn't say. He, too, went to look at the dead creature. It was like a fawn from tail to shoulders, but from the shoulders up its "neck" was more a tapering torso, with short, childlike arms and six-fingered hands. The face was also childlike, which is to say very nearly human. And it was female.

"Haggie would have eaten this?" Angela was appalled.

Varre looked at her curiously. "But it is an animal, a beast. It is meat."

"Like a small centaur." Gill shook his head in wonder, gently closed the large, sad, lifeless eyes. And to Varre: "Meat? Of course it is. So is Angela. So are you." He shook his head again. "I couldn't touch this. It would be like eating a legend, a kind of cannibalism."

"You think so?" Varre lifted his eyebrows. "Come now, hardly that!" He licked his lips again, insisting, "And it *is* meat."

"If you want it," Gill told him bluntly, "you carry it." He turned away and with Angela started up the side of the dune. A moment more and Varre came scrambling after them.

"Actually," he said, "or even amazingly—I'm not especially hungry!"

"A sign!" Clayborne whispered as they reached the top. The American was pointing at the low range of grey mountains shimmering on the horizon. Under the crags, something burned silver in the shadows with an intensity that hurt their eyes. "Do you see it? Do you know what it is?"

Turnbull whispered in Gill's ear, "This bloke's condition is becoming serious!"

"A burning bush!" Clayborne cried, his eyes blazing in their dark orbits. "I told you I would lead you up out of hell, and I will! We were like children in a wilderness—like the Children of Israel, wandering in the wilderness—but soon we shall find a land of milk and honey. . . ."

Varre scowled at him. "They wandered for

forty years, didn't they? The Children of Israel?"

And Turnbull added, "Yes, and a hell of a lot longer since then! Better calm yourself down, Miles. Christ, you'll be demanding a burnt offering next!"

Clayborne glowered at him, and at Varre. A vein pulsed in his neck and he began shaking with rage. But then his eyes went wide and his jaw fell open. He gasped. "Out of the mouths of babes! But don't you see? We were *given* a fatted calf to make our offering—and we abandoned it!" Before the others could say or do anything to stop him, he'd gone scrambling back down the side of the dune.

They watched him go and Anderson said, "Let him get on with it. He's mad as a hatter, anyway—and treacherous." He glanced sideways at Varre. "He was treacherous when he was in his right mind, so God only knows what he'll be like now."

He turned away and started off along the crest of the dune. In front of him the desert stretched in wave after white wave, and to his rear the others followed in his tracks. There was nothing much else for them to do. . . .

CHAPTER TWENTY-SEVEN

Sith of the Thone had not been following the progress of the seven; he had other things to do, and anyway the synthesizer was monitoring them, recording all that transpired. Sith would enjoy their various predicaments later, during editing. But for the present, while he was kept busy with his programming and with thoughts of his glorious future as Grand Thone, they simply adventured in those alien worlds which could support them, however marginally.

So far they had had the (random) choice of those worlds; Sith had not yet interfered with them, not substantially. He had little doubt that some of them would "die" during the course of their adventures between the synthesizer's foci; indeed some of them might already be "dead"— but that made no real difference. The manner of such "deaths" would have been recorded, for editing later, and all would be seen to have expired ignobly, without honour. They were an ignoble species.

Because he had not kept tabs, Sith was unaware that Haggie had been taken out of the game until the correction construct brought his unconscious body back to the control room. The correction construct had access to all stored worlds and had been "hunting" for Haggie ever since his accidental incarceration here. Hunting was not its normal function: that was the removal of extraneous refuse from (and the general tidying up of) stored worlds *after* contamination by any particular group of beings under test. In this way the synthesizer's memory was kept clean and uncluttered by events that had taken place since the original recording and storage. Thus the correction construct was a sort of erasing cursor moving across and within the entire scale of the synthesizer's multiscreen. Its hypodermic stinger was a refinement Sith had built into the construct to facilitate its handling of Haggie.

When the construct arrived via one of the control room's many projection ducts, Sith was on the point of entering the Bannerman construct in order to reinsert himself into the game. He couldn't leave it too long, for he desired to be present—indeed to be responsible—when both Gill and Turnbull met up with and were consumed by the Unthinkable; desired to let them *know* he was responsible, and so square the account. It was not Thone-like to behave in this manner, and Sith knew it. But it was Sith-like: the minds and mores of all individual creatures are individual. And so Sith was annoyed that he must now deal with Haggie before proceeding further with his plans.

At first, in his annoyance, Sith considered destroying Haggie, disposing of him utterly. That was no real problem: Sith might simply transmat him far out into space, or into the heart of this system's sun. But . . . in fact Haggie had been something of a bonus. If all Earth's billions of inhabitants were of his stamp, then none of Sith's subterfuge was necessary in the first place! He could have simply recorded the vileness of the place and commenced planetary restructuring out of hand. Yes, for Haggie's capacity for wrong thinking and doing was simply astonishing; the dark depths of his incredibly complex criminal mind were as yet unfathomed. So . . . perhaps Sith might yet find a use for him in the scheme of things to come.

Of course, Haggie was quite different from the other players in Sith's game. For one thing—and quite apart from the fact that he was a self-confessed criminal—his presence there at all was completely unscheduled, an error. He had put himself in the game. (Or the "examination," as Sith should rightly think of it. Except that now he preferred to think of it as a game. His game.)

And because Haggie had not been processed, his needs and requirements remained exactly what they had been before he was taken: he required to eat, drink, sleep, and perform all the other human-animal functions he'd performed before. The others didn't; the synthesizer had taken care of all such matters; but of course they had no way of knowing it. Unless by now they'd started to work it out for themselves. . . .

Sith stored Haggie—not synthesised storage but the real thing—by placing him in suspended animation: hypersleep, as the Thone knew it, when they journeyed out between the stars. As he did so, he checked the little redhead's numerous parts for any permanent damage and found none. Small degrees of dehydration, hunger, and the resultant fatigue were only to be expected; while he slept, the hypersleep chamber's placenta would adjust to his needs and make up any deficiencies. Sith quickly programmed it to do just that.

Finally all was done and he could now reenter the game. He used the control room's rapid-scan locator to check the whereabouts of the six, discovering them on a desert world which for the past thousand years had been the domicile of three medium-rank Thone theosophists. In such close proximity, each could argue with the others the various merits of his philosophy to his core's content. This balanced the disadvantage of overcrowding.

Of course, the six humans only occupied a projection of that world as it had been before Thone colonization, a synthesised "memory" of it. It was nonetheless real within the parameters of its three dimensions, its mass and all its content, but it did not occupy space as the humans were aware of space. It was instead a synthesised world occupying synthesised space.

Sith decided to take the easy route: he would emerge up in the mountains, at the focus which they had made their destination. But before leaving, he must check a small matter of programming. It had amused him to wonder what would happen if the adventures of the six were shaped by their own fears and beliefs, their own phobias and fallacies; and to that end he had programmed the synthesizer to produce effects corresponding to each individual's character. The trigger was to have been the mind of whichever one of the group first passed through a door.

Now, on checking, he was delighted to discover that on this occasion Clayborne had been the first. Clayborne with his vertigo and his ghosts, his religious and paranormal passions. For what the mind of any sentient creature could imagine, the synthesizer could make real. And right now it was working to make real all of Clayborne's worst nightmares. . . .

To the diamond blue eyes of the birds of prey fanning high overhead, the six people plodding the dunes formed a straggly line of black dots on an aching white backdrop, leaving prints like punctuation marks behind them. Two dots to the fore, like the head of some strange lizard, three in the middle, the lizard's squat body, and one bringing up the rear like a stubby tail. Anderson and Varre were the head, Gill, Turnbull and Angela the body, and Clayborne, carrying the dead quadruped over his shoulder, the tail.

Despite the fact that they'd been tramping the dunes for close on two hours, still the small, hot sun seemed scarcely to have moved in the sky. Sweat rivered them, causing Gill to wonder out loud, "Where the hell does it all come from? I mean, did we really drink this much on our way down the escarpment? And if we did, why haven't we found an easier, quicker way to be rid of it?"

"Don't talk about drink," Turnbull groaned. "Lord, I could murder a pint!"

"Really?" Gill said. "Are you dying for one?"

Turnbull looked at him. They'd had this conversation before. "No," he eventually answered, perhaps reluctantly, "not really. Frankly, I don't think I need a drink. It's just that I know I should, and I remember what a pint tastes like."

Angela walked between them, half a pace to the rear. She looked from one to the other. "Am I supposed to know what you two are on about?"

Gill managed a grin, if only for her sake. He wiped the dust from his upper lip where it clung to the sweat. "We're on about something we've discussed once before," he said. "About not needing to shave, eat, drink, sleep, go to the loo, et cetera. About me being a dying man—and never feeling so fit in my life! And Anderson being overweight—but belting along there like an athlete only slightly behind in his training. And you, a 'slip of a girl,' as the saying goes, having the energy of a war-horse!"

Turnbull took over. "We're talking about cuts and bruises that heal in hours, and presumably lethally poisonous stings that knock you down but don't kill you, and about being sick to your stomach from eating inedible fruit, yet an hour or so later running a ten-mile cross-country marathon!"

"In short"—Gill again—"we're talking about something being very wrong—or right?—with our bodies! So what do you make of it?"

She considered it and said, "I had noticed

those things, I suppose, but hadn't really worried about them. There's always been so much else to think about. In fact we did sleep, in that cave back in that other world, but now that I think of it, I'm not sure we needed to. I don't think I did, anyway. We did it out of custom, out of habit. As for calls of nature . . ." She shrugged. "I for one haven't been called. Which for me is strange, to say the least. I'm like most women: I spend my pennies frequently. Or I used to."

"And yet," Turnbull put in, "when Haggie slept on top of the escarpment, it was because he was quite genuinely exhausted. Also, he'd grown a straggly beard and his hair had gone a bit wild. And I noticed that when he slaked his thirst, he really went at it. By comparison, we only took sips."

Gill nodded. "He needed food, too. *Really* needed it! He was actually drooling when he killed that poor wild centaur thing."

"And he . . . made water," Angela added. "Twice in the forest, he . . . went. I just walked on a little way and waited for him."

Turnbull frowned, wiped sweat from his forehead. "So what's the big difference between him and us?"

"I don't know," Gill answered, "but maybe we should be thankful for it. Whatever the difference was, that hunting machine didn't much like it!" He came to a halt, shielded his eyes, and gazed up ahead. Another mile and the mountains began, rising maybe a thousand feet to sharp, craggy crests. Gill's eyes narrowed as he let his sixth sense come into full play.

"And talking about machines," he said, "Clayborne's 'burning bush' is just such an animal!"

Turnbull and Angela stopped, too. They all three squinted their eyes to gaze up into the shadow-streaked flanks of the shimmering range. The unknown glinting, fire-flashing object was still there, a bright jewel of painful light reflecting out from shadowy darkness. Clayborne, coming from behind, caused Gill to start where he brushed by. He mumbled incoherently as he passed between the three, his "sacrifice" draped limply over one shoulder. They let him get out of earshot.

"A machine?" Turnbull finally said. "You can feel it from here?"

Gill nodded. "Oh, don't be mistaken, there's 'machine' all around us, just like before—a background of machine static that tells me we're still inside the House of Doors—but it has its focal point up there. Take my word for it: it's there, waiting for us. . . ." He started forward again and the others kept pace.

"What sort of machine?" Angela wanted to know.

Gill slowly shook his head. "I only wish I knew," he said, a little peevishly, angry that any sort of mechanism should elude him. "The sort of machine that's sitting there right now on the slopes of Ben Lawers. It didn't have any doors—not on the outside, anyway. Castles within castles, worlds within worlds. Chinese boxes that fit inside each other." Again the angry, frustrated shake of his head. "Russian dolls, making more space on the inside than there is on the outside. Houses of Doors enough to build a city, and each one of them the same—the *self-same*—House of Doors!''

He looked at Turnbull, then Angela, and grimaced. Either the puzzle would crack him or he'd crack the puzzle. He forced himself to offer them another grin, and nodded. ''That's what's up ahead,'' he said. ''A Russian doll within a Russian doll within . . . et cetera. With no apparent rhyme or reason to it.''

''Well, I know one thing.'' Turnbull took up the lead, striding out as the ground became firmer underfoot. ''I may not be clued up on Russian dolls, but I once played Russian roulette. And each time we use one of these doors, that's what it feels like. So far the hammer keeps falling on empty chambers, more or less. But what happens when we reach the loaded one? That's what I'd like to know.''

Gill had no answer to that, just another question. *What I'd like to know,* he kept it to himself, *is who loaded the bloody thing?*

Sith saw them on his screen, toiling up the mountainside, and for the moment delayed his reentry into the game. Nightfall would be soon enough. Human eyes weren't equipped for night, for which reason they tended to fear it. And because they were true primitives, night in an alien place would be that much more fearful.

So far there had been no manifestations; that, too, was because it was still daylight, and Clayborne was comparatively happy with the situation. But as night fell and his hagridden, half-crazed mind got to work—and the darkness expanded his mind's terrors larger than life—so, too, the synthesizer would get to work.

Perhaps Sith-Bannerman's sudden eruption onto the scene might also trigger things. Sith was anxious to obtain the best results possible. . . .

CHAPTER TWENTY-EIGHT

With Gill and Angela close behind him, and having overtaken all the others, Turnbull was the first of the party to get a good look at the shining object. Having taken what had seemed the most accessible route up the flank of the mountain, they'd eventually been obliged to traverse in order not to overshoot. Even so, they had in fact gone a little higher than was necessary, so that when Turnbull reached the jagged crest of that last spur, he found himself looking slightly down on the thing. It lay bedded in rubble, in the shadows of a scree-filled reentry between twin spurs, and it was not what had been expected. The climb down to it looked easy enough, but for the moment Turnbull found it difficult to tear his eyes from the object itself.

Gill had been quite right, it was a House of

Doors—of sorts. But it was also the weirdest one they'd come across so far.

Giving Angela a hand, Gill hauled and pushed her up alongside the big man, then climbed up to stand with them. And they all three stared at the—crystal?—together. Now that the sun was off it, the thing was a dull, slaty colour, like a gigantic, polished, many-faceted jewel with a heart of stone. It might simply have grown there, except it was more perfect than nature would have made it, and there were aspects she could never have incorporated. It was a magnificent alien crystal on an alien world; but it was also, unmistakably, a House of Doors. Its facets, around the perimeter where it was bedded in the scree, were oblongs; and central in each oblong was a black, obsidian door. Even from here they could see the knockers—shaped like gargoyles?—set in large, skull-shaped panels of veined quartz, themselves set high in the otherwise blank obsidian slabs.

The effect was beautiful in its simplicity, ugly in its implications, frightening in its clear purpose—which was to frighten. Like the warning hieroglyphs on some ancient pharaoh's tomb, the skull and gargoyle motifs cried out: Don't touch! *Or perhaps*, Gill thought, *abandon hope all ye who enter here.*

"Well?" said Clayborne, panting under his burden as he clambered up level with them. "Well?"

Gill shook his head. "Sorry, Miles," he said. "No burning bush, I'm afraid." But his voice held no trace of sarcasm.

"Of course not." Clayborne's eyes opened wide as they spied the giant crystal House of

Doors. "The Lord works in mysterious ways. Did you really think to find a burning bush as such, on a . . . world with . . . no vegetation?" He paused and the colour drained from his face. He had become aware of the ominous aspect of the thing. "But this—"

"Is no work of the Lord." Anderson finished it for him as he joined them.

Varre was last up. "A House of Doors," he said quietly. "But where the others were merely awesome, this one is . . . menacing."

"What now?" Turnbull looked at Gill.

"I should have thought that was obvious." Anderson puffed himself up, became "leader" again. "We proceed!"

Gill looked at him and in an even tone said, "Off you go then, boss. Me, I'm proceeding nowhere."

"What?" Anderson frowned. "You intend to stay here?"

"For now, yes," Gill answered. He looked from face to face and they waited for him to continue. "Look, right now we don't seem threatened in any way—unless it's by that," and he nodded down the incline towards the House of Doors. "Apart from a few birds and a strange-looking lizard or two in the desert, we've seen nothing of local life-forms. If there were any, and if they were unpleasant, they'd probably have found us before now. We must have stuck out like sore thumbs coming across those dunes. So it appears that we're safe for the moment. We're nowhere, but we are safe."

Turnbull said, "You don't think we should be quite so eager this time, right?"

Gill nodded. "I think we'd be wise if we rested

up for a couple of hours—maybe until morning—before taking the next step. Let's face it, if we *are* threatened during the night, we can always try our luck then. Personally, I'd like to take the opportunity to feel this thing out. I'd like to just take it easy, give my mind and body a break, and . . . see what happens."

The others had taken in what he'd said and he saw from their faces that they agreed—all except Clayborne. He probably hadn't even heard him. "We should worship," the American said. "You must give me your clothes—all of them! I am commanded to make a burnt offering to my God, and this shall be your personal sacrifice, that you give up your clothes that I may burn them." He pointed a shaking finger at the giant crystal. "That is the devil's work! There are devils in the very air of this place—can't you feel them? But we shall drive them away with a fire and the sacrificial offering of this lamb." He stroked the beast lying stiff on his shoulder.

Turnbull looked at him with narrowed eyes, knotted a huge fist and gritted his teeth. It was obvious that he intended to knock the other cold. But Gill caught his eye, shook his head. Clayborne saw the look that passed between them. "What? Do you plot against me? Do you *dare* deny the Lord God His—"

Gill had drawn out the thorn stinger from its holster. Now he jabbed Clayborne in the thigh and gave the bulb in the root of the thorn a gentle squeeze. Clayborne's eyes stood out like marbles. He coughed once, sighed, and simply crumpled down into himself. The centaur thing slid from his back, went cartwheeling all the way down the scree slide to the jumbled depression between the spurs.

"Okay," said Gill, "let's get him down there as gently as possible. Maybe when he wakes up, he'll be over it. If not"—he shrugged, sighed—"then I really don't know what the answer is."

"There *is* an answer," said Varre, avoiding their eyes, scowling at his cracked, dirty fingernails. "Clayborne is a liability, useless to us. Why should we allow him to jeopardize our lives? That place down there—that House of Doors—is clearly different from the others, possibly dangerous. It bears the skull and crossbones of the poison bottle. I suggest we simply go along with whatever Clayborne says; except, of course, we do not give him our clothes. But when the time comes, and if he desires to use one of those menacing doors, then we . . . put no obstacle in his way. At least that way he will have contributed something." He looked up from the examination of his fingers.

Blank-faced, Turnbull and Angela looked away. Anderson said nothing but raised a speculative eyebrow. Gill said, "You're a cold-blooded bastard, aren't you, Jean-Pierre? Thanks for your . . . suggestion, anyway. But from now on I step very carefully."

"You?" Varre looked surprised. "But why?"

"In case I should accidentally break a leg," said Gill. "That's why. . . ."

Gill came awake knowing that something was happening or about to happen. He sat with his back to a depression in a sloping slab of rock, his feet shoved down into loose scree which formed a brake against any sliding. His arms were round Angela where she snoozed beside him, with her head on his chest and one arm thrown carelessly across him. He remembered very little of their settling down in that position, and nothing of conversation.

Turnbull was close by, chattering gibberish to himself in his sleep. In the east the first stars were coming out in a palid sky, a small scattering of them that threw their reflections into the great crystal's many facets; far to the south the tiny secondary sun was setting, leaving a floating ring of bright light like a halo to mark its passing; a lone kite wheeled over the highest crags.

Anderson and Varre were already awake, yawning where they got to their feet a little distance away. A nine-inch grey lizard with a yellow frill along its back went streaking down the slope, taking a tiny avalanche of dust and pebbles with it. Fifty feet away, Clayborne was standing in front of the House of Doors. He was quite naked and raving again, which was what had disturbed Anderson and Varre. But Gill had been awakened by something else. He could sense the House of Doors stirring. It, too, was coming awake.

Clayborne's clothing was piled a short distance from the giant crystal, and the madman had put the dead centaur on the pile and set fire to the lot. Flames were licking up, and black belches of rolling, stinking smoke.

Turnbull woke up and saw what was going on. He looked around and saw Gill where he gently shook Angela awake. "Where'd he get the makings?" the big man mumbled. Then he patted his jacket pocket and gave a snort. "He stole my matches!" he said. "Well, no, actually they were his."

Angela was awake now and Gill could move her and get to his feet. "So much for not needing sleep," she said, stretching. "Our bodies mightn't, but out brains certainly do."

"Miles," Gill called out, stiffly making his way towards the American. "Clayborne, you should get away from there right now. It's not safe there." He tried to make his advice sound urgent without causing Clayborne to panic. He spoke quietly, as if he feared that the House of Doors itself was listening. And maybe it was, for certainly it was gearing itself towards something.

Clayborne turned to face him. "Keep back, Gill!" he thundered. "I know what I'm doing—and I know what you would do, too! Put me to sleep, would you? Fool—that way lies eternal damnation! Don't you know we tread the rim of the very pit? I make obeisance. Man, it will be the saving of our souls!"

He stood between his fire and the crystal. Gill was close now but something warned him to go no closer. For the first time he noticed that the doors were numbered, and how they were numbered: in multiples of one hundred and eleven. Those which were within view bore the numbers 888, 777, 666, and 555, left to right in an anticlockwise direction. Clayborne stood before door number 666, and Gill couldn't help but wonder if it was significant.

In fact it was, for now Clayborne turned towards the door and pointed at it, shouting,

"See? The devil is revealed. The Lord my God has shown me his number, which is the number of the beast! Now I turn my back on him"—he did, and facing the fire threw his arms wide—"saying, get thee behind me, Satan!"

"Clayborne!" Gill hissed, aware of the vast crystal crouched there like something about to spring. "For Christ's sake, man!"

"For Christ's sake?" Clayborne howled across smoke and flames. "Yes, and for yours, and for mine. Great merciful God, now hear this sinner and show to him a sign, that he shall know he is forgiven and made welcome to Thy bosom. . . ."

It was coming—*now!* Gill threw himself flat.

Door number 666 slid swiftly, silently down out of sight—and hell itself was visible behind it. Red and orange fires rumbled and roared in there—and now roared *out* of there! A great shaft of fire belched out like a thick, dripping tongue, and licked Clayborne for long seconds head to heel. He disappeared screaming in liquid light and heat, and Gill felt his own hair and eyebrows singeing as he scuttled frantically away on belly, knees and elbows. Then the tongue of fire was retracted and the door hissed shut to contain it, and for a few brief moments splashes of fire dripped sparks from the rim of the obsidian panel.

Amazingly, horrifyingly, Clayborne still stood there—but only for a few seconds. Then he crumpled. He was like a plastic doll tossed on a bonfire by some spoiled child, and dragged back out again as the child felt something of the doll's agony. He was a candle that dripped its wax and slumped under the blast of a blowtorch. He was a dying *thing* that screamed a bubbling, boiling lobster scream as he fell in a smoking, steaming pile on the scorched scree.

And the House of Doors stood there as before, an alien evil under alien stars. . . .

CHAPTER TWENTY-NINE

Gill felt unbearable horror, and more than horror. It was as if Clayborne and the House of Doors were connected, but by much more than the fire which had reduced him to red and black ruin. Gill felt it, was on the point of grasping it, when Turnbull came running.

"Oh, *shit*!" The big man was gasping, his Adam's apple bobbing. "Oh my *God*! What the hell happened?" He had seen everything but hadn't taken it in. He ran to Clayborne, went down on one knee. His huge hands fluttered helplessly. "I can't ... don't ... where can I touch him?"

But he was now within range of door number 666, and the thing was still working; Gill could feel it. "Jack!" he called out warningly.

Clayborne had lifted his smoking head and opened his eyes. His back had been to the blaze.

When the tongue of fire had engulfed him, he'd closed his eyes and so saved them. But they were all that had been saved. And perhaps something of his mind, too. "I . . . I've been a bloody fool," he gurgled. "But I believed. I believed. I should have known. How could there be a God in a . . . godless place like this, eh? Hell is the devil's domain."

"Don't speak," Turnbull told him, aghast. But Clayborne wasn't only speaking, he was trying to get to his feet.

"H-help me . . . up," he said, his agony reaching such a crescendo that it became nothing. "Let me do it, before everything welds together, seizes up."

The House of Doors did nothing, it *waited* as Turnbull somehow got Clayborne to his feet. Gill felt it waiting. He stood up, ran forward, helped Turnbull guide the staggering, dripping thing that had been a man. Huge blisters burst and released their contents; fluids fell from the roasted body like rain; barbecued, blackened ribs were visible in the steaming mass of Clayborne's back.

"Six, six, six," Clayborne mumbled, his face a molten mask. And between Turnbull and Gill he staggered like a crippled robot, aiming himself at the door. "Let it . . . finish what it started!"

Gill could feel the affinity. The House of Doors waited for Clayborne. More than that: he was its guideline! "Jack!" Gill hissed. "We have to leave him now—right now—or we're dead men, too!"

They released Clayborne but he continued to shuffle forward. "Finish it," he told door number 666 as Gill and Turnbull backed off. "Put . . . an end to it." This time the door slid to one side, and there was no fire. Instead there was the vacuum of space. Stars like jewels hung in the vast, unending void of it. And Clayborne was sucked in.

They saw him go tumbling head over heels, a blackened thing falling forever into his own ultimate nightmare of vertigo. And this time when the door slammed shut, its rim was rimed with frost. . . .

"He was controlling it," Gill told the others. "Inadvertently. He didn't know, had no idea. But that machine was in tune with him. It still *is* in tune with his line of thought. Its programming is based on his worldview."

"His netherworld-view," said Turnbull, and Gill nodded.

Varre looked sceptical. "And just like that"— he snapped his fingers—"all of a sudden, you 'know' these things. Is that what we're to believe?"

Anderson said, "Jean-Pierre, you haven't seen Gill's talent in action. I have, so I'd advise you to hear him out. Please go on, Spencer."

"I don't know why he was chosen for the pattern, for copying," Gill continued, "but he was. It could be because his mind was the most chaotic, the best suited to produce horrific results. But—"

"Could it be," Angela cut in, "that it was simply a question of whoever was first through that door from the forest world? You'll remember, he was first." She shrank a very little as all eyes turned in her direction.

"That's a distinct possibility," said Gill at last. "That point had escaped me. It's definitely worth keeping in mind."

"I'm sorry," she said apologetically. "I broke your chain of thought. You said 'but'?"

"But"—Gill gathered his thoughts—"to accept the idea that Clayborne was chosen because he was unhinged, because his perception of things would produce monstrous effects, is to accept that we are being deliberately misused, manipulated—"

"But we *are* being manipulated!" Anderson snorted. "Surely that's obvious."

Gill nodded. "By whatever alien intelligence controls the House of Doors. The question is, to what end? I mean, why torment us?"

"To see what kind of stuff we're made of?" Turnbull raised his customary eyebrow.

"The Castle has stood on Ben Lawers for some considerable time," said Gill. "Given that it's a device that's come across light-years of space, its builders or controllers aren't stupid. They *know* what we're made of."

Varre remained unconvinced about something. "This thing about Clayborne having shaped this world with his mad mind," he began.

"Not this world," Gill cut him off. "Just what happens in it. Or specifically, what happened to himself, and what happens to us."

"But nothing has happened to us!" The Frenchman's frustration was getting the better of him.

"Yet," said Gill coldly. "Nothing has happened to us yet. But less than half an hour ago Clayborne was disfigured and murdered hideously—I said murdered!—and if we wait long enough, events will shape themselves in representation of the supernatural forces and powers of evil in which he believed. Forces which will turn themselves on us."

"You *know* this?" Varre snapped.

"Can you hear your watch ticking?"

"Eh? When it's working, of course!"

Gill nodded towards the House of Doors. "That place is ticking," he said. "Like a bomb!"

Varre felt reality slipping—felt the terror of his cynic's worldview being erased with giant strokes—and fought against it. "Proof!" He blurted the word out. "There's no proof. You can show us nothing!"

"Clayborne feared two things worse than all others put together." Gill was relentless. "The devil and all his works, and falling. Hell and high places. Hellfire burned him, and he fell into space forever."

For long moments there was silence. The dusk was eerie, with only a handful of nondescript stars to light it. And now to the east the rim of a lesser moon was rising, its light a faint, pastel yellow tinged with red. Finally Anderson asked, "So what are you suggesting? Surely we aren't simply going to wait here for something else—something even more monstrous—to happen to us? Where do we go from here, Spencer?"

"I've told you how things are," Gill answered. "I could be wrong but I don't think so. I *felt* that machine working with Clayborne, and working against him. Now I suggest we each think it through. Five heads have to be better than one. Any ideas—all ideas—are welcome."

"And meanwhile, if something does . . . come up?" This from Angela.

"Then we'll be obliged to use a door," Gill answered. "And maybe that's a good starting point: figuring out which door to use. Now I suggest you all get on with it. And if anyone comes up with anything at all, well, for God's sake don't keep it to yourself! Me"—he looked at Varre—"I'm just going to sit here and listen to that thing tick. If you choose not to believe me, that's your problem. Do your own thing." He walked off some little distance and found a boulder to sit against.

After a while Turnbull came to him. "We still haven't told them about Bannerman," he said, keeping his voice low.

"No," said Gill, "and I don't think we should, not right now. Hell, there's enough confusion! Anyway"—he shrugged helplessly—"I'm not even sure about Bannerman."

"What!"

"It might have been machine static. I mean, we're inside a machine! My mind's confused no less than anyone else's—maybe more so. Christ, if I'm to believe everything my senses are telling me right now, then you're not entirely human either, Jack! You're giving off the same kind of half-machine aura I sensed around Bannerman. And so are the others. And I just *know* that girl's the most human creature I ever met!"

Turnbull grunted, perhaps disappointedly. "But there was still that business at your flat," he said, "and I'm fairly certain it was him. And where did he vanish to, eh? So he saved my life, and Clayborne's—but where's Clayborne now?

Jesus, *someone* has to be playing a game with us, and Bannerman fits the—"

Gill held up a hand. "*Shh!*" he said. And a moment later: "It's building again, preparing itself. Arranging . . . something."

Breaking his conversation, Angela came slipping and sliding across the scree slope. She had Anderson and Varre in tow. "Spencer!" she called out excitedly. "An idea."

He looked at her blankly.

"Numerology!" she said.

"What?"

"Clayborne would have been interested in numbers, wouldn't he?" She was breathless. "Their occult meaning and application?"

"So?"

"The numbers on the doors: he knew the number of the beast in Revelations."

Gill's expression didn't change. "I should think that just about everyone knows the number of the beast in Revelations."

"But it was *his* number, too!" she said. "Clayborne's." And she quickly went on to explain the Hebrew system of numerology, where numbers are substituted for the letters of a name to divine a person's destiny or affinities. She broke down the alphabetical values in the following manner:

1.	2.	3.	4.	5.	6.	7.	8.
A	B	C	D	E	U	O	F
I	K	G	M	H	V	Z	P
Q	R	L	T	N	W		
J		S			X		
Y							

"Miles Clayborne adds up like this," she said: "Four, one, three, five, three, three, three, one, one, two, seven, two, five, five. Which equals forty-five. And four plus five is nine. Six-six-six equals eighteen, and one and eight makes nine. He and the door had the same number. It was his door and he couldn't avoid it. That's where that old saying comes from: his number was on it! Also, in various types or 'states' of numerology, nine is the death number—as in the nine of spades. . . ."

Gill shook his head, looked mystified; but the action of the House of Doors had steadied again, enabling him to give her his attention. "So where do we go from there?" he asked.

"We need to work out our numbers," she answered, "to discover which door is most applicable—most propitious—to whom! For instance, I'm a six. My door would be two-two-two. That's a good one: the number two stands for peace and harmony, tranquility and sincerity. And if it's good for me, it should be good for all of us."

Gill frowned. "That was damn quick reckoning!" he said. "How come you know all of this, anyway? I mean . . . Hebrew?"

"I've always been interested in numerology, astrology and the like," she explained. "The Hebrew system's the one I know best, that's all."

Gill nodded. "So what's my number?"

"You're a five," she answered with certainty. "I already worked it out. You occasionally live on your nerves, but you're also resourceful, resilient, multifaceted—just like the crystal. You can be sexy, too, and irresistible"—Varre snorted—"and clever. Sometimes you're not too considerate, but you are well meaning. And you love travel."

Dryly, Varre said, "World-hopping, for instance?"

Gill looked sideways at him, said, "What about him?"

"His number?" She worked it out. "Fifty-one! He's a six, like me. Door number two-twenty-two—again. But he has *three* names. The three tempers the two: ambitious, proud, sometimes overbearing."

Jack Turnbull totalled thirty-eight, which equalled eleven, or two—yet again. And David Anderson was a three.

"If we were to take this seriously," Gill said, "door number two-twenty-two would seem the best choice."

"You don't take it seriously?" She seemed to be disappointed.

But Gill surprised her. "Yes, I do!" He grinned.

"You do?" Her excitement was back again.

Anderson and Varre couldn't believe their ears. They looked at Gill as if he were raving mad. "What?" said Anderson flatly. "You actually believe all of this rubbish we've just been subjected to? Gill, I begin to have serious—"

"Hold it," Gill cut him off. "It's not what *we* believe, it's what *he* believed, Clayborne. The machine—crystal, House of Doors, whatever it is—shaped things to his way of thinking, his beliefs. And if it's still working along the same lines—if it's now tuned in to what *we* believe—"

"Two-twenty-two's our door," said Turnbull. They moved as a body, stepping carefully in the dark, around the curve of the great crystal. And as they went, so doors number 444, 333, and 222 came into view.

"Incidentally," Gill said as they came to a halt at a safe distance from the crystal, "what would Jon Bannerman's number have been?"

Angela worked it out. "He was a seven," she said. "But like threes and fives it won't split down. Door number seven-seventy-seven would have been his door. Seven is the number of the scholar, the philosopher, the thinker. They're reclusive and keep themselves apart—which he did. They're reserved and self-controlled, and powerfully intelligent. Seven's aren't quite of this world—of Earth, I mean—and they generally consider the great mass of humanity in a poor light."

"All of a sudden I'm interested in numerology!" said Turnbull. He glanced at Gill's dark silhouette. "So Bannerman was a seven, eh?"

His remark was like an invocation. Gill sensed it coming just half a second before it happened. . . .

CHAPTER THIRTY

Sith of the Thone had made several mistakes, was guilty of certain omissions. One mistake had been the loss of a surgical tool on the night he'd tried to kill Spencer Gill; another had been not to worry about it. He hadn't because he'd known that no human being could ever understand it, divine its purpose, put it to use. He had omitted to credit Gill with that ability. Or perhaps in the back of his mind he had so credited him, only to put such thoughts aside because the chances were astronomically against Gill's understanding. What—a simple rod of silver metal, dented, useless? Even if it were found, it would be tossed aside, buried in some scrap pile, lost. The human race was as negligent in its use of metals as in its misuse of liquids!

Another omission had been his failure to check on the progress of the test group. If he had—or if he'd checked the synthesizer's recordings—then he might have hit upon one of those moments when Gill produced the tool to study it, perhaps even that moment when it had self-repaired. He would know that Gill had it, and might guess that he knew how to use it. Similarly he had failed to note the fact that the correction construct had lost its hypodermic; again, Sith might have checked the recordings to discover just how it was lost. But having done none of these things, he'd placed himself at a slight disadvantage—of which as yet he was completely unaware.

The one mistake he did know about, to which he must regrettably admit, had been a quite deliberate act at the time: to leave the Bannerman construct undisguised, in its original form, following that clash with Gill and Turnbull in Killin. Sith had been satisfied that merely restructuring the hand would suffice to disconnect him from that event. That had been sheer arrogance, an exuberant gesture of his superior psyche and entirely un-Thone. But he'd been bested by them once and so had desired to taunt them, almost to *defy* them to recognise him—which he believed Turnbull might finally have done. Well, what was done must now be undone. Sith must try to convince Turnbull that he was mistaken, and as soon as possible after reinserting himself into the game. The way he planned it, it shouldn't prove too difficult. He'd already made his arrangements and inflicted a little necessary damage on the construct.

But to Sith's great annoyance and just as he was about to vacate the control room through a duct into the synthesised world of the crystal,

Miles Clayborne arrived. He was very badly burned, bursting out of his skin, and rimed with the hoar of deep space. In short, he was quite "dead". Sith was not only annoyed but also surprised—and *very* curious. Obviously the synthesizer had been active to an extraordinary degree! What in the universe had Gill and the others—and especially Clayborne—been up to? Eager to find out, Sith sealed Clayborne's disgusting remains in a storage web and at last entered the duct. . . .

The House of Doors had nine sides at ground level, with doors numbered 111 to 999. Since Gill and the others stood back a little way from door number 444, number 777 was just out of sight, hidden by the curve of the great crystal. Therefore no one actually saw Bannerman emerge from 777—but they did all hear Gill's hoarse cry of alarm in the instant before he grabbed Angela to him and carried her bruisingly to the hard, cutting scree.

After that there had sounded the reverberations of a great door slammed, its echoes bouncing off the mountains, and in the weirdness of the ensuing, ringing silence human cries of terror—cries for assistance—from around the crystal's curve.

Shaken and trembling, Gill was on his feet again, helping Angela up and urging her away from the crystal, when Bannerman appeared. He came staggering from behind the House of Doors, his clothes in tatters and feet a bloody mess inside flopping, shattered shoes. He held his arms out wide before him, claw hands groping at the air, feeling his way like a man in total darkness—or like a blind man.

"Help!" he called again, hoarsely, croakingly. "For God's sake—is anyone there?"

Paralysed with shock and horror, they could only watch as he stumbled on sharp stones, collided with a corner of the crystal and fell. But as he climbed painfully, groaningly to his feet again, they moved towards him in a body and began to understand something of his condition. His hair had been scorched to stubble on his head and his hands were blistered, raw and bleeding. He looked like he'd crashed headlong through a burning thorn tree. And his eyes ... were the colour of sour milk and quite blank, reflecting only the pale yellow pulse of the freshly risen moon.

"Blind!" Anderson gasped—and Bannerman heard him.

"Anderson?" His voice was almost childlike, pleading, wanting to hope but scarcely daring to. "Is that you? Why don't you speak to me?" He came stumbling towards them.

Angela flew to him, a sob in her voice as she said, "Oh, you poor man! Yes, it's us, Jon. All of us—except Haggie and Miles Clayborne. They're ... not with us."

"Angela? And ... the rest of you?" Now he believed.

"We're here, Jon," said Anderson as Angela took Bannerman's hand.

He grasped her, clasped her to him, cried, "Then it's a ... a miracle! God, I was never much of a believer, but I believe in you now!"

Gill and Turnbull swapped glances, Turnbull's a little sheepish. But Gill still wasn't quite sure. Here in the vicinity of the House of Doors—especially now, with the crystal still active, if temporarily stable—alien machine presence was just too great to distinguish between Bannerman and the major source of activity. Gill's sixth sense was swamped by his awareness of the crystal.

"Sit down before you fall again." Angela found Bannerman a seat on a flat stone. "Here, let me help you. There." She had to crouch beside him, because he wouldn't let go of her hand.

"What happened to you?" Varre was over his astonishment. "The last time we saw you was in that cave on the escarpment, when we settled down to sleep."

"What happened to me?" Bannerman's voice was a little deeper now, more the voice they would normally associate with him. His terror and hysteria were ebbing, relief and exhaustion flooding in to replace them.

And Gill thought: *If this is an act, it's a good one.* And: *Would he really go so far as to blind himself?*

"I'll tell you what happened," Bannerman continued. "I thought I heard something. Whatever it was, it woke me up. I left the cave and went to the rim of the escarpment. Down there in the forests, things were on the move, shrieking and fighting. Then I saw something—an impossibly huge insect thing—climbing up the cliff towards me. It had reached an overhang and was having difficulty bypassing it. I thought it might have smelled us out and was on its way up to get us!"

Gill asked, "Can you describe this thing you saw?"

Bannerman nodded and gave the description of the hunting machine. "I found a loose boulder and rolled it to the rim," he continued. "The thing had just about manoeuvred itself up over the obstruction when I toppled the boulder down on it. I knocked it loose, thought I'd done for it. But . . . it fell only a little way, onto a ledge. And it clung there. It looked up at me with its faceted eyes, and they shone on me like powerful beams—like lasers! They blinded me in a moment, and the pain was so terrific that I . . . I must have blacked out. Since then . . . God, you tell *me* where I've been!" His voice had started to break.

Angela tried to comfort him, and in a little while he went on. "I've been in deserts where the sun burned me, swamps where *things* like flatfish clung to my thighs, a place where everything I touched was sharp as broken glass. Finally I was finished, had given up hope. Then . . . I found myself in a place of fires and terrific heat; and when I was just about ready to lie down and die, then I heard a voice." He turned towards Angela where she crouched beside him. "I think it was your voice. I forced myself to move in your direction, and—" He paused, shrugged, blinked his blind eyes in the bland moonlight. "Here I am."

"She spoke your number," Turnbull told him. "She . . . called you through a door? Door number seven-seventy-seven."

Gill said, "Jack, will you come with me?" As Turnbull joined him, Gill looked at the others.

"Stay here. Take care of Bannerman. We'll be back."

They walked round to the front of the crystal, to door number 777. At its base the scree had been disturbed. Several slabs of loose stone had been sliced through like blocks of cheese; their flat faces lay flush against the door's obsidian panel. Next door, 666 was the same. Both doors had been activated; since they knew about 666, obviously Bannerman had emerged from 777. Gill shook his head in blank astonishment. "If Clayborne's mind really did help fashion this place," he said, "then it was a weirder mind than even we suspected. What bothers me especially is that he's still influencing things. Damn it, this was *his* world! We're not just inside a machine, but a machine programmed by a madman!"

Turnbull looked at Gill's moon-yellowed silhouette. "And Bannerman? What do you think?"

"I don't know," Gill answered. "Part of me is inclined to say he's okay, but there's another part—"

Both men gave massive starts, felt their hearts start to race in their chests. From far away along the ridge of the mountains, a blood-curdling sound had reached down to them, a sound awesome enough in its rightful place, but one which should never be heard in a place like this. It was a howling—but very different from that howling they'd heard in the world of the great escarpment. This one was a deep, throbbing, ululant baying. And it seemed entirely familiar.

They weren't the only ones to hear it. "Gill,

Turnbull!" Anderson's fearful voice came echoing. "Get back here—quick!"

They returned to the main party. As they went Gill advised, "Jack, just forget about Bannerman for now. Stay vigilant, but not up front, if you follow me. If we were wrong about him, fine. If not—well, we may have his measure anyway. Forewarned is forearmed." He allowed Turnbull a glimpse of the silver cylinder before thrusting it back into his pocket.

By the time they got back, the night was alive with the howling, some of it echoing from afar and some from quite close at hand. Too close. "What do you make of it?" said Anderson, obviously a mass of nerves.

"Don't ask them," said Varre, "ask me." And without any hesitation: "Wolves! There is no other sound quite like the howl of a wolf. I have relatives in Canada—in the far north, where I've visited them—and that was where I heard it. Timber wolves."

Anderson grabbed his arm. "Are you serious? Timber wolves—in a world with no trees?"

"None that we've seen." Varre angrily shook him off. "But so far we've seen nothing—not even the other side of this range of mountains. They are wolves, I tell you. I would stake my life on it!"

"How about all of our lives?" Turnbull's voice was grim, heavy with foreboding. "Look up there."

They looked. In the darker cracks and crevices of the mountain's flank, many pairs of eyes burned yellow as tiny triangular lamps. A shaggy shape was silhouetted where it loped between outcrops of rock. Now there could be no doubting it. "My God!" Anderson backed off a pace on legs like jelly. "A pack of the bloody things!"

"I don't understand this." Even Turnbull was unnerved. "I mean, we've seen nothing to explain how—"

"And look down there!" Angela's shuddering gasp cut him short. Down on the floor of the desert, converging upon the same trail which had led the party of human beings to this place, strange streams of flickering lambent fire—like massed ignes fatui or sentient St. Elmo's light—eddied and flowed where it (they?) followed their trail like bloodhound trackers.

"Sniffing us out," said Varre in a series of gulps. "But what are they?"

"Who cares?" said Turnbull. "Me, I think it's high time we decided which door we're taking out of this place!"

"I vote for Angela's door," said Gill, backing towards the House of Doors. "Door number two-twenty-two."

Anderson hopped from one foot to the other, dancing like a girl in his anxiety. "But we can't be sure," he said.

"One thing's certain," said Turnbull. "We're not using six-sixty-six or seven-seventy-seven. Angela, what do you think?"

She made no answer. They looked at her where she sat beside Bannerman, clutching his hand. Her eyes were wide and terrified; they were fixed on the scree slope which they'd all descended from the spur. And coming down that slope—a naked man! The light of the alien moon was full upon him. He smiled as he stepped easily, unerringly down through the sliding scree. And behind him came other human forms. All naked, all smiling.

"Clayborne's world!" Varre suddenly hissed. "A world full of supernatural powers. Gill, Anderson—these are not men. And the wolves are not wolves. They're—"

"Werewolves!" said Gill. . . .

CHAPTER THIRTY-ONE

Gill's reaction—the way his voice had filled with horror and disbelief as he said the word "werewolves"—wasn't merely a shot in the dark; for he had seen with his own eyes the first of many transformations. So had the others. The first of the naked men (the leader of the pack?) where he stepped down from the slope, had fallen into a crouch, then gone to all fours; and in place of a man, there had hunched a great grey wolf! The metamorphosis had been instantaneous: man to beast in less time than it took to think about. And snarling, the flame-eyed creature slinkingly advanced.

"Gill! Turnbull!" Anderson cried, all pretence of leadership utterly flown.

The leading werewolf paused; others, changing from men to beasts, took up their places on his left and right flanks; the shadows of cliffs and slopes all around were alive with their bright three-cornered eyes.

"Gill?" Turnbull echoed Anderson.

"Back off," said Gill. "But slowly. Towards the House of Doors. Can you get Bannerman?"

Turnbull said, "Jon, try to relax. We have something of a problem here. It will be easier if I carry you." He grunted as he hoisted the other man onto his back in a fireman's lift.

Varre's deeply ingrained scepticism and sarcasm were quickly evaporating. Reality had all but disappeared here, and the Frenchman felt himself vanishing with it. "Those corpse-fires," he babbled, and paused to utter a brief, breathless prayer in his own tongue, "they're coming up the mountain!"

"But what are they?" Angela clung to Gill, backed with him towards the great crystal.

"Clayborne's powers of evil," Gill answered. "Ghosts, malevolencies, evil spirits."

"There are no such things!"

"He believed there were."

"We have to use the door!" Anderson shrieked. He turned and headed straight for door number 222. "Follow me!"

The werewolves edged closer; their fangs were yellow as their eyes, dripping saliva; the ruffs of fur along their backs were ridged, erect, threatening. *Then one of them barked!*

It wasn't a howl but a bark. A smaller animal was tobogganing down the scree slope, bringing an avalanche of dust and pebbles with it.

Gill backed up to Anderson at door number 222. "What are you waiting for?" he said. But Anderson could only stand there and gurgle inarticulately. Gill risked taking his eyes off the closing circle of werewolves, glanced at Anderson—then at door number 222.

It was 222, then 333, then 444, 555, and so on! The numbers were flashing and changing like strobe lights, transferring themselves from door to door, circling the great crystal's perimeter facets and speeding up with every passing second. Then 222 came flashing onto the door again, and Anderson lifted a trembling hand to the knocker—but already the number had changed. 333, 444, 555, 666 . . .

It was like a crazy carousel. Gill shoved Anderson out of the way. Faster and faster the circling numbers winked on and off, until they began to blur. "Take a chance!" someone, Turnbull, yelled in Gill's ear.

Do it! Gill told himself. *Take a chance—while there's still a chance to take!*

Cries of horror reached him as he grasped and lifted the great gargoyle knocker. He held it, turned his head and looked back. Beyond the sloping field of scree where it fell into shadows and darkness, a curtain of fluorescent blue and green light like aurora borealis sprang up from the desert's floor. It lit up the entire shelf of scree in an eerie, flickering weave of pastel patterns. And in the shifting, dancing folds of the curtain, vast faces were forming themselves of its energies: faces with eyes that leered, and gaping mouths and nostrils black as pits. Human faces, and yet inhuman faces, and upon their foreheads—horns!

Again there came the barking; something scampered, yelped, came bounding high over the circling wolves; it crashed into the group of humans where they cowered at the door. Gill felt himself jostled. The numbers were a blur before his eyes. He let the knocker fall.

Upon the instant, the numbers stopped revolving—at 555. Gill's door, according to Angela—which in the next moment cracked open like giant jaws to snatch them all inside. . . .

Gill had hit his head against something. Not hard enough to cause him serious or lasting damage, but sufficient to raise a lump like an overripe plum about to split its skin on the left side of his forehead at the hairline. Angela was sobbing, cradling him in her arms. He lay in a pile of sharp, hard, angular debris and gritty, flaky stuff. Opening one eye where his upper torso lay across Angela's thighs, head lolling, he saw that the flaky stuff was reddish brown and knew that it was . . . rust?

Varre was screaming. "*Mon Dieu! Mon Dieu!* For the love of God, get it *off* me!"

Anderson was answering him, "Keep still, Jean-Pierre. Give us a chance."

"The pain!" the Frenchman howled. "My leg, my leg!"

"Listen, Frog!" Turnbull's voice growled. "You have a choice: keep still and we'll get this bloody thing off you, or keep leaping about and wear it for the rest of your fucking life!"

Bannerman was quieter, almost plaintive, saying, "Where are we? What happened? Are we safe? Won't someone please tell me what that was all about?"

Gill moved, tried to sit up and see what was going on; and Angela cried: "Spencer? *Spencer!*" She hugged him to her and sobbed all the harder. "I thought you were seriously hurt. Tell me you're not." She kissed his neck, his ear, the bump on his forehead.

"I'm not," he croaked, hoarsely, and paused to spit more of the rust out of his mouth. Then: "Hey!" he said. "I thought I was supposed to be the sexy one?"

As Gill's head stopped spinning he looked about, tried to take in something of their surroundings. At first he thought they'd emerged in some sort of cave. In fact they had, but no kind of cave Gill or any of the others might ever have imagined. Light, a sort of hazy, dusty daylight, entered the place through a gaping oval hole in one wall, also in smoking beams through holes in the ceiling. *A cave?* Gill wondered. *Or a nuclear shelter that took a direct hit from a big one?*

There were pipes and cables, and broken plastic and metal conduits hanging everywhere, like twentieth-century stalactites, and the floor was littered with rusting levers, nuts and bolts, pistons and jacks and metallic scrap of every and all descriptions. *A junkyard?*

"A junkyard!" This time he shouted it out loud, tried to struggle to his feet.

But Angela kept a tight hold on him. "Take it easy, Spencer," she pleaded with him.

"But don't you see?" he said. "This place is a junkyard! I mean, this is the debris of civilization. Can you imagine all this on an alien world? This *has* to be Earth!"

She shook her head, carefully got up and helped him to his feet. "No," she said. "No it doesn't. And it isn't. I thought so, too—until I looked out there." She nodded towards the great oval gash of an opening in a wall of piled mechanical bits and pieces.

Gill would have gone to the opening at once, but now he'd seen Bannerman propped in one corner, trembling and asking his blind, pitiful questions where he leaned against what looked like a great engine block. And he'd also seen what Anderson and Turnbull were doing—or trying to do—to Varre. They'd torn away his trouser leg from his right thigh. Fastened *through* the fleshy part of his leg, a great wolf's muzzle was clamped there in death. The creature's head, shoulders and forelegs were intact, but beyond that it had been guillotined clean through its trunk. Its blood slopped everywhere.

Turnbull looked up as Gill stumbled over. "Are you okay?" he asked, and Gill nodded. Anderson was sitting on Varre, trying to hold him down where he writhed in his agony. Turnbull's fingers were bloody, locked in the jaws of the wolf, straining to force them open.

Gill guessed what had happened: this creature had attacked the Frenchman as he came through the door—which had then closed on it, cutting it in half. Now . . . sweat rivered Varre's agonized features; his teeth were grinding behind lips drawn back in a rictus of pain. Gill grimaced and took out the thorn hypodermic from his pocket.

But at that moment Turnbull hissed his horror and jerked up and away from Varre. Anderson too. The Frenchman gave a scream of sheer terror. The wolf's head where its teeth were locked on his thigh . . . was now a man's head! A man's bust, with arms intact, that flopped obscenely as it crashed down where Varre tossed it. "Jesus! Jesus!" he cried shrilly, his fingers fluttering over his lacerated thigh.

Gill and the others stared wide-eyed at the inhuman remains, at the grinning death mask of a face, shoulders and trailing arms—which at once dissolved away, turning to dust and smoke in a moment.

"What . . . ?" Anderson and Turnbull mouthed the word almost in unison.

"It had no place here," Gill hazarded a guess. "It was something spawned in Clayborne's world, a thing of his imagination. This place is . . . somewhere else, where creatures like that don't exist."

As if to defy his logic, something came bounding in through the oval gash in the wall. Gill gave a massive start and drew air in a gasp—but Turnbull grabbed his arm and steadied him. "A dog," the big man told him. "Only a dog."

"Eh?" Gill still wasn't sure. Then he remembered the barking, scampering creature in Clayborne's world. "A dog? It came through with us from there?" The other nodded.

In a frenzy of joy, the animal jumped and frolicked around Angela's legs. It barked excitedly, wagged its stump of a tail madly, then left the girl and came snaking for Gill. He stooped to give it a tentative pat on the head and it got up on its hind legs, licking his face with a wet, feverish tongue. Then it got down again and backed off. Between bouts of barking it whined, skittered nervously, sidled this way and that. "He's finding us just as unbelievable as we find him!" said Gill.

He sat down on a pile of junk and fondled the

dog's ears, and it at once curled itself into his lap, whining for all it was worth. Angela said, "He has a collar."

She was right; there was an identity tag, too. "Barney," said Gill wonderingly. And the black and white mongrel barked and wagged his stump that much harder. "He lived in Lawers. . . ." Gill frowned. "That rings a bell."

"So it should." Anderson nodded. "The first man to report the presence of the Castle on Ben Lawers was one Hamish Grieve. He complained that the Castle had 'taken' his dog, called Barney!"

"And he's been here ever since?" Angela's voice was full of compassion. "In . . . in this place? Here, Barney," she called. "Here boy!"

"What about me?" Varre cried out. The junkyard cave was weighing on him and his claustrophobia was surfacing again. "Damn it, that's only a dog!" Turnbull had fixed the Frenchman's leg with a bandage torn from his shirt. He growled low in his throat as he tied the final knot, jerking it tight. "Ow!" the Frenchman protested.

"I'm really going off you, pal," said Turnbull warningly. "Only a dog? But he's stayed alive a couple of years longer than we're likely to last. We might be able to learn things from this dog—which means he's worth a sight more than you! Anyway, he's an Earth dog. Where I'm concerned that makes him next to human."

"Idiot!" Varre muttered.

"Can you walk?" Turnbull asked him sharply.

"I'm not sure."

"Well *get* sure, because I'm not going to carry

you and Bannerman both!" Turnbull was coming to the end of his tether.

Gill said, "Easy, Jack. We'll take turns with Bannerman. And we're all in the same boat, remember?"

Turnbull looked at him and the harsh lines in his face grew a little softer. "Yes, we are," he finally agreed, nodding. "But we're not all trying to sink the fucking thing!" Angela looked away and Turnbull rubbed his chin, shrugged. "I'm sorry," he said. "Polite conversation was never my forte, anyway. . . ."

Varre had got to his feet. He limped a little but seemed mobile enough. And he was eager to be out of this enclosed space. "Very well," he said to the others, "let's get out of here and see where we've landed. . . ."

CHAPTER THIRTY-TWO

"Where they had landed" was possibly the strangest of all worlds, and Gill knew what Angela had meant when she'd said—the *way* she'd said—that this wasn't Earth. A junkyard is one thing, but a planet-sized junkyard is quite another. Standing on the rusting iron rim of the broken wall and looking out on a skyline which would have been quite impossible and therefore totally unbelievable just a few days ago, still he knew exactly what he was looking at and felt the wrenching effect of several terrors combined. Later he might find himself compelled to acknowledge them, but for now:

"Well?" Angela said, breaking the silence of Gill's awe and astonishment, drawing his mind back from the precipitous brink of fear.

And in a little while he nodded, but his voice was still shaking when he answered, "I'm still not sure about your numerology thing, but you were certainly right the first time."

"The first time?" She failed to understand.

"What are you talking about, Spencer?" Anderson was still trying to be king of the castle—or Castle?

"She said maybe the last place was shaped by Clayborne because he was first through the door." Gill answered without turning his head, continuing to study the skyline. "It seems to me she was right. This time I was first through."

"What is it, Gill?" said Bannerman tremulously. "What can you see?"

It's more what I can feel, Gill thought; but out loud he answered, "I can see a machine world, most of it falling into decay. A world crammed full of machines, with nothing of grass or trees or anything so healthy as stone; no mountains except mountains of machine junk, and no streets except giant iron catwalks, and skyscraper gantries spanning everything like bridges to the end of the world. We're up high and the horizon's a long way off, but as far as I can see there's only metal and some plastic and dead machinery, and—" He paused for a moment for breath, focused his eyes on part of a nearby skyline, and in a quieter voice continued, "And some machinery that isn't dead!"

The others traced his line of sight and he felt Angela's fingers tighten on his arm. "Spencer," she whispered, "what is that ... thing?" It might be a crane on tracks, or a steam shovel, or a giant mechanical woodpecker—but Gill didn't answer because that was a part of the terror: the fact that he didn't know. It was his worst nightmare come true, to be surrounded by machines or machine parts and not understand the workings or principles or purpose of a single one of them—including *that* nodding monstrosity! That was part of it. And the rest of it was that this was—

"Your world, Spencer," said Turnbull, sighing, picking the thought right out of his head. "You were first through, and this place was shaped by your mind."

"By my fears," Gill corrected him.

"Your fears?" Varre was quick on the uptake. "There are things here to be afraid of? What are you saying, Gill? What do we need to be afraid of?"

"You?" Gill looked at him. "Nothing much, I suppose. No, you're lucky. This place is my nightmare, not yours. And I'm not like Clayborne, if that's what's bothering you."

"Your world! Clayborne's world!" Anderson threw up his hands. His voice was full of barely controlled anger, seething frustration, and more than a little fear. He looked back into the iron cave and licked his lips. "But where does it go when we come through? I mean, there was a crystal whose facets were doors. We came through one of them, but now the crystal's not there anymore. So . . . where is it?"

"One-way doors," Gill answered. "Like one-way mirrors: now you see 'em, now you don't."

"No"—Turnbull shook his head—"more like a quagmire. With quicksand there really is only one way to pass through. And you don't stop till your feet touch bottom. . . ."

Angela frowned at him and said, "That's morbid—and unscientific. We're agreed that none of this is supernatural, not even on Clayborne's world. It's in the mind, or it has come out of the mind. And it's all controlled by the House of Doors. The crystal was just another projection of it, another cross section through the same basic structure. It didn't disappear just because we came through. It's still there on Ben Lawers, and in the world of the escarpment it's the mansion, and in Clayborne's world it's an evil crystal. Here . . . it's out there somewhere." She stood beside Gill and gazed out upon a desolation of metal run wild, but mercifully run to a standstill. Most of it . . .

Gill felt the horror of the place, which the others were incapable of feeling. They felt only its strangeness, but to Gill it was undiluted horror. His brain collided with each new machine or piece of machinery and was unable to grasp it. It was the Castle all over again, but magnified a million times. The only mercy was that he had a safety valve, he could shut it off. He did so now: squeezed his eyes tightly shut and shook his head, and denied it.

No, he told himself. *No, it's not going to get me. I didn't build it—it's just an enlargement of my innermost fears. It's someone's deliberate ploy to drive me crazy: to put me in a world where my machine mind is surrounded by the unknown and completely unknowable! Except . . . it could be that same someone's big mistake.* Gill clung tight to that idea: that this could be his best chance yet to come to terms with and understand an alien science. Because if he could only get inside—get his mind inside—these weird machines, then maybe—just maybe—he could begin to make them work for him.

"Spencer? Are you all right?" It was Angela.

Gill opened his eyes, nodded. "Yes, I'll be all right. But ... what did you say just then? A cross section through the same basic structure? A projection?"

"I was talking about the House of Doors," she answered. "It's like a beam switched off the moment we use it, and redirected somewhere else. The lamp is still there, but pointing in another direction." She blinked, shook her pretty head, said, "Ignore me. I don't know what I'm trying to say."

"You make sense to me," Turnbull grunted. He was very bitter, sharing Anderson's and everyone else's frustration. "It's a false lighthouse built by wreckers, and like doomed ships we fall for it every time—and go crashing on the rocks."

"We're like rats in a maze," said Varre, "who smell food on the other side. But when we get there they change the maze around and put the food somewhere else."

Gill's patience was used up. Not only must he keep a tight rein on his own terrors but pacify these people as well. He was starting to feel smothered. "So what do you want to do?" He rounded on them. "Quit? So go ahead, quit!"

"We *can't* quit!" Anderson clenched a fist, shook it at nothing. "How *do* we quit, anyway? Lie down and die? You can't even die in a place where you don't need to eat! I can't see how this is happening to us—I don't even *believe* it's happening!"

"Oh, it's happening, all right," Gill told him. "Clayborne died, remember? And probably Haggie, too. You want to know how to do it?

Just throw yourself down there. That will do it."

They looked down through a tangle of girders to a wide iron catwalk far, far below. Anderson drew back at once. "It's just . . ." he started to say, "just that . . ."

"It's just a bastard." Turnbull finished it for him. "Like someone wanted to kill us, but didn't want to do it himself. As if he wants us to do it for him . . ."

They all thought about that—until Bannerman said, "Can someone please guide me? From Gill's description of this place I could very easily hurt myself. I'll be burden enough without that." For the moment his misery took their minds off their own.

More than that, it successfully steered them away from a potentially dangerous line of enquiry. . . .

They climbed down towards the nearest "roadway," a giant catwalk ninety feet wide and . . . how long? It stretched away in both directions, out of sight. The climb wasn't difficult; without Bannerman it would have been the simplest thing. There were great metal ladders, dangling cables, pipes and pylons everywhere. It was as if at the core of this world (*was* it a world? Or was it like this all the way through?) a giant robot factory had gone wild, churning out machines and machine parts until it had buried itself, and that it was still down there, its production lines unceasingly manufacturing meaningless machinery.

The spaces between great engines as big as city blocks were bridged by gantries; huge metal spiders with round, square and triangular "wheels" at the ends of their jointed legs abounded, all stiff and immobile; TVs the size of cinema screens were protected by metal grids, not all of which were dead. When Turnbull, in a mood of destructive defiance, picked up a huge iron bolt and hurled it at the centre of one such screen, there came a bright flash of electrical energy and the bolt was shattered and deflected. Blobs of metal splashed down and sizzled on iron surfaces, skittering like solder. After that they avoided all such grids.

Barney had already left them. As the climb had become steeper, the dog had gone off on his own along a safer, horizontal route. When he'd looked back, wagged his stump anxiously and barked for their attention, Angela had offered her opinion that: "He wants us to follow him."

Impatiently Varre had snapped, "Of course he does! He desires our companionship. Dogs are not good climbers. He knows he can't follow us and so wishes us to follow him." It was the last anyone would see of Barney for some considerable time.

Almost down to catwalk level, they found one of the giant screens that was still working—in a fashion. It showed a slow whirl of muddy colours, like dull paints stirred in a giant's caldron, interspersed with flashes of white light. And Anderson asked, "Who is it for?"

Gill looked at him. "What?"

"The picture, the screen, the information—if there was information and not just that sickening . . . static? Who would it be for? I don't feel that there are people here—"

"There aren't," said Gill, with certainty.

"—so who needs TV screens?"

"But that's the whole point," said Gill. "From what I've seen, I'd say that there's no rhyme or reason to any of this. It's my biggest nightmare come true: a million mad machines, an entire worldful of them, and not one of them serving any recognisable purpose. They don't *have* a purpose—unless it's to drive me crazy—which is why I'm trying to ignore every damned one of them!"

"Listen!" said Angela.

They had climbed down through a vast tangle of partly collapsed scaffolding to rest for a while on a sheet-iron platform some forty or fifty feet over the road. A nervous silence fell as they followed Angela's instructions and listened. But after a little while Anderson shook his head impatiently and said, "I hear nothing."

"Try feeling it, then," said Gill. "It's in the metal, coming up through the platform, the soles of your feet."

And now indeed they could feel it: a dull, distant, metallic thumping, like the beat of some unseen mechanical heart; and in another moment they began to hear it. "It's coming from the road," said Turnbull. "Like the sound of a train transmitted along a track."

"Look down there," said Gill, pointing at the tremendous catwalk below. "There are tracks—two sets of them. So now it appears that there are things in this bloody place I can understand after all! But now I have to ask myself, what runs on tracks like those?"

Twin, parallel sets of steel rails each a foot wide, with a gage of at least forty feet, were bolted to massive iron sleepers along the full length of the road. Bright, fat metal ribbons, they narrowed into the distance in both directions and disappeared down canyons of colossal, corroded components. Turnbull observed, "Everything else down there except the tracks is covered in rust, swarf or oil. So whatever it is, something does run on those tracks."

"And . . . and here it comes!" said Varre. Gaunt-faced, he pointed at the mouth of the nearer canyon.

Gill strained his eyes, shook his head in bewilderment, finally said, "It's like . . . like nothing I ever saw before. Just a huge metal box on wheels, not going anywhere very fast and making a hell of a lot of noise about it."

"A *spiky* iron box on wheels," Turnbull corrected him. "It has bits of junk sticking out all over it. Arms, hooks, grapples." He, too, shook his head. "What the hell is the thing?"

"Listen," said Gill resignedly. "Get used to one thing: it's no good asking me what anything is. For the last time, they don't have any real purpose. I don't see how they could have, seeing as they're my bloody fantasy!"

"That's as may be," said Varre, "but your 'fantasy' is on our side of the tracks. It will pass directly beneath us."

"Hadn't we better get down from here?" Anderson was hopping from one foot to the other again, scared for his life. His breath came in explosive gasps. "Even at this distance that thing is . . . huge! The noise it's making is hellish. Why, we could be shaken right off this platform!"

Gill and Turnbull got down on their stomachs and looked over the platform's edge. The structure was supported by a square iron stem at one corner. It might just be possible to climb or slide down it, but even if there was time Angela was going to find it very difficult and Bannerman simply wasn't going to make it. "We'll have to climb back up a ways," said Turnbull. "A little way, anyway—until we spot an alternative route down."

But the gigantic mechanism on the rails was closer now, and its clanging that much louder. Gong-*bang*! Gong-*bang*! Gong-*bang*! It made it hard to think.

Nearby, something suspiciously like a crane on a gantry came suddenly to life. It trundled along its own tracks and swung a huge iron dinosaur-head bucket with steel jaws directly at the tower and platform. Gill and Turnbull were on their feet again, but as Angela yelled, "Get down!" they grabbed Bannerman and joined the others on the deck, where they clung for dear life to projecting bolt heads. At the last moment the crane lifted its head and came jarringly to a halt, leaving the jaws creaking and swinging like a rusty pendulum directly overhead.

"Shit!" Turnbull shouted. "Now I know what we're standing on. It's a fuelling platform!"

Gill knew that he was right. It was obvious. So obvious that he'd missed it—because he'd believed there was nothing here that he could grasp.

Gong-BANG! Gong-BANG! The thing on the tracks was passing beneath the shuddering platform; the jaws of the crane dipped lower; Gill thought: *It's going to tip its load right on our heads, and we're going to end up as so much fuel!*

He looked up, saw the grinning steel jaws crack open, and closed his eyes. . . .

CHAPTER THIRTY-THREE

Nothing came out of the jaws except dust and grit and a powdering of iron filings. The machine had been working, but it had nothing to deliver. Silently, Gill began to thank someone or other—probably God—but his thanks were premature. The jaws extended to a gape and lowered themselves to press down on the platform's iron surface. For a moment Gill and the others were enclosed by huge blunt metal teeth.

Meanwhile, clanking and snorting, the—engine?—on the tracks had come to a halt. In the top center of its box body was a shallow hopper, waiting to be filled. The jaws pressed down harder yet on the platform, which cracked open in the middle. It was hinged, spring-loaded. "Hang on!" Gill yelled as the weight of the jaws forced the trapdoor open. But . . . there was nothing to hang on to, except each other.

They fell through in a tangle of gasping, flailing bodies, and crashed down into the engine's hopper. The huge metal plate where they landed was also a trapdoor; for a moment it gave an inch or two under their combined weight, then held. They weren't quite as heavy as a load of fuel. Below them, in the body of the thing, they could hear a grinding and a hissing, a frustrated meshing of unthinkable machine parts.

Then the engine gave three short, shrill hoots, and recommenced its journey along the great track. The racket it created as it proceeded was brain-shattering: Gong-*bang*! Gong-*bang*! Gong-*bang*!

Turnbull was first on his feet. Groaning, he staggered to the rim of the hopper and looked over. There was a sort of shallow perimeter moat some fifteen inches deep. He dipped a finger in a residual coating of black sludge and sniffed it. It smelled like fish oil. He rubbed it on the sleeve of his torn jacket and waited; it left a stain but that was all. So it wasn't corrosive.

The others joined him one by one, Bannerman and Varre crawling. Gill and Angela were last, lifting and guiding Bannerman as they came. All were bruised and battered. Turnbull had meanwhile hauled himself up into the gutter or moat. He flopped there with his head on the rim, weary to the bone. The others got up with him, dragging Bannerman and Varre behind them. And eventually the monotony of the engine's dinning took away a little of its own pain, until it became a "background" clamour against which they could begin to hear themselves think again, and even to speak.

"Follow the, follow the, follow the, follow the, follow the shining steel ribbons," sang Turnbull tunelessly, his voice dripping with inward-directed sarcasm.

Gill looked at him. *The Wizard of Oz?*

Turnbull nodded grimly. "Except that this time the wizard and witch are one and the same, and the bastard's got us exactly where he wants us. *And* we don't know where that is!"

"And no Emerald City waiting for us," said Angela. "Just another House of Doors."

"If we're headed in the right direction," said Anderson, with none of his usual authoritative ebullience.

"Oh, we are," said Gill, nodding. "We always have, haven't we? The way I see it, it's out of our hands." They began to look around as the machine world slipped by.

They passed into a canyon of gigantic cog-wheels and pistons, rusting ratchets, scabbed girder scaffolding, whose walls towered up on both sides like cliffs of condemned, corroding, incomprehensible clockwork. And Anderson was prompted to ask, "Spencer, is this what you meant when you said we were inside a machine?"

"No." Gill shook his head. "We're still inside *that* machine. This entire machine world is inside *that* machine. But everything you see here is commonplace by comparison. This junk came out of me." He tapped his skull with a tired finger.

Turnbull gave a snort. "You mean this stuff isn't alien?"

Gill stroked the furrows out of his brow, left sludge in the shape of a hand upon his forehead. "Weird but not alien," he answered. "It's like those machines that bothered me so much when I was a kid: Heath-Robinson things that couldn't possibly work, or worked to no end. Illogical perpetual motion machines that don't do anything. Mechanical mobiles that turn endlessly and without purpose. Idiot things. Executive toys that click and whir and do sweet—"

"Nothing," Angela interrupted.

"That too." Gill nodded ruefully.

"You were about to say 'fuck all,'" said Angela, quite matter-of-factly. "I don't know why I stopped you, except that I hoped you hadn't given up hope yet. I'll know that you have when you . . . well, when you let things go."

"Can you come over here?" said Gill.

She crawled to him through the fish-smelling oil and he wiped grit and dirt from her face, then kissed her soundly. In her shredded, dirty ski pants, greasy, knotted shirt, and completely incongruous very feminine bra, she looked like some demonic urchin—but he kissed her anyway. And she responded fiercely. "Don't let me let go," he said, when their mouths at last parted.

"Is this really the time for . . . canoodling?" Varre was tenderly examining his torn, puffy thigh.

"You lick your wounds," said Gill, but without malice, "and we'll canoodle. Time moves far too quickly in this place. Right now we're taking a break . . . from everything!"

The engine shuddered and clanked and gong-banged on its way; Turnbull sat with Bannerman and patiently explained what was happening; miles slipped inexorably by; they

came out of the canyon into rust-scabbed sub-
urbs of ferro-degenerable debris. . . .

Gill had been dozing. Angela shook him insistently. He opened his eyes and looked around.
The others lolled and nodded, sleeping where it
was almost humanly impossible to sleep. "Look
at the sun!" said Angela. Gill did—and understood the look on her face.

In front the tracks stretched interminably on,
shining into the sunset; behind, on the horizon,
a spiky metal mound glowed red and silver; on
both sides stretched dunes of red rust, with
here and there girders protruding like broken
teeth from bleeding, rotten gums. And sinking
towards the horizon at ten o'clock of where they
were heading, the "sun" put the whole mad
scene in perspective where it covered the land
with its warmth and light. Its entirely unnatural warmth and light.

For it was no "sun" that Gill had ever imagined—and yet it must be, for it was "his" sun.
Twice or three times as large as Earth's sun, it
hung there in the sky and defied acceptance. It
was a giant, silver ball-bearing a million miles
across, peppered with blow holes which blasted
out spokes of fire and light and radiation—a
never-ending chain reaction of nuclear energy—a *machine* sun set centrally in a machine
system of worlds!

Gill looked away, shook his head, refused to
consider it; but in the next moment he narrowed his eyes as they lighted upon a lesser,
more acceptable wonder. Coming towards
them, but on the other track, gong-banged a duplicate of the great engine whose back they

were riding. Gill woke up the others with a warning: "Don't ask me about the sun, for I don't know. But here comes another Heath-Robinson mobile."

A mile away, the thing stopped. A twisted tower of metal lay collapsed on the track directly in front of it. Appendages at once commenced to work: great piston-driven arms that shoved and jostled, pincer claws tugging and lifting, a giant sledgehammer fist that hammered and battered. Finally the obstruction was broken up; and their own engine gong-banged its way towards the other, rapidly narrowing the distance between.

But now the second engine began carefully piling the twisted rubble of its success onto the other track, in the way of its passenger-carrying colleague! It made an untidy pyramid of the stuff, then came gong-banging on. As the two engines passed each other by, so they toot-toot-tooted derisively.

"That's better!" said Gill. The others looked at him. He nodded. "It makes no sense, what that machine just did. If it had made sense, something would be wrong. Heath-Robinson, remember?"

They had reached the rubble-piled section of track; their engine came to a halt, began piling the wreckage back where it had been; it finished the job and stood as if appraising its handiwork, then thrust a pincer deep into the rust on one side of the tracks and drew out a huge iron girder, which it rammed haphazardly into the stack like a stanchion.

"That'll teach him!" said Turnbull, almost hysterically.

And then they were off again: Gong-*bang*! Gong-*bang*! Gong-*bang*!

An hour later and the atomic sun was that much closer to the horizon. The tracks beelined along an elevated gantry over a desert of rust dunes, where the shadows were growing longer by the minute. For the past half hour the engine's human cargo had seen nothing of note: no collapsed towers or twisted girders, no burnt-out boilers scabbing their way to oblivion, no metal parts at all except the gantry and interminable tracks stretching fore and aft. And upon all sides wave upon wave of red rust, sifted as fine as sand.

Then, on the horizon up ahead, three dark nodules or knolls became apparent, seeming to grow up from the rust desert as the engine gong-banged towards them. Because they were the only irregularities in an otherwise monotonous vista, Gill and the others took special interest in them, watching them enlarge and expand as the distance narrowed down. They were gigantic, oddly shaped, spired like mountains or castles painted by an artist of the fantastic, with nothing regular or mechanical about them at all. In short, while they did not appear to be junk as such, neither were they of a mechanical construction. On the other hand, nor were they *man*ufactured. Natural? It seemed unlikely, in this most unnatural of places.

The track-runner gong-banged a little slower now; it put up a tall, telescopic periscope from its flank and surveyed the—land?—around. There came a thick, glutinous gurgling from the rear of the moat, and Gill crawled over to that section to take a look. The moat was deeper here, where the bottom sloped off into a massive funnel welded onto the rear of the engine. Gill wrinkled his nose; the funnel was full of the fish-smelling oil.

Oil began to spray from a system of sprinklers down by the wheels, a fine stinking mist of the stuff that clung to rails and gantry, permeated and darkened the rust from ten to fifteen feet outwards from the desert-bordered rim of the track.

Turnbull joined Gill, suggesting, "Protection from the rust?"

Gill looked at him and frowned. "That would be the obvious answer," he said. "The logical answer . . ."

"Spencer!" Angela's voice calling over the racket of the track-runner held a note that trembled a little, and Gill thought: *Oh, yes—too logical by far!* He looked where she was pointing.

Out in the desert to the left of the tracks, maybe fifty yards away, something was *creating* a new dune! Red rust was being thrust aloft in a straight line that kept pace with the engine, building a long, shuddering barrow of the stuff like a mole run in a country garden. Turnbull, checking the other side of the tracks, said, "Oh-oh—flanked! We have an escort."

More runs appeared even as they watched, parallel lines of rust forming themselves as if by some weird seismic force just beneath the surface. The one on the left suddenly changed course, came angling in towards the tracks. Then it hit the oil-soaked belt and hastily veered away again, keeping a respectful distance. "Things that burrow through loose rust at fifteen to twenty miles an hour," said Gill, "against which these tracks and engines are self-protected by use of this stinking oil."

"Creatures?" Turnbull was tense. "Animals?"

"I get on with machines." Gill was as thoughtful as a man could be under the dinning of the engine. "I used to, anyway. Machines are the tools that lifted man up from ignorance. I'd hate to see machines threatened. This is my nightmare. In this world they're not only being threatened but devoured, turned to rust. All of them. This rust desert is encroaching on the machine cities, with only the tracks and engines left to link them together across endless graveyards of long-dead metal."

"Iron to filings," said Turnbull, "rust to rust, amen. What are you getting at?"

"I'm not sure." Gill shook his head. "But it's just dawned on me that this bugger"—he rapped his knuckles against the metal wall of the moat—"must be rapidly running out of fuel!" The gaps between each gong-*bang*! were definitely lengthening.

"*My God!*" Anderson cried his alarm. One hundred yards out, rust erupted volcanically— scabs and flakes and tons of grains of the stuff hurled aloft—as one of the fantastic burrowers thrust up its snout and emerged. . . .

CHAPTER THIRTY-FOUR

The thing was a telescopic worm of dull grey metal eighty feet long and five feet thick. Its upper head was flat, spadelike, with eyes like auto-inspection lamps behind protective grilles. Under the eyes a tapering snout, and beneath that a huge mouth like that of a basking shark, gaping and scoop-shaped. Inside the scoop bright flashes of sputtering purple energy made a curtain of "teeth" between the upper and lower jaws.

"Metal-eater!" Gill breathed.

"Eh?" Turnbull's enquiry was more an exclamation, a gasp of amazement. But then what Gill had said got through to him. "How do you know?"

I don't know how I know! Gill thought, his skin prickling. *But I do.* It was as if something had suddenly slotted itself together in his mind, a piece of the Big Jigsaw falling neatly into place. He "knew," for example, that this was a new order of machine. It was of his mind, yes, but at the same time it was alien. He *and* the House of Doors had built it. This time it wasn't just Heath-Robinson but more truly alien. It was of that same generation, that same origin, as the Castle, the silver rod weapon, and the thing that had hunted Haggie. But Gill had "made" at least part of it, and therefore he could understand it—almost. Certainly he knew what it was: a metal-eater.

Gill stared in fascination at the thing where it reared up and swayed as tall as the gantry, its head moving this way and that like a cobra's head. He tried to get inside it, understand it, divine something of its workings. It was seamless and yet its telescopic segments were flexible; it *was* a machine, but it "thought" like an animal and probably—no, unquestionably—reproduced its own kind. Gill *knew* these things were, but he didn't know how they were.

He looked at it and felt its parts flowing like mercury, yet solid as steel. The answer was close. It was the difference between fractions and decimals. One-third may be expressed as ⅓ and as such it is a complete concept; but as a decimal it's .3333333 and so on forever. So that no one can ever *really* visualize one-third as a decimal because no one can picture or ever have the time to picture a line of threes marching to infinity. Gill knew all the fractions. All he had to do now was convert them to decimals and the problem would cease to be. He would know how the House of Doors and its machinery worked, which would be half the battle.

"Nests!" Turnbull gasped, destroying Gill's concentration and drawing him back to the present. "Christ, look!"

The nearest knoll was now little more than a mile away. The machine sun was setting between its lumpy spires and those of its closest neighbour. A little way beyond both of them, the third anthill was a dark blot, reduced by the sun to a silhouette with one scintillant-gleaming edge.

Rust worms came and went around the bases of the two closest, half-mile-high stacks, so that they seemed enveloped in dust storms. And for all that the strange termite towers reared tall and precipitous, still they were holed and tunnelled to their topmost spires like giant wedges of Gorgonzola cheese. Worms were active on the outside as well as the insides of their nests, to-ing and fro-ing between the myriad circular holes like bees in a honeycomb.

"Hives," Gill corrected Turnbull. "Rust-worm hives."

The tracks had now split up, the one snaking to the right and theirs to the left, carrying the labouring engine around the hives in what could be the beginning of a wide circle. Rust-worms accompanied the track-runner for a little of the way, then slowed and gradually fell behind. When none of them remained to be seen on the ground, the periscope folded itself away and the gurgling in the oil sluice stopped; funnel and sump were seen to be half-empty. Gill and Turnbull rejoined the others, who had come to their own, similar conclusions.

Anderson said, "Are we to take it that this engine 'knows' when these damned things are about?" The track-runner seemed too rustic to him, too far removed from his idea of a computer, to have any "intelligence" of its own.

"It has its periscope," said Gill, shrugging. "It must be programmed to spray when the worms are on the go. Maybe that's the purpose of the tracks and engines in a nutshell: to encircle the worms and confine them to their stacks, stop them from spreading."

"Wrong," said Varre. "Those metal beasts were on both sides of the tracks, inside and outside your circle—if it is a circle. And anyway, wouldn't that explanation be just too logcial, too easily understood?"

Gill shook his head. "The difference between logic and lunacy is instinct," he said. "And it's also where they meet—in all worlds. Does a madman stop breathing just because he's mad? No, because breathing is automatic, instinctive. It's a question of survival. In order to survive, the machines must keep the worms caged. Except now they seem to have broken out. Or . . . maybe I *am* wrong!" He shrugged again.

"You're not wrong," said Turnbull, too quietly. "Look up ahead there."

They looked. Half a mile in front, close to the third hive, the gutted remains of an engine lay toppled on its side, half-buried in rust. The worms had piled up rust on the inside of the circle until the wall was higher than the gantry. Then, when the track-runner had come along, they must have avalanched the stuff down onto the gantry, wrecking it and throwing the engine off the track. There was still a large party of worms in attendance, dismantling the crippled machine and making off with claws, pistons, hammers, iron plates, and other unidentifiable bits and pieces. Then one of them reared up and spotted the new prize where it came gong-banging to its doom. And as if someone had fired a starting pistol, the things came burrowing at the double.

"Why doesn't this crazy bastard back up, then?" Turnbull urgently demanded of no one in particular. "I mean, if survival's the driving force, this bloke's not much of a driver!"

Gill thought that the question, like an accusation, had been aimed at him. "Christ, I don't *know*!" he said. "But right now if I were you I'd worry about your own survival."

Gong . . . *bang*! Gong . . . *bang*! Gong . . .

The track-runner gave a last gasp and clanked to a halt. Deep down inside, strange gears clashed and clattered; iron guts grated and groaned, crying out desperately for fuel to convert into energy and receiving none; there commenced a trapped, hysterical, mechanical screaming.

"She's going to blow!" Gill cried, drowning in a sudden wave of empathy. He felt entirely helpless, forced himself to surface, fought to maintain a measure of control. His Adam's apple bobbed as he gulped, "Here's where we have to get off!"

"Get off? You're crazy!" Anderson floundered about in the fish-oil moat.

"Over here!" Turnbull called to them. He'd hauled himself slitheringly around the moat's perimeter to the right-hand side of the hopper, was looking over the rim. As they made to join him he stood up, shouted, "Here goes nothing!"—and jumped.

On that side the rust-worms had been busy; they'd piled up rust in a great wave, presumably to use in the same way they'd used it up ahead. The drop was about thirty feet; Turnbull had thrown himself far out, landed just beyond the crest, gone tumbling in a rust storm down the other side of the wave. "It's fine as flour!" he yelled, spitting the stuff out where he sprawled.

They jumped. Gill saw the other men and Angela on their way, and watched with his heart in his mouth until the girl had landed safely, then spoke to Bannerman. "Jump for all you're worth," he said. "Jump forward, not down. Gravity will do the rest."

Amazingly, Bannerman did as instructed, and as he leaped Gill gave him a massive shove in the back. By then the track-runner was shuddering convulsively as its engine continued to pound itself to pieces. Gill jumped, and as his feet left the rim of the hopper he looked far out across the rust desert and saw the third hive clearly illumined in flashing rays from the setting sun—saw it, briefly, as something other than a silhouette—saw, in fact, that it wasn't a hive.

He landed—flew head over heels down the powdery rust slope—rolled to a standstill close to the others. By some miracle of good fortune, no one had been hurt. And in the same moment that Turnbull hauled Gill to his feet, but on the other side of the worm-piled dune, the track-runner blew. A terrific explosion hurled metallic debris into the sky in a sheet of fire, black smoke and a spray of foul oil. But the blast had been contained by the wall of rust, and most of the shrapnel rained to earth on the other side.

"What now?" Turnbull yelled, over secondary rumblings and explosions.

"That way," said Gill, pointing. "Let's get away from here, and quickly!"

Almost knee-deep in powdered rust, they climbed a dune. Near its crest, Varre came to a halt and gasped, "But surely we're heading in the direction of the third hive. Shouldn't we go back across the tracks and move *away* from the—" He paused as he climbed one more step and his head came up over the top of the dune. Gill stood there, pointing. And now Varre's jaw fell open.

Turned red as a scene from hell by swirling rust and the atomic sun's lancing rays, the third hive was roughly the same size and shape as the others, but its purpose was entirely different. Steep ramps of solid red rust fanned out like spokes from its more or less circular base, and at the top of each ramp, set back in arched-over, cavernous recesses—

"Doors!" said Angela.

A whole houseful, Gill silently agreed with a nod of his head. And taking her hand, he plunged with her down the far side of the dune.

After that . . . in a muscle-wrenching, maddeningly slow-motion march—floundering in the soft rust like beetles in a sand pit—the group made its weary way across the doomed-metal desert towards the House of Doors. . . .

Finally, exhausted, they arrived at the foot of the nearest ramp. From behind, throughout their gruelling trek across the rust dunes, savage rending sounds had carried to them in the red twilight: sounds of ruptured iron and dismembered steel. But so far the worms had not bothered with them. They'd seen runs snaking under the dunes and the occasional flurry of rust as a worm's back broke the surface, but that was all—until now.

Almost on the ramp, suddenly a pile of rust erupted to one side of them not fifty feet away, and a monstrous flat head emerged, basket jaws fully extended. The worm fixed them with its headlamp eyes and snaked closer. Its head reared and commenced to sway from side to side. The movement became more rapid, a threatening vibration, a bunching of metallic muscles. In the gaping mouth, rods of electrical fire made a brilliant blue and white mesh where "teeth" of energy crackled between electrode jaws.

"Freeze!" Gill croaked. "It thinks we're machines. We have to be because we're moving. So freeze . . ."

Everyone froze—for a little while. But as the great head swayed closer and its vibrations became a blur, so Anderson cracked. "Not me! Not me!" he cried. He broke and ran—or staggered—up the ramp. The worm snaked after him along the base of the ramp, its head reaching up to his level; he stumbled and fell; the thing's scoop mouth took him—and spat him out! Screaming, he bounced on the ramp and lay still.

The worm reared back; Gill took a chance and ran up the ramp towards Anderson, waving his arms and yelling hoarsely at the metal monstrosity. The worm backed off more yet, seemed confused, undecided. Suddenly it made a dive down into the rust and started a run which disappeared under the nearest dune. As quickly as that it was over.

"The fish oil," said Gill. "Worm repellent. We've got the stinking stuff all over us—thank God!"

They picked up Anderson under his arms and dragged him without ceremony up the ramp and into the cave at its top. There were scorch marks on his tattered clothing, and his face and hands were crisscrossed with a fine mesh of burns, as if he'd run into a section of white-hot chicken wire. But apart from that he was breathing and seemed to have suffered no serious injury.

Now, in the rusty red gloom of the cave, Anderson was temporarily forgotten as finally they looked upon a door of grey slag five feet in diameter and round as a plug in a hole. There was no knocker and no number, just the door itself set in a wall of compressed, congealed rust.

"Is this ... ?" said Varre uncertainly. "It doesn't look ... I mean, is it really ... ?"

"A door like all the others?" Gill finished it for him. "Yes, it is." He could feel that it was; he *knew* it was. "Not exactly like the others, no. They've all been different, anyway. But this is the House of Doors, all right. And this *is* a door."

Angela stepped forward. In a voice that was tiny, which yet echoed, she said, "My turn, I think."

"Wait," said Gill, taking her arm. "I think it is your turn, yes—but first you'd better tell us if there's anything we should worry about. I mean, we know how this game is played now. So it's only fair that we should know if there's anything you're desperately afraid of."

She turned her face away. "It's nothing for you to be afraid of, anyway," she said. "I don't think it's something men really worry about."

"Can we be the judge of that?" Varre snapped harshly. "Are we supposed to coax it out of you? Come on, girl, speak up."

"Violation!" She rounded on him and spat it out. "My husband was . . . he was a pig!" She turned to Gill. "Spencer, I—"

"We understand," he said simply. "And for what it's worth, I'll go down before I see that happen to you again."

Bannerman stumbled, came blundering forward. "What's going on?" he said. "Won't someone tell me what's happening?" He stumbled again, flew forward.

"Be careful!" Gill cried, but too late. He and Turnbull were supporting Anderson, were unable to move fast enough to stop it from happening. Bannerman had already crashed into the slight figure of Varre, hurling the Frenchman against the door!

Behind the group the roof of the cave crashed down in massive chunks, completely blocking the entrance. And ahead of them—

—The circular slab of fused slag simply disappeared, and a Stygian darkness fell on them like the Primal Dark before there was ever light. . . .

CHAPTER THIRTY-FIVE

"Gill?" Turnbull's voice echoed rumblingly in a darkness that was absolute. "Where in the name of all that's . . . ?"

"Anderson's lighter." Gill breathlessly ignored the other's half-formed question. "Hold him up while I find it." Angela's trembling hand was on Gill's arm as he frantically searched Anderson's pockets and found what he was looking for. And Varre was utterly silent apart from his rapid, frightened panting.

But at last the Frenchman found voice. "I . . . I came through first!" he whispered. "*Mon Dieu*—I was the first!"

But for the moment Gill wasn't worried about any of them; or if he was worried at all, it was about Bannerman. Back in the machine world Gill's sixth sense had been more or less useless—had been drowned out in meaningless, alien machine static—but here it was working properly, and even in the dark he knew that one of the group was other than human. His first instinct had been correct: Bannerman was *part*-human, part-alien mechanism, and possibly part something else. And Gill and the others were in the dark, in close proximity with him.

Fingers all thumbs, Gill worked the lighter.

Light flared and thrust back the wall of darkness. Controlling himself, presenting a comparatively calm front, Gill looked first at Bannerman. The—blind?—man was slumped against a seamless stone wall, a tightly curving wall that formed a perfect circle up the line of his back, overhead, down, and underfoot. They were crouched in a tube of stone only five feet in diameter—a tunnel through solid rock

"*Jesus!*" Varre screamed then, and threw himself to the floor. "No! No! *Noooooo!*" He pounded with his fists on the solid stone floor, and his terrified cries came echoing deafeningly back—and again—and again.

"His phobia." Turnbull was aghast, understanding only too well where they were: underground, trapped in a claustrophobic hell of the Frenchman's own making.

"What's going on?" Bannerman asked, his voice hushed and gasping. "What is it?"

He's still playing his little game. Gill was relieved. Relieved and furious—but for now he'd go along with it. "We'll put you in the picture when we get sorted out," he told the supposedly "blind" man.

"Sorted out?" Varre sat up. In the flickering light of Anderson's cigarette lighter his eyes were staring, starting orbs. "But we can't *get* sorted out, Gill—not ever! Don't you know where we are? We're under a million tons of rock! We're buried alive, man, buried al—" He couldn't go on, burst out sobbing.

Gill passed the lighter to Turnbull, got down on one knee beside Varre. Unseen, he took out the thorn hypodermic and used it to sting the little Frenchman in the arm . . . and in the next moment gentled him down onto his back on the curving stone floor. "Better this way," he said, looking up at the others. "This place is bad enough as it is, without him making it any worse. We know what Clayborne conjured up in his world, also that it killed him and might have killed us. I'd prefer *not* to have Varre do the same sort of thing."

Crouching and holding the lighter out before him at arm's length, Turnbull had meanwhile turned in a full circle, illuminating their immediate surroundings. Behind them, where they'd entered the cave and seen the roof come crashing down, now there was nothing, no rubble at all. The tunnel finished there in a smooth wall of stone. It was as if a rock borer had come this far and then been withdrawn along its own bore. In the other direction . . . the tunnel disappeared into darkness.

"Not much of a choice," Angela whispered.

Gill thought: *God, she's got guts, this one!* For her sake, if only for her sake, he mustn't show what he was really feeling. "Jack," he said, "can you sling Anderson over your shoulder? And Jon, I'm going to ask you to do your part, too, okay?" It seemed a good idea to bring him into things, keep him busy.

"Anything, anything," said Bannerman at once. "Glad to be able to help."

"No—*uh!*—need for that," said Anderson as Turnbull passed the lighter back to Gill and made to pick him up. "I can—*uh!*—manage very well, thank you." With Turnbull's help he got to his feet and propped himself against the wall for a moment or two.

Another remarkable recovery! Gill thought; and he asked, "Are you all right?"

"My face and hands feel . . . burned?" Anderson gingerly examined his hands, touched them to his face. Turnbull quickly explained what had happened with the rust worm, and how they now came to be where they were. "My own fault entirely," said Anderson. "I should have heeded you, Spencer. I'm lucky to be alive."

"Varre probably wouldn't agree with you there," said Gill. "But I reckon we'll still let Jon here do his share of the work. He's a strong man after all. And the rest of us have been having a pretty rough time of it." As he spoke he looked at Turnbull and narrowed his eyes a little, briefly, warningly. The big man made no comment.

"You see, Jon," Gill continued, "in this place there's nothing for you to fall over. We're in a horizontal tube drilled through solid rock. You can't very easily stumble, and you can't head off in the wrong direction. There is only one direction. Okay?"

"Anything you say." Bannerman was still willing. "It will be a relief to be of some use to you."

And so they started off. Anderson, having repossessed his lighter, took the lead; Gill and Angela followed immediately behind; Turnbull was next, and Bannerman last of all, holding on to Turnbull's jacket and with Varre tossed over one shoulder.

They had covered only fifty to sixty paces when Anderson said, "Up ahead. Is that . . . natural light?" He cupped his hand over the lighter's lifesaving flame. And maybe thirty or forty paces ahead there was indeed light: a pale haze of yellow, looking like dusty sunlight slanting into the mouth of a cave.

Eagerly they moved on, their footsteps echoing, and after a few more paces Anderson was able to snap shut his lighter and so conserve its fuel. The yellow light brightened rapidly as the bore carried them to its source—which was not what they'd hoped for.

Anderson came to what looked like the end of the shaft, paused, leaned out into the soft haze and looked around. "What . . . ?" he said then, simply and quietly. But it was more a puzzled exclamation than any sort of question. He stepped down maybe twelve inches onto the flat stone floor of a domed hemisphere of a chamber, paced falteringly forward a little way, then came to a halt and shielded his eyes to look straight up at the source of the light. And this time when he spoke it was definitely an exclamation—of total disappointment and frustration. "*What!*"

Angela and the others joined him, but Gill hung back and just a little to one side in order to observe Bannerman emerge from the tunnel. Caught up in the suspense of the moment, no one had thought to say anything to the blind man by way of warning, but still he stepped down unerringly into the chamber without a moment's pause or thought. And:

Got you! thought Gill. But now wasn't the right time for any big exposé or showdown. That would have to wait.

Turnbull, slowly turning on his own axis, took in the layout of the place and said, "Spencer, what do you make of it?"

Anderson at once bridled. The impression was that all authority had now passed to Gill, indeed that it had been that way for some time! But he would see about *that*! "Why, obviously it's a junction of tunnels," he said. "I mean, really, Jack—does it need an explanation?"

Turnbull scowled at him. "Anderson, you're not often right but you're probably wrong again," he said, without humour. "Spencer, on the other hand, is more often right than wrong, which is why I'm asking him."

Gill looked around, said, "Can someone mark that tunnel we just emerged from? Pointless to make a stupid mistake and end up going back in there!"

Angela stepped back to the mouth of the first tunnel, licked her finger and put an X on the wall to one side of the circular bore. The mark was cut very clearly into the dust. "Which leaves us with four more to choose from," she said. "Or five—except the fifth one is impossible."

The fifth was straight up, perpendicular, the source of the light. Squinting his eyes, Gill could just see its rim shining on high, like the rim of a well, maybe fifty feet overhead. And she was quite right: five feet wide, the shaft was too big for a man to jam himself inside and climb. Also, the domed ceiling's centre where the shaft was situated was at least fifteen feet high. The other four tunnels were exactly the same as the first one, horizontal, disappearing into darkness.

"The way I see it," said Gill, "we're in a maze. But it seems to me there has to be a way out—or the game finishes right here. If we're to proceed to the next House of Doors, then there *has* to be a way out."

"Why a maze?" Angela wanted to know.

Gill shrugged, pointed at the slumped figure of Varre where Bannerman had put him down. "I reckon that's his doing. His claustrophobia on the one hand, complicated by this entire situation. Earlier he said we were like starving rats in a maze, and every time we get to the food they put it somewhere else and change the system. Obviously the idea stayed with him, manifested itself here. This is Varre's big nightmare. Anyway, we're wasting time. We should be figuring out what to do next."

Angela said, "We don't yet have enough experience of this place to try using any sort of logic or perhaps develop a geometrical system. Which I suppose leaves guesswork. Trial and error. Since we're all in the dark, as it were, I suggest we let Jon pick our route. Light or dark, it's all the same to him." She touched Bannerman's arm. "I didn't mean that to sound uncaring."

But Gill shook his head. "I think we can do better than that," he said. "Jon stays here with Varre. Jack and I, we take a tunnel and explore it—*only* for a hundred yards or to the next junction, whichever comes first. Angela, you and David take another tunnel and do likewise: one hundred paces, or the next junction, and then back here. Okay?"

Turnbull nodded. "That makes sense," he said. "And that way we might get a better idea of the layout of this place."

"I'd like to think so," said Gill. "And even if we don't, we can use the same method to try out the last two tunnels. Finally, if nothing at all comes of it, *then* we can take Angela's suggestion and let Jon choose our route. Who's to say a blind man's instincts aren't the best anyway?" *And if he intends to continue the game, then he'll have to lead us out of here....*

They split up, marked their new tunnels with a *Y* and a *Z*, and proceeded as planned. Gill and Turnbull had no light, but now that their eyes were more accustomed they found that the darkness wasn't absolute after all. A very little light from the vertical shafts was filtering its way into even this darkest of places.

About a hundred yards down their chosen tunnel, they came to a domed chamber identical to the first. Turnbull marked their exit with an *X2* and was about to reenter and return along it when Gill stopped him. "What is it?" Turnbull asked.

"It's Bannerman," Gill answered in a whisper, a finger to his lips. "We were right first time. The machine world kicked my senses out of play for a while, but as soon as we came through into this place I picked him up again. He isn't human."

"What? But he's blind! I mean, why would he—"

"*Shhh!*" Gill warned. "Not only is he fully sighted, he isn't deaf either!"

"But you've seen his eyes; they—"

"You're still thinking human." Gill cut him off.

Turnbull thought about it. "Supposing you're right, what do we do about it?"

"We go back, offer him the chance to lead us out of here. Certainly we can't afford to confront him here. If he wants to carry the game on, to whatever end, then he'll be obliged to see us safely through this—at least as far as the next stage of the game."

"I'll give the bastard 'game'!" said Turnbull grimly. "And what makes you so sure he knows the way out?"

"I'm not sure," said Gill. "But I'm assuming that if he didn't know the way out, then he wouldn't have pushed Varre in here in the first place!"

"*Pushed* him . . . ? You're right! Of course he did!"

"Time we got back," said Gill. "But remember: play it as close to your chest as possible, just the way it comes. . . ."

"You took your time," said Anderson, when they got back.

"We didn't have your lighter," Gill answered. "We found a place just like this one, identical. We marked it just in case we end up there again, from a different direction."

"Ditto," said Angela. "So what now? The last two tunnels?"

Gill pursed his lips, appeared to give it some consideration, finally shook his head. "I've a feeling we'll find exactly the same setup," he said. "That's the nature of mazes, isn't it? That every which way should look the same? No, I reckon it's time we tried it your way, Angela, and gave Jon his head. What about it, Jon? Are you game?"

Bannerman shrugged. "Whatever you say," he said.

"*Ohhh!*" Varre groaned, stirring where he lay on the stone floor.

Gill frowned and took out the thorn hypodermic. He checked the bulb in the thorn's root and found it soft and flacid. When he squeezed it with his thumb, only a single drop of liquid fell from the thorn's tip. He tossed the thing disgustedly aside. "So now we're going to have him to deal with, too," he said.

Angela took Bannerman to the first untried tunnel. "We can try this one," she said, letting him feel the edge of the opening, "or—"

"That one will do," he answered, before she could show him the other tunnel. "It feels . . . right." Behind him, Gill and Turnbull exchanged brief glances.

"Very well," said Gill. "Jon takes the lead, with David right on his heels with the lighter. Then Angela, with Jack and myself bringing up the rear and looking after Jean-Pierre. Okay, let's go. . . ."

CHAPTER THIRTY-SIX

It appeared that Gill must be right about the nature of mazes: after about a hundred paces they came to another junction cave, exactly the same as all the others. By that time, too, Varre had struggled back to consciousness, so that Turnbull could sit him down on the cold stone floor, and Anderson was beginning to worry about the fuel in his lighter. "These things are meant to light a thousand cigarettes," he said, "but they're *not* meant to burn for minutes on end! I've turned the flame as low as it will go, but there can't be a lot of time left in it."

Varre said, "A . . . a cave?" He got up and staggered to the centre of the floor, stood swaying where he gazed up the vertical shaft at the haze of softly flooding light.

"A whole series of caves," Angela answered him. "There appears to be one of them every hundred yards or so, all with five tunnels radiating from them and one central, vertical shaft to the surface. Except of course they're not really 'caves' as such; we only call them that. Obviously they're too regular to be caves; their walls are too smooth, too perfectly hemispherical. It's a maze someone has fash—" And she came to an abrupt halt as she suddenly remembered who she was talking to.

Varre nodded, continued to stare up the shaft into the flowing yellow light. "Which *I* have fashioned, right?"

"It looks like it," said Gill. And an idea came to him out of nowhere. "Jean-Pierre, since you're the, er, architect, as it were, maybe you can tell us the secret."

Varre looked at him. The Frenchman's eyes were dark-circled, deep now and less fearful, yellow where they reflected the suddenly sinister light. "Horizontal tunnels," he said, "and five to each junction point. How many of these— call them 'caves', if you will—have you visited? And did you cross any side tunnels en route?"

"This is the fourth," Turnbull told him. The big man shook his head. "No side tunnels."

"And the tunnels run in straight lines?"

"As near as damn."

"Impossible!" Varre grinned, but it wasn't a natural grin. He looked sick.

"What?" Anderson stepped forward. "Did you say impossible, Jean-Pierre? How do you mean?"

Varre shrugged listlessly. "Obviously there is no mathematician amongst you," he answered. "No *geo*metrician!" They looked at each other blankly and Varre sighed. "Try drawing it," he

331

said. "In your minds or in the dust. With *four* tunnels to each junction it will function perfectly—like a simple system of squares, for example—but not with five. If there are *five* radiating tunnels, then one of them either stops short every time, or it *must* cross another tunnel!"

"Murphy's law!" Gill gasped, looking like he could kick himself. "We tried every tunnel but the last one—which was probably the right one."

"What do you mean, the right one?" Turnbull frowned.

Gill nodded, indicating Varre. "He designed the thing—however unconsciously—and he's also provided the clue. If the fifth tunnel in each set doesn't join up with any other, then where does it go to?"

"It rises through an incline, perhaps?" said Angela. "To the surface?"

"Or . . . it stops short," said Varre ominously. "A dead end. It's my world, remember? And you know what I am. . . ."

Alarmed, Gill went to him. "Jean-Pierre, don't talk like that. Don't even *think* like that!"

Varre looked at him and grinned again, vacantly. Or perhaps not vacantly. There was something sick but at the same time very sly about him. He scratched absentmindedly at his scarred thigh where his trouser leg had been torn away. "Gill," he said, "Spencer—we've always known, haven't we, you and I?"

"Known what?" Gill tried to fathom the man's mind.

"About the House of Doors." The other shrugged. "Aided by your talent, you could feel it all around us, and oppressed by my phobia, so could I. We've always known. We have that in common, at least."

Gill nodded. "That and the fact that we've been through hell together—all of us. And that we're now trapped in your nightmare. Oh yes, we have several things in common."

Varre also nodded, and narrowed his eyes. He seemed to come to some decision or other, licked his lips and began to blink rapidly. He looked at the others where they watched him curiously, backed nervously away from them. "Gill," he said, his voice suddenly urgent, "Spencer, I need to talk to you . . . in private!"

Turnbull stepped forward and out of the side of his mouth said, "Spencer, this bloke is trouble. He's better off asleep. And we'll be better off, too." He made a grab for Varre, who avoided him and darted into a tunnel.

Gill caught Turnbull's arm. "No," he said sharply. "First let's see what he has to say. He's already given us a few things to think about, so now let's find out if there are any more." He went to the mouth of the tunnel and saw Varre's silhouette crouching there a little way along it. "Jean-Pierre?"

"I need to talk to you, Spencer," the little Frenchman said again. "But in private. In here . . ."

Gill joined him and they moved out of earshot of the others in the main cave. "Spencer," said Varre in a whisper, "I forgive you for putting me to sleep. I can see that it was necessary. And while I was out I seem to have compensated somewhat." He looked shudderingly about at the tunnel's confines. "My phobia is active, obviously, but at the moment it's at least controllable. While I was asleep, though, I dreamed . . . strange dreams."

"Oh?" Gill waited.

"Spencer," Varre continued in a little while, "what do you know of the legend of the werewolf?" There was that in his voice which made the short hairs rise at the back of Gill's neck.

"I know it's just that," he answered. "A legend, a myth. There are no such creatures. What we saw in Clayborne's world was of his own mind. You shouldn't worry about things like that." And to himself: *Maybe Jack Turnbull was right and we'd all be a lot better off if you were still asleep, Jean-Pierre.*

"But . . . that awful thing *bit* me!" the Frenchman insisted. "It bit me *in* Clayborne's world, and its weight pushed me through the door." He felt his thigh. "The wound has almost healed now— which would normally be impossible in itself— and yet I have this feeling that . . . that . . ."

"Jean-Pierre." Gill tried to stay calm, started to make his way back along the tunnel to where the others were waiting. "You really mustn't dwell on such things. Not in this place." He didn't like to take his eyes off Varre, but he couldn't very well back along the tunnel. That would be as good as admitting that the Frenchman's worst fears were real. And so he looked at him one last time, at his yellow eyes in the gloom of the place, then deliberately turned his back and paced away from him. But in his pocket, Gill kept his right hand firmly clenched on the silver rod of alien metal. "Better come out now," he said. "Time is wasting."

"You're right, of course," Varre answered.

And Gill heard the pad of the Frenchman's feet as he began to follow him. A moment later and they stepped back into the junction cave; Gill began to breathe again; his nerves quit jumping and his pounding heart slowed into something like its normal rhythm.

"Spencer," said Angela, taking Gill's elbow. "We've been talking about what Jean-Pierre said. And it looks like he's right. These tunnel mouths are not equidistant. Four of them go off at right angles, making the grid of squares that he mentioned. But the fifth falls between two of the others. If you look at those three tunnel mouths there you'll see what I mean: the one in the middle is the one we want—*and* it's the one we didn't try in the first cave."

"It *might* be the one we want." Gill gave her his attention. "Look, I don't want to put you down, but there's really only one correct solution to any maze. If each and every junction has one possible escape route, we could end up trying out an awful lot of them before we discover the one that will lead us to the surface—before David's lighter runs out of fuel! But I agree: we have to start somewhere, and it might as well be with this odd-tunnel-out as with any other."

"I'll try it," said Turnbull. "The rest of you stay put. I'll go faster on my own." He disappeared into the tunnel mouth.

They waited for him, and looking from face to face Gill could see how the strain was working on them. Angela was dirty, a mass of bruises from her falls and scratches from the rust; despite the fact that the maze wasn't really cold, still she shivered persistently. Anderson was haggard; his grey face twitched and his lips trembled. Bannerman was ... simply Bannerman. His blank, leaden eyes hid a great many secrets, Gill was sure, and distracted one's concentration from his actual expression. But in fact Bannerman had never had much of an expression of any sort. And Varre—

The little Frenchman was back in the column of hazy light that shone down from on high. Head tilted, he stared directly up the shaft, perhaps longing to be able to climb it, longing for the freedom of the surface. *Poor bastard*, Gill thought. *He's living out his nightmare, stuck like a fly in the molasses of his mind.*

"Jean-Pierre," said Angela, "you shouldn't stare into the sun like that. Even indirectly, it can damage your eyes."

He glanced at her, and the way he tilted his eyebrows made his eyes seem slightly slanted. He smiled a queer, lopsided smile. "Sunlight?" he said. "But what makes you think it's sunlight, my dear? Oh no, no—not sunlight." He stepped from the shaft of light into a haze of floating dust motes, and for the first time Gill noticed the length of his jaws, the way he seemed to crouch down a little—like an animal at bay—into himself.

"Not sunlight?" she repeated him wonderingly.

"Moonlight!" said Varre. "Most certainly the light of the full moon ..."

Oh my God! thought Gill—but at that precise moment Turnbull came scrambling out of the tunnel. He was obviously badly shaken; he turned to look at the tunnel mouth, backed away from it, gulped audibly and tried to speak.

"Jack?" Gill prompted him.

Turnbull found his voice. "Fifty paces and the tunnel slopes, all right—but downwards! A few more paces and it plummets. I got the hell out before it tipped me to blazes! Also, it narrowed down a lot. Even coming back I got the feeling that . . . that . . ." He stared wide-eyed at the tunnel mouth, then whirled and stared at the other tunnel mouths. And: "Spencer," he gulped, "for Christ's sake tell me I'm seeing things, will you?"

Gill looked, as did the others, but what they saw only confirmed Turnbull's horror. With wild, anxious, inarticulate cries, they all rushed to the mouths of the tunnels and touched them, grasped and strained at them, attempted uselessly to reverse the monstrous, inexplicable process taking place. But they couldn't.

The five tunnel mouths were visibly smaller. They had been something like five feet in diameter—but now they were only a little more than four!

CHAPTER THIRTY-SEVEN

"It's that crazy bastard!" Turnbull yelled, pointing accusingly at Varre. "Spencer, you should have let me deal with him."

He's right, Gill thought, *but would it have made any difference?* In any case, it was too late to "deal with him" now. The House of Doors was reacting to the Frenchman's fears, magnifying them out of all proportion. Gill knew it was too late, but the fact had obviously escaped Turnbull. The big man leaped for Varre—only to pull up short and fall back.

Varre had gone into a crouch. Long-snouted, lean-bodied, slant-eyed, he fell to all fours and backed towards a tunnel. His features seemed to melt and flow. His clothes slackened around him and he stepped out of them. Yellow eyes burned and a yellow tongue lolled, and Varre was no longer a man. The great wolf bunched its muscles.

Gill swept Angela behind him, tried to shut everyone's cries of shock and terror out of his mind. He brought into view the silver cylinder and let his machine instinct take over. The weapon whirred in his hand, glinting where it reflected the yellow light from the shaft. "Jean-Pierre," he said, "if you can understand me at all, then understand that this will kill you. It's not a silver bullet, no, but it will slice you up as small as mincemeat. Don't make me do it." He swung the weapon in an arc before him, slicing left to right, and the wolf backed into the tunnel mouth directly behind it. In another moment it had turned tail and fled. Its howl, long drawn out, reverberated back to them in the laden, constricting air.

"Bannerman," Gill growled, turning now to the "blind" man. "Varre's not responsible for any of this; you are."

Turnbull herded Angela and Anderson to Gill's rear, and Gill held out his weapon towards Bannerman where he stood with his back to the curving wall. For a moment the man's face remained impassive, but then he smiled. It was a smile utterly devoid of human emotion. "You're a clever man, Gill," he said, "but only a man. And as you seem to be aware, I am something quite different and entirely superior."

"The tunnels," Anderson babbled from behind Gill. "They're down to three feet in diameter. The whole cave is that much smaller!"

"Bannerman," said Gill, "this was once your weapon. You know better than anyone what it can do. Now you have a choice: get us out of here or I use it on you." He crowded Bannerman, thrust out the whirring weapon like a knife towards him.

"Fool," said Bannerman, with neither malice nor emotion, making it a simple statement of fact. "You don't need me to get you out. Did you think the House of Doors would make it that easy for you? Did you think that this was the end of the game? When you finally break, Gill, *that's* the end of the game—but not yet for a while, not yet. Just how long it will take depends entirely upon you—and upon the others, of course. As for myself, it's time I left you to your own devices."

Gill lunged at him. Bannerman's eyes came alive, glowed like coals; his breath whooshed like a great bellows; he floated up off the floor, drifted towards the vertical shaft directly overhead.

At first astonished, finally Gill sprang forward, made a flying leap upwards with his weapon hand outstretched. The weapon struck Bannerman's right thigh halfway between hip and knee, slicing the entire leg from his body as if it were papier-mâché! The severed limb thumped heavily, soggily down between the four still entirely human beings, slopping its juices and rolling a little on the floor. And Bannerman screamed.

It was a *sound* formed in a man's throat but having origin in an alien mind. A hideous thing to hear, it grated like chalk on a blackboard, like a shovel in cold ashes. Bannerman floated on high, screaming still as he passed out through the ever-narrowing shaft and was gone.

A pattering of liquid droplets, some of them blood, fell from the yellow haze.

"Shit! Oh, shit!" Anderson was on the point of fainting. "The bloody walls are closing in!"

"Spencer, hold me!" Angela clung to Gill. He put away his alien weapon and crushed her to him.

But Turnbull was still thinking, still actively seeking an answer, a way out. "Gill," he shouted as the walls continued to close on them. "Bannerman said it wouldn't be finished until we had broken. So for fuck's sake *don't break now!*"

They heard a pitiful mewling, looked towards the tunnel down which Varre had disappeared. He was in there, one scrabbling paw extended, slavering wolf's muzzle framed in a nine-inch tube of rock. The horror of his situation got through to Gill: the fact that his nightmare from Earth—from birth, probably—was crushing him here in an alien world.

"Oh, Christ!" Gill cried. He knew he must make a quick end of it for Varre. He snatched the weapon from his pocket, took two swift paces to the wall and tube where the wolf was being pulped. But even as he got down on his knees the hole closed. Gill saw it happen: solid rock, a wall of the stuff, sealing itself like a pebble dropped in fine wet concrete. It closed with a sound like a fat child crunching a large apple, or ripe bladders of seaweed bursting underfoot, and the extended paw was nipped off and fell to the floor.

Gill straightened up and was pushed back as the wall advanced. He stood with Angela, Anderson and Turnbull, back-to-back, and the gap between their faces and the curving, tightening wall was only fifteen inches. Gill looked at the whirring weapon in his hand, then at the blank wall, and said, *"Fuck you!"*

He sliced with the weapon, carving at the wall as if in a last desperate bid to dig his way out. And that was the answer!

It was similar to putting the like poles of a pair of magnets together: they opposed each other, wouldn't interact, held each other at bay. The whirring weapon was like a catalyst—it signalled a change—and the synthesizer, waiting, put the change into immediate effect. Where there had been a tightly curving wall, a tube of rock closing on the four, now there were—

"Doors!" Anderson's voice was a sandpapered croak. Somehow, through all of this, he'd managed to hold on to his lighter and keep its flame steady.

"Four of them!" said Turnbull as the flame of Anderson's lighter flickered and sank to the merest spark.

"But they're still closing in!" Angela cried as finally the flame expired.

Shaped like coffins, like the carved lids of sarcophagi, the square of stone doors squeezed the four together like stripes of toothpaste in a tube. The House of Doors gave them no choice, no chance to make up their own minds. Each had his or her own door, all four of which opened simultaneously to snatch them through . . .

Gill heard a distant, insistent whining. Mechanical or animal he couldn't for the moment say. It was accompanied by a wet slapping sound and the feel of soft leather moistly applied to his face. In the back of his mind, as the whining grew louder and clearer, Gill wondered how long he'd been out. Then ... he realized he was now awake, remembered what had happened, snatched himself back from whoever it was was doing whatever to his face.

The back of his head came into sharp, cracking contact with something hard and metallic, something which clanged and shed flakes of rust. And almost before Gill had opened his eyes he knew where he was and understood how he came to be here. "Barney!" he gasped as the dog backed away from him, yelping and furiously wagging its stump of a tail.

And then Gill looked all around at the interior of the iron cave and the junk heaped everywhere, and shook his head in despair. Where to go from here (*was* there anywhere to go?) and what to do next? Obviously the House of Doors had returned him to his personal nightmare, the world of mad machines. And Angela, Turnbull, Anderson—what of them?

They (no, she, for if he had to admit it, Angela was the only one who had really come to mean anything to him) she, then, was separated from him now by entire universes. Or by a world, two worlds, at the very least. And was one of them, he wondered, the world of her worst nightmares of violation? He prayed that it wasn't, for her sake. And then he put it out of his mind. He had to, for now he must worry about himself. He must survive if he was to help anyone else survive. He *must* survive, if only for the sake of revenge, a chance to balance the score.

Bannerman, he told himself bitterly then,

whoever or whatever you are, you've a lot to answer for. And if there's any justice at all, I'm the one you'll answer to!

He made to struggle to his feet and put down his hand on something soft, wet and fleshy. He hissed and jerked his hand back, and scrambled away from the thing he'd inadvertently touched. It was Bannerman's amputated leg, lying there amidst the junk where it had come through Gill's door with him. And beside it, Varre's forepaw. Except that the latter was now a perfectly normal human wrist and hand again.

Gill grimaced. He forced himself to handle Bannerman's leg, to prop it up so that he could examine the severed cross section. If Bannerman was an alien machine, some sort of robot, then it really ought to show. Something should show, for he had screamed when Gill cut him. Gill's weapon had sliced *his* flesh as well as imitation or synthetic flesh. Gill looked: he saw skin and red, sliced flesh, fat and sinew, veins and arteries—but no bone! Where the bone should be was now a tube of metal, indenting when he touched it but always returning to its original cylindrical shape as soon as he released the pressure. Alien metal. And inside the cylinder—

Liquid!

He lifted the thigh, poured out the contents of the tube-metal "bone," watched it splash onto a rusted iron surface. It was inert; it seeped into the rust, darkening it; it reacted with the ferrous oxide and began to evaporate.

Liquid? Gill wondered. *The blood of an alien—or his flesh? Just how alien is the bas-*

tard, anyway? Then, disgusted, he kicked the stump aside.

Barney was still wagging furiously. He barked, growled, yelped, skittered here and there. "It's okay," Gill told him, trying to calm him down. "And don't worry, this time I'm not going to leave you. We'll stick together." Maybe Turnbull had been right in the first place. What was it he'd said, about the dog being more valuable than Varre?

"He's stayed alive a couple of years longer than we're likely to last," the big man had said. "We might be able to learn a few things from this dog. . . ."

And Angela: hadn't she thought that Barney had wanted them to follow him? Gill knew he was on the track of something, and he probed at something else—a loose connection—wriggling there in the back of his mind. Then he had it. When they'd opened that door on the as-yet-unexplored world of mists, out of which Haggie had staggered like a ghost into their arms, they had heard in the distance the howling of a dog. Not the sound a predatory wolf makes but a perfectly acceptable howling; the mournful voice of a lost, miserable animal. Barney's voice? And if so, then how had he made his way from that place to this one?

Just how *had* Barney survived? What secrets were locked in his dog's brain? Gill fondled his ears and thought, *God, how I wish you could talk!* Well, he couldn't—but talking wasn't the only means of communication. Old Hamish Grieve had been a gillie, hadn't he? And if Barney's master had been a gamekeeper, then the dog could well be a tracker, sniffer, finder, all

345

manner of things. Gill wished he knew more about dogs and their specialist abilities. But certainly Barney must be of above-average intelligence.

Gill yawned and his mind suddenly felt quite light, detached almost, incapable of concentration. *Knackered*, he told himself, nodding. Not physically but mentally. He went to the iron cave's mouth and looked out. The atomic sun was still setting, with maybe an hour left to darkness. That had to be wrong but Gill didn't question it. It was his belief that these worlds were made to order, by the House of Doors or whatever controlled the House of Doors. Whether one arrived in daylight or darkness was a matter of chance. The worlds were freshly created each time, for each visit. They were ... projections on a 3-D screen? Where that idea came from Gill couldn't say.

He shook his head and blinked rapidly; but it was no good, he couldn't think straight. "Barney," he said, "we're going to rest, you and I. Or I am, anyway." He looked at the rust-scabbed metal junk lying all around, and at the *un*metal debris of Bannerman and Varre. Dismembered machines and men. "Sleep," he said, "yes—but not here."

Some little distance from the cave they found a large bin with a curved bottom. It had circular portholes in its sides, a hinged, galvanized lid, and as a bonus it wasn't attached to any other piece of machinery. Shivering a little as the atomic sun set, Gill climbed in and Barney joined him. And through the rest of the night they shared each other's warmth. . . .

CHAPTER THIRTY-EIGHT

Gill dreamed, and in his dreams tried to resolve certain problems. Bannerman's empty face smiled his unsmile as he drifted aloft. He had only one leg, and his stump dripped blood and steaming, alien fluids, but he smiled his unsmile. Under the flesh—the synthetic flesh—of his guise, he wore a harness which defied gravity, sustaining his liquid body. And he passed unsmiling into the heart of a many-faceted sphere, through a door formed of one of the facets.

Then the dream changed. A projector whirred and Gill was part of the huge screen that flickered into being. He lay flickering on the side of a flickering dune in a flickering rust desert. A door opened in the dune and Varre's flickering hand came crawling out of it, crawling towards Gill. The unseen projector settled down; the

*whirring and flickering ceased; Varre's hand
formed itself into a fist and shook itself at Gill—
then opened into slavering wolf jaws that lunged
at his face!*

Gill started awake in a cold sweat, and
snatched back his face out of the beam of faint
coloured lights which crawled into his refuge
through a porthole. Then, cautiously, shivering,
he looked out and saw that it was night in his
machine world. Barney was sitting watching
him, yellow-eyed in the galvanized steel bucket's gloom. Gill propped himself up on one elbow, looked out again through the porthole and
saw that there was life here—mechanical life—
even at night. But so weird that it was almost a
continuation of his dream.

Against an indigo-turning-black horizon, a
distant skyline of rusting rods, corkscrew spires
and slumped scaffolding was lit by red- and
orange-pulsing fires, like a row of coke ovens or
blast furnaces roaring in the darkness. Their
fire bellows voices reached to him faintly across
miles of silence: *Whoosh! Whoosh! Whoosh!*
Closer at hand but deep down in the bowels of
the junk, a great hammer gonged dully like a
subterranean pile driver: ker-*thump*! Ker-
thump! Ker-*thump*! Its vibrations came up
through the bottom of the bucket like blood
pounding in a sleeper's ear.

Shifting his position, Gill looked out from a
porthole on the other side of the bucket; in that
direction the machine city's silhouette had a
scattering of lights, white and yellow and green.
Set against a great patch of darkness, something gigantic nodded twin, shining hammer-
heads monotonously over a revolving yellow

light. Chains rattled rustily, clanked into silence, then rattled again—and so on. Some strange wheeled thing on a gantry trundled to and fro, with lights fore and aft that changed colour with each change of direction.

In the sky the stars were bright silver ball bearings, all the same size, radiating their light in faint, aurora waves. . . .

Nothing made any sense, not now that Gill was awake. But he remembered his dream, and part of that at least had made some kind of sense. *Dreams*, he told himself, *are the junkyards of the mind, where subconscious vacuum cleaners suck up and dispose of the wrack and rubble of the waking world. But occasionally there may be nuggets in the junk, diamonds in the dust and the cobwebs.*

Gill's mind was clean and fresh now. His body might be dirty, bruised, pitted, but *he* was brand new. He took out the silver-cylinder weapon and looked at it in the faint beam of coloured light weaving in through the porthole. Why, compared with the machines out there— those utterly worthless, aimless, futile machines of his nightmares—the tool in his hand seemed hardly enigmatic at all! *They* were the fractions which wouldn't convert into decimals. *They* were the aliens. At least this tool had a purpose. In this world, it was the only tool with a purpose.

The weapon seemed suddenly alive in Gill's hand; his mind touched it . . . he understood it. He let it lie across the palms of both hands, rolled it in his fingers, felt of its essence. And like the links of a Chinese puzzle it fell into two perfect halves, one in each hand!

Gill looked at one of the halves: three inches long by three-quarters of an inch in diameter, blunt-tipped. The business end. *This is where the power is focused.* He touched a fingertip to the freshly exposed metal, which indented like mercury. But when he tilted the tube it didn't run, and when he flicked it with his fingernail it was hard as steel. *Each molecule knows its task: to intensify and pass on the current to the point of application, the cutting edge.*

He looked at the other half of the cylinder. *This is the power source, the battery.* A ten-sided crystal as big as the last joint of his little finger, so green that Gill must shutter his eyes against the intensity of its colour, floated to the surface of the now fluid metal. It lay there exposed for a moment, and Gill checked that it was fully charged. He "knew" that it was fully charged; and once he had checked it, it sank back out of sight again.

And when power is beamed to it, this is its receiver. Gill touched the end of the rod in a certain way, as simple as pressing the stud on an electric cigarette lighter, and a tiny mesh of filaments composed *of* the liquid metal rose up *from* the metal for inspection. Gill saw that it was perfect, that the weapon—the tool—was in proper working order. He had completed his inspection. Hardly daring to breathe, he put the two halves together and they fused into one.

Then he went through the entire process again, but faster, with a new dexterity. He applied an alien touch to an alien machine and it responded. There were no nuts and bolts here to be coaxed or forced, no screws to be unscrewed; to *know how* was the whole trick; to understand was to master. Now Gill could visualise the line of threes marching to infinity. He felt that if he were a mathematician, he could square the circle, could realise pi to its last decimal place. Uncluttered by mundane machine preconceptions, his machine mind had learned, had acted, instinctively.

Even a newborn baby, who knows nothing, knows enough to breathe. All he needs is a pat on the backside to start him off, and after that it's a question of survival. And Gill knew that he'd just received his pat on the backside.

"Barney," he said out loud, but softly, wonderingly, "go back to sleep, boy. Tomorrow's another day—with any luck." Barney did sleep, but for Gill it was much harder. The word "projection" had stuck in his brain like a tomato seed in his teeth: it had been there all the time without his knowing it. But his dream had brought it back to mind, and now he remembered how and where and who had used it.

Angela, when she'd said that the House of Doors was a projection, and that each materialisation was just another cross section through the same basic structure. She'd also said that each door was like a beam switched off the moment they used it; and that the lamp—the projector—was still there but pointing in another direction. Obviously these things she'd said had made an impression on Gill, which had finally crystalised in his dream.

But . . . a projection needs a projector—a lamp—and it also needs a screen. Gill tried to picture it: a 3-D projector, projecting solids, using entire synthesised worlds for its screens? But why not? Gill was after all contemplating

351

a science which could replicate flesh into facsimile human beings, and motorise them, *and* use them as the transports or vehicular appendages of the alien creature inside!

And so, with these things and one other on his mind, Gill found it hard to sleep. The other thing was Angela herself: he kept wondering about her—where she was now—and hoping that she wasn't where he thought she might be. For if it was *that* place . . . he could (but refused to) imagine what it must be like. In their worlds it had killed Varre and Clayborne. They had died from their own worst nightmares. Which was why Gill found it hard to sleep, because he knew that when he did, this time he'd probably dream of Angela dying of hers. And right now, and for as long as it took before they were together again, Gill knew that this would be his worst nightmare, too. . . .

Sith of the Thone was furious, outraged, injured. Not only had he been damaged in a physical sense, but also in a place where it hurt almost as badly—in his pride. Twice now the ingenuity of men, their savage instinct for survival, had undone him and made a mockery of his planning—and that was twice too often.

So far the game had been played more or less in accordance with the rules. Oh, there had been unforeseen circumstances (such as the criminal Haggie, and Barney the dog, which were not properly part of the scenario) but given that the combinations were almost infinite, the rest of it had gone fairly well to schedule—for the most part. Two members of the test group had reached their personal breaking points and allowed themselves to be forced out of play: they had "died". But instead of weakening the resolve of the survivors, this had seemed to serve only to intensify it. Occasionally their logic moved dangerously close to truth, their extrapolations furnished glimpses of fact.

By now, all of them should have been eliminated; by surviving they had in effect passed the tests. Individuals had fallen but as a group—and more importantly as a race—they had proved themselves worthy. At least according to the book of rules. But Sith was gamesmaster here, and the rules no longer applied. He could bend them any way he liked, even break them entirely. Which was precisely what he intended to do.

Adding to his fury—heaping fuel on the fire of his frustration—was the sure knowledge of his own fallibility, the irrefutable evidence of his errors. To have lost a Thone tool was bad enough, and that the man Gill should have found it, kept and learned how to use it was worse, but that it had now been used on Sith himself . . . unthinkable! And yet Sith could only blame himself, in that he had failed to appreciate the full potential of Gill's talent, failed to consider all of the possibilities.

And yet who could have foreseen it? If a human being accidentally allowed a machine gun to fall into the hands of a chimpanzee, would he really fear that the creature might of its own accord learn how to load, aim and fire the thing? But Gill had learned, and was presumably still learning. And that was a process which must be terminated just as soon as possible.

Except . . . it would seem a very impersonal

sort of revenge, to let the synthesizer do all the work. And this was now a very personal thing—indeed, a vendetta. Sith not only desired to be there when the end came, he wanted Gill and Turnbull—yes, and the others, too—to *know* that he was there, and that he was the author of their destruction.

Rules? There could be no more rules. It was time now to apply real pressure, to set the grinder working that much faster and rapidly reduce these "survivors" to so much mindless refuse—as he himself might easily have been reduced to a stain! It was a terrible thought, that last: that the future Grand Thone had almost fallen prey to a primitive! But if Gill had cut the Bannerman construct higher, if he'd sliced through the nerve chain between brain and motor system . . .

Well, it had not come to that; Sith had lost only the lower half of one of his three mobilizers—a tentacle tip. But even that had been sufficient to destabilise his system and cause him the human equivalent of great pain. If it had been the other leg, then that were even worse. That limb had housed both of Sith's remaining tentacles, and his pain and outrage would be that much greater.

As it was he'd been obliged to synthesise the missing portion of the mobilizer, which would be shed when his mainly liquid body replaced it. A matter of days. Thus the physical pain no longer existed, but the damage to his pride remained.

In the synthesizer's control room, Sith commanded the master locator to seek out the individual members of the test group. The search was made at random and with reflex rapidity, and Sith viewed with keen interest the plight of Angela Denholm on one of his screens.

Her own, personal nightmare was being enacted on a world of oceans and beaches, blue skies and seas, grassy plains and flowering forests. The world's creatures, which variously walked, flew and swam, were in the main small, pretty, and fairly unintelligent things. With some small changes the planet would have made a perfect Thone habitat; alas, its parent sun was rapidly evolving and showing signs of that process which must soon—in some several thousands of years—destroy it. Recorded long ago and now reproduced by the synthesizer, it might well have been the girl's idea of paradise—with a certain exception. And that was the very essence of her nightmare: to have her beautiful world, her existence, marred and brutalised by her husband, Rod Denholm.

Now she fled from him—fled indeed from a great many Rod Denholms—through the forests and waterways of that world. The world was real enough, but her pursuers had never lived there; they were the product of the synthesizer, enhanced and given loathsome sentience only by Angela's own conception of Denholm's mind. But as long as she fought and fled she would overcome, win, survive the test. For she was a strong one, stronger far than Varre and Clayborne had proved to be, and Sith had no doubt but that she *would* survive it—or would have, according to the rules. But not according to his rules. For now he contemplated the introduction of a new element into the game, over which the synthesizer would have no control whatsoever.

Towards that end he now graphed one of Angela's pursuers and fed the resultant profile to a secondary locator. Scanning externally, the locator radiated its beam sweepingly outwards from the Castle on Ben Lawers and found the real Rod Denholm awaiting trial in his cell in a Perth police station. . . .

CHAPTER THIRTY-NINE

David Anderson—who, for a high-ranking MOD minister, was now as disreputable a sight as anyone could ever wish to see—had felt the sudden rush of air as the coffin-shaped door sucked him in; he'd closed his eyes and heard the door's sepulchral *clang* as it slammed shut behind him, and a moment later had gone sprawling to his hands and knees. Then—

There was noise all around him, tumultuous noise, which at first served only to further alarm him. His confused brain had not known what to expect; but whatever it might have expected, it was certainly not this. Still clutching his cigarette lighter in a palsied hand, finally Anderson wincingly, cringingly opened his eyes.

Sight and sound coordinated, and the resultant revelation was almost too much for him. He looked out into a street, one of the world's

357

most famous streets, and could scarcely believe his eyes.

"Oxford Street?" he said then, his jaw hanging slack and his eyes starting out. "Oxford bloody Street?" He drew air in a huge gasp, and let it out in a shout of joy. "Bloody wonderful for-God's-sake *Oxford Street*!"

"It's a good sign, that, sir," said a knowing, mildly caustic, booming bass voice. "Knowing where you are, I mean. It means you haven't quite managed to kill 'em all off yet. Not all of 'em, anyway."

"Kill them off?" Anderson answered automatically, without looking up. On all fours, he continued to gape out into the busy flow of traffic like a blind man whose sight has suddenly returned to him.

"Brain cells, sir," said the booming voice. "Booze does that, you know, in large quantities. Kills 'em off."

Anderson knew that someone stood close by, and that others skirted him where they passed in chattering streams in both directions along the pavement. Now he dragged his eyes from the bustling traffic to stare hard at a pair of shiny black boots. He blinked his eyes and shook his head but none of it went away. He was really here, really back home. Back home in London!

His eyes traced a line from the boots up the sharp creases of blue uniform trousers, to the jacket and shiny buttons, the frowning, shaded, narrow-eyed face beneath the familiar Bobby's helmet. A policeman: an ordinary, everyday, metropolitan God-bless-him-forever policeman! "My God! My *God*!" Anderson cried. "Oh my good, *good* God!" He clutched the policeman's leg and wept hot, salty tears down his trembling, grimy jowls.

A strong hand reached down, took him under the arm, and with some difficulty lifted him to his feet. "Now then, my Old China," said the policeman, displaying a great deal of patience. "See, you're either to show me that you're a nice responsible sort of chap and start behaving yourself, or I'm to fix you up with a nice cool uncomfortable place to sleep it all out of your system. It's entirely up to you."

Anderson *was* back home, back on Earth, in London, and he knew it. It appeared to be summer, or a very warm day in the spring at least, and that wasn't quite right (indeed it was quite wrong, and rang small warning bells in Anderson's head, which for the moment, in his extremity of joy, he ignored) but everything else was perfectly normal. This was his place—yes, *his*, not Clayborne's madhouse or Varre's labyrinthine lunatic asylum—and he had power here. Nor had he forgotten how to use that power. He dabbed away his tears of relief, puffed himself up and shook off the policeman's hand.

"Constable," he said, fighting hard not to dance and laugh, and so make an even greater spectacle of himself, "I don't suppose for one moment that you'd accept or even understand the only explanation I can offer for my present appearance. But as you now see for yourself I am not, as you so obviously suppose, under the influence of alcohol. Nor am I drugged or in any way . . . unbalanced. I am in fact a Minister of the government of the day, which I can prove easily enough. Indeed, I may very well need to do just that, for in all fairness to you, you could hardly be expected to recognise me under all this dirt! As to why I appear as I do: that is for authorities somewhat higher than your own, and it's imperative that I report to them as soon as possible."

The policeman nodded, smiled understandingly and again took Anderson's arm. "I see," he said, "and you're the Minister for Crawling Along Pavements, are you? Well, best if you simply come along with me, Old Lad—and nice and quietly, if you don't mind."

Once more Anderson shrugged him off, and quickly produced his wallet containing almost two hundred pounds in twenties and some smaller notes, his driver's licence, and several other identifying documents; but chiefly his stamped, signed ministerial security card with a recent photograph welded into the plastic laminate. There could be no mistaking or denying that.

The policeman studied Anderson's papers, and Anderson himself, scratched his jaw and shook his head, finally handed the documents back. He was still uncertain, but . . . under the grime and stink, certainly Anderson's clothes were expensive. And his upper-class public-school accent was very much in evidence. "Well," he said at last, "I've had some daft things happen to me in my time, but—"

"Constable, I completely understand," Anderson told him. "And this does appear 'daft', I agree. But now that I'm back I have many important things to do, and—"

"Back?"

Anderson sighed. "Look, I really haven't the time to explain. Now, you've seen for yourself who I am. Do you really want me to phone the Chief Constable—who happens to be a personal friend of mine—and let him take charge of matters? Or may I now consider myself free to go?"

"You always have been free to do whatever you like, sir," the policeman at once replied. "Within the law, of course, and as long as you do it on your feet and we know what's what. But as for going somewhere—might I ask where? For if you ask me, sir, I'd say you'd first better . . . well, sort yourself out a bit—before going anywhere!"

Anderson looked down at himself. "I didn't ask you," he finally replied, "but . . . I'm forced to agree. Very well: first I shall visit the gent's outfitters there, second a place where I can clean myself up, and then straight to my club."

The constable took out his notebook. "Your club?"

"My residence," said Anderson, and he gave his Knightsbridge address.

"Very well, sir," said the policeman. "And you're sure I can't be of further assistance?"

"Perfectly sure," the Minister answered. "Thank you very much." He backed off a pace, turned and walked a little unsteadily through the sidewalk's milling crush to the door of the outfitters, and entered.

"Sorry, Bertie." An unsmiling shop assistant immediately loomed close.

"Bertie?" Anderson was nonplussed.

"Burlington Bertie, innit?" The Cockney tilted his head on one side. "From Bow? Come off it, Chief. Outside, if yer don't mind. The bins are round the back."

"Bins? I'm here to buy clothes!" Anderson waved money at the man, whose expression changed on the instant. And now the Minister was sure he was back home, because where nothing else would have worked, money had turned the trick in the blink of an eye.

He fitted himself out with shoes, socks, underclothes, a shirt, blazer and trousers, and a tie with a stripe which resembled as closely as possible that of the Old School. The clothes were off the peg and hardly of the finest cut, but they were clean, new, and inexpensive. Wearing them, Anderson gave a sigh of relief and began to feel much more like his old self.

His next stop was a public lavatory where he paid the attendant for a little privacy in a back room and did his best to spruce himself up. Finally, looking a lot more presentable if not one hundred percent himself, Anderson took a taxi to his club.

In the back of the taxi, he picked up a cast-aside newspaper and scanned the headlines. The Castle was big news again, apparently (only to be expected, really); but in fact the story contained nothing about Anderson himself and had an odd—no, an *old*—ring to it. He checked the date: July 1994. However crisp and new looking—*and* smudgy with ink, after all this time—the paper was in fact more than eighteen months out of date. That gave Anderson pause, and again alarm bells chimed in the back of his mind. The date was or should be (how long had he spent . . . *there*?) oh, late February or early March 1996. But the sun striking through the taxi's windows felt more like a July sun to him. And the driver was in his shirt sleeves, with his window wound down.

"Driver." Anderson leaned forward. "Er, would you happen to know today's date?"

They'd reached Anderson's club and the driver jumped out, opened his door for him. The Minister got out and paid the fare, and repeated, "Well? The date?"

The driver nodded, smiled, got back into his taxi. "That was today's paper you was readin', guv," he said. "Bought it meself, I did. But don't worry, there's no extra charge!" And before Anderson could ask any further questions, he'd driven off.

"Today's paper?" the Minister muttered, shaking his head. "Twenty months out of date?" Had it been a misprint? Could he have made a mistake? Had the driver perhaps made a mistake? Anderson snorted, headed for the canopied entrance to his rather exclusive club, and nodded his usual (or perhaps slightly more worried than usual) nod of greeting at the elderly but immaculate commissionaire. "Good afternoon, Joe."

Joe Elkins, beribboned veteran of some ancient conflict or other, frowned back at him with a visible uncertainty and touched his chin wonderingly. "Er, good afternoon, Mister . . . ?"

God! thought Anderson. *The man's been on extended sick leave for so long he's forgotten the names of the bloody members and residents! Why do we employ such doddering old cretins?* "It's Mr. Anderson, Joe." (No reaction.) "David Anderson? Minister? Or are you perhaps hint-ing that I may have forgotten your fiver this week, eh?"

That did it. "Ah, of course, stupid of me!" the old fool at once sputtered. "Mr. Anderson, yes, certainly!" He nodded, beamed, squinted this way and that and looked Anderson up and down, and finally saluted. But as the Minister made to pass he placed himself just a little in the way and held out his hand.

"Later, Joe, later." Anderson brushed by him. "On my way out, perhaps. This evening. But right now I'm in a terrible hurry."

Old Joe Elkins, he thought, frowning as he crossed the wide, airy foyer to the desk. The receptionist was absent (nothing unusual) but Anderson leaned across and lifted his key from its peg. Suite 37. *Old Joe Elkins, with a piece of shrapnel in his back, whisked off to the hospital, oh—how long ago? Seemed like years since he'd given the old fart his last weekly fiver!* But Old Joe's face had been a familiar one, and everything familiar was like a warm, welcoming handshake.

Almost sprinting up the wide, sweeping stairs, Anderson passed Lord Cromleigh coming down. "Good afternoon, Sir Harry," he said, but without pausing. The old duffer was an ex–Minister of Defence and had a habit of cornering him for hours on end about the modern "shambles" at MOD. But glancing back he saw that Cromleigh had stopped and was looking up at him, looking in fact completely mystified.

"Eh? What? Hmm?" the portly lord was muttering.

Senile! Anderson thought. But at the top of the stairs he almost collided with Simon Matherly, a mincing chat-show host whose too-easily earned millions couldn't conceal the fact of his glaring indifference to women. They were neighbours (Matherly had Suite 38) but Anderson had always kept him at a distance; the creature positively gushed! But knowing Anderson's preferences, Matherly had never much bothered to cultivate him. Now, however, the man literally fawned on him.

"*Dreadfully* sorry, Old Chap!" Matherly grasped Anderson's hand in his own warm paw. "My fault *entirely*—should watch where I'm going. Almost had you flat on your back just then, which would never do, eh, eh?" Twinkling, he gently elbowed Anderson's midriff. And then, low-voiced: "Er, you're new here, aren't you?"

Anderson pushed him away, sidled around him. "The clothes may be new," he replied, "but I'm not. You must have been drinking, Simon—or maybe it's time you got your pince-nez seen to." He hurried on to the top of the stairs and looked back. Both Cromleigh and Matherly were staring after him now. Were his clothes *that* different?

Opposite the first-floor landing was the billiards room; its doors stood open and George (Brigadier) Carleton-Ffines, the club's president and founder member, was engaged in a game with some snot-nosed aristocrat yuppie. Anderson remembered seeing this young man here once before some years ago. For all his money and silver-spoon background he'd been denied membership: something about his making the fatal mistake of beating the Brigadier at billiards! Perhaps he was now having another go at it. And maybe this time he'd let the old fraud win!

But the Brigadier was the president, and Anderson liked to keep on good terms with him. Actually, he believed Ffines quite genuinely liked him, and he had little doubt but that when he saw him he'd throw down his cue in astonishment and roar like a bull. "Now where the devil have *you* been, young Anderson?" he'd roar. "And what *is* all this twaddle about a castle or something up in Scotland that eats people? Eh, eh? I mean—damn me—Scotland's full of the bloody things, but they don't all run around eating people now do they? What?"

The Brigadier had just potted red, a fluke if ever Anderson saw one. But: "Oh, *shot* sir!" he said, stepping in through the open doors.

Ffines glanced at him. "Eh? D'you think so? Well, I suppose it was, really."

"What?" His young opponent was plainly astonished. "Shot?" He laughed. "A good shot? Why, I've never seen such a fluke!"

The Brigadier grunted something inaudible, went a little red in the face, put down his cue and began to twist his moustaches. A sure sign that he was annoyed. He looked at Anderson again and his expression was unmistakable. *Now who the bloody hell's this?* he was thinking.

Suddenly Anderson felt cold. It was as if a breeze from outer space had just blown on his spine. He felt cold and weak and faint. And powerless, which was worst of all. In desperation he looked around the room. On one of the chairs he spied a copy of the *Financial Times*. In a place like this, that one would have to be right up to date, this morning's paper. Two strides took him to the chair and he snatched up the paper in hands that were trembling again. 24 July 1994. And now things fitted together, and he remembered, and he knew. . . .

The Brigadier's young opponent had meanwhile spotted the red ball. "Well . . ." He spoke to Ffines. "It's still your shot. I suppose you do intend to claim that fluke?"

"They all count, young fellow-me-lad." The Brigadier rounded on him. "And anyway it wasn't a fluke." And then he rounded on Anderson, too. "Incidentally, just who the blazes are you and what are you doing in here? Press, are you? Somebody or other's secretary? Here to arrange an interview? I've an office for that sort of thing, don't y'know!"

Anderson fell into a chair and let the newspaper go flying. Eyes staring from a chalk white face, he said, "You don't know me, do you?"

"Eh? What? Haven't I just said as much? Know you? I never saw you before in my life!"

The House of Doors, thought Anderson. *The bloody House of Doors! My own personal hell. I should have known it*. He hadn't lost five months but gained twenty of them, gone back in time. And this wasn't the planet he was familiar with. Oh it was "Earth," all right, but it wasn't his Earth. In this world he didn't exist, probably hadn't even been born. Old Joe the commissionaire hadn't recognised him; of course not, for he wasn't a member and never had been. Not of *this* club. Joe Elkins, yes—who'd gone into hospital and never come out again. That had been eighteen months ago, but it hadn't happened here yet. Anderson's brain whirled as it tried to balance the facts and come out even. Why, he remembered now how he'd given a fiver into Joe's widow's fund. He'd considered it a bargain, that last fiver, instead of one each week.

"Are we still playing, or aren't we?" The yuppie type had definitely soured now. And so had the Brigadier.

"Game's finished!" he snapped. "And so are you. Out! Come back when you know how to lose gracefully."

That too, thought Anderson. *Except this isn't the young idiot's second go but his first.* "Jesus! Jesus!" he burst out, leaping to his feet. "That policeman should have known me. If not through all that filth, from my photograph at least. I don't exist here. I'm nothing here. Power? I don't even have an identity here!"

He advanced on the Brigadier. Ffines saw him coming: a madman, eyes starting out, frothing at the mouth, mumbling and shrieking. Backed up against a wall, he snatched up his cue and prodded Anderson in the chest with it. "Eh? Eh? What?" he bellowed.

Anderson growled low in his throat and knocked the cue aside, sent it clattering to the floor. He pounced on the Brigadier and held him up by his lapels. It was worth one last try. But something was bending in Anderson's brain, first this way then that, bending and weakening like a paper clip at a board meeting. "I'm Anderson," he grated. "David A-n-d-e-r-s-o-n. MOD. A minister of the government of the day. You are Brigadier Ffines, president of this club. I'm a member and resident here, Suite thirty-seven. Now then . . . *tell me you know me!*"

"Eh?" Ffines spluttered, turning purple. "Are you mad? Carruthers has thirty-seven. He's our man at MOD. David Anderson? I never bloody *heard* of you!"

Anderson snarled and tossed the Brigadier aside. "But it's still a world *like* mine, at least!" he cried. "It's still Earth or a sort of Earth! I came up from nowhere before and I can do it again. Power? I'll show you power! I'll get there yet!"

The receptionist and a porter ran in. They were both big men. They jumped on Anderson and bore him down, and the Brigadier sat on him. "Raving lunatic!" Ffines roared. "Who the hell let him in?"

"I did," the receptionist gasped. "I was on the phone, sir. Message from the police—a warning—about this Anderson bloke coming here. They said they'd checked him out and he'd probably be impersonating a minister from the MOD. Except the MOD don't know him! This must be the bloke."

"It bloody well *is* the bloke!" Ffines exploded. "Out with the sod! Down the stairs and out the door! And make sure he bounces when he lands!"

The paper clip in Anderson's brain bent one last time and snapped. He gave a wild shriek, threw them all off, fled out the billiards-room doors and went bounding, floating, gibbering down the stairs, across the foyer, and—

Outside, under the canopy, talking earnestly to dead Old Joe Elkins—there was the policeman Anderson had bumped into in Oxford Street. Anderson's face split wide open in a mad, frothing grin. "Bastard!" he howled. "Oh, you bastard! Why . . . don't . . : you . . . *recognise* . . . meeeee!"

He reached out long, eager arms, with straining hands shaped into talons, and hurled himself straight at the swinging glass doors. He crashed right through them—

But behind him they gonged shut, which wasn't right. And outside, it wasn't Knightsbridge. . . .

Chapter Forty

It was midnight in the police station in Perth, a Thursday night and quiet. In the rest·room the three-man standby patrol took it easy, played cards and drank coffee. The mobile patrol Alpha One prowled in the town, crisscrossing the cold, damp streets with its headlights, occasionally coming up on the air in a crackle of hissing static to state its location and pass on desultory situation reports. Nothing much was happening.

Police Sergeant Angus McBride was on desk duty, keeping himself busy by checking out yesterday's traffic accident reports. Eight more hours before his shift ended and he'd be free to go home, and by the time he got in his wife would already be on her way to work. Hell of a life! Maybe during the coming weekend they'd find some time to do something together.

McBride heard the outer door open and close, heard hesitant, uncertain footsteps cross the floor of the now empty advisory annexe to the door of the Duty Room. He waited expectantly until the buzzer went and a light started flashing over the door, then pressed the electronic release and heard the door click open. McBride watched the figure of a man enter and cross to the desk. Making no attempt just yet to look at his night visitor too closely, the Sergeant wondered what the trouble would be.

A missing person? A lost child? Burglary? Theft? This time of night it was usually a stolen car. Yobs thrown out of the pubs were wont to go joyriding—and sometimes they were wont to smash up the cars they took and kill people with them. The accident report he'd just been checking had been one such case: drunk steals car, mows down old lady. What a bastard!

The stranger had come to a halt now in front of McBride's slightly elevated desk. They looked at each other. The Sergeant saw a man in an overcoat, tall and blockily built, with dark brown hair, faintly foreign eyes and a mouth without emotion. There was a sort of half-smile hidden in the face, but lacking any genuine warmth. The sergeant gained an impression of strength—rather of power, heat—like a blowtorch on stone. There seemed to be a deal of contradiction in the man. And in that McBride was very observant.

"Can I help you in some way?" he said.

His visitor had scarcely studied McBride at all; he saw just another human being. "Possibly," he answered. "You're holding a man called

Rodney Clarke Denholm. I'll be representing him. My name is Jon Bannerman."

McBride sighed and looked this way and that; he tried hard not to show his disgust. "Do you know what time it is?" he said. "I mean, we don't usually allow visitors—not even solicitors—at this time of night, Mr. Bannerman."

"I did phone earlier, at about ten this morning," Bannerman lied. "I've come up from London. Missed several connections due to snow on the rails. And the trains I did manage to catch were all delayed. I'm sorry if I'm putting you to any trouble."

"You phoned, you say?" McBride opened the telephone book, began to check through the entries.

Bannerman took out his locator, looked at it in the palm of his hand like a man glancing at a pocket calculator. He saw that there were three men in a back room several rooms removed from here, and another man, alone, in one of a block of six cells down a corridor leading off from this control room. That would be Denholm. There was no one else around.

The radio came to life in a sputter of static. "Alpha One," the caller announced himself, "it's dead out here. ETA your location figures five minutes, over?"

McBride answered, "Zero, roger so far, over?"

"Alpha One: put the coffee on, out."

Five minutes, Sith thought. *It will be enough.*

McBride looked at him again. "Patrol's coming in," he said. "But I'm afraid I can't find any record of your call. Ten this morning, you say? Nothing here . . ." He shook his head. "But look, if you care to wait a few minutes until the patrol's in, one of them will let you in to see Denholm and wait outside until you're through with him, okay?"

"No." Bannerman shook his head. "Not okay, and I don't care to wait. Do you have the keys to Denholm's cell?"

Suddenly McBride was very much aware of the man's size. He was big and strong, and seemed wound up as tight as a steel spring. Like a cat ready to leap out from the long grass on some unsuspecting sparrow. "The key?" He inadvertently glanced down at the bunch of keys dangling from his belt.

Bannerman saw the flicker of his eyes and nodded. "I want to see Denholm now. You'll take me to him and open the door."

Trouble! the Sergeant thought, and his hand strayed towards the alert button connected to the standby room. Bannerman's reactions were lightning fast; he reached across the desk and trapped McBride's wrist in a fist like a vise; with his free hand he knocked the policeman's flat-topped cap flying and sank his fingers into his hair, then yanked him bodily up and over the desk, hurling him to the floor. Crashing down on his head and one shoulder, the sergeant was knocked unconscious.

There hadn't been a lot of noise. Bannerman cocked his head on one side and listened a moment, heard nothing out of the ordinary. He bent down and tore the bunch of keys loose from McBride's belt, crossed silently to the door to the cells and opened it. And a moment later he stood in the corridor outside the occupied cell.

Denholm woke up when he heard the key grating in the lock. He was still lying on his back on a steel bunk bed when Bannerman put on the light and moved to stand beside him. "Rodney Denholm?"

Blinking and rubbing his eyes, Denholm sat up. He clasped his bandaged right arm, which was still stiff from the graze Turnbull's bullet had given it, and looked at his visitor. "What?" he mumbled. "Yes, I'm Denholm. But who . . . ?"

Bannerman caught his arm under the shoulder and jerked him to his feet. "You are to come with me," he said—but even as he spoke, behind him the cell door slammed shut!

Bannerman released Denholm, leaped for the door. He'd left the keys dangling in the lock. Sergeant McBride, weak, staggering and white as a sheet, was trying to coordinate himself sufficiently to turn the key. Barely conscious, he still hadn't sounded the alert and acted more out of instinct than common sense.

In the upper section of the steel door was a grid of iron bars formed of nine eight-inch squares. Bannerman's eyes glowed red and his breath began to whoosh. Calling on his construct's reserves, Sith caused him to reach through the bars with both hands and grab McBride—and commence to drag him through them!

Bannerman's right hand crushed the policeman's throat, tore his windpipe and Adam's apple loose and *into* the cell in a welter of blood and gristle. His left hand hauled on the sergeant's right arm until it was pulled out of joint at the shoulder. And furiously Bannerman dragged pieces of McBride into the cell, including his head, from which the bars sheared off his ears. Finally, quite dead, the policeman hung there like a mutilated scarecrow, one-third of him on Bannerman's side of the door.

The door was still unlocked; Bannerman turned the handle and kicked it open; he looked back at Denholm and motioned him into activity. "Out," he said, his voice cold again and the fires dying in his eyes. "Quietly—and quickly!"

Denholm was frozen to the spot. His mouth had fallen open and his tongue flopped about in his throat, but no words came out. He was trying to scream and couldn't, gurgling like a man in a bad dream who fights to wake up. And Bannerman saw that he was quite incapable of acting or accepting instructions. He struck him in the stomach and, as he folded, rabbit-punched him unconscious.

From the midnight street outside the police station, Alpha One radioed, "One for Zero, we're home. Where's the coffee?" The driver parked up and switched off; he and his Number One got out of the patrol car and entered the police station. As they crossed to the duty room, Bannerman stepped out from behind the door and carrying Denholm across his shoulders vanished into darkness. One of the two constables thought he heard something, turned quickly and looked. But the outer door was already swinging shut.

The other policeman pressed the buzzer for admittance and waited—and waited—and after some little time began to yell.

Eventually the standby patrol sent a member to find out what all the noise was about. . . .

* * *

Jack Turnbull was sucked through the coffin-shaped door into inky darkness. Then . . . he was inside a stone water chute, being hurtled like a spider down a plug hole into some monstrous subterranean sump—or into his own personal hell. As suddenly and terrifyingly as his ride had started, so it ended and he was shot out into jet black space . . . and down into water as thick and as black as midnight mud.

Surfacing, he gulped cold, reeking air into starving lungs, and treading water he turned in a slow circle. In all directions save one there was only darkness, but in that one direction he saw stalactites like stone daggers descending from a domed dripstone ceiling, and a ledge of slimy stone, all fitfully illuminated by the flickering yellow flaring of a torch or torches.

And in an instant he was back in that mountain cave in Afghanistan, where his torturers weighed him with rocks and submerged him in the underground river, and left him there for— God, how long?—before hauling him out and questioning him again.

He'd been caught with a Mujehaddin outfit in the hills close to Kabul, disguised as one of them. The Russians had been tipped off: a gun-runner ferrying near-sentient American stingers through to the guerrillas was with them right now in the hills, teaching them how to shoot down Soviet transports out of Kabul. It was their chance to hit back against "foreign intervention" and teach Turnbull and those like him a well-deserved lesson, also to even the score for a lot of dead or missing Russian aircrew.

Whoever it was had blown the whistle, he

377

*must be Mujehaddin, one of two men employed
as information gatherers, who had occasional
jobs in the city. Turnbull had known both of
them and one had been a close friend: the big
man had saved the guy's life in a misplanned
foray against a Russian fortress down in Zam-
indawar. He hoped to God it wasn't Ali Kandamakh who'd shit on him. Not that it would make
much difference now. Turnbull had been the
only survivor of the ambush, and only then because the Russians had wanted him alive. But
at the same time they hadn't wanted to dirty
their hands, which was why they'd given him to
their Afghan puppets, who in turn had handed
him over to their torturers. . . .*

Turnbull swam towards the ledge, through
water that glopped like glue, and saw in the
shadows of stalagmites and stalactites a
bearded, flame-eyed crew waiting for him there.
And he guessed—no, he knew—that it was going to be the same all over again. He understood the principle of the thing; Gill's
explanation had been one hundred percent correct; the House of Doors was testing them—
testing *him*—to the breaking point.

Well, Jack Turnbull hadn't broken that time
in Afghanistan—though he'd been no good for
anything since then, except as a tame watchdog
to puffed-up clowns—and he certainly wasn't
going to break now. Not now that he knew he
was only fighting against himself, against his
own worst nightmare. But—

*He remembered how it had been: the cold,
rushing water, and the rocks holding him there
on the bottom, bound hand and foot, feeling the
water sluicing by while his lungs screamed for*

air and his nostrils gaped and his heart pounded in his chest like it was trying to tear itself free and break out!

What did they think he was, these torturers? A pearl diver? A Japanese sponge fisherman? It was all in the mind, he knew—the ability to hold your breath underwater—but those guys did it for a living, and they had the psychological advantage of being able to surface whenever they wanted to. And Jack Turnbull? He had no advantages. Just ropes and rocks and water that wanted to be into him like—like a stiff prick into a willing virgin! Christ, it had no conscience at all, that water. . . .

And this water was just as bad. It was different but just as bad. It *would be* as bad, when he had no control over it. Stagnant but deep. Thick but cold. Made of a great deal of oxygen, true, but also of far, far too much hydrogen, in a combination just as deadly as sulphuric acid—if you happened to be lying under it. He was closer to the ledge now and could see that the raggedy types waiting for him there had ropes, and rocks in nets. Just the same as before. Or . . . worse?

Turnbull was suddenly aware of things moving about his legs. Fish? Blindfish? Cavernicolous catfish come to sniff at this intruder and see if he was edible? He trod water and reached down along his right thigh. Something as big as a plate had fastened itself to him like a giant sticking plaster. He tore it free, brought it up into the light of the torches on the ledge. *Jesus!*

The thing was a kind of leech. They were all over his legs, his belly, back and thighs! And over his screams he could hear those bastards on the ledge laughing!

They'd laughed in Afghanistan, too. Four times they'd submerged him, and each time they'd brought him up they'd laughed. But he hadn't talked, not a word. What good would it do to talk? The sooner he'd let it all out the sooner they'd let him out—all over the floor of the cave. Which was why he'd decided that the next time they sank him in the water, he was just going to open his mouth and drink the fucking stuff. It would be like drinking whisky except it wouldn't taste so good and would knock him out that much faster—forever! But it was coming anyway and at least this way it would be on his terms.

Then one of the bastards had yelled: "I spicking English! I insulting you in your own tongue pig-bastard shit-eater!" And Turnbull had known the voice, and when its owner came closer, he'd known the gap-toothed, wicked grin, too! Ostensibly checking his ropes where they bound his hands behind him, the Afghan had sliced them through and pressed the knife into Turnbull's eager hand. God bless you Ali Kandamakh, you old mountain wolf! And a moment later they'd kicked him back into the underground river.

Down on the bottom he'd freed his feet, sliced through the ropes which bound him to the weighted nets, then clung tight to the bundles of stones, waiting for them to drag him out again. And when at last they did . . . this time Turnbull had been the one with the psychological advantage.

He'd come out of the water like a salmon and into them like a knife. Exactly like a knife! Ali

*took one and Turnbull two, which left the one
who put his knife in Ali's back and through his
heart. Then Turnbull got that one, too, and it
was over. All over for Ali.*

*After that . . . Turnbull had been into the hills
and gone like a ghost, listening to the choppers
overhead until nightfall, then heading for the big
rebel camp up in the Hindu Kush.*

A month later and he'd been back in London. . . .

But all of that had been nine years ago and
this was now. And now as then these jokers on
the ledge *thought* they had the advantage. For
which reason Turnbull screamed his throat raw
and tore more of the leeches off his body and
begged them with every gasped breath to drag
him up out of this scummy soup. They had
knives, too, just like the ones his Afghan torturers had had. (Of course, for that was his recur-
ring nightmare, from which he still hadn't
managed to free himself.) But when they saw
his terror—the fact that he was totally un-
manned—they relaxed a little and some of them
put their knives away.

Not the one who reached down a hand to him,
though; no, for that one kept his long, curved
knife handy just in case. He reached a hand
down to Turnbull, but at the same time showed
him his dully glinting knife. Turnbull came half
up out of the scum, tightened his grip on the
man's hand, braced his feet against the ledge—
and yanked! He yanked himself up and his
yelping would-be torturer down! And as that
grimacing scarecrow fell, so Turnbull snatched
his knife from him and sprang at the others on
the ledge.

Oh, there were too many of them to make a go of it; he could only hope to slow them down a little, put the fear of Christ into them; but nonetheless he was like a lion amongst lambs while it lasted. He gutted one and hacked the throat out of another, and then he was off and running through the dripstone maze, following a path of flaring flambeaux. And as he went, so he cut down the torches and stamped them out on the dusty floor, leaving only smoke and reeking darkness, screams and shouted oaths in his wake. Then, as he passed through the last of the stalactites where the stone ceiling came down low and the cave bottlenecked—

—The way was blocked! It had been a tunnel, but now it was plugged with a mighty slab of black stone. One last torch flared where it lit the plug with its yellow light. And Turnbull saw that the slab of stone had ... a knocker? A knocker, yes, in the form and shape of a huge iron question mark!

Footsteps pounded behind him and a ragged panting that seemed to sound right in his ear. He tore loose the last leech from his ribs and turned, ducked, slammed the thing like a wad of bloody red dough into a snarling heathen face, then leaped for the knocker—

—And knocked ... !

CHAPTER FORTY-ONE

Angela slept. She hadn't intended it when she'd climbed the tree, but once at the top and when she'd seen the great soft cup formed at the heart of the palmlike branches, then she'd known that she had to sleep. Her reason for climbing the tree had been simple: to spy out the land around. To see if any of the Rod Denholms had picked up her trail. And if they had, to choose the best direction in which to run from them.

For this was her nightmare world, the world of her very blackest dream: a beautiful world marred only by the presence of her bestial, lusting, loathsome husband. Made so much more monstrous by the fact that there were dozens of him!

The climb had been easy. Like a palm, the bole of the tree had been regularly serrated where older branches had died and fallen away. The horny, cusped stumps of these shed branches had been hard on her now naked feet, but that had been the least of Angela's concerns; she'd learned as the others had learned that wounds healed quickly in these worlds created by the House of Doors; and in any case, torn feet would seem a blessing in comparison with the tearing her body would suffer if the Rods caught her.

But at the top of the long, gracefully bending trunk where the new branches grew out in a great fan to droop like exotic green and yellow plumage—in the very heart of the hugely spread leaves—there she'd seen the central cup and had gratefully settled her scratched, bruised and bloodied body into it. Lesser fronds angling inwards overhead had provided shade from the sun, and a breeze off the achingly blue sea had served to cool the fever of her body—but not of her heart and soul. For despite all of its undeniable beauty, this jewel world had proved beyond the slightest doubt that it was also capable of the utmost horror!

Before allowing herself the luxury of sleep (which her mazed and staggering mind needed, if not her poor body) Angela had thought back a little on the somewhat blurred sequence of events she'd experienced since her arrival here.

Of the arrival itself:

Sucked out of Varre's claustrophobic, crushing rock tomb by her own sarcophagus door, Angela had found herself thrown down in shallow salt water on the rim of an ocean so perfect as to make the loveliest oceans of Earth seem dull. Washed in soft, white-foaming wavelets, she'd come reeling to her feet on sand as white as marble, on a beach where a million alien shells lay drying in the warmth of a golden alien sun.

And at once she'd known that she was not alone here, for there on the beach were fresh footprints in the sand, and out in the shallows—

A dark head bobbed like a cork on the gentle swell! At first her heart had given a great leap inside her. She'd thought: *Spencer!* Or perhaps Jack Turnbull! Anderson? Then the swimmer had turned to face her—to see her and come swimming in towards the beach—and as he'd climbed up out of the waves she'd realised the full cruelty, the perversity, of the House of Doors. For it wasn't Gill or Turnbull or Anderson but her husband, Rod Denholm. Strong, handsome, leering Rod Denholm, his eyes turning to slits as the frown lifted from his forehead and he smiled . . . one of *his* smiles!

Naked, even as he'd splashed up out of the shallows towards her his lust had become apparent, and his face had twisted into that same vile mask she'd seen him wear so many times before.

She was a woman, alone on a world of her own making (or if not of her making, inhabited by her fears) and now for the first time she felt a woman's weakness. It had been different when the others were there, all in the same boat, all pitting their wits against whatever it was that controlled them. Even in the darkest circumstances they'd given each other strength, hope to carry on, companionship of sorts. Yes, even with Haggie there had been that. Oh, he had been much of a kind with Rod—in *that* respect, anyway—but however he might have misused her, Angela doubted that he'd have killed her.

But Rod was something else. That look on his face said it all: he would take her, repeatedly and savagely, and *then* kill her!

At that point she might simply have given in, surrendered herself to whatever fate was waiting—which would have signalled the end. Thone directives would have come into operation and the game would have been over; the synthesizer would have removed her from this world—or this world from Angela—and recorded her failure; all memory of her travails with Gill and the others would have been erased and she would be returned to her own place and rightful existence no worse off. All of these things would have been . . . *if* the normal rules had applied. But they no longer applied. The directives had been overruled: Sith demanded that failure be paid for in full. Clayborne had failed, and "died"; likewise Varre, a terrible, unthinkable death; and now the girl. Except she wasn't about to give in.

For as the Denholm clone came lolling arrogantly up the beach, his arms already reaching, Angela had remembered what Turnbull had said to Gill just a few minutes ago (a few *minutes*! God!) as the rock walls closed to crush them: "It won't be finished until we break," he'd said. "So for fuck's sake don't break now!"

For fuck's sake? A certain irony in that!

She'd backed away from the advancing Denholm, tripped and fallen on her backside—but as he sprang she'd hurled sand straight into his glittering, lusting eyes!

Don't break now! Turnbull's words kept repeating in her brain as she ran for the palmfringed forest where the sand turned to loamy soil. *"Don't break now!"* For somewhere in this place—on the surface of this planet—there would be another cross section, another projection, another manifestation of the House of Doors. And while there were other places into which she might escape, then she wasn't finished yet.

And not once had she asked herself how Rod came to be here: as well ask who was Bannerman? What was he? Or a dozen other of the hundreds of questions she felt rushing through her whirling head. No use asking who this—facsimile?—was; she knew *what* he was and what he would do. He'd told her clearly enough on the telephone that time, hadn't he? And even if he was only part of her nightmare—no, *because* he was that nightmare—she knew that he or it would do it.

She'd looked back once and seen him staggering and stamping on the beach, clawing at his eyes and screaming her name with Rod's voice. "Angela! Oh, you bitch—*Angela*! Run, sweetheart, run—but I'll find you. *We'll* find you, Angela!"

The "we" had made no sense to her, not then. But in the forest, shortly, and suddenly, it would.

As she entered the cover of the trees, so beyond them she'd seen green mountains rising through a ragged tree line to yellow and ochre peaks bathing in warm sunlight. Since there seemed little chance of finding the House of Doors in the woods or along the beach, she determined to cut straight through the trees to the mountains. At least from up there she'd have an excellent view of the land all around;

and if the thing she sought was to be found (in whatever shape or form it would take this time) then perhaps she'd see it.

Also (it had dawned on her) in each of the episodes or on each world so far visited, she and the others had come upon the House of Doors almost without trying. And usually just as they were reaching the borders of human limitations. So that she'd wondered: *Is that the way this game is played?* Well, if it was, then she hadn't reached her limit yet—not nearly.

The trick of it was not to break. To win one must first play, and give it all one had. Gill wouldn't break, she knew that. Nor Turnbull. And she wondered where were they now, especially Spencer Gill. Was he in a fix as bad as hers? Probably, for that seemed to be the nature of the thing. But at that stage she still hadn't known exactly how bad her fix was. . . .

The whipping branches of trees and shrubs lashed and cut her where she burst through them; vines tripped her and pitched her headlong into the mud beside a stream; the stains of pulpy exotic plants tinted her body where she fell amongst them, crushing their leaves and flowers. And the air rasped in her throat and lungs as she drove her body to even greater excesses—to such excesses that she really couldn't believe that this was Angela Denholm at all, performing like an athlete!

And yet she knew that while this was her nightmare, still it wasn't a dream but a *living* nightmare. It was as real as all the rest of it had been. For however vivid the dream, and however true it may seem, dreaming pain is not an easy thing to do. Dreams may hurt emotionally, but rarely physically. And in this place—and in just about every place—Angela hurt like hell!

Then she'd come across the river, a broad belt of glistening water flowing between well-formed banks and over a pebble bed, and the sight of it had given her a big boost. She was a fair swimmer and knew she could make it across if she just took her time and moved diagonally with the river downstream; but the beauty of it was that this was sweet, clean, deep *water*! And if any woman had ever felt that she needed a bath—not to mention a drink—that woman was Angela Denholm.

Her bra had finally had to go; it had suffered and was no longer as form-hugging as a swim costume; its cups would act as brakes. Spencer's now tattered shirt would tuck down inside what little remained of her ski pants. And that was that, the sum of her otherworldly possessions! Bare-breasted she'd taken to the water, and almost swooning from sheer pleasure and relief as it laved her cuts and bruises, swum out across the placid deeps. In a little while she'd felt the current take her; not fighting it she'd simply gone along, at the same time gradually cutting through it towards the opposite bank.

This was a tropical world, however, and Angela did worry a little about cannibal fishes or perhaps crocodiles; but since she personally had never considered these to be "nightmarish" creatures but simply "things of nature," her fears were not exaggerated. Nor for that matter had been her fear of Rod—not now that she was clean away from him—but two-thirds of the way across, that had been about to change.

"Angelaaa!" The long halloo had echoed out

mockingly over the river, disturbing dragon-flies where they skipped the water. But ... it had sounded from in front of her! Impossible! How could Rod have crossed the river ahead of her? Angela trod water, lifting herself up to scan the bank ahead. And there he was, naked, rampant, stepping down into the river and wading to meet her. "Sweetheart," he'd called. "I can see you're all ready for me. Those lovely firm breasts of yours—but they'll be puffy purple bags when we're through, Angela my love!"

That "we" again—or did he simply mean he and she? Then, this time from behind her: "Don't swim so hard, Angela. Why waste your strength on running and swimming? You're going to need all the strength you can find in a little while, Angela."

She'd churned wildly in the water, losing her rhythm, caught up in a suddenly strengthening current. And then behind her she'd seen a second Rod Denholm—or the first?—even now diving cleanly into the water from the far bank. *Two* of them? And now it was a nightmare and she felt herself squeezed in the grip of sheerest terror.

Spun dizzily by the quickening current, she saw more Rods on the banks: displaying themselves as he had used to do, or simply waving at her and smiling their leering smiles, or diving into the river. A dozen of him. Two dozen!

Upriver, heads had bobbed and powerful arms knifed the water; she'd turned downstream, deliberately driven herself into the fastest-flowing part of the current, been swept away from him and him and—

Only her will had kept her going then. Her

will to survive, to win. He hadn't got her in her own world and he wouldn't get her in this one. Not while there was an ounce of strength left in her. Ahead of her she'd been aware of white water, a foaming, but whatever was there had to be better than what was behind. Now she made no effort to swim, was simply swept along unresisting to her fate—but at least not *that* fate.

Behind her the Rods were swimming back towards the banks, but it was too late for Angela to do the same. The current had her, was racing her back towards the sea. She remembered then how she'd climbed up from the beach through the forest. It had been the steepness of her climb which gave the river its impetus. Ahead, black shining rocks broke the surface; between them passed a tumult of tossing water; the rocks had rushed closer and she'd slipped through—into space. Torn air and rushing water and the roaring of the falls! And then the downward plunge into cool, green depths that galvanised her once more, sending her swimming underwater away from the falls, to surface in comparatively placid waters some little way beyond.

Exhausted, she'd flopped over onto her back and floated, and up there at the crest of spray-wreathed cliffs had seen a line of Rods like soldiers on the wall of a fortress, all following her progress. Then the river had taken her round an overgrown bend and the trees and foliage had intervened to separate her from the view of her tormentors; and ahead, shortly, the forest gradually opened to ocean, and the river swept grandly to the sea. . . .

Chapter Forty-two

Along the sandy shore of the river where it shallowed out, the first palms were growing. That was where Angela had dragged herself wearily ashore, pausing only sufficiently to recover a little of her strength before climbing the nearest tree. Its bole actually grew up out of the sweet water and so she left no tracks on otherwise virgin sand. From the top of the tree she'd scanned the beach in both directions, seeing nothing either to alarm or especially interest her; and then, finding the soft cup at the heart of the wide, spreading leaves, she'd lowered her body in and quickly fallen asleep.

Her dreams—nightmares within nightmares— had been full of Rod, an entire army of Rods; so that now, as the dream became more violent, she started awake. But only to discover that the dream persisted, and that now it was real again.

It was nighttime, and along the beach fires had been lit, flaring up here and there as far as the eye could see in both directions. And in the warm darkness she could hear his voice—his many voices—calling from both beach and forest alike:

"Angelaaa! Why are you hiding, Angela? You know you like it, so why not get your fill? Let us fill you, Angela. You've let everyone else, you little cow, so why not all of us? We're hard for you, Angela. We're all so very, very hard for you. . . ."

Swine! she thought, gasping her fear from between clenched teeth. *Great swines!*

She moved her aching body a little—and froze. From below, almost directly below, she'd heard the sound of someone snoring. Moments passed while she held her breath, but the snoring continued unabated. Parting the branches, she peered down. By the light of a scattered handful of small, variously coloured moons, she saw him: Rod, of course, or one of them, sprawled out on the sand close to the foot of her tree, with one foot washed by the water gentling oceanward. And in his wide-flung hand, a bottle. But . . . a bottle, here? Also, this Rod wore clothes—his own clothes—and he looked just as exhausted, perhaps even more so, than Angela herself!

Now what kind of trick was this that the House of Doors was playing on her?

She crept out between two of the great leaves, turned herself about and commenced her descent, and inch by painful, agonizingly slow inch lowered herself to the ground. The cusps left by dead branches hurt her feet as before, but she could do nothing about it, and certainly not cry out! Finally she was down; turning from the sea and keeping a low profile—especially in the vicinity of the still-sleeping, dishevelled, fully clothed Rod—she headed for the fringe of the forest where the sand of the beach turned to loam.

Her intention was to skirt the woodland, using the shadows at its rim for cover, and so make her way along the ocean strand to a place—anyplace—beyond the area of the campfires. There were Rods in the forest, too, she knew, but in that she had a small advantage: they were noisy, and she was only one and they didn't know where she was. Or so she thought.

But as she reached the trees she heard a low panting from close behind, and looking back in cold fear she saw him: the one in the clothes, with the light of the small moons on his face and in his frightened eyes. Frightened, yes, and suddenly she knew for a certainty that this was the real Rodney Denholm.

The fact was confirmed as his wide eyes swept over her moonlit face and figure. He gasped: "Angela? Is that you? Is it really you? I woke up on the beach and saw you, and I couldn't believe it was you. But . . . Jesus Christ, what *is* this place? Where are we, Angela? God, what's happening to me?"

To him, always himself. Not what was happening to them but to him. As if no one else in the entire universe mattered a damn! But at least while he was frightened like this he'd be no threat to her.

"*Shh!*" she cautioned him. "Be quiet! Can't you hear them calling? They're after me."

"After you?" He stepped closer, his voice questioning, suspicious, hardening a very little. "Those men?" But in a moment he was lost again, bewildered. "Angela, have you seen them? They all look like me!"

Yes, and I'll bet they all act like you, too! And yet suddenly she felt she could cope with him, and far better than she might ever hope to cope with the pseudo-Rods. His fear gave her the edge over him; for the first time since the day she'd married him, she had the upper hand.

He was like a lost, petulant child. The neck of a bottle stuck out from his jacket pocket, but he seemed sober enough. It would be a difficult thing, to get drunk in a place like this. He'd tried, though, for she could smell it on his breath. Or maybe he'd slept it off. Now if only he could stay sober, perhaps he could be of some use to her yet.

"Rod," she whispered, "I have to get away from here—but quickly and quietly. You can come with me if you like—but only if you do as I say. God knows you never protected me before, the opposite in fact, but right now I could use some protection. You're a man and you're strong. You could be if you wanted to. So these are my terms: look after me as best you can and you'll benefit from my knowledge of this place." (That was a joke!) "And if there's a way out, maybe we'll find it. It's up to you, take it or leave it. But now I'm on my way."

"Angela!" he gasped, and she guessed he'd scarcely heard a word she'd said. "But don't you understand that something terrible has happened to me? I was in the police station in Perth. A man came in the night. He . . . he killed a policeman, horribly! He pulled him through the bars of my cell—literally *pulled* him to pieces! I—"

"I haven't the time, Rod," she said, feeling sickened. Not by what he'd said but just by the fact of him. "I should have known you wouldn't be able to look after yourself, let alone me." She turned into the shadows.

"I'm coming!" He stumbled after her. "Don't leave me, Angela. I'm coming!"

"Quietly, then!" she hissed, her heart lurching with its terror. He took her hand in trembling fingers and the touch of him felt like slime. She shook him off and said, "Very well. Stay right behind me. But Rod—don't touch me, do you hear?"

"How long have you been here?" she asked him, when they were past the last fire and the calling voices had fallen far behind. They trudged along the beach under alien moons and constellations, and Angela guessed that theirs were the first human footprints to ever mar these strange sands—and probably the last. Those other Rods back there: they weren't human, couldn't be, for the human Rod was right here beside her. And even he wasn't her idea of human. Not anymore.

He shrugged. "I woke up on the beach back there with these clothes I stand in and two full bottles. I saw some of those men—saw that they could all be my twins, or whatever—and thought I was dreaming. They were calling your name and searching for you, but sort of aimlessly. When it dawned on me that I wasn't dreaming, then I thought I was mad. And what had happened at the police station, maybe that was my madness, too. So I drank one of the bottles and passed out. When I woke up again, it was dark and I saw you. It seemed to me you were my last hold on sanity, or proof of my insanity, and so I followed you." He looked at her. "You still haven't told me where we are, or how we come to be here."

"There's a castle on Ben Lawers," she answered. "Not a real castle but an alien thing. It's a sort of trap. We call it the House of Doors. It took us in, absorbed us—don't ask me how. Since when we've been to many different places, all of which were terrible. And finally I'm here."

"We?" He uncorked his bottle, took a swig.

Watching him drink, Angela couldn't hide her disgust. Now that they were away from the other Rods—now that there was no "competition" and his fear of the unknown was fading—he was beginning to sound and behave like his old self again. His true self: his swinish, overbearing self. "Me," she finally answered, "Spencer Gill, a man called Jack Turnbull, an MOD minister called David Anderson—oh, and some others. It's all very confused and confusing. I might have been here for a couple of days, a week, even a month for all I know."

He thought about it, nodded. "All of that time," he said, "with all of those men." His voice had thickened; she could almost feel his eyes on the loll of her breasts where Gill's shirt barely covered them, coveting them. He pulled on the bottle again, drinking deep. "Dressed like that, and with all those men . . ."

The beach had narrowed to a strip of sand fifty feet wide between the sea and the forest. Away out across the ocean a faint silver nimbus was forming on the horizon. Dawn was about to break. Angela brushed dangling ringlets of jet hair out of her eyes. "I must have slept the night right through," she said. "That's how badly I needed it."

"Needed it?" Rod repeated her, chuckling gruffly. "You, badly in need of it? That'll be the day! Oh, *sleep*! I see what you mean!" And suddenly his voice was thick with sarcasm.

Finding the firm, ocean-washed sand easier going, Angela walked faster. It had dawned on her that she was stronger than Rod, or at least that she had more stamina. There was that to say for the House of Doors at least: it built up your stamina!

"I suppose you realise," he said, panting as he hurried to catch up, "that we're pretty much like Adam and Eve in this fucking place? I mean if we can't get out of here, if we're actually stuck here, we—"

She whirled to face him, her deep, dark eyes alive in the first ray of light from the rising sun—but alive with anger, not fear. "I realise a lot of things," she snapped. "Like what a cheap, shitty, bullying bastard you were! Like just how bad it was with you! And like how it will *never* be that way again, not on any world! A Garden of Eden? Is that what you were thinking? Well forget it, Rod. I'd have those mindless clones of yours before I'd ever have you again!"

He grabbed her arm, brought her to a halt. His face had twisted into that familiar, ugly, lusting snarl she knew so well of old. "You're still my wife," he reminded her, his voice guttural now. "You can't deny me anything. And especially not here." He took another long pull at his bottle, which was already three-quarters empty. "God, how I've missed pouring myself into you—Angela, *sweetheart*!"

Something snapped. She drew back her arm, balled her small fist and hit him. But it was more shock and astonishment than pain that felled him. Snarling obscenities, he scrambled upright again. But before he could say or do anything further—

"*Angelaaa!*" a voice called from the forest. "Where are you, sweetheart? Just think of all the good times when we find you, Angela. Why you'll be able to have us three at a time! It will be fun while it lasts, anyway. While *you* last, Angela . . ."

"They *know* you!" The real Rod drunkenly blurted his accusation. "They've had you—you can't deny it. But you'd deny me, wouldn't you—bitch!"

Naked figures stepped out of the trees, and others were coming from back along the beach. For a moment Angela was frozen in horror—with the horrific futility of it all—but only for a moment. It still wasn't her time to give in, not yet by a long shot.

She turned from Rod and ran through the shallow water and softly lapping wavelets. Alarmed by her thudding footsteps, and possibly by the renewed burst of calling from the forest and beach, great strange night-feeding crabs came trundling out of the ocean-fringing palms, tumbling each other in their eagerness to make it back to the safety of the sea. They were timid things, all of a foot long but carrying no pincers, and they reared up and cowered back from Angela where she ran and Rod as he pursued her.

"Bitch!" he shouted after her. "Cow! It's the end of you, sweetheart. You'd better believe it—*the end*!"

She tripped on what looked like a length of slimy rope—which immediately snaked across the wet sand and was sucked down out of sight! It was the siphon of some great clam, which had been sent up like a snorkel to lie on the surface of the quaking sand. Then she saw what was happening: the great crabs, scuttling down to' the beach, were triggering the clams. Vast hinged shells were opening, and the crabs were tumbling into their scalloped cups; and when they had their fill, then the shells were grinding shut again. But huge? Why, these things could surely take a man! Some of them must be all of ten or twelve feet across, and the shell of the horny valves was at least eight inches thick! And yet, while there was an obvious danger in it, there was nothing sinister; it was Nature at work and nothing more.

Again Angela stepped on some wriggling, snaking thing, and a shell opened immediately in front of her. Sand and salt water fountained as the huge bivalve yawned like a trapdoor; inside, pink and grey flesh pulsated and a mantle full of black, saucer-sized eyes flopped and writhed. Angela leaped to one side—straight into the arms of Rod! He grabbed her shirt and tore it from her, then threw her down and nailed her writhing body to the sand with his own superior weight.

"You ... *bastard*!" she spat at him, but he caught her breasts in his hands and squeezed.

"Hold it right there, sweetheart," he said, "and hold it very still. Or I swear I'll pulp these tits of yours!" He would and she knew it. She did as he demanded—for now—relaxed and lay quite still. He pinned her throat with one hand, tore open his trousers with the other. Nothing happened. Made impotent by the liquor, he was no threat.

But Angela was. She brought up her knee as hard and as fast as she could, ramming it home between his thighs. Screaming like a gelding he flopped to one side and curled up, holding himself. She scrambled to her feet. And through the expanding dawn light she saw them coming. But where Rod was impotent, the pseudo-Rods most certainly were not.

She turned this way and that. They were everywhere. Rod grabbed her ankle, screaming, "She's here, she's here! The bitch is here! Come and get your fill!"

She yanked back her foot, broke free of his grasp, turned to run. But where to? Rod was up on his knees; he lunged at her and staggered to his feet, then slipped on a writhing siphon that slurped down out of sight into the sand. He grabbed her arm—and a great shell cranked open to one side of them. Rod teetered on the brink of the monster Tridacna; Angela kicked him again in the same place; he fell, gagging, into suffocating slop and constricting muscular tissues. And the upper shell lowered itself and ground shut.

The pseudo-Rods were converging on Angela.

She had nowhere left to run. "Fuck you all!" she screamed at them, shaking her balled fists.

Then, close by, another shell opened. But inside it there was only the yawning blackness of a great pit. It was the colour of space out between the farthest stars. But Angela knew that in fact it was a door, a tunnel to another world.

And even as the Rods came leering and loping towards her, she gave a glad, mad cry and toppled herself in. . . .

CHAPTER FORTY-THREE

Spencer Gill woke up to a weird dawn on a weird mechanical world which was half the creation of his own mind and half the work of an alien machine called a synthesizer. A machine which could synthesise anything, even space itself. Many of the worlds it made were or had been real worlds: it recreated them not in space as we know it but in the space *between* the spaces we know. Gill woke up and felt the Thone instrument in his pocket and remembered how to use it, master it, understand it. And that was important, for it was a step towards the understanding of all such machines.

In the hour or so leading to waking his mind had broken barriers of new knowledge. Lying just under the surface of his conscious machine mentality, subconscious instinct had released a flood of alien ideas: he had been allowed to glimpse new techniques, had felt his abilities enhanced, expanded, had more fully grasped that basic understanding which was the key. But like all things dreamed he knew that such skills would fade without practice, that the ephemeral would pass without reinforcement. Jewel insects turn to dust in a year, but preserved in amber they last out the aeons.

"Amber," said Gill to Barney, who already understood quite a bit of what his new master still had to learn. "I have to find some amber, Barney—or else my dragonflies might crumble. Last time we were here you wanted to show us something. All right—so show me."

Through the higher levels of the rusting, rotting machine city or factory they made their way under a rising nuclear sun to a place Barney knew of old. The dog led the way, and even if Gill hadn't followed him, he would have gone on his own. He had to, because unlike Gill he needed to eat. He was here in error, and Sith of the Thone had not caused him to be processed, altered. In short, he was *all* dog, a real dog, and dogs get hungry. And in some of the synthesizer's reconstructed worlds at least, there were good things to eat.

A mile from the rusty iron cave Barney reached his objective and stood before it, yipping and wagging his stump of a tail. Gill came after, crawling through a tangle of twisted girders and rust-scabbed, buckled steel plates, and finally stood up before one of the giant TV screens. It seemed no different to all the others Gill had seen: housed in a dull, grey metal frame, it was as big as a large cinema screen and showed alien "static" in the form of colours all muddied together in a vast whirl, like the strange galaxy of some surrealist painter. Protecting the screen was a rusty iron grid formed of bars two inches thick. The squares of the grid were maybe two feet across, so that Gill guessed he could angle himself through if he wanted to. But first he had to be sure that he wanted to.

He wondered if the grid was live and tossed a length of frayed copper cable at it to find out. It was: the piece of cable was hurled sputtering aloft, spraying molten golden droplets everywhere. Barney yelped and cowered back; Gill, too, asking, "So what's this, Barney? Are you showing me a quick way to end it all if I get desperate? Maybe we're here to admire the pretty pictures, or something?"

Or something, obviously. Barney approached the grid, stepped nervously through a square, padded closer to the screen. Then, only a foot or so away from the flat picture, he paused and stood frozen, as if fascinated by the slow, monotonous distortion of colours in meaningless motion. Gill watched, wondered, and thought: *Maybe it isn't meaningless after all.*

Finally there came one of those infrequent flashes of white light—at which Barney leaped straight forward, directly *into* the screen! In a moment he'd disappeared, and the screen's colours continued their tortured, muddy swirling. It was as if Barney had never been there.

Gill waited for some minutes but the dog didn't return. Was he dead or what? A dog, committing suicide? Or had he simply known the exact moment to make his move? Gill got down on all fours and, with the short hairs prickling at the back of his neck, crept through one of the squares at the bottom of the grid. There were inches to spare but he didn't draw breath until he was through. And as he stood up on the other side—

—Barney came back! He stepped out of the screen like coming through a waterfall, except he wasn't wet. *A door?* Gill wondered. *Is this a door like all the others in the House of Doors— or is it unlike all the others? Obviously it goes somewhere, for Barney went there. But this door seems to be part of a two-way system. And Barney has a return ticket!*

Indeed, Barney had more than that. He had a rabbit, too—or something suspiciously like one, despite an extra pair of legs—freshly dead and dangling from his clenched jaws! Wagging his rear end, the dog came and laid his offering at Gill's feet. The rabbit-thing gave a final twitch and lay still.

Gill shook his head, partly to refuse the gift and partly out of bewilderment. Mostly the latter. How come the dog had figured out things which still mystified him? Was Barney *just* a dog or maybe ... something else? Part of the game? Gill looked at the animal through narrowed eyes; he called him, checked his name tag, automatically fondled his ears. And then he sighed. No, the dog was just a dog—with fleas. And he was hungry.

"You go ahead." Gill gave him back his offering. "Thanks but I'm not hungry. Not for food, anyway." But he was very hungry for knowledge.

He looked at the screen and thought about it. He thought about the machinery which governed it, tried to get his mind inside the thing. Nothing. On their way here, Gill had let the jungle of stupid mechanisms and pointless machine parts—the futile, purposeless robots of his nightmares—eradicate the last spark of his instinctive inspiration. He had dreamed that he had all of the answers, but now it seemed they'd slipped away. Like a man who dreams he can fly, and *knows* how to do it even after he wakes up, only to find as he stumbles from his bed that gravity has robbed him of his talent. The mundane world gets in the way, and this immundane world had got in the way of Gill's expanding machine consciousness, robbing him of dormant, as-yet-unidentified skills.

Or then again, maybe not . . .

Between the energised grid and the enigmatic screen, Gill and the dog shared the weirdness of the moment. Barney who knew (knew something, at least) and Gill who wanted to know. Barney who had managed to stay alive here, even now gnawing on his rabbit, and Gill who knew he might very well die here. But maybe not.

With fingers that trembled he took out the silver cylinder from his pocket. If only he could revitalise his dream, bring back the knowledge he'd so clearly understood there. He let go of conscious effort and rolled the Thone instrument in his hands, and felt it not only with his fingers but with his mind. The tool came apart in his hands as easily as a fountain pen; he had opened it like opening the back of a watch—no, easier than that. And once again he understood it. And he remembered his dream.

He had been afraid that he'd dream of Angela

in her own world of nightmares—a world of black rape and red death—but that had not been the case. Instead his subconscious mind had gone back to wrestling with its basic obsession, his most immediate and burning problem. It may be selfish of him, but he'd dreamed only of alien science and alien mechanics.

There had been no buttons to press in that dream, no switches, no plugs or sockets, nuts or bolts. Fluid mechanics was all that there had been. Nothing solid, for solidity requires effort, and maximum efficiency should be effortless. The dream had simply reinforced his earlier findings, when he'd opened the silver cylinder to examine it for the first time. Except on that occasion he'd actually been trying too hard. But now he had the answer again, the key which was right here, waiting to be turned in its mental lock. And indeed that *was* the key: do nothing physically, do it mentally!

He looked at the two halves of alien metal in his hands—just looked at them—and they flowed together, fused, became whole. And as he put the cylinder back in his pocket, he looked at the screen again. Except that now he believed it had lost something of its mystery. And he believed he knew why.

A wheel is a wheel. Whether it draws water from a prehistoric well or balances an expensive modern watch, it still performs only one function: to turn. And the alien machines were like that; they might be simple or sophisticated in their own terms, but one principle governed all of them. And it was the same principle for the instrument in Gill's pocket as for this screen, this portal between alien spheres of existence.

Forcing the Heath-Robinson smog from his mind, Gill gingerly reached out his hands towards the screen. He closed his eyes and felt the nearness of the thing—its alien energy—tingling on his sweating palms. It was a door, yes, but it was a window, too, on all manner of stored, recorded worlds. More, it was an index, a catalog of contents, a quick search-and-scan tool. A locator.

But how do I make it work? How did Barney make it work?

Answer: he didn't. It was already working. The dog had simply smelled a world he knew, a friendly one, and jumped into it before it could go away. And suddenly Gill knew that even in a House of Doors, this most certainly was not just any old door.

There are many kinds of doors. One will take you from one room to another. But pass through a door onto a train and your exit point is limited only by the number of stations along the line. The white flashes were stations, switchover points between worlds. And the swirling colours were the sum total of those worlds before fine-tuning and visual definition.

All right, thought Gill, superimposing his will on the transdimensional multinode which was the screen, *now let's see what I can locate here.* It was like using a telephone: all he had to do was dial a number—but with his mind. Any number would do for starters. He gave a mental shrug, and dialed—

And at once the colours on the screen separated and a picture, a real picture, firmed into being. Gaping, Gill took two full paces to the rear before remembering the energised grid. At the same time, unnerved by the "memory" he'd activated, he released his mental grip on the locator. The muddy colours flooded back, but not before he'd got his fill of what the screen had shown him.

A tossing, throbbing, tropical jungle planet, where green and purple and poisonous yellow flora writhed and fought in hybrid horror, and mighty medusae drifted on mud oceans, and the atmosphere was thick with the spores and pollens of plants in their teeming millions. It had been like a vast, semisentient swamp, or a mad, mutated greenhouse.

Finally Gill moistened his dry lips and closed his mouth. Maybe he'd better dial a number he knew. Or . . . why not dial one-zero-zero and get the exchange?

He frowned as the idea took root and finally nodded. The exchange, yes. Where there are screens to be viewed and records to consult, someone—something—had to be there to view and consult them. And the thought occurred: *Why, maybe I'm being watched right now!* By Bannerman maybe? By the alien creature Bannerman contained?

Basing his design on what Haggie had told him of it, he pictured a control centre; also, he pictured the redheaded criminal's description of the alien intelligence he'd seen there, Haggie's "spook". And the colours on the screen obligingly warped into another picture.

Gill saw what the screen held, and at first it was almost too much to take in. But this time he refused to be shaken loose and hung on to it with his mind. And this is what he saw:

It was . . . kaleidoscopic. Whatever else Haggie might or might not have been, certainly he'd been articulate. His description *was* the control centre of the House of Doors. The walls crawled; they were formed of flowing, ever-changing patterns. And they weren't true walls but screens, like this very screen. And the metamorphic scenes they displayed weren't just surrealist pictures but unformed statistics and computerised components of worlds! Gill's mind staggered—but stayed upright. With the exception of three things the picture on his screen would be as meaningless to him as his Heath-Robinson horrors; and the three things were these:

One: he had the basis for understanding what he was seeing. And two: Bannerman and Sith of the Thone were there to give the picture size and shape and definition. He saw the naked, sexless, flesh-and-blood robot thing which was Bannerman, standing there with its chest laid open and its alien machine innards showing; and also the floating jelly creature which was Sith, swaying and gyrating before a screen much like Gill's own. And three: he saw what *that* screen contained:

A moving, living picture of Angela Denholm—on Clayborne's world!

She lay sprawled at the foot of a dune, mostly naked, gleaming damp and with the sand clinging to her, eyes wide in a weird mixture of emotions, relief and joy and terror. Halfway up the side of the dune was the mark of her recent arrival: a bite taken from the sand where it had collapsed under her weight and sent her tumbling to the bottom. Yes, and there were other marks, too.

Human footprints, a good many of them, all fairly recent, all starting here and heading off towards the mountains and a certain something that glittered up there. Others had landed here before Angela, and Gill thought he knew who they might be. Anderson and Turnbull? God, he hoped so!

Hope, however, was all he had time for. Nothing else. No time for elation or intense emotion of any sort. For he saw that it was already afternoon in that place, with evening only a few hours away and night just one hour beyond that. And Angela was there, on Clayborne's world.

Which was no longer a safe place for anyone to be at any time, but especially not at the fall of darkness. . . .

CHAPTER FORTY-FOUR

Gill called up other worlds and locations onto the screen, practiced his newfound skill, felt the edge of his talent sharpening in his mind. Finally he located the great crystal node—the variant House of Doors—in the mountains of Clayborne's world. And then to Barney he said, "Well, are you with me or not?" Maybe Barney could see what was on the screen, the great sinister crystal, and maybe he couldn't. But certainly he could sense Clayborne's world and his memories of the place were not good ones. Stifflegged, he backed off. "Barney," Gill told him, "you've been too long on your own." He took hold of the dog's collar. "Now I say we're going there." And dragging Barney after him he stepped through the screen.

For a moment Gill reeled, and he heard a door slam shut behind him. It was door number 777,

of course, with the dust still settling as its reverberations died away. He had supposed it
would be so. Doors in an ordinary dwelling
house allow movement from room to room, but
if someone desires to move covertly he may use
a secret passage, whose doors are known only
to him. Number 777 was the door from which
Bannerman had emerged the last time Gill and
the others were here. It was in effect a "secret
passageway" to and from the alien control centre.

But Gill asked himself: *What if that last time
we'd accidentally entered 777 instead of 555?*
Then he pulled a wry face and shook his head.
Out of the question! With the alien intelligence
at the controls it had already been fixed, programmed. The display of revolving numbers
had simply been part of the game. No matter
where Gill had let the knocker fall it would always have come out 555. As well try to stop a
one-armed bandit on a jackpot combination!

Now that Barney was here (and even though
he hadn't especially wanted to be) he quickly
settled down and stuck close to Gill. "What the
hell," Gill comforted him, "we can always move
out again if we want to, can't we?" Couldn't
they? He checked with the great crystal and
found that it was so: door number 777 was a
gateway to all the other doors. At the moment
it was inactive, but Gill guessed that the controller—the gamesmaster—could reactivate it
at any moment. Which led to another thought:
Gill had spied upon this place, and so presumably could be spied upon. .

He reached out his hands to the crystal,
closed his eyes and mentally "felt" his way in-

side. He flowed with the fluid mechanics of the thing and asked: *How may I remain undetected, shield myself from discovery in this location?*

The crystal stirred into life and showed him. Activated in a certain way, its energies would cause interference in the event of a locator being used to scan this region. And so Gill activated it in just that way. Nothing appeared to happen, but Gill could feel the great crystal working—this time for him, not against him. So . . . he now had some protection, from prying alien eyes at least. Now all he could do was hope that the controller didn't actually scan this area and wonder why he was having trouble with his locator—and perhaps investigate.

But one thing at a time; worry about what is, not what might be; check out how the others are doing, then make some plans. Any sort of plans, for Christ's sake!

He climbed to a ridge and looked out across the desert. Something less than three miles away, a tiny dot struggled towards the foot of the range. Perhaps a mile beyond that, another dot, smaller still, trekked the dunes. That one would be Angela, last to arrive here through an "ordinary" door. And the closest one would be Anderson or Turnbull. But there should be three people down there. Gill narrowed his eyes against the glare of a small, blinding white orb which was settling towards the far horizon, and gave the dunes and the foothills his closest scrutiny. Nothing. Then—

Small rocks came tumbling from somewhere higher up the slopes. Gill started, ducked low and hid behind a rocky outcrop, turned his eyes to the heights. Then he saw who was coming down from above and gasped his relief. He stepped back out into view and called, "Jack— Jack Turnbull!"

The big man slid the rest of the way on his backside, sending the loose scree clattering, and Gill and Barney were there to meet him when the dust settled. The two men hugged each other and slapped backs like long-lost brothers, and almost simultaneously said, "God, it's good to see you! I—" They paused—and then they laughed together, too.

Finally they stood apart, not knowing what to say, shaking their heads. Gill looked out and down across the desert. "Anderson," he said, pointing. "And Angela. It's as much as I can do to stop myself running down there to see how they're doing. But I guess they're all right. We all have been so far."

"There's nothing you could do to help them anyway," said Turnbull. "And you'd only have to climb back up here again. As for being all right: yes, we have been. But only just!" And he quickly told Gill what had happened to him in his nightmare world. "But I came through it," he finished, "and here I am." He showed Gill the black puncture marks of the leech things on his thighs. "Ugly bastards!"

"I had nothing like that." Gill felt almost guilty. "I went back to the machine world. But . . . they don't bother me anymore. And now it seems we're all back here. Those of us who've survived, anyway."

"Right," said Turnbull. "And how do you figure that one, eh? I mean, why have we all ended up back here?"

Gill took a stab at it. "Apart from our own

personal nightmares, this world—Clayborne's world—was the worst. That's arguable, of course; but Varre's claustrophobic maze was a one off, and he's gone now. Presumably his nightmares have gone with him. Also, Varre's world was a no-hoper—a dead end, literally—and the House of Doors likes to play games. The place you feared most after your torture world was this one, and so here you are. Which doesn't bode at all well for us. I would guess something especially monstrous is in the works for us."

Turnbull nodded, looked at the slowly moving dots down on the white sprawl of the desert. "And of course the same goes for them, too."

"They've survived their own little hells," Gill answered, "so whatever else has been set up for us, it happens here. We all face it together." Then he told Turnbull about his breakthrough with the alien science of the House of Doors. Turnbull understood part of what he said, at least.

"Fluid mechanics? Machines whose working parts are liquid? *All* liquid? Is that possible?"

Gill shrugged. "It's the way it is. Super hydraulics."

Turnbull shook his head. "I don't see it. I mean, I can understand the power, the energy, in falling water, or in any liquid under pressure; hydraulics if you like. But entire *engines* of liquid? What drives them? Did you ever see water run uphill?"

"Not water," said Gill. "These are alien liquids, manufactured like we make nuts and bolts. Look, for the sake of argument, let's just say that there's this liquid—like mercury, perhaps—whose molecules can be programmed like microchips. Are you following me?"

Turnbull looked glum. "Over my head," he said.

Gill sighed. "Yes, and mine too. But I'm getting there. And anyway, at the moment I'm not so much worried about the how of it as the why. Why would creatures with this kind of technology want to put insects like us through hell? I intend to get there, too—eventually. Let's go back down to the crystal."

On their way back down into the hollow between the spurs, Gill asked, "What were you doing up there, anyway?" He indicated the higher slopes.

"Looking for caves, dens, droppings," said the other.

Gill raised an eyebrow.

"Werewolves," Turnbull explained.

"You know about that sort of thing?"

"No, but I figured forewarned is forearmed. We had that trouble with them last time we were here, and I wanted to know what tonight would bring. I was thinking like, you know, better the devil you know. I arrived here early this morning and I've been scouting around ever since. I've covered some miles. This place has a long day, because of its two suns, I suppose. Anyway I didn't find anything. Maybe Clayborne's influence is fading."

Gill doubted it. Clayborne had programmed the place. *But of course, I can always try deprogramming it, through the great crystal.*

"These liquid machines of yours." Turnbull cut into his thoughts. "The science is completely different, right? I mean, didn't these aliens ever discover the wheel?"

"No." Gill shook his head. "I don't think they ever did. And I don't think they could have used it if they had. Let me ask you something: how do *you* see a machine, an engine?"

Turnbull shrugged. "You put fuel in, which produces energy, which performs a job of work easier and faster than you could do it using just your muscles."

"That's right," said Gill. "We build machines to work like we work. We eat for fuel, turn the fuel into energy. And because we understand the principles involved, we construct our machines along the same lines. They work the way we work. So what if we were intelligent plants? Would our machines work by photosynthesis?"

"Solar cells?" said Turnbull. "We have them."

"What I'm asking is this," said Gill. "Do *all* intelligences build their machines after themselves? To function like themselves? I believe they do—because it's natural for them to. And I've seen the jellyfish who's in charge of this lot!" He opened his arms expansively. "He's mainly liquid; so are his machines. They have no switches or levers because he doesn't have the physical strength to throw them. So what he does is this: he controls them with his mind! Each molecule of their makeup is 'intelligent'. For machines they'd make good polyps: each smallest part is an individual performing functions to the benefit and for the prolonged existence of the entire organism. And if our alien's machines are polyps—"

"So is he? Are you telling me we're being shafted by intelligent slop?"

"I've seen him, remember?" said Gill. "That's *exactly* what I'm telling you! His only drawback—and our advantage—is his physical weakness. . . ." He paused and frowned. "Something you said . . ."

"Oh?"

Gill snapped his fingers. "About water running uphill! You remember the way Bannerman lifted himself out of Varre's labyrinth through the vertical shaft? Antigravity!"

"What?"

"He made himself weightless. Now think of that: self-repairing machines made of 'clever' liquid that can control gravity. How do they work? *That's* how they work! And you'd better believe they can run uphill!"

"Eh?" said Turnbull.

"Never mind," said Gill, shaking his head. "But thanks anyway. Jack, you're a genius."

Turnbull scratched his head.

They were down into the hollow. Gill sat on a boulder in the slanting sunlight and let his mind drift, fuse with the great crystal. There were many things he wanted to ask it. It was mainly a matter of how to frame the questions. . . .

Evening began turning to night and still Gill sat there. Turnbull had watched him for almost two hours before leaving him to it and climbing back up the spur to wait for the others. Even without understanding what Gill was trying to do, he had realised its importance and hadn't wanted to interfere. And in the end he'd feared that even his close presence might be a distraction. But in fact Gill was totally absorbed and didn't even realise that Turnbull had left. Barney lay with his head on his paws and whined now and then, watching Gill where he sat hunched on his boulder. The dog was perfectly sure they shouldn't be in this place, but he accepted that he and Gill were now a team of sorts.

Up on the ridge Turnbull watched Anderson struggling up the steep, final rise, following the same route they'd all used once before. He didn't call down his encouragement for fear of disturbing Gill; but in any case it wasn't necessary as Anderson had already seen him; the heavy, overweight man—still overweight, for all that he'd been through—had paused and looked up, and offered a sort of nod. And Turnbull had thought he couldn't have had such a bad time of it: he appeared to be wearing new clothes, anyway.

A full moon, huge, cratered, was rising from behind the mountains; its rim was orange turning to yellow across its pocked disk. Its upward creep was slow, however, and Turnbull was glad for that. In a place like this, a free-floating full moon could be very significant.

Turnbull glanced down at Gill on his boulder, and at the great crystal lying dull and apparently disinterested, half in its own shadow. He supposed that he could have been out of here easily enough, through any one of nine doors, at any time during the course of the long day. But at the same time he'd known that some of the doors were extremely dangerous—possibly all of them—and he'd learned like all the others that it was best to use them only as a last resort. There was always the chance that the next place would be just as bad, and possibly worse, than this one. Also, he'd always clung on to the small hope that some of the other survivors would somehow make it here. Which they had.

Anderson's puffing and panting drew Turnbull's eyes from Gill to the Minister where he laboured up the last few feet of stony slope. He reached down a hand to him; looking up, Anderson grasped it. Too late Turnbull saw the look in the other's eyes. Then Anderson had drawn himself up to Turnbull's level and lunged at his throat with both hands. "Who am I?" He frothed at the mouth, crushing the big man's windpipe with the strength of a madman. "Now you tell me, you miserable wretch: *who . . . am . . . I?*"

Turnbull forced his hands up and outwards between Anderson's, breaking his hold; and while Anderson teetered, off balance, the big man went to deliver a blow to his face. Somehow Anderson avoided it, fell on Turnbull, and both of them went tumbling and fighting down into the hollow between the spurs, bouncing and sliding in the scree and the dust all the way to the bottom.

At the same time Gill felt the last rays of the sun fade from his hands where they rested on the boulder, and his eyes were drawn to the long shadows spreading like stains as they blotted their way across the hollow and left it gloomy and hagridden. Looking up, Gill was in time to see Turnbull haul Anderson to his feet and deliver two telling blows: one to the belly to fold him over, and the other to the jaw, straightening him out again. For the moment, Anderson was out of his misery.

Cramped from his long session with the crystal, Gill started to his feet—and at once groaned. Barney groaned, too—but not from stiffness of the joints—and began to growl low in his throat. He'd felt something in the air, something that rasped like a rusty file on his doggy nerves. Nor was he mistaken.

A full, bloated moon had now fought free of the mountains and floated like a fat decayed face in space. In the distance, the first forlorn howl went up from a throat which was only half-human. . . .

CHAPTER FORTY-FIVE

Gill and Barney crossed to where Turnbull stood panting over Anderson's outstretched form. "What was all that about?" Gill wanted to know.

"When I saw his new suit of clothes, I thought he must have had an easy time of it," the big man answered. "But it seems I was wrong. He's mad as a hatter, went for my throat. He tried to kill me!"

Echoing wolf voices joined the first as the twilight deepened. "Look after him," said Gill. "There might be hope for him yet. But not for Angela if I don't get to her before they do. She was a mile behind him last time I looked. If she was moving faster than he was, she should be just about here. I'll go give her a hand, and we'll see you back at the crystal. But if we don't—"

"Good luck, Spencer," said Turnbull.

Gill climbed the spur to its crest, paused and deliberately silhouetted himself there for her to see, and called out, "Angela! Up here! Hang on—I'm coming!" His voice carried far out, came echoing back. At first only the calling of wolves answered him, but then her voice came floating up the side of the mountain.

"Spencer! I'm here. . . ."

Twilight is a bad time for vision: it distorts shapes, confuses distances. Gill saw a pale shape moving between the shadows of outcropping rocks some two hundred yards down the mountain. On the level it was a distance he'd expect to cover in less than thirty seconds; here, in the poor light, even knowing the route, it was treacherous work and frustratingly slow. Or should be. But Gill couldn't afford to waste any time.

"Barney," he said, "I'm going down. She must be just about all in. Come if you want to, or go back to Jack." It would be a great shame if the dog had survived so long only to meet death on an alien world in the jaws of his inhuman cousins tonight—just because he'd found himself a new master.

Gill went sliding down through the scree, balancing on his heels and windmilling his arms for stability, and Barney went with him. As he descended in this fashion, Gill slowed himself periodically by deliberately colliding with looming boulders; it was bruising work but effective, and the distance between himself and the climbing pale shape rapidly narrowed. Until finally, as Gill caromed from a boulder back onto the track, they met—and he saw that it wasn't Angela.

425

A smiling, naked, handsome young man stepped out of a patch of shadow into Gill's path, and he was moving too fast to avoid him. As they headed for a collision, the youth timed it perfectly and stepped aside, and grabbed Gill's hair as he went skidding by. Yanked flat onto his back, Gill looked up into a grinning, moonlit face that changed even as he dipped into his pocket.

Great paws weighed on his shoulders and slavering jaws descended towards his throat, but Gill had the alien cylinder in his hand. Barney hit the werewolf from the side, and Gill struck upwards from beneath. His weapon whirred softly but bit like a shark's fin slicing water. Barney sent the wolf's body toppling one way, and its head fell the other. And as Gill climbed shakily to his feet, then Angela came.

She came panting up the hill, her body gleaming with sweat in the weird moonlight, naked except for the tattered shreds of her ski pants. "Spencer!" she gasped when she saw him. "Behind me . . . !"

But he'd already seen them, two of them, lean grey shapes with yellow triangle eyes, loping in her tracks and almost on her. He grabbed her, thrust her behind him against the face of a looming slab of rock, and faced the pair of wolves even as they rushed him. Snarling, Barney went for one of them, which served to distract it. The other leaped—and Gill met it head-on with his whirring weapon. Blood and brains splashed him as the beast was cut through snout, muzzle and head to crash against him before falling twitching to the dust. The second wolf crouched over a yelping Barney, its teeth dripping saliva. Gill paced forward, sliced downwards—and it was done. Two slashes had severed the beast's spine in two places. Jerking and twitching, it flopped over onto its side, scrabbling in blood and dust until Gill decapitated it. And after that—

—The climb was a nightmare by any standards. Gill half-dragged the exhausted girl back up the steep slope, and the only encouragement he had was the dancing, barking Barney urging him to greater effort. Eyes were gleaming yellow as lamps in the shadows of the rocks; lean quadruped silhouettes stood gaunt and quivering along the crests, their muzzles thrown up to the moon, howling their lost, self-pitying howls; grey shapes flitted from shadow to shadow on the slopes, each moment closing the distance between themselves, the man, girl and dog.

But finally they were at the top, and descending again into the hollow of the crystal. By moon and starlight Turnbull saw them coming, but the light was poor and deceiving and he wanted to be sure it was them. "Gill, Angela? Is that you?" His hoarse shout carried to them.

"It's us," Gill croaked, then tried again and managed to shout the words across the space between. "Jack, tear Anderson's shirt into strips. Make a rope."

"What?" came back Turnbull's answer. "A rope?"

Gill almost carried Angela the rest of the way, with Barney dancing round their sliding, slipping feet. They met Turnbull at the crystal and the big man at once gave the girl his jacket. She accepted it gratefully enough, but told him, "It's getting so that it hardly matters anymore, isn't it?"

"Everything still matters." Gill was grim. "We've still got everything to play for, believe me."

"I already had his shirt off," said Turnbull. "Tore it up to bind his hands and feet. He's still out, so I tied him up while I had the chance. Here's what's left." He handed Gill a bundle of rags.

"Tear it up." Gill gave him it back. "Knot the pieces together," he panted, fighting to get his breath. "Then tie one end to the knocker of door number six-sixty-six—but for God's sake be careful! Don't let the knocker fall!" And to Barney: "Good dog—watch 'em, Barney!" Barney moved off into the shadows, sniffing here and there, guarding against the gathering wolves.

"You think a mongrel dog can do much against that lot?" Turnbull worked at fashioning a rope of sorts.

"No," Gill answered, "but at least he'll warn us when they're coming. Now listen, both of you: I know this will sound crazy, but I have to communicate with the crystal. Don't ask me about it, just take my word for it. I *can* do it. So unless the mountains themselves start coming down on us, don't disturb me. Just let me get on with it, okay?" He sat down with his back against the boulder where Angela perched shivering, put his head in his hands and fell silent. And in a little while his ragged breathing grew even again.

Angela got down from the rock and went to Turnbull. He finished making his rope and showed her a length some eight feet long.

"Weak as shit," he said. "You couldn't swing a cat on it. I hope Gill knows what he's up to." The big man was nervous—even him—and his voice was beginning to break a little. "I mean, what the hell's it for, anyway?"

"A remote knocker," she answered, taking the looped, knotted rags from him. "Give me a lift and I'll do it. I probably have a softer touch than you."

He lifted her piggyback on his shoulders and moved to stand before door number 666, where she carefully formed a knot around the ring of the gargoyle-shaped knocker. "There," she said as he let her down. "And now we can knock from one side if it comes to that. Well out of the way of the result."

Now Turnbull understood. "A flamethrower? But what if it's space in there, like when Clayborne fell in?"

"Maybe that's what Spencer is trying to fix," she answered.

Barney came back just then; creeping, cowering, ears flat, his stump of a tail depressed and quivering. "Oh-oh!" said Turnbull. Down in the hollow, forming a wide circle all around, yellow eyes glared hungrily out of the darkness; wolf shapes made a creeping, living silhouette on the crags on both sides and at the back of the crystal.

Angela took Turnbull's arm. "They could take us right now if they wanted to," she gasped. "Spencer, too, even with that cutting thing he's got. There are just too many of them. So what are they waiting for, Jack?"

"You shouldn't have asked," he groaned. And he pointed down the mountainside, where even now a weird luminosity had sprung into being and was advancing up the slopes. It was the aurora effect they'd seen before, but this time it was different. Lighting up the mountain it came, a curtain of cold, eerie fire, its pastel shades merging and separating, dancing like a live thing as it lifted to meet the sky. But in the shifting, shimmering folds of the curtain, the vast white faces that were forming were not the horned devils that Clayborne had made. They weren't evil spirits or demons at all—or at least they hadn't been, *not when they were alive!*

"Varre's face!" Turnbull cried, his mouth opening into a gape. "Jesus—*look!*"

But Angela didn't need telling. She was already looking, couldn't draw her eyes from those of the vast faces in the glowing, weaving corpse-fire curtain. Jean-Pierre Varre was there, certainly, but his ears were those of a wolf, his eyes feral, and his teeth when he laughed—they were bone daggers! Nor was Varre alone: Alec Haggie was with him; licking his lips, his puffy bloated face leering, eyes alive with lust. Likewise Rod Denholm, his face a snarling mask of hatred.

"Rod!" Angela couldn't stand against this, not anymore. She went to her knees. "Dear God!" she sobbed.

"And Clayborne!" Turnbull croaked, his Adam's apple bobbing. "Shit, what a nightmare!" Clayborne's face was blistered, split open to the bone, rimed with the frost of deep space—but he leered and laughed like the others. For without exception, the faces in the sky were each and every one that of a raving madman.

Turnbull lifted Angela up, hugged her to him—as much for his own comfort as for her safety. She was human where nothing else appeared remotely so. She hid her face from what was happening all around them. Tight in his arms, she was, he sensed, on the verge of complete collapse. "I . . . I can't take any more," she whispered. "A door—any door—has to be better than this."

Wolves came loping—a handful, five or six of the lean, slavering beasts—their tongues lolling from slavering mouths. They made straight for Turnbull and the girl. He hugged Angela to him, backed up and to one side of door number 666. And as the wolves began snarling and crowded to the attack, so he yanked on the rope of rags and knocked.

The door opened and fire leaped out in a withering tongue of belching, gouting white and yellow heat! The wolves were caught in it, set alight, crisped where they stood or sent yelping off like living fireballs in all directions. And in another moment the door had slammed shut again. But the same fire from hell had burned through Turnbull's rope; now he was left with nothing but his sanity, and that beginning to fall apart.

"Spencer!" the big man yelled. "For fuck's sake, *Spencer*!" But there was no answer from Gill.

Again the wolves held back; but as the huge faces in the sky lost cohesion and melted back into the curtain of eerie light, so a new terror commenced. Without warning, door number 222 opened and vomited something unbelievable into the hollow. It was pulped flesh, broken bones, the remains of some crushed thing—and it lay steaming under the light of the weird moon and writhed with hellish life!

The fragments of white bone came together like the pieces of a grisly puzzle; flesh lapped over them redly and clothed them in raw red meat, which itself became sheathed in skin; a man screamed his dreadful agony where he wriggled like a snake with a broken back in the dust and the scree. But in another moment he lay still, lifted his head and looked all about, finally got to his feet and swayed a little before standing steady. It was Jean-Pierre Varre, naked, his right forearm missing from just below the elbow.

"Varre?" Turnbull couldn't take it in. But the Frenchman only smiled and backed off, joining the wolves where they lay in a circle, like furry, fearsome spectators. And as he got down on his belly with them, so his form changed yet again and he became one of them.

Angela tried to free herself from Turnbull's arms and run to Gill, but seeing her intention the big man held on to her. "No," he said. "If he was going to do anything he'd be doing it; he would have answered me when I called to him. So let's give him this last chance. Don't break in on him now."

Even as he spoke door number 666 slid to one side. No fire in there now but the deeps of deepest space. Something came sliding out of the star-flecked darkness beyond the door and tobogganed a little way out onto the scree of the hollow. It was the blackened, ruptured figure of a man frozen solid, beginning to steam as temperatures clashed. And both Angela and Turnbull knew exactly who it would be.

"Two-twenty-two was Varre's door," she whispered, "and six-sixty-six was Clayborne's, remember?"

Turnbull nodded. "So . . . we're all here now," he said.

"No," she answered, "I don't think so. There were four faces in the sky. One of them was my husband. I know well enough that he's a twelve. His door would be four-forty-four."

She was right. As Clayborne's hideously disfigured body rapidly defrosted, 444 hissed open and Rod Denholm came staggering out. He saw Angela in Turnbull's arms and at once said, "Angelaaa! What's this, sweetheart? *Another* boyfriend?" But the remark had no sting, because she knew for a certainty that it was programmed.

Her fingers bit into Turnbull's arm. "He's not real," she said. "He's a pseudo-Rod. None of these things are real or natural. They've all been caused to appear here—made to threaten us—for the entertainment of whoever is running the show!"

Turnbull put her behind him. "Well let's see if he's real enough to feel this," he said. And he hit the synthesised man with every ounce of muscle and energy in his body. The clone was lifted off its feet and knocked down like a felled tree, and Turnbull winced as he clutched his fist. He wouldn't be hitting anyone else that hard for a while, for sure.

"Only one left," said Angela. "Alec Haggie. I've worked it out and he's a three—door number one-eleven." Again she was right: 111 opened and Haggie came bounding through. But he was no threat.

"Oh, Jesus! Jesus!" he screamed, leaping away from the crystal. And right behind him, scuttling from the door before it slammed shut, came the lobster-scorpion hunter, pursuing him still where he fled screaming through the startled ranks of wolves.

"That has to be the lot," said Turnbull. "The cast is assembled. The Big Show can start."

"No," said Gill, standing up and swaying, leaning a little against his boulder. "There's still someone missing. The conductor. The one who orchestrates the whole damn thing. The one with the key to *all* the doors! Jack, Angela—get over here."

"Well, did you learn anything?" Turnbull asked as they stumblingly joined him.

"Almost everything," said Gill. "Once you get into it, it's like hacking a computer. I know all the whys and wherefores, and all I need now is the who. And he'll be along shortly—through door number seven-seventy-seven."

"Bannerman?" Turnbull knew he must be right.

"The same." Gill nodded. "And if he wants the job done, finished, this time he'll have to do it himself."

Angela believed she understood. "It was you who stalled the wolves and these other horrors?"

"I've stalled everything," Gill answered. "I've

thrown a hell of a spanner in this alien bastard's works. So now we wait until he comes to clear the obstruction. We wait just as we are, right here, and see if he has the guts to play the game out to its end."

Nor did they have long to wait. . . .

CHAPTER FORTY-SIX

Clayborne's crust of ice melted away and he sat up. His face was a mess and his guts flopped like sausages out of his trunk; he sat there examining them in apparent astonishment as they slithered through his fingers.

"We can be horrified," Gill said, turning away, "but no longer menaced. The frighteners are off. I've seen to that, at least. The House of Doors had orders to drive us to madness and the very edge of death—and over the edge, if it was in the cards. But we wouldn't actually die. We were to be tested to see just how much we could take, and how we faced up to it. But somebody reprogrammed things so that we could actually die—except that he waited too long to do it and now I'm onto him. Which is why I say that if he still wants it done, he must do it himself. You'll see what I mean if we survive that final showdown. But there are still a good many ifs, so we'll have to take them one at a time."

"Why don't you just call him Bannerman?" said Turnbull.

"Because that's the human name he chose," said Gill. "What's underneath isn't human."

"You say we can die 'now,'" said Angela. "But Varre and Clayborne *did* die—they are actually dead."

"It wasn't them." Gill shook his head.

She didn't understand and he didn't enlighten her. On top of everything else, that might be too much of a shock. Later—if there was to be a later—would be soon enough.

"Are you saying it wasn't Varre who got changed into a werewolf, got himself pulped, and is lying there with that pack of hungry bastards right now?" Turnbull wondered if maybe Gill, too, had finally cracked.

"In a way it was him," said Gill. "But that thing over there isn't him, no. You know it isn't. Human guts don't reconstitute themselves like that. Human beings don't change into wolves."

"And this isn't Clayborne playing with his entrails like they were oozing out of an overripe gooseberry?" The big man's voice quavered on the edge of hysterics. "Clayborne, mad as a hatter and amusing himself with his own guts?"

"Same answer," said Gill. "It is and it isn't. Save it until later."

"But my real husband was there in that nightmare world of mine," said Angela. "I mean the *real* Rod Denholm!"

"Possibly," said Gill, "if you say so. I don't know about him."

437

"And Haggie?" Turnbull was still trying to find a starting place.

"Haggie's different—the poor bastard," said Gill, but with nothing of emotion. "He's here by mistake. It may have been him that came out of door number one-eleven with the hunting machine after him, and it may have been something else. It all depends."

"On what, for God's sake?"

"On the controller's sense of humour," said Gill.

"What about my sense of humour?" said Anderson, causing all three to start. "Believe me, I don't find it funny being tied up in a place and at a time like this!" They'd forgotten him where he lay with his hands tied behind him and his feet lashed together.

Gill went to him where he lay in the shadows close by. "Are you okay?"

Jack Turnbull said, "Whatever he says, don't trust him."

"I'm fine . . . now," said Anderson. "I . . . I acted crazy because I thought I was crazy. And I probably was, until Jack hit me. But just before I passed out, I realised that I'd been hit by something very solid and very sane. And everything became real again. Even this unthinkable situation, real. So . . . I'm okay now. I'm sure I'll be able to face anything else that happens to me here. It was just that I couldn't face what happened to me . . . there."

"There?"

"In my nightmare world, in London."

Gill took a chance, tugged at Anderson's bindings until they shredded and came loose. Groaning, Anderson lay where he was, gingerly moving his hands and feet to get the circulation going again. "You see," he began to explain, "my nightmare was to lose—"

Door 777 banged open, and a moment later slammed shut—and Bannerman stepped out of the great crystal's darkest shadows.

The Bannerman construct was naked, more than "entire" in its own right, and entirely alien. Sith had given his vehicle extra "arms," snake-like appendages one to each side of the trunk, midway between hips and shoulders; and these were tipped with bone or chitin scythes. Sexless, his groin was simply smooth, hairless synthetic flesh where the thighs met the body. His "blind" eyes had been removed so that deep-seated scanners glowed premanently red in their otherwise empty sockets. The sound of his breathing, which was not breathing at all but the roar of alien hydraulics geared for maximum exertion, was a whooshing such as bellows make. In his right hand he carried a silver metal cylinder, which had the dull gleam of lead in the light of the moon and stars. It was similar to the one Gill had already snatched from his pocket—but where Gill's was like a fat fountain pen, Sith's might be a walking stick!

He advanced upon Gill, Angela and Turnbull, and they found themselves caught in a triangle: between Sith, and Clayborne, and the wolves. Despite Gill's assurances, instinct made them steer clear of the wolves—even Gill himself— and around the mad, ruptured Clayborne; and in this manner Sith herded them back towards the House of Doors. Gill's alien instrument whirred, but its sound was almost drowned out by the angry buzz of Sith's.

"Jesus!" Turnbull breathed. "He grows new limbs like a bloody starfish!"

"No," said Gill, "he synthesises them. In fact he synthesises everything."

The Bannerman construct's mouth opened wide in a soulless laugh. "You are a clever man, Mr. Gill," he boomed. "Possibly the cleverest of your race. And indeed under different circumstances you might well have been the saviour of your race. But events have determined otherwise."

"You came to test us," Gill answered, slowly backing away. "I've confirmed that much. But there were limits which you've exceeded. Your synthesizer had a built-in code of conduct, which you've seen fit to overrule. Why?"

Again Sith laughed. "Amazing! I am interrogated on 'equal' terms by a life-form so low in the scale of things that I find it almost contemptible! But I'll answer your questions. Why am I intent upon the destruction of you and your entire race? To make way for a superior, more worthy race, the Thone; and also because the needs of my destiny are greater than those of a planetful of primitives, that is why."

"And am I such a primitive?" said Gill, again backing off as his inhuman adversary stepped a little too close. "I've learned how to communicate with your machines. How to control them. Given a little time, I might even do it better than you."

"Because you are unique of your kind," said Sith. "A freak or mutant. In my race, when errant strains appear, they are put down. I see no reason to make any exception in your case."

"So you'll kill us," said Gill, aware of the

crystal's facets—and their doors—so close behind. "But why have you prolonged it? Did you
enjoy torturing us? Is that the measure of your
'superiority?' "

The Bannerman construct paused and its
weapon buzzed with redoubled energy. Gill and
his two companions backed off a further pace.
"You yourself are responsible for that," Sith finally answered. "You and Turnbull—you
brought it on yourselves. Because of your . . .
skills, which might prove troublesome, I came
to kill you. You damaged my construct and
fought me off. I am not one to be thwarted by
inferior creatures! And again, in Varre's tunnel
world, where you discovered my real identity,
you dared to employ a Thone tool to injure both
my construct *and* myself! When you did that,
what had been a mere amusement became a
duel in earnest—albeit one which you couldn't
win." He lifted his arms a little, his coiled tentacles, too, and inched forward.

"You're a coward—not to mention a black-
hearted, slimy jellyfish bastard!" Gill accused,
standing his ground. "You sent constructs to do
your dirty work. The Clayborne-thing to
frighten and weaken us; likewise the Varre
changeling; and a likeness of the girl's husband
to menace her. Only when all else failed have
you yourself come on the scene."

Bannerman bared his teeth, said, "Well, *you*
most certainly are no coward, Mr. Gill." His
voice was soft now, and very menacing.

"Very few human beings are," said Gill.
"Given a fair trial, we'd come through it every
time. But you? Even now you make yourself un-
beatable by use of a hybrid form and a superior

weapon. What a small, wretched thing you really are, if the truth's to be told!" Gill sneered these last few words, crouched down a little and indicated to the others that they should spread themselves out. "And do you really think we'll die so easily, even now? Haven't you learned even *that* much about us?"

Bannerman's appendages uncoiled, fell to the ground and writhed like snakes to his rear, lethal whips ready to be called into action. "Keep talking, Mr. Gill," he said. "For you're talking yourself to death. Oh, I admit you've exerted a certain influence over this region's node: the synthesised crystal behind you. But what I do by instinct is to you still something of an effort. And you can't talk and think *and* exercise your talent at the same time. But I can. And already I've untied most of the knots which you so cleverly put in my system."

Gill knew it was so. He could feel his contact with the crystal slipping. The wolves were creeping forward again. Clayborne had stopped examining his innards and had turned his hideous face towards the tableau now in its ultimate stages of enactment. Even the Denholm construct, seriously damaged by Jack Turnbull's powerhouse of a blow, was stirring and trying to rise to its feet, calling: "*A-a-angel-aaa!*"

"The House of Doors is waiting, Mr. Gill," said Sith-Bannerman, "and I shall have the pleasure of ushering you in across the very last threshold that you shall *ever* cross. Only look behind you and see what I mean."

The oldest ploy in the world and Gill fell for it. He stole a glance—and even as he knew that he'd been duped, he saw that all the doors now bore the same number: 666!

"*Gill!*" Turnbull yelled his warning. Gill ducked, held up his weapon protectively before his face. One of Bannerman's tentacles whipped overhead, brushing his hair, and Gill's Thone weapon sliced through it like a strand of mist. The severed chitin scythe went clattering and Sith-Bannerman howled. He pointed his own weapon and Gill's turned red-hot in his hand! He dropped it and it spattered and flowed like a blob of mercury where it hit the scree, completely deenergized.

Sith-Bannerman coiled up his wounded, dripping extension and advanced. "You first," he hissed. "The door is behind you. Knock now, at once, or I finish it right here."

"Spencer!" Angela cried, but Gill shook his head. He knew it was all over.

"He has control." He ground the words out. "And he's lifted the limits right off the top. The sky's the only limit now. Behind these doors lies death for any—for all—of us!"

"Correct," said Sith. "No one—no sentient creature—may pass through one of those doors now without experiencing his own worst nightmare all the way to the end. No escape, no mercy, just the inevitable end." He pointed his buzzing weapon at Gill's chest and stepped forward—

—And Anderson hit him from behind!

On his own, Sith would have known—his sensors would have alerted him—but encased in the Bannerman construct he was restricted by its limitations. He could only "see" to the front.

In the last split-second Gill had seen the dark

blot of Anderson's figure erupt from even
darker shadows, had seen it hurtling forwards.
Struck with all Anderson's weight, the monstrous construct was lifted up and thrown forward; Gill hurled himself sprawling to one side;
Bannerman toppled and, turning as he fell,
struck Anderson *through* the waist with his
weapon. And the Minister's death scream coincided precisely with the back of Bannerman's
head striking the knocker!

There came a *hiss-ss* as the door opened like
the sucking snout of some immense vacuum
cleaner, following which . . .

Bundled head over heels like a page of news-
print down a windy, early-morning city street,
Gill prayed: *A soft landing, God—that's all.* And
while he'd never been much of a believer, still
his prayer was answered. He came down in
knee-deep snow in a howling blizzard. The landscape was white as far as the eyes could see
(which was maybe twenty-five feet in any direction), the sky grey, and the cold as biting as a
razor-edged knife.

Still disoriented, Gill got groggily to his
knees—and was immediately knocked down
again as Angela piled on top of him. In the same
moment, Turnbull crashed down in a drift close
by. Then everything stopped spinning and Gill
stood up. He looked all around through eyes
slitted against the blinding snow and let his machine consciousness—his alien machine awareness—reach out. Something was there, quite
close but slowly moving away, and Gill knew it
for the only thing it could be. Dimly glimpsed,

a bulky figure lurched through slanting lances of snow at the very edge of vision.

"This way!" Gill howled above the frantic shrieking of the storm. And plunging through the drifts like a madman, he went after Sith-Bannerman.

We have maybe ten minutes in this, Gill thought. *Fifteen if we're lucky*. Following which they'd be part of the permafrost.

Gill lunged after the lurching figure—which already had stopped moving and stood swaying, leaning into the icy blast—and wondered why his body felt made of lead. And a moment later knew why as the whole truth of the situation hit him. For this was a cold world and a world of high gravity.

And as Gill had supposed it would be, it was indeed his enemy—the enemy of his entire race—who leaned like the stump of some strange lone tree out of the deep snow and against the blast. The Bannerman construct and what was inside it: a murderous alien intelligence who had been first through the door, triggering the synthesizer's automatic and inexorable response. And here he was trapped in his own version of hell, his own worst nightmare: a cold, high-gravity world.

No escape, he'd said; and who would know better, for he was the one who'd programmed it. What was more, the House of Doors had improvised: it denied Sith the use of his antigravity harness, refused to beam power to it. Likewise his Thone instrument, which was now useless to him. To allow these things would have been to provide an escape route, and Sith's instructions had been explicit. To top it off he faced the ignominy, the ultimate irony, of dying before the very eyes of the one he'd most desired to destroy.

But . . . no mercy. The stored power in the construct's battery was almost expended and the cold was seeping in, and the one thing above all others in the entire universe which was guaranteed to terrify any member of the Thone was to freeze. To lie undead forever, turned to ice, and to know the gradual petrifaction of the aeons!

Gill stumbled up to him, saw the fading red glow of his eyes, and knew the truth. *Got you, bastard!*

Sith forced the last ounce of energy from his construct, lifted his death-wand. It was merely warm where its tip prodded Gill's chest. He knocked it aside, out of the construct's unresisting fingers. And: "Which way?" Gill shouted into Bannerman's almost immobile face. "If you want to live, tell me where's the node?"

For answer Sith tried to lift the construct's arm again and point. The arm came up like a rusted robotic lever, stuck, and overbalanced he fell facedown in the snow.

Turnbull and Angela came stumbling out of the blizzard. "Spencer, we're done for!" Turnbull yelled, his words blowing away in streaming white plumes.

"Not yet," Gill shouted back. "Help me with this bastard."

"What? There's somewhere to go? So why take him along?" But still Turnbull grabbed one of Bannerman's arms.

"Because he has the last of the answers, and I want them. Without him we can't solve the puzzle. And there's a hell of a lot hanging on it. Anyway, save your breath and *work*, you big sod!" Angela helped, too; with one arm crooked round Bannerman's thick neck, she shared the load as they hauled him over the snow. And in her other hand she carried his walking-stick weapon.

It was maybe a hundred yards to the node, but it felt more like a thousand. Ten more yards and they wouldn't have made it. Later Gill would think back on it and wonder why the node was so handy, and he'd reason that in a place like that Sith would naturally want exits placed at frequent intervals; even under normal conditions, with all of his support systems working, he'd feel uncomfortable in that sort of Thone hell.

But eventually the node did loom up out of the storm: a House of Doors in the shape of a block of ice! It was simply that, an ice cube of nine-foot sides, a crystal-clear cube containing nothing but ice—apparently. And it didn't seem to have any doors.

Frustrated, all in, unable to concentrate his new, alien knowledge, and almost willing now to accept death in any form, Gill hammered with his naked fists on the cube's nearest face— and the ice caved in! It was a quarter-inch thick, no more. They dragged Bannerman across the shattering threshold, and—

CHAPTER FORTY-SEVEN

"Frostbite!" said Turnbull, when at last he could speak again. "We should at least be frost-bitten." He examined his hands with an almost childlike astonishment. "Nothing! Not even a chilblain! But what the hell ... another five minutes of that and it wouldn't have mattered anyway. God, do you know how lucky we are to be alive?"

"Are we lucky, Spencer?" Angela wanted to know. "I mean, is it over, or is there more still to come?" She looked all around and most of what she saw made her feel sick, so that she half-shuttered her eyes to diminish its confusion. "In a way I almost hope there *is* more to come—or at least something different to this!"

"A hothouse," said Turnbull, his voice gaining strength. "One extreme to the other. Where the hell are we, anyway? Inside one of those screens we saw on the world of mad machines—on your world, Spencer?"

"Something like that, yes," Gill answered. "In fact we're at the nerve centre. This is the control room. Part of it, anyway. It's just like Haggie described it, remember? You'll find it easier to take if you ignore the 'walls' and concentrate on the floor. The walls are screens, of a sort. Scanners. The swirling colours are unformed scenes, that's all. They are memories of worlds, some of them. The House of Doors doesn't keep its records on tape but as frozen actualities which can be recalled, synthesised, down to the smallest detail. But some of these scanners are focused on our world, too. When I've dealt with this bloke, I'll try to show you what I mean."

"Dealt with him?" Turnbull repeated him. "You mean put an end to him?" Now his voice hardened. "Just a few minutes ago we saw him 'deal' with Anderson. You know what mercy we could expect from him, so what are you waiting for?"

Gill shook his head. "No," he said, "I'm not going to kill him—unless I have to. Indeed I'm keeping my fingers crossed that he's still alive. But if he is, I intend to disable him. Power is flowing back into this weapon of his, this tool, even now; and it's doubtless flowing back into the construct, too. This human—or inhuman—figure is the alien's exoskeleton, his vehicle. The controller's inside. And he also controls the House of Doors. But not anymore, because I'm not going to give him the chance."

Angela barely had time to avert her eyes as Gill used the Thone instrument to shear through the construct's tentacles where they joined with the body. And at that Bannerman rolled over onto his back and sat up. Turnbull gasped and Gill bared his teeth and stepped back a pace; but as the construct's empty eye sockets began to glow again with a red life, Gill took a grip on himself. This wasn't mayhem; he was slashing the alien's tyres, that was all. Removing his rotor head, immobilising him.

He struck through both of the construct's legs at the knees and kicked the bleeding pieces aside. At which Sith-Bannerman shuddered violently, balanced himself with one hand on the floor, and held up the other in a sort of horror, as if to hold Gill back. "No more!" he croaked. "If you cut the construct any deeper, then you also cut me. My fluids are already more than sufficiently depleted. Or . . . if you're intent upon destroying me, then at least do it quickly: simply strike the construct through the chest."

"We didn't save your life out in that frozen hell just to kill you here, Bannerman—or whatever your name is," Gill told him. "We saved it because there are things only you can tell us. But first, snail, I want to winkle you out of that shell of yours."

"Out of my . . . ?" Then Sith understood. "You want me at my most vulnerable," he said. "I shall come out, if you wish it—but there ends our conversation. I speak through the construct's system. My own has neither the articulation nor the volume. The Thone do not converse in that manner."

Gill nodded. "Then since I need to talk to you, you'd better stay where you are. First I want to know about Clayborne, Anderson, Denholm, Varre and Haggie. Where are they?"

Turnbull and Angela had found their feet; averting their eyes from the flowing, liquid-colour walls, they looked at each other. Angela was plainly mystified by the question Gill had asked of the captive alien; Turnbull, equally at a loss, could only shrug.

"Clayborne, Anderson and Varre—I can show them to you," Sith Bannerman answered. "Or I could have, before you took away my mobility. Now I can only direct you."

"Liar!" Gill snapped at once. "Your antigrav is working. I can feel it like my own pulse. You're only waiting for a chance to use it, that's all. You could lift yourself and that wreck up off the floor and be gone out of here in a moment—but not before I'd cut your construct and you in half a dozen pieces!"

Turnbull said, "What the hell's going on? He can show us Clayborne and the others? Is there something I've missed?"

"Something we've missed," Angela corrected him. "What's happening here, Spencer?"

Gill said, "You're in for a shock, you two. And so am I—probably. I mean, I know what's coming, but I'm not sure how I'll take it. Anyway, if my butchering of this thing offends you, look away for a moment. I can't trust him while he has hands."

Angela saw Gill's intention and quickly looked away; she heard Turnbull's sharp intake of breath; when she looked back Gill didn't have to worry about trusting Sith-Bannerman. With certain exceptions, there wouldn't be a great deal that he could do anymore.

Gill looked a little pale but his voice was as

hard as ever. "Very well, and now maybe you'll show us the others."

"*And* yourselves," said Sith-Bannerman, causing the construct to grin its soulless grin. He floated up from the floor and Gill took a firm hold on his left elbow.

"No higher than that," Gill warned. "And no tricks. The first inclination I get that you're up to something . . . you won't be up to anything. Understand?"

"Oh, yes, I quite understand," Sith-Bannerman answered. He pointed the stump of his right hand into the kaleidoscoping colours and led Gill and the others a short distance into the control centre's mazy interior. They passed between banks of living screens and around several "corners"—until finally they were there.

"I told you it would be a shock," said Gill, his voice very small.

Standing upright against a backdrop of coloured motion, suspended there with their arms crossed on their chests and apparently asleep, were six fully clothed people. Their chests rose and fell; their flesh was a natural, healthy pink; pulses were visible and they were quite clearly alive. Three of them were Miles Clayborne, David Anderson, and Jean-Pierre Varre. *And the other three were Spencer Gill, Jack Turnbull and Angela Denholm!*

"Clones!" Turnbull gasped.

Gill shook his head. "Sorry to keep contradicting you," he said, "but they're the real thing—we're the clones! You—" he held his weapon close to the floating alien, "—you're responsible, so you explain it to them."

"You are not clones," the alien said. "Nor are

you constructs as such, for you are governed by your own brains. That is to say, your memories are true memories and not created artificially, and apart from the fact that your recent experiences are yours and yours alone, you *are* the beings you see here in repose. In short you are duplicates, synthetically copied to resemble in almost every respect the original pattern or creature."

"We're not . . . *creatures*!" Turnbull scowled. "Not the way you use the word, anyway."

"On that point we beg to differ," said Sith-Bannerman. "Should I continue?"

"Get on with it," said Gill.

"Indeed you are superior to the original specimens . . . will you allow me the use of that term, specimens? Good. Several microsystems were introduced into you at the moment of duplication to assist with your primitive healing processes, to change your metabolisms, to remove many of the weaknesses inherent in your race. The Thone cannot abide physical handicaps or abnormalities: 'illnesses', as you term such disorders. But your psyches, your mentalities, were left quite alone. For it was these that I was testing. But physically? When a Thone invigilator examines a specimen group, he is bound to ensure that they have every possible advantage. Most of the worlds you have seen were poisonous to you in one way or another: their atmospheres, pollens, species, some or all of these things could well have proved fatal to you. Without the alterations I have mentioned, the examination would be invalid. You could all very well be 'dead' by now."

"Like that runt Haggie?" Turnbull again interrupted. "Is he 'dead'? Why isn't he here?"

"And Rod—what about him?" Angela wanted to know.

"Alas," said Sith-Bannerman, "Haggie came here by error. He was not synthesised. The man you know is the true man. And a remarkable man! Somehow he has avoided the more poisonous places, found sustenance for himself, kept one jump ahead of his pursuer, the machine I sent to find him so that I could expel him."

"But it did catch up with him once," Gill said. "You could have expelled him then—but instead you tossed him back into the game. Which was murder pure and simple. He *will* die out there, somewhere, eventually."

"Presumably." There was a shrug in Sith-Bannerman's response.

"And Rod?" Angela had to know.

"I introduced your husband into this in order to . . . add flavour," Sith answered. "But please, do not accuse me of *his* murder! No, for I believe that was your doing. . . ."

Suddenly it was all too much for Angela. Her knees wobbled; she swayed and sat down at the feet of her likeness—no, at her *own* feet! Gill and Turnbull turned instinctively towards her—and Sith took his chance. He used his antigrav to its full, jerked upwards toward the ceiling haze and out of Gill's grasp. Gill made a wild leap, his weapon buzzing angrily, and missed by all of twelve inches.

Sith drifted away into the high haze of soft light and was gone. . . .

For a few moments Gill raged, but silently. At first furious beyond words, he hurled down the Thone weapon and shook his fists, then finally commenced cursing himself for a fumbling, bumbling clown. All of his frustration poured out of him in seconds, leaving him pale, limp and trembling.

"My fault!" Angela was aghast. "I'm sorry, Spencer. But when he—"

"No," he rasped, shaking his head. "Nobody's fault. Or mine, if anyone's to blame. He would have escaped sooner or later. This is his place, not ours. And we aren't up to his sort of trickery. Not even in the same league."

"He wouldn't have escaped if you'd killed him," said Turnbull matter-of-factly, but without accusation.

"I couldn't, Jack," Gill told him helplessly. "Not because I didn't want to or he didn't deserve it, but because it wasn't my place to kill him. I wanted—I don't know—to bring him to trial? Yes, I think so. But trial by his own kind. You see, I'm pretty sure that they'd consider him a criminal, too. There were rules to this game and he broke every one of them. But to kill him out of hand . . . that would simply be to invite their wrath."

"So what now? Do we hunt him down?"

"In this place? We're the ones who'd be hunted! We don't know what he has here, what he can do." Suddenly Gill felt trapped—even more so than when he'd been a true prisoner of the House of Doors, in worlds utterly beyond his control. "Jesus," he panted, throwing up his hands, "there'll be stuff here he can use against us! And . . ." He paused, chewed his lip and gradually fell silent, became thoughtful.

"And?" Angela prompted him.

"And . . . stuff I might be able to use against him!" Gill's smile was grim when finally it came. "The synthesizer—the House of Doors—is just a machine after all. Think of it as a car, and the alien as the driver. But I'm an unwilling passenger and I can give him real problems."

"Like fiddling with the knobs on the dashboard?" said Turnbull. "Stamping on the brakes, and so forth?"

"Maybe even the accelerator," Gill answered.

And as the big man helped Angela to her feet, Gill in his turn sat down. He offered them one last hot and harassed glance—and even managed the ghost of a smile—then closed his eyes and put his head in his hands. And all around them the House of Doors was a great maze of eerie, multihued mobility, and very, very quiet. . . .

But in Gill's mind—within the world of his machine mentality—it was not quiet. Sith was already at work, mobilising the synthesizer to the attack. And Gill could feel the alien's agile "fingers" at work as surely as the hand of some careless thief in his pocket. Careless because he thought he had Gill's measure, and that this merely "human" being was more or less helpless. Gill knew this and was determined to prove him wrong.

Poisonous gases were in the process of being produced; which Gill channelled from their target—his area of the control room—into an unspecified but long-dead world many light-years *away in the synthesizer's memory. Frustrated, Sith answered by "dimming" the lights and other life-support systems; and Gill at once cancelled his command and "switched" them on again. Sith located his grotesque correction construct (even now pursuing Haggie across a frozen, alien ocean, where now and then great whale things would crash upwards through the ice to spout) and ordered it back to the House of Doors. Gill countermanded the instruction, told the hunter to bring Haggie to the control room with all possible speed—and then to pursue Sith! An order which Sith at once cancelled.*

And so it went: with the alien on the offensive and Gill in defence, it was stalemate. But as Gill's base of experience widened and his skill improved, he began to take the initiative. And soon Sith began to discover what a two-edged sword the synthesizer was.

Gill had two big advantages, and when the opportunity came he used them in concert. As Sith sensed his opponent's growing strength and felt the changes taking place in the House of Doors, finally he knew that there was no alternative but flight.

In an antigrav harness made unreliable through Gill's interference, and feeling the temperature of the control area plummeting, Sith made his way to the transmat. He had no option now but to abandon the House of Doors to the three human beings. He could not simply "take off" in the synthesizer, for that required both concentration of attention and complete mastery of the necessary manoeuvres, which were things that Gill would deny him; and anyway, he was aware of something which his enemies knew nothing about.

Gill did know, however, the precise moment when Sith departed: he felt the surge of alien machinery and immediately asked the synthesizer for an explanation. The answer came back as quickly as his request, and:

"Gone!" he said then, opening his eyes and climbing wearily to his feet. "Gone back to his own kind, to the seat and centre of all Thone power."

"Gone?" Turnbull echoed him, no longer doubting anything that Gill said, but still questioning the meaning of it. "He abandoned all of this as easily as that?"

Gill laughed, however shakily. "Easy for you!" he said. And then he frowned. "But he does seem to have been a bit hasty, yes. And I can't help wondering why."

He turned to the ephemeral "walls" and called the whirling, unformed scenes to order, focusing the screens on Ben Lawers outside the Castle, and others upon the nearby towns of Kenmore, Killin, and Lochearnhead. It was midday out there, with grey skies and fine, soft snow falling to coat the mountain slopes. But as the pictures came clearer Gill and the others were at first puzzled, then shocked to their roots.

"What the hell . . . ?" Turnbull gasped. Men in radiation suits moved on the slopes of Ben Lawers, all around the Castle. A tower of scaffolding stood almost as tall as the Castle itself, with a platform bearing the weight of an ominous grey-metal mass. Scientists in white smocks stood on the tarmac of the lakeside road, binoculars to their eyes, gazing at the Castle and the tower both. Apart from which the place seemed deserted.

And even as Gill, Turnbull and Angela watched, the handful of scientists and technicians began to take their departure, going down to the road and driving off in their various vehicles. TV cameras mounted on poles turned this way and that, televising the whole scene. As for the towns around the loch—and isolated farms and settlements nearby, and other towns even farther out from the centre—they were quite empty.

"Oh my God!" Turnbull finally croaked, the very look on his face causing Angela to fly into Gill's arms.

"Spencer," she said breathlessly, "surely they don't intend to . . . ?"

"I think they do," said Gill, "unless we can stop them. They're going to blow the Castle right off the face of the Earth!"

CHAPTER FORTY-EIGHT

"Doors," said Gill, starting off through the weird maze of the place, wanting to run but feeling the floor sucking at his feet like so many giant sponges. "We have to find the doors. Some of these walls are locator screens and storehouses and God knows what else, but others are doors. I don't know the layout of the place or I could find them. And the synthesizer's idea of 'direction' is different from mine. So it's trial and error; we search until we stumble across them. Or we try to backtrack along the route that alien bastard took to bring us here, and I use the synthesizer to tell me when I'm warm."

"We believe you," said Turnbull, "just keep going. It's a good job I got an *A* in gibberish!" The big man was right behind Gill, almost tripping on his heels. "But shouldn't it be easy? The Castle isn't that big, surely?"

Gill didn't even bother to look back. "Don't you remember what Haggie said? About seeming to walk for miles in this place? This is *synthesised* space, Jack—space within space. And it's bigger on the inside than on the outside. Christ, it's a projection room for entire galaxies!"

"Shit!" Turnbull laughed, his hysteria very real. "The House of Doors! And you can never find one when you want one!"

"If Barney was here, he'd sniff me one out," said Gill, directing his machine awareness ahead of him.

"Barney?" said Angela. And: *"Barney!"* she gasped. "But where is he?"

"Last we saw of him was in Clayborne's world," said Gill. "But if I know Barney he'll be okay. Those horrors on Clayborne's world were for our 'amusement,' not his."

Turnbull caught Gill's elbow. "Spencer, how long will it take those boffins to get clear of ground zero? I mean—"

"How much time do we have? How should I know? It could be days or only hours. It just depends when she's scheduled to blow."

"Or . . . minutes?" said Angela.

But Gill made no answer. . . .

In fact it was half an hour.

The thermonuclear device was a small one (a "tactical" weapon and relatively clean) which would take the Castle, most of that face of Ben Lawers's scanty topsoil, and a deal of the mountain's rock with it to hell. But the scar wouldn't be permanent, and within a week people would be able to move back into their homes inside the twenty-five-mile zone.

The decision had been taken to destroy the Castle utterly following the disappearance of Anderson, Gill, and the others—but especially Anderson. A Minister from the MOD—in the hands of alien aggressors? Not only did Anderson have knowledge of Britain's defence systems but all of NATO's and most of the world's as well! When word of his abduction had leaked, then the outcry had been international and the demands undeniable, however undesirable. Martial law had been declared in the area, the tower built, the people moved out.

At Strike Command HQ in a commandeered hotel in Pitlochry, the countdown was into its last minute when a technician glanced at the bank of TV monitors and gasped, "What the . . . will someone tell me I'm seeing things?"

In the background, over a tinny Tannoy system, an unemotional voice continued the countdown: "Zero minus forty-eight . . . zero minus forty-five . . . zero minus forty-two . . ."

All eyes were now turned to the screens, all mouths falling open in shock. "Turnbull!" someone shouted. "Jack Turnbull—one of the group of people who were taken. He was Anderson's minder."

"Minus thirty-six . . . minus thirty-four . . . minus thirty-two . . ."

"Are you sure?" the four-star General I/C Operation was on his feet, staring.

Someone yanked out a drawer and its contents went flying; magazines and newspapers were tipped in a pile on the floor; a copy of *The Observer* was snatched up, thrust under the

General's nose. It had pictures of the Castle's victims.

"Twenty-six ... twenty-five ... twenty-four ... twenty-three ..."

On the screen, Turnbull waved his arms frantically, shouted at the top of his voice without making any sense or sound. For while the site was wired for sound, all electricity had been switched off—except for power for the TV monitors, and of course the main cable to the tower. Turnbull couldn't know that and he danced and screamed like a madman in the thin snow on the slopes of Ben Lawers. He was a mess: dishevelled, dirty, a tramp in a handful of soiled rags. But he was unquestionably Jack Turnbull.

"Nineteen ... eighteen ... seventeen ..."

Turnbull climbed a pole, pushed his face right up to the TV screen and mouthed: *Shut—the— fucking—thing—off!*

"Jesus!" said the General.

And someone took the initiative and pressed the abort button when the count was down to twelve.

On Ben Lawers, Turnbull got down from the pole but continued to dance and rave until a speaker finally came crackling alive and boomed, "Okay, Mr. Turnbull, we see you. The operation has been aborted. Stay right where you are and someone will come and get you. ..."

"You should have gone with him," Gill told Angela. They had watched the cars come back, and Jack go down to the road to meet them. But he had not left the area of the Castle, and wouldn't until he got the word from Gill. If that word didn't come ... at least he'd be able to tell them what it was all about. And perhaps help them a little with their preparations . . .

"Why?" she asked; and immediately nodded, answering herself: "Because I'd be safer out there. But no, I think I'd prefer to know that you're safe, too. So when you leave, I leave."

"When I leave," said Gill, "it may not be to go out there, with Jack. I might be going . . . out *there*, instead. What I have in mind—I don't even know if it's possible. But I have to try it. You see, this place—this spaceship, synthesizer, House of Doors—it's like an examination room at a university, where the students take their final exams. And I do mean final! The Thone use it to decide which races live and which die. That's the long and short of it. Whole planets are judged right here. If their races are found worthy—if they have intelligence, wit, the will to survive—then they're okay. Now as far as I'm concerned we've passed all our tests with flying colours. But—"

"The Thone need room. They're expanding through the universe. If they find a world they can take and mold and change into something which to them is home, then they'll take it—*if* its peoples don't come up to scratch. But this invigilator we've been dealing with, he broke the old rules and made some new ones of his own. And right now he's back home, lying his head off about what a bad bunch we human beings are.

"So . . ."

"You're going after him," said Angela, "to put the picture straight."

"If I can, yes." Gill nodded.

"And I'm coming with you."

Gill shook his head. "We don't know what's out there. And anyway, you really don't want to waste your time with me. Spencer Gill's a lost cause. In this body of mine—no, in *that* body of mine"—he nodded towards the sleeping figures—"I have maybe a couple of years left. And that's it. Lights out."

"And what about the body you're using now?"

"This body?" Gill looked down at himself. "I've thought about it and . . . it isn't me." He shook his head. "And that isn't you. Later, when I've found out how to put our minds back where they belong . . . I mean, I want to be me again."

"I know what you mean." She sighed. "And anyway, we really don't know how long we're . . . well, built for, do we? But in any case, I still want to come with you."

He shrugged and sighed. "We can argue about it later. And right now no one is going anywhere until I find out just exactly what the synthesizer can do, and how it does it. Now I'm going to programme the thing, and then I'm going to sleep. While I'm asleep it will teach me all I need to know—I hope. I think it's possible because I know the synthesizer can beam energy, create solids, send messages, ideas." He shrugged again. "And when I wake up, maybe I'll know what else it can do. So . . . why don't you get some sleep, too?"

She smiled, not coyly, not seductively— perhaps a little nervously—and answered, "I thought you'd never ask!" And before that could sink in: "But Spencer, can we sleep on my world? Just one night? It was—will be—a paradise without those clones of Rod. I'd like to swim in that warm sea with you, watch the sun go down with you, and then sleep with you. Is that possible?"

And from the look on his face she knew that it was. . . .

They woke up to a beautiful alien dawn in the cup of the biggest palm they'd been able to find. Climbing down to the sand, cool where the sea had crept in overnight to cover the beach with its gleaming ripples, Gill felt completely alive; a feeling he'd not known since he was a boy, and one he'd thought was gone forever. Angela was his, for however short a time, and whatever the future would bring, somehow he felt it had all been worth it.

While they had slept, the synthesizer had filled in the blank areas of his new knowledge; he was now *aware* as no man had ever been before him, the source of a science which—if it was to be—would eventually take men to the stars. Not in Gill's lifetime, for his expectations were short, but eventually. If things went according to plan. The ifs were still there. . . .

The first intimation he had that things were not going to plan came as he and Angela started out along the beach. He could sense the locations of several nodes in his near vicinity, but the idea of a giant clam as a door fascinated him and he wanted to see it for himself. And there on the beach, that was where Gill's so recently acquired mental alarm system first began clamouring.

She felt his hand stiffen where it held hers, glanced at his face. "Spencer?"

"The House of Doors has visitors," he said. "Several!"

She clutched at his arm. "Visitors?"

He nodded. "And we've been summoned." His gaze went beyond her, in the direction they'd been heading.

She looked where he was looking, along the beach, and saw something forming there: a shimmering oblong figure, like a doorway made of air, hovering over the sand. It moved towards them: a mirage of heat haze in the shape of a door. They could see the sand underneath it, the sea to one side of it and the jungle to the other, and the blue sky overhead—but within the shimmering oblong itself there was nothing. Light entering it struck on nothing and made no reflection.

Gill drew Angela close as the door dipped down towards them, flowed forward and enveloped them. . . .

Frozen, immobilised—held in a temporary stasis which allowed thought but denied physical movement, and which neither Gill nor Sith before him had known the synthesizer possessed—the human couple were drawn into the control centre and the travelling door collapsed around them. With their backs to the same wall of coloured motion where stood the six sleeping people of the original test group, Gill and Angela came face-to-sensors with the Grand Thone himself, and with several senior members of the Thone Council. Calming thoughts washed over them, easing their troubled minds, as the Principal Power of Thonedom communicated through the synthesizer.

"Sith is confined, and I have come to see for myself what damage has been done, and what reparation may be made. The synthesizer has told me all. There has been loss of worthy, sentient life, and other atrocities for which I am sorry. Never in Thone history was any machine put to such perverted use!"

"Never?" Gill found his thoughts flowing from him like speech; they conveyed his feelings, his meanings, but more lucidly than words or actions might ever have done. For any and all sorts of reasons, a man may hold back words he might like to use, but he may not hold back his thoughts. "But you don't know that. How many Thone invigilators are loose in the universe, seeking new worlds for you? And how many of them, like—Sith?—are misusing their power, for the glorification of the Thone? For *your* glory? We have a saying: Power tends to corrupt, and absolute power corrupts absolutely."

"We, too, have a saying," the Grand Thone countered. "Before a teacher may instruct, first he must be instructed. Upon a time, I was an invigilator. And I was tempted, and instructed in my temptation. But like the Thone majority, I did not succumb. From that time to this there have been safeguards. As the invigilators test, so are they tested."

"Really?" said Gill. "But I, too, have communicated with the synthesizer. And I know that Sith was short-listed for absolute power, that he was in fact a candidate for your own position as the Ultimate Thone Authority! That is why he broke the rules: to impress you with a stolen world—*my* world—and so improve his chances."

If a mind may smile without a face, that was

when the Grand Thone smiled. "That," he said, "was the test—and he failed it! I have no inclination, just yet, to abdicate the crystal pedestal. . . ."

Gill couldn't be consoled, placated. "But there have been deaths—murders! A man called Haggie floats miles deep under a frozen sea on an alien planet, and another named Denholm—"

"I know these things," said the Grand Thone. "And . . . murders, yes, of which you are not aware, because you were specific in your investigations. These things are inexcusable, and Sith will not be excused. But alas, they are beyond reparation. Even I cannot undo what is done so completely."

"But you can ensure it doesn't happen again."

And after a long moment: "Perhaps. Obviously the safeguards must be made . . . safer."

"I would ask you for your word that they will be!" said Gill.

There were shocked stirrings from the Thone Councillors, but the Grand Thone brought them to order. "You have my word," he said. "But you should know, Spencer Gill, that we are not alone in our expansion through the universe. And there are some who are not governed by our ethics. Oh, I know it could be argued that even our ethics are not all they could or should be, but by comparison . . ."

"*The Ggyddn!*" the Thone Councillors whispered.

"Ggyddn?" said Gill, feeling their mental shudders. But they hid what was in their minds.

"Let us hope you never come across the Ggyddn," said the Grand Thone, "and that they never find you. Space is a big place. But now,

Spencer Gill, we must go. You are a man of honour, and this world is yours, not ours. May I take it for granted that you will deenergize the synthesizer?"

"Yes," said Gill. "But . . ." and he paused.

"Yes?"

"There's just one thing that still puzzles me. You Thone have the science, the power to synthesise whole planets. Why then do you seek to colonise the worlds of other races? Why not simply inhabit synthesised worlds?"

"It takes energy," the Grand Thone answered. "The very presence of the synthesizer here in your world will have drained away thousands of years of the planet's life span." A mental shrug. "Nothing compared with the billions it has left. But you see my point. Uncontrolled, such waste would speed the devolution of the universe. Also, there is always the chance of power failure. To live permanently on a synthesised world would be too risky."

Gill's thoughts were sour now. "And you don't like taking too many risks, do you, you Thone?"

For a while the Grand Thone was silent, but then he said, "At least you, personally, have not lost by your experiences here in this House of Doors. That much may be said, at least."

"Not lost?" Gill was astonished. "I've been through hell! All of us went through hell!"

"But you were also terminally diseased," said the Grand Thone. "You were going to die, before your time."

"*You* WERE *terminally diseased*," the message slowly sank in. "*You* WERE *going to . . . ?*"

"We abhor illness," said the Grand Thone as he and his councillors prepared to take their departure. "Here in the synthesizer, where at all possible, all such malfunctions are automatically corrected."

Then they had gone, leaving Gill and Angela staggering together as their will over their limbs at once returned. . . .

Gill found Barney where he knew he would find him: in a world of rolling plains, great forests and six-legged rabbits. He found the synthesised remains of Clayborne and Varre, too, where Sith had stored them, and recovered Anderson's clone from the world of the great crystal. Not that this was necessary, for their minds were now part of the synthesizer; only their bodies—their synthesized bodies—had died. As for "Smart" Alec Haggie and Rod Denholm: there was nothing he could do for them.

Then he sent Angela outside onto the slopes of Ben Lawers to bring Turnbull back in, and finally he instructed the synthesizer to return all of their minds to the sleepers and then to deenergize—in a fashion.

Gill had seen to it that Anderson kept all of his memory, for that would be needed for corroboration; Varre and Clayborne remembered only that they had gone to see the Castle, and then that it had vanished before their eyes. Nothing more. Both of them had failed the Thone tests and their minds had caved in. To retain their memories intact could easily have driven them mad all over again.

But Angela and Turnbull: they kept everything, and because of it and with Gill they were made that much stronger.

So there they stood, six people and a dog, on

the slopes of Ben Lawers, and the Castle fading like a mist until it disappeared and the mountain was itself again. But as Barney rushed off, barking wildly, on his way home to the master he'd missed for far too long, and as the Castle's staff of technicians, military men and scientists came running, Gill stooped, picked something up and put it in the pocket of his good clothes.

He had promised to deenergize the synthesizer and that was all. And the thing in his pocket was a tiny miniature Castle. To anyone seeing it, it would seem an incredibly detailed model, exquisitely carved in granite. But only Gill would know that it was bigger on the inside than on the outside. A *lot* bigger.

And for the moment and for quite some little time to come, he would say nothing at all about it.

Nor about the Ggyddn . . .

Epilogue

In Shantung Province, Ki-no Sung yawned as
he rolled up his reed bed and took down from
the bamboo walls two great bundles of nets. He
carried the first armful out into the dawn light
flooding from the east across Hwang-Hai, the
Yellow Sea, and looked down upon the narrow
strip of beach separating the jungle from the
ocean. His boat sat there as at the rim of a mill-
pond, calm in the gathering light, with never a
ripple to rock it. Except for when the storms
came, it was always like this, a scene that never
changed.

Ki-no Sung went back inside, put on his wide-
brimmed hat, took up the second bundle of nets
and carried it outside—and dropped it!

Down the beach his boat had disappeared,
been swallowed up. Ki-no Sung saw a splendid

pagoda, half in, half out of the water, rearing a hundred feet high! Impossible! He rubbed at his slanted, sleep-filled eyes and looked again. And it was still there! It was real! A mighty, wondrous pagoda. But—

It had no windows. And no doors . . .